To (

CW01430022

RAVENOUS

H N Pashley

Welcome to a very dark Victorian London.

All best.

For Amy, Aaron and the crew of the Andiamo

*"Vengeance is in my heart, death in my hand,
blood and revenge are hammering in my head."*

WILLIAM SHAKESPEARE

CHAPTER 1

Cover her Face

23 November 1890

Ada lifted her mourning veil, the better to examine the body of Elizabeth Fellowes. The young woman lay on her marriage bed, her face screaming silently at the ceiling. Her death had been neither swift, nor painless.

'What do you see, Ada?'

She took a deep breath and turned to her father. 'I think it likely she was murdered by the same individual that killed the others.'

'I would tend to agree. Our observations should align with those of the previous three victims. Are you ready to assist me?'

'Yes,' she said, watching as he opened his casebook, the nib of his fountain pen hovering over a fresh page. Despite his outwardly professional demeanour, his hand shook and sweat beaded his forehead.

'Shall I take notes while you dictate, Papa?'

Henry Phillips hesitated a moment, then handed the book and pen to his daughter. 'That would be helpful,' he said, but offered no further acknowledgement of his infirmity. Clearing his throat, he set about the grim task of describing the crime scene. 'The victim is Elizabeth Fellowes, aged eighteen years and resident at 2 Station Row, Limehouse. She was found by her husband, Reginald Fellowes, at eleven o'clock this morning, Sunday, 23rd of November. He is a signalman on the adjacent London and Blackwall railway. The body is lying...'

Henry was interrupted by a man's agonised sobbing from outside the cottage. Ada looked at her father. His mouth hung slightly open, as if he wished to say something but was unable to do so. His eyes brimmed with unshed tears and his neat, handsome face grew pale. This is too much, too soon, thought Ada, for both of us.

'May I suggest that I also make the observations on this occasion?' she asked. 'I believe it would be instructive.' Her father nodded, folding his arms across his chest as he composed himself.

Ada let her gaze range across the bed, noting every detail before she spoke. 'The body is lying supine with the arms outstretched at right angles to the torso. The index, middle and ring fingers on the left hand appear to be broken. The right arm is fractured just above the wrist, with damage to both radius and ulna. The bones have not pierced the skin. Both sets of injuries are recent and were likely sustained during the attack on her person.'

She raised her eyes to her father for confirmation.

'Please continue,' he said softly.

'Elizabeth is wearing a...'

'The victim,' he said. 'I know it seems unfeeling but you must not personalise matters. It is for your own good, believe me.'

'Yes, Papa, my apologies. The victim is wearing a white, linen nightgown. It has been torn open from neck to hem and the torso and pelvic region laid bare. The garment is stained with blood, predominantly at the neck. The legs are splayed, with livid contusions present on the inner thighs. There are no external indications that she has been violated; this can be confirmed during autopsy. There are multiple, shallow lacerations on the torso and abdomen, although none appear to be deep enough to be the cause of death. The edges of the wounds are smooth, indicating they were inflicted by a sharp blade of some kind, probably a knife. Her mouth is open and tightly filled with what appears to be a cotton rag. It is likely her assailant did this to prevent her from crying out.'

Ada paused to write, the nib scratching its way across the fine paper; a litany of torment detailed in such a matter-of-fact way that she almost found it offensive. She left the observations regarding the victim's head until last. The injuries were similar to those of the other victims, but this time the killer had gone to extremes. Under the circumstances, the grief of Reginald Fellowes as he mourned his new wife was more than understandable.

'Around the circumference of the victim's neck is a deep, narrow cut. Significant blood loss is evidenced by the staining of the pillows and bed linen, indicating possible rupture of the carotid arteries. In addition, the trachea is partially severed just below the larynx. As per previous findings it is likely the assailant used a wire garrotte. It is not clear whether the victim died from suffocation or exsanguination.'

'And what is different this time?' asked Henry.

Ada forced herself to look at Elizabeth's face. She had been a remarkably pretty, young woman; according to her husband, her eyes were as blue as cornflowers. Given the nature of the injuries sustained in the attack, Ada had no way of confirming this was true. 'The victim's eyes have been roughly excised. There is significant damage to the orbital cavity and surrounding tissue, although it is not clear if the organs were removed pre or post mortem. Dear God, Papa, he must have hated her to do such a thing.'

'That is supposition,' he replied. 'Although it is likely the murderer is male, we cannot state such a thing categorically. As for hating her, how does one judge the state of mind of a person capable of such atrocity?'

'But…'

'Just the facts please, Ada,' he said, his voice weary. 'You have every right to feel anger at such a violent crime, but if you are to be a doctor you must learn to distance yourself. Objectivity is everything.'

'Yes, Papa.'

Ada and her father stood in silence for a moment, offering mute acknowledgement of the suffering Elizabeth had endured. There was a gentle knock on the bedroom door.

'Come in,' said Henry.

The door opened and a young police officer entered. 'Sorry to disturb you, sir, miss, but the photographer is here. We need to get plates of the scene before the body is moved to the mortuary.'

'Very well,' said Henry, 'we shan't be long.'

'Thank you, sir. I'll tell Mr Price he can come in shortly.' He hesitated. 'Beggin' your pardon, but is this one the same as the others?'

'As in, do I think the same person killed all four women?'

'Yes, sir.'

'I shouldn't really comment, Constable Bennett, but the evidence is consistent. That's all I can say for now.'

'Of course, sir, I'll leave you to it.' With a polite nod he left the room.

Ada stared at the body. The previous murders had been just as vile, yet the removal of Elizabeth's eyes was beyond barbaric. Seeing a linen chest under the window, Ada bent down to open it.

'What are you doing?' Henry asked.

'The only thing I can.' Inwardly she dared him to reprimand her for a lack of objectivity.

'I understand, my daughter,' he said, kindly.

Fetching a cotton sheet from the chest, Ada draped it across the bed with her father's help. After taking one last, sad look at the poor young woman, she carefully drew the sheet over Elizabeth's face, hiding the violence that had been inflicted upon her.

'We should go now, Ada,' said Henry, 'I have much to do and the photographer is waiting.'

She nodded, and in strange solidarity covered her own face with her mourning veil. Stepping into the fading light of a winter's afternoon, Ada glanced at the restless crowd behind the police cordon. She had no doubt they wanted this murderer caught and hanged, but with every new victim, their faith in the authorities dwindled. She wished she could tell them just how hard her father was working to assist the police, but she knew her pleas would fall on deaf ears. The people of the East End had been let down before, and they had long memories.

Sitting on the ground nearby was Reginald Fellowes. Head in his hands he rocked back and forth, weeping as solicitous neighbours did their best to comfort him. Ada wanted to say something, anything that would ease his pain, but all that came to mind seemed facile and empty. Perhaps her father was right: dispassionate observation was the only way to stay sane when faced with such awful brutality.

'The coroner's finished, Mr Price,' said Constable Bennett. 'You can go in now.'

Ada watched as the police photographer was ushered inside the cottage. She hoped he would treat the body with respect and replace the sheet once he had finished. It was a small thing, yet important. Taking her father's proffered arm, she walked to the hansom cab that sat waiting for them. With some encouragement from Bennett the crowd parted, and once clear of Station Row the cab headed for Shoreditch.

'I'll drop you off on the way to Scotland Yard,' said Henry, rubbing a hand over his face. 'Chief Constable Halloran wants my initial report as soon as possible. He's desperate to avoid another Whitechapel; isolated murders seem oddly pedestrian when compared to a series of killings committed by the same person.'

'Halloran is asking too much of you, Papa. Mother's funeral was barely over before these killings started. Can't Doctor Bond take over?'

'He isn't the coroner for H division, I am for my sins. It's my responsibility.'

Ada nodded, unwilling to pressure him any further, but her concerns regarding the chief constable remained. He had objected to Ada's presence at the crime scenes – on the grounds that a woman had no place in the medical profession – but her father had paid him no heed. She hoped that decision would not have unpleasant consequences, for either of them.

'Do you think he was there today?' she asked.

'Who?'

'The murderer. It is said they tend to return to the scene of their crime.'

'That's always a possibility, but why they would want to do so is beyond me. It is a pity we cannot see into the hearts of men. Perhaps then we could stop these terrible things from happening.'

'If only that were the case,' said Ada. 'I imagine there will be another salacious headline in The Standard this evening?'

'It's sadly inevitable I'm afraid. I do wish they would refrain from giving murderers such sensational names. One cannot help but feel it glorifies them somehow, and that is obscene. The Limehouse Strangler indeed!'

'I couldn't agree more. I hope the police catch him before he kills again.'

'As do I. Every new victim brings with it a sense of a failure on my part.'

'You're doing your best, Papa.'

'*We* are doing our best, Ada. Do not forget that. Your assistance in this matter means a great deal to me.'

She smiled at him. 'Thank you, Papa.'

Arriving at their townhouse, Henry bade Ada goodbye before continuing on to Whitehall. Standing on the pavement, she watched until the cab was lost from sight. Praying that her father would come home at a reasonable hour she turned to go inside, but stopped as the skin on the back of her neck prickled. Ada had never been one for the wild imaginings of her less academic peers, but the sensation that she was being observed was both immediate and overwhelming.

Doing her best to remain calm, she glanced casually up and down the street. Dusk was falling, the gas lamps were being lit and a thin mist hung in the chill air. Nothing and nobody appeared out of place, yet Ada could not avoid the morbid thought of how easy it would be for a stranger to slip a wire garrotte around her neck. Unable to scream for help, she could die on her own doorstep; another life snuffed out, another family rent asunder.

That night, before climbing into bed, Ada barred the shutters on her first floor window, something she had not done since she was a child.

CHAPTER 2

Mourning Black

A da woke later than she would have wished. Her sleep had been fitful at best, her dreams filled with images of Elizabeth Fellowes' maimed body. The curtains were half-drawn, and weak morning sunlight filled the room. Her maid had clearly been in while she slept.

There was a soft knock at the bedroom door. 'Breakfast is ready, miss. Will you be coming down?'

'Yes, Milly, I'll be there shortly.'

'Very well, miss. I'll tell Mrs Crane to expect you.'

Ada sighed. It was supposed to be a day for celebration, yet she had never felt less like doing so. Putting on a dressing gown, she splashed some water on her face and followed Milly downstairs. In the parlour, a fire was burning cheerfully in the grate; the table was set for one, and propped against the cruet was a folded sheet of notepaper, her name written upon it. She smiled and picked it up, reading the contents.

"Happy birthday, my darling. I cannot believe you are so suddenly twenty one years of age. How

quickly the time has flown. Despite all that has happened we cannot allow this day to pass us by. You are my joy, and I have no words to tell you how proud I am of what you have achieved. I have reserved a table at Claridge's for lunch at one today. Please meet me there; I have a surprise for you. All my love. Papa."

It was heart-warming to read her father's words. Given the pressure he was under, it meant much to her that he could put work aside, if only for an hour or two. There was a soft snuffling from the hall, and an elderly Great Dane appeared in the doorway. Upon seeing Ada he gave a soft bark and padded over. 'Hello, Hamlet,' she said, stroking his head, 'I'll take you for a walk later.'

'That would be a good idea, miss,' said Mrs Crane, striding into the parlour with a breakfast tray. Sombrely dressed as befitting a household in mourning and with her grey hair pulled into a severe bun, the housekeeper peered at Ada over the rim of her *pince-nez* spectacles. 'A dose of fresh air will put some colour in your cheeks. You look pale. Did you sleep well?'

'Not particularly, Mrs Crane,' said Ada, 'but thank you for asking.'

'Your father told me what you discovered in Limehouse; a poor night's slumber is hardly surprising.'

'It was unpleasant, but I cannot shy away from such things. It is part of my training.'

'I know,' said the housekeeper, 'but it is no easy thing to face such tragedy. On a lighter note, Milly and I wanted to offer our best wishes on such an important birthday. I know circumstances have been challenging of late, but your mother would be very proud of you.' She set a small plate of kedgeree on the table, and beside it, an orchid in a tall, glass vase. 'Milly thought you may like a flower to brighten your morning, so she took the liberty of cutting an orchid from your mother's greenhouse. I hope that was appropriate?'

'It's beautiful,' said Ada, touched by her maid's kindness. During rare, lucid periods, her mother had spent many happy hours cultivating an array of orchids, and the specimen of *brassavola nodosa* that sat in the vase was quite exquisite. 'Lady of the Night was always mother's favourite. I shall thank Milly later.'

Mrs Crane smiled. 'That would mean much to her. Please enjoy your breakfast, miss. When you're finished, Milly will help you dress. If you will excuse me, I have matters to attend to.' With a polite nod of her head, the housekeeper turned and left.

The events of the previous day had left Ada with little appetite, but she forced herself to eat at least some of the food that had been prepared for her. Thin as she was, she had no desire to appear gaunt. The scent of the orchid hung in the air, filling her with a sudden, intense nostalgia. Tears ran down her cheeks; it was her 21st birthday, and her mother wasn't there to witness her passage into adulthood. Clara Phillips had been absent in many ways for many years, and now that she was truly gone, Ada could only mourn every missed milestone, every moment not shared. In the six weeks since her mother's funeral, Ada had lost count of the times she had woken in a cold sweat, burying her face in a pillow so Milly wouldn't hear her crying. Grief was indeed the price of love, she thought.

Hamlet whined softly and pressed his head against Ada's leg. The solid warmth of the dog was comforting, an anchor to normality in a seemingly chaotic and indifferent world. She let her fingers drift across the fur on his back, giving silent thanks for his presence. He had been part of her life for over a decade, and always knew when she was unhappy. God willing, it would be some time before he left her too. Glancing at the clock on the mantelpiece, Ada saw that it was almost eleven. Lunch with her father beckoned, and it wouldn't do to appear melancholy on such a special occasion. Drying her eyes with a napkin, she ruffled Hamlet's ears and returned to her rooms to run a bath, praying that hot water and steam would help soothe the ache that filled her chest.

Sitting at her dressing table, Ada looked at herself in the vanity mirror. A pale, hollow-eyed reflection peered back at her.

'Did you like your flower, miss?' asked Milly.

'Yes, it was very thoughtful. Thank you.'

The maid smiled as she ran a brush through Ada's damp hair. The gentle, rhythmic tug on her scalp was almost enough to lull her to sleep.

'It'll be lovely for you to see your father today; at Claridge's no less. I've never seen inside, it looks very grand.'

'It is. I shall be surrounded by women in the finest of dresses, daintily sipping wine and judging everyone around them. Given what I have to wear, I'm sure I shall be the subject of their whispers.'

'Oh, miss, I know it's not fashionable but it's…'

'Tradition? Yes, Milly, I'm aware I have a responsibility to mourn publicly. Society expects nothing less, yet it feels like an invitation of pity, and that is something I require from no one.'

'I understand, miss.'

Ada silently berated herself for sounding so abrupt; Milly, more than any of them, had suffered enough. 'I am worried about Father,' she said, changing the subject. 'It feels as though he's been holding his breath since the funeral. He has no time for his private patients and his coronial duties would test anyone, let alone a man who is recently bereaved.'

'I've been trying my best to be kind to him, miss.'

'I know you have, dear one.' Ada turned, taking Milly's hands in hers. The maid kept her gaze low, peering out from under the brim of her bonnet.

'You can look at me, it's all right.'

Milly raised her head. She didn't stare at the floor out of deference but of shame, and knowing that twisted a knife in Ada's heart. From the corners of her mouth to the lobe of each ear, a livid, still-healing scar cut a vicious divide across Milly's pretty face, a cruel smile she could never escape. Ada reached out, and oh-so-gently traced the line of damaged tissue on the maid's left cheek. The wound had been stitched by an expert hand, the delicate skin knitting as smoothly as anyone could have hoped for given the severity of the injury. Milly flinched, but didn't pull away.

'It's healing well,' said Ada. 'Another few months and you'll barely notice. The young men of London will be fighting over you.'

Milly blushed. 'You're being too kind, miss,' she said. 'I have your grandfather to thank for saving my face. Sir Edmund is a brilliant man.'

'He is,' said Ada. 'After what happened it was the least he could do, the least any of us could do. I hope you can forgive us, Milly.'

'Nothing to forgive, miss,' said the maid, 'you're my family. Mother is in service at Rookwood with your grandfather and I belong here with you. It's the way it's supposed to be.'

'You are a saint, Millicent Fletcher,' said Ada, standing to give the embarrassed maid a hug. Milly hesitated before returning the gesture. 'Thank you, miss. Now, I need to get you ready. You can't go to Claridge's looking like a scarecrow.'

'Indeed not,' said Ada, returning to her seat. She sat in silence, waiting patiently as Milly expertly combed her long, dark hair into a fashionable *chignon*. Once finished, she bade Ada stand, and helped her into the requisite prison of a whalebone corset, laced just tightly enough to be able to breathe without overt discomfort.

'Now for the dress, miss.'

Once clad in a simple yet finely-tailored garment of midnight-black, Ada turned to face the cheval mirror that stood against the wall. The image she saw was one she still didn't fully recognise.

'It's quite beautiful in its own way, miss.'

'It is.' Yet to Ada the cut and cloth meant nothing; it was what the dress represented that mattered, a statement to the world that she was in mourning, a public acknowledgement of private pain.

'Just a touch of powder, miss? Black does drain your colour.'

'I think that wise,' said Ada, noting the dark circles under her eyes. She may not have a say as regards the dress, but she would rather her complexion did not betray her state of mind. With a practised hand, Milly swiftly applied a thin layer of cold cream to Ada's cheeks, followed by just enough pink powder to hide the tell-tale signs of sleepless nights.

'Just one more thing,' she said, pinning hat and veil to Ada's hair, 'and we are done. There, you look lovely.'

I look like an angel of death, thought Ada, but she smiled at the maid regardless. A bell rang in the hall.

'That'll be your cab.'

Ada nodded. 'I appreciate your help, Milly.'

'My pleasure, miss.'

Making her way downstairs, Ada found Mrs Crane waiting by the front door. 'Enjoy your lunch, miss,' said the housekeeper, 'and happy birthday again.'

'Thank you. I shall put on a brave face, for Father's sake.'

'You will do splendidly. Hold your head high; the opinions of anyone outside this family mean nothing.'

'You sound like Grandfather.'

'I take that as a compliment.' With unaccustomed familiarity, Mrs Crane took Ada's hand, giving it a gentle squeeze. It was a simple act, yet profound, and it lifted her spirits more than she could say.

'Would Mother really be proud of me?' she asked.

'Without question,' said Mrs Crane. 'I am sure she watches over you. You are not alone, miss, remember that.'

'I shall,' said Ada, and ignoring the curious glances of passers-by, climbed into the waiting cab.

CHAPTER 3

The Masks We Wear

With a gentle lurch the hansom joined the traffic of Shoreditch, heading to Brook Street in Mayfair. Resting her head against the quilted-leather interior, Ada watched the bustling city as it passed her by. It was only in the heart of the great metropolis that she felt truly alive, but she was under no illusions as to what lay beneath the surface. During the day London was an attack on the senses, a mélange of sights, sounds and smells, yet at night it changed character utterly. Gas lit and seductive, it offered every vice you could name, and in the East End, life was cheap indeed. Once that fog-bound darkness descended, a sense of foreboding came with it, like a burial shroud being drawn across the face of a loved one. Ada shook her head; she had no wish to dwell upon that particular memory, not today.

The cab came to a stop alongside the grand portico of Claridge's. Paying the driver, Ada took a deep breath and entered the lobby. Painfully aware that she was a single point of black amidst a rustling sea of colourful silk and crinoline, she sought out the *maître d'hôtel*; he stood by a lectern at the entrance to the restaurant, his expression one of practised imperiousness.

'Good afternoon,' said Ada. 'My father has a reservation for one o'clock in the name of Phillips.'

He nodded, and after running a pen down his list, neatly drew a line through her name. 'He is already here, miss. Please follow me.'

Ada could feel eyes upon her as she walked to her father's table. The attention was unwelcome but she understood it. No one wished to be reminded of the frailty of human existence during an otherwise civilised luncheon.

Her father stood as he saw her approach. 'Happy birthday, darling,' he said, embracing Ada and kissing her cheek.

'Thank you, Papa.'

The *maître d'hôtel* pulled out a chair, and once Ada was seated he bowed smartly before hurrying back to his lectern. Lifting her veil, she smiled at her father across a sea of crisp linen and shining cutlery. A white-aproned waiter appeared at Henry's elbow, and after a brief perusal of the wine list, her father ordered a bottle of vintage Bollinger.

'Today we celebrate in style,' he said. 'You look positively radiant by the way. I take it you slept well?'

'I feel quite rested, Papa.' The lie slipped from

between her lips as easily as breathing. Milly's application of cosmetics had patently been a good idea. Henry nodded, and Ada studied him as he absently toyed with his napkin. Tall and strong, her father had always seemed so resilient, but it was becoming increasingly obvious that recent events had taken their toll. The new lines on his face, the sunken cheeks, the slight yet visible tremor of his hands; they were all signs of incipient nervous exhaustion, cracks in his mask of Victorian male stoicism.

'How was your meeting with the chief constable?' asked Ada, hoping there had been some progress with the case, some glimmer of light at the end of the tunnel.

Henry sighed. 'It went as expected. Halloran is a weak man and it shows in his attitude. He wants the killer caught and will use whatever methods he deems necessary. It's all about appearances; such is the nature of politics.'

Ada's heart sank. If Halloran was getting desperate then her father would feel duty-bound to assist, regardless of the cost to his health. 'Have you thought of retaining a locum for the Harley Street practice?' she suggested. 'At least then you will know your patients are in good hands while you have so much else to deal with.'

'I am considering it. Your grandfather returns from Paris tomorrow so I shall speak to him; see if he has any recommendations as to suitable candidates. I must admit I have missed his presence these past weeks. Halloran tends to be more reasonable when he knows Edmund is nearby.'

'I think that's a splendid idea,' said Ada, reassured by the thought of seeing her grandfather again. He had left London to lecture at the Sorbonne just after the first of the Limehouse murders, and was not a man to be trifled with. 'You cannot flinch in the face of horror,' he had told her as she bid him farewell at St Pancras station. 'You spit in its eye and use your rage at such injustice to further your understanding. The medical profession is no place for the timid.' He was right of course, but as she had discovered, objectivity was no easy thing to master.

The waiter arrived with their champagne, and with consummate skill opened the bottle with a ceremonial sword before filling two exquisite crystal flutes. 'To you, my darling,' said Henry, raising a glass to Ada. She smiled and raised her own glass. 'To *us*, Papa.' Once the waiter had taken their orders, they sipped in good-natured silence until Ada's curiosity got the better of her. 'So, what is this surprise you mentioned in your note?'

Henry chuckled. 'I was wondering when you would ask. Well, it comes in two parts. Firstly, I have taken the liberty of speaking to

Doctor Elizabeth Garrett Anderson, at the London School of Medicine for Women. With both my endorsement and that of Edmund, she has kindly agreed that you may begin studying for your medical degree early next year. To be candid, she could hardly refuse. With the knowledge and experience you hold, you have a significant advantage over her existing students.'

'That's wonderful news. Thank you so much.'

'You have earned it, my daughter. Your skills could help shape the future of medicine, save lives, ease suffering. It is a worthy calling, but one should not go into battle unarmed.' Reaching under the table, Henry pulled out a neatly-wrapped package and handed it to Ada.

'This should help you achieve great things.'

'What is it?'

'Open it and see.'

Carefully tearing away the brown paper, Ada gasped as she saw what lay beneath: a pristine medical bag of black, Italian leather, the ornate lock engraved with her initials.

'It contains all the material you should need,' said Henry. 'I chose the instruments myself – the finest quality of course.'

'Oh Papa, it's beautiful. I will carry it with pride.'

'I would expect nothing less.'

The food arrived, and as Ada devoured her

lunch, she discussed areas of further study in preparation for the start of her career. Her father's gifts could not have been more fitting nor more timely; a renewed sense of purpose was exactly what she needed. All too soon the meal was finished and Henry glanced at his fob watch. 'I'm afraid I have to go. I have a meeting at Whitehall. The Home Secretary wishes to review the evidence we have collected, see if there is anything we may have missed.'

'I understand,' said Ada. 'Come, escort me out.'

Henry proffered his arm, and together, father and daughter walked out to the hotel steps. 'I'll be late back tonight,' he said, seeing Ada to a cab. 'I'll likely have dinner at my club, so please tell Mrs Crane not to prepare anything for me.'

'I will, Papa.' She kissed him goodbye, and as the cab made its way to Shoreditch, she stared at the medical bag on her lap. She had been gifted the accoutrements of a doctor and now it was time to act like one. The more she thought about it, the more convinced she became that a locum for her father's practice would not be enough. He had to step down as coroner before he crumbled beneath the weight of his responsibilities, but persuading him to do so without injuring his pride would be difficult. She needed advice as to the best course of action, and as luck would have it she knew just where to turn. Her grandfather would have the answers. He always did.

'I'm glad you had a pleasant lunch, miss,' said Milly, brushing out Ada's hair in preparation for bed, 'and such fine presents from your father too.'

'I am lucky, Milly. It's been months since I asked him if I might start my degree; I assumed that with everything that has happened he had forgotten. I should have had more faith in him.'

'And you have a party at the Hunter's tomorrow night. That's something to look forward to. I'm sure Miss Dora has missed you. I'd love to go to something as fancy as that.'

Ada sighed. Upon her return she had found an invitation to an evening soirée at the house of an old friend. Dora Hunter was both worldly and kind, but the gaggle of preening, society women that surrounded her would no doubt be irksome at best.

'Dora may appreciate my desire for a career, Milly, but the rest of her guests are unlikely to be of the same opinion. Their minds are like a blank canvas, just waiting for someone to paint something pretty on them.'

The maid giggled. 'I think I know what you mean, miss.'

'Just be glad you don't have to spend an evening in their company, pretending to be interested in the latest fashions and who is courting whom. I am content for them to view me as something of a bluestocking as long as they're polite, otherwise I may say something I'll regret.'

'I wonder what Mrs Crane would think of that?'

'She'd remind me that maintaining our family reputation was something Mother insisted upon.'

For the briefest of moments Milly's hand faltered.

'I'm sorry,' said Ada, 'I shouldn't have mentioned her. It was thoughtless of me.'

'No need to apologise, miss. I wish she was still with us, truly.'

Ada nodded, wondering how the maid could be so sanguine after what had been done to her. Some scars healed, some just festered.

'Will that be all, miss?' asked Milly once she had finished.

'Yes, thank you. Sleep well.'

'And you, miss.'

Sliding her legs into bed, Ada lay back on the pillows and closed her eyes. Life had felt so bleak for so long, it was difficult to imagine any other way of being, yet there was always cause for hope; if she worked hard enough, she may indeed make the world a better place. 'I will be a good doctor,' she whispered as she drifted away, 'and I will not flinch in the face of horror.'

CHAPTER 4

Ill Met by Moonlight

The dream was always the same. Ever since her mother's funeral it had haunted Ada's nights, an unwelcome guest that refused to leave. Dead leaves swirled about her ankles as she walked through a moonlit garden, seeking the last resting place of Clara Phillips. There, beneath the bare branches of an ancient oak, a plain, marble headstone was enclosed by a wrought-iron fence.

Ada came to a stop at the foot of the grave, hands clasped, head bowed, filled with questions to which there were no answers. The dead owed nothing to the living. She would stand there, silently aching for her mother's love until the mist rolled in and she fell into deepest sleep. The dream was always the same, until it wasn't.

Ada froze, heart in her mouth, as a man stepped out from the shadows beneath the tree, shreds of darkness trailing behind him like ebon cobwebs. He was tall, slim and dressed for the opera, complete with top hat, kid gloves and a cloak lined with burgundy silk. Ada couldn't see his face; it was covered by a finely-sculpted mask of white velvet, the androgynous features as beautiful as Michelangelo's David, yet with lips pursed in the most extreme disapproval. In his right hand he carried a medical bag, identical to the one that her father had given her.

'Good evening, Miss Phillips,' he said. 'I've been looking forward to meeting you for quite some time.'

Ada wanted nothing more than to turn and run, yet her body refused to move. 'You do not belong here,' she said, trying to remain calm. 'This place is for me alone.'

'Then I beg your forgiveness for my intrusion.'

'Why do you disturb my grief? What is it you want from me?'

'Simply to talk. We have much to discuss.'

Beneath her dress, Ada's skin prickled as a dreadful thought crossed her mind. 'Are you him?' she asked, her words sounding hollow and slurred. 'Are you the one responsible for killing those women in Limehouse?'

The man chuckled softly behind his mask. 'I am not. Such actions are anathema to me.'

'Then who are you?'

'Now there is a question,' he replied. 'I will answer it in time, but first I need to ascertain your worth, your capabilities.'

'Why would you wish to do that?'

'Like you, I seek an end to suffering.'

'Are you a doctor then?'

'Of sorts, although surgeon would be a more fitting title. I need you, Ada, but I have to know if you deserve my gifts. I have to know if you are stronger than your mother.' The man turned his head to look pointedly at the grave.

'M… my mother?' Ada stammered. 'What has she got to do with you?' Her eyes widened as the man placed his bag on the ground, opened it, and took out a long-bladed amputation knife.

'Fear is a powerful emotion; become its master and you are free to do anything, remain its slave and the world will tear you apart. This is the challenge that lies before you. What will your choice be, I wonder?'

Nausea filled Ada, a swelling sickness that curdled her stomach. She had watched her grandfather use such a knife on many occasions, and knew exactly what it could do. 'Please, just let me go,' she begged. 'I do not want to stay here any longer.'

'NO!'

Ada recoiled at the sound. She had never heard such command in a human voice, such a terrible mix of anger and contempt, all held in check by the most fragile of threads. The man stepped in close, limned with moonlight as he towered above her.

'I am someone to watch over you, a means to cut away that which holds you back.' He pressed the knife to Ada's veil, gently running the tip down her cheek. She shuddered, unable to stop him from brushing the cold steel across her lips.

'I know you can feel it,' said the man, 'the infection beneath your every step. London is riddled with it. I have never known so much corruption in one place, it is… overwhelming.'

'I don't understand.'

'Oh, but you will. If you saw the world as I do, you would know how hard it is to show restraint. How I yearn to sate my hunger, to know peace in my heart once again.' He lowered the blade and turned away. 'There is much to be done. Vengeance *will* be had and you, Ada Phillips, can either accept it, or fail. Please don't fail, I beg you.'

His tone had changed; now Ada heard nothing but love.

'It is time for you to show your mettle as a doctor,' said the man, opening his arms wide, 'to prove that you have what it takes. Come join us, Henry.'

To Ada's disbelief, her father stepped out of the night and sank to his knees in front of her. Clad in a bloodstained surgeon's gown, he looked at his daughter with pleading eyes, his face etched with bone-deep misery.

'Papa?'

'I cannot bear it, dear one,' said Henry. 'I am broken. I will fail you as your mother did. Please, end my pain.'

'Papa, no.'

'Do as I ask, I implore you. I cannot go on; to do so would only shame our family.'

Ada wanted nothing more than to embrace her father, to tell him that everything would be all right, but her efforts were in vain.

'Free him,' said the man.

'What?'

'Free him. He wants to die, so honour his wish. Why would you hesitate to offer such blessed release? Here, let me help you.'

Ada felt something heavy in the palm of her hand. Looking down, she saw that her fingers gripped the handle of a shining, new amputation knife. Bile burned the back of her throat. This was impossible, this was not right.

'I cannot do it,' she whispered, her mouth dry. 'I will not.'

'So you fear to land the killing blow, and in so doing remain shackled by weakness. Perhaps you are not familiar with the appropriate technique? Please, let me demonstrate.' The man moved to stand behind Ada's father, and with a gentle touch that was almost a caress he tilted Henry's head back. Ada fought to break free of her paralysis, but the sheer presence of her tormentor held her fast. With a cry of anguish, she watched helplessly as her father closed his eyes and smiled.

'Wonderful,' said the man, slowly drawing his knife across the breadth of Henry's throat, cutting deeply and with purpose.

Ada stood aghast as blood fountained from the open wound, soaking the front of her dress. She could feel its warmth, smell the iron, hear the soft pattering as it dripped to the ground at her feet. 'Papa!' she gasped, weeping hot tears as her father fell prone, his life pooling beneath him in a crimson flower.

'Do you see how easy it is,' said the man, 'how precise, how full of grace?' Stepping over the steaming body, he placed himself in front of Ada, watching her from beneath the brim of his hat. 'I ask you a question. What would you do to someone who tore from you that which you loved most? What passion would it stir within you? What revenge would you seek?'

Ada's fear drained away, only to be replaced by the unfamiliar sensation of cold and utter hate. The implacable will that held her in place shattered, and with a swift, sure hand she raised her own knife.

'I ask you again,' said the man, his voice soft and encouraging, 'are you stronger than your mother?'

'Murderer!' hissed Ada, and with all her strength drove the razor-sharp steel into the left eyehole of his mask. There was a moment of resistance as the knife hit bone, followed by a soft crunch as it slid into his brain. The man's head rocked back, the blade that had killed Henry spilling from his hand.

'At last,' he said. 'Perhaps there is hope for you yet. Let us see just how far you are prepared to go, shall we?' With a gentle sigh his body dissolved into sparkling motes of dust, leaving hat, cloak and dinner suit to collapse in upon themselves. Atop the pile lay his mask, the lips slowly drawing themselves into a devilish smile.

Ada took a deep, ragged breath and lowered her arm, knife still clutched in white-knuckled fingers. She looked for her father's corpse but it too had disappeared, as had the blood on her dress. Shivering as the adrenaline left her veins, Ada wiped her eyes and prayed for the mist that always came to carry her home. It failed to materialise; the night remained clear, the moon full, but in the distance, beyond a swathe of ornamental gardens stood a great house, light shining from a single window. 'Grandfather,' Ada whispered, the utterance of such a simple word offering her much needed comfort. On unsteady feet she walked slowly toward the house, following the gravel path. As she drew nearer she could see her grandfather in his study, tumbler of brandy in hand, firelight bathing the room in a soft, warm glow.

Ada smiled, and was about to call out to him when she heard the sound of running feet. Turning with treacle-thick slowness, she saw a man sprinting along the path toward her. Dressed in nondescript clothes his face was a blur, a flickering zoetrope that refused to stay still. He was everyone yet no one, and in his outstretched hands he held something that chilled her to the core; two wooden handles connected by a length of taut wire.

For one awful moment Ada was overwhelmed by sheer terror. Mouth dry and with her heart beating a strident tattoo, all strength fled as a monster from the waking world bore down upon her. Forcing herself into motion, she turned her back on him and ran toward her grandfather, towards safety, towards somewhere she thought of as home. Dragging chill air deep into her lungs, she opened her mouth to cry out for help, but her desperate plea remained stillborn as something thin and impossibly strong looped itself round her neck. Drawn tight, it pulled her backward and up until she stood on tiptoe, breath locked in her chest. The most appalling stench enveloped her; foetid beyond imagining, it spoke of something worse than the corruption of the grave. It was the darkness at the top of the stairs, the unexpected shape looming out of the fog, the rot beneath the poisoner's floorboards. With sick certainty Ada knew what held her; it was evil itself, and it would give no quarter.

'You have lovely eyes,' it said. 'I shall take my time with you.'

Unable to scream Ada flailed at her attacker. Not a single blow found purchase, and with blood thundering in her ears, she reached out to her grandfather. Mere yards away, he stood staring out into the night, his bearing that of an officer and a gentleman. Turning his head he looked at Ada, the expression on his face one of expectation, as if he was waiting to see what his granddaughter would do. Help me, Ada mouthed, but he did nothing except take a sip of brandy and watch her, as if studying a patient in his care.

The wire drew ever tighter, cutting into her skin, and Ada's vision began fading to grey. Faced with the same fate as that of Elizabeth Fellowes, she reached inside herself for something, anything that would allow her a way out. She found it in her grandfather's parting words as he left for Paris, a single point of clarity with which to defy the inevitable. I shall choose my own end, she thought, I will not give this creature the satisfaction. *I will not flinch.* Placing the amputation knife against her chest, she gripped the handle with both hands and drove it straight through her heart.

Torn violently from her nightmare, Ada sat bolt upright in bed. With bile filling her throat, she flung her sodden bedsheets aside and rushed to the bathroom. Sinking to her knees, she vomited into the toilet bowl before curling up on the tiled floor and sobbing like a child.

CHAPTER 5

The Cold Light of Day

'**M**iss? Are you all right? What on earth happened?'

Ada woke with a start. Milly was kneeling on the bathroom floor next to her, eyes wide.

'I'll fetch your father, miss, he's just finished breakfast.'

'No!' said Ada sharply, grabbing Milly's arm as she made to leave. 'I'm all right, really. I must have eaten something that disagreed with me then fainted. This is nothing to bother Father about.'

Milly remained where she was, but Ada could see the indecision in her face. She was biting her bottom lip; she always did that when she was unsure. Ada held out her hand, and with the maid's help got slowly to her feet. Her mouth tasted sour, and a dull ache nestled uncomfortably behind her eyes. Bracing herself against the sink, she groaned and massaged her stiff neck. 'Please tell Father I will be down shortly,' she said. 'I want so see him before he leaves. I just need a few minutes to make myself presentable.' She offered the maid what she hoped was a reassuring smile.

'As you wish, miss.' Milly dropped a quick curtsey and scurried away.

After rinsing her mouth and splashing cold water on her face, Ada threw on a dressing gown, tied her hair back and followed the maid downstairs, hoping she looked less unsettled than she felt. She had suffered night terrors before, but what she had just experienced was of a different magnitude entirely. It was fading, yet what she could remember filled her with dread. Taking a moment to compose herself, she took a deep breath and entered the parlour.

'Good morning,' said Henry.

'Good morning, Papa,' she replied, seating herself opposite him.

'I've already eaten I'm afraid, I have a very busy day ahead. Shall I ask Mrs Crane to bring you something?'

'No thank you, I'll just have some tea.' She reached for the steaming pot of Earl Grey, hoping her father wouldn't notice that her hands were shaking.

Henry nodded absently, glancing at the clock on the mantelpiece.

'I didn't hear you come in last night,' said Ada. 'Did you work late?'

'Yes. Mercifully the Home Secretary is a practical man. He knows everyone is doing their best to find this murderer, but Halloran is like a dog chasing its own tail. All he's really worried about is his career should civil unrest occur. You know how awful the situation is; if there is another killing, I dread to think of the consequences.'

Ada looked at her father as he nervously drummed his fingers on the table. The skin on his face was sallow and he had cut himself shaving, leaving a thin red line to one side of his neck. Ada shut her eyes as images from the nightmare replayed themselves in her mind: steel parting flesh, the bright spurt of blood, the begging for death. The brief moment of shared happiness the previous day was swept roughly aside, leaving only the ominous feeling that if she didn't act, and now, something truly terrible would happen.

'Papa?'

'Yes, Ada.'

'Forgive me if I speak out of turn, but I need you... no, I beg you to resign your position as coroner.' Tears ran down her cheeks as she spoke. 'You need to be away from this case, away from all of it. Can't you see what it's doing to you? Is duty more important than living? Than me?'

Getting to his feet Henry came to kneel at Ada's side, taking her hands in his. 'It may surprise you, my daughter, but last night in my club I had an epiphany of sorts. I was sitting there, nursing a whiskey, and one of the stewards – a new chap who doesn't know who I am –

actually asked me if I needed to see a doctor. The irony of such a statement is not lost on me. I am quite aware that my health is failing, and if my condition is so apparent to others then I have no choice but to step down.' He paused and swallowed heavily, as if admitting to such a thing made him less of a man.

'There is no shame, Papa,' said Ada. 'I could not respect you more for making such a decision.'

Henry nodded and smiled at her. 'However, Edmund used his influence to obtain the position of coroner for me, and it would reflect poorly on both of us if I simply left without proposing a replacement. To that end, I will make discreet enquiries among my peers. It will not be immediate, but given that Halloran has never liked me much anyway, I would imagine that I should be able to return to Harley Street within the next month. Does that reassure you?'

'It does, thank you,' said Ada. She had half-expected her father to deny that anything was seriously amiss, but his response to her plea came as a great relief; perhaps now they would have the opportunity to mourn in peace. At the sound of footsteps in the hall, Henry let go of Ada's hands and retook his seat. Mrs Crane entered, and Ada watched as her father swiftly replaced his veneer of professional dispassion. Showing his feelings to her was one thing, but he would never reveal himself in such a manner to the staff.

'Would you like something to eat, miss?' the housekeeper's archly-raised eyebrow indicating Milly may not have been as discreet as Ada would have wished.

'Just some toast, please.'

'I must be away,' said Henry, finishing the last of his tea. He bent to kiss Ada on the cheek. 'We will talk tonight,' he whispered in her ear.

Once her father had gone, Ada ate in silence before returning to her room and rinsing away the dregs of nightmare with hot water and soap. Donning her black dress, she made her way downstairs with the intention of sitting in her mother's greenhouse and studying among the orchids. She was just passing the front door when the visitor bell rang, and on opening it found a familiar face grinning at her.

'I know it's a day late, but happy birthday.' A tall, athletic man in a plain suit and brown derby hat held out a small, yet beautifully arranged bouquet of winter flowers.

'Rory! I wasn't expecting you. Thank you, they're exquisite.' Ada took the flowers and kissed him on the cheek, the ginger whiskers of his beard tickling her skin. 'Come in.'

Doffing his hat he stepped inside. 'I would have come yesterday, but this is the first day's leave I've had in a week. Things at the station have been desperate.'

'Well, you are a sergeant now, you can hardly

disappear when you feel like it,' said Ada, leading him through to the parlour. Curled up on the floor by the dresser, Hamlet raised his head and gave a soft bark.

'Hello, old boy,' said Rory.

'I heard the doorbell, miss. Was there anything I... oh, hello, Sergeant Canavan.' Milly dropped a neat curtsey and blushed furiously.

'Rory brought me a birthday bouquet. Would you be so kind as to put it in a vase for me?'

'Of course, miss.' Milly scurried from the room, unable to look Rory in the eye.

Ada smiled. 'I think she finds you rather dashing.'

'I do have a certain Celtic charm,' he said, his Dublin brogue self-evident. 'I was wondering if you fancied taking the dog for a walk; it's a fine morning and I could do with the distraction.'

'That's a good idea. I didn't get the chance yesterday and I need to talk to you. Let's take Hamlet to that park two streets down, the fresh air will do me good.' He nodded, waiting patiently as she affixed her veil and hat. Once outside, Ada took her friend's arm, a leashed Hamlet walking obediently at heel. 'So, how is the investigation progressing at your end? I didn't see you at Station Row.'

Rory puffed out his cheeks. 'It's fecking hideous, that's what it is. I haven't known anything like it since Whitechapel back in '88. If

41

this bastard kills again it'll get even worse. I've been spat at, had stones thrown at me; anyone would think I was just sitting on my arse while some mad fecker butchers these poor lasses. I was still dealing with the last murder when news of Mrs Fellowes came through. If I'm honest, Ada, I feel completely helpless.'

'I understand,' she said, giving his arm a squeeze. 'This is all new for me too. Assisting Father at the last scene was... difficult. You know the killer took her eyes this time?'

'Yes, George Bennett told me. Poor bugger finishes his training as a constable, and a couple of weeks later he's up to his neck in this. Still, at least he doesn't puke his guts up at the sight of blood anymore. I've seen your da a couple of times recently too. I hope you don't mind me saying, but he looks ragged.'

'I know, Rory. I spoke to him this morning. He's going to step down as coroner, and not a moment too soon in my opinion.'

'That seems like a sensible thing for him to do under the circumstances. When a man doesn't allow himself to grieve it eats him away. We can be sorry specimens in that regard.'

Arriving at the park, Ada found a secluded bench and freed Hamlet from his leash. 'We've known each a long time, haven't we?' she said, turning to Rory.

'Ever since your grandfather saved my sorry

arse from an even sorrier end. Did I ever tell you what he said to me?'

'I don't think so. What pearl of wisdom did he have to offer?'

'He said I had three choices of destination: the army, the police force, or the end of a rope.'

'That sounds very much like him. He is nothing if not direct.'

'I'm very grateful of course. If *my* grandfather hadn't saved Sir Edmund's life in India, I'd probably be bleeding out in a Dublin back street just like my da. Now here I am, a reputable Irishman in a disreputable city. Isn't fate a strange thing?'

'It is, but the thought that one's life is subject to such intangible forces is unsettling. Take these murders in Limehouse for example what did the victims do to deserve such horrible ends?'

'Absolutely nothing that I can see,' said Rory. 'Sad though it is, these things just happen sometimes.'

'They do, but knowing that is no comfort. There is something about this case that makes my skin crawl. If I am honest, I do not think I have ever felt so afraid, even though I cannot fully explain why.'

'You're being too hard on yourself, lass. You've seen what this lunatic can do right up close, and all of them young women, just like you. If you weren't a bit scared, I'd be questioning your sanity.'

Ada nodded. 'That's true, but after coming home from Station Row I had this awful feeling I was being watched, studied even. What if the killer has seen me attending with Father, what if he decides he wants to taunt the authorities by garrotting me too?'

'He's targeting new brides, lass, you don't fit his pattern.'

'We're dealing with an insane butcher, Rory,' snapped Ada. 'Just because he's only murdered brides so far, doesn't mean that every other woman is safe. The worst thing is that he could be anyone, any man is this park and we wouldn't know. A monster on the inside, chances are he looks as innocuous as a bank clerk, acting in a perfectly respectable manner except when he's killing. If I can't see him coming, how can I stop him?'

'Ah, I'm sorry, lass. I didn't mean to sound flippant. You're right of course; I was seeing it as a rough and ready policeman, not as a young woman might.'

'I know,' said Ada, taking his hand. 'Forgive me for sounding so brusque, I didn't sleep well and I'm very tired.'

'Are you having that dream about your mother's grave again?'

'Yes, that's actually what I wanted to talk to you about. It was different this time and I don't know what to make of it.'

'How so?'

Hoping that Rory wouldn't think her deranged, Ada told him about what she had experienced: the masked man, her father's despair, and the decision to take her own life rather than let herself become a victim.

'Jesus Christ!' said Rory, once she had finished, 'that's no dream, that's a full-fledged night terror. Look, lass, you're the cleverest woman I've ever met, you make me feel positively dim in comparison, but you know where all this comes from don't you? Clara's illness and suicide, Milly, and now this business with the Limehouse Strangler. Your da isn't the only one who needs time away from it all.'

Ada reached up and touched his cheek. 'Thank you. You do have a way of putting things in perspective.'

'That's the benefit of being Irish, lass. We're on first-name terms with tragedy, so we know how to deal with it.'

They sat in silence awhile, watching the dog chase pigeons, enjoying the simple pleasure of sitting on a park bench and letting the world turn. All too soon it was time to leave.

'I should be getting back,' said Ada, wishing she could stay longer. 'I have an evening function at the Hunter residence and Mrs Crane will start to fret if I am late. Would you be so kind as to walk me home?'

'My pleasure, lass.'

With Hamlet once again at heel, Ada left the park arm-in-arm with her friend, yet even with Rory by her side she knew she wouldn't feel truly safe until this murderer was caught. All it took was a moment's inattention, a length of piano wire, and what was left of her family would be utterly destroyed.

CHAPTER 6

Bluestocking

Ada sat at her dressing table, trying to drum up some degree of enthusiasm for the evening ahead. It had been almost a year since she last attended such an important social engagement, and it was the first time that her mother had not been there to help her get ready. Clara would have been in her element as she fussed over dresses, arranged hair, offered advice as to protocol. Steering her daughter through the intricacies of Victorian society would quiet her mania, give her a reason to leave the pit of despair in which she languished. Ada treasured those memories, but they were wholly outweighed by the anguish of having to watch her mother suffer. She hoped that madness could not be inherited. The concept of treading the same, agony-strewn path was too awful to contemplate. Physical pain was one thing, but losing one's mind was a different matter entirely.

'I have laid out a suitable garment for you, miss,' said Mrs Crane. 'It's restrained but not overly formal; I thought it may help you feel less conspicuous. Given this is a private function attended by your peers, I don't think it necessary for you to wear a veil.'

'Thank you,' said Ada, 'that it most thoughtful and I agree. It will be a welcome change to not feel like a storm crow. If you would be so kind as to send Milly up, I shall try to make myself presentable.'

'Excellent. A coach will be here for you in two hours. I know it's only a few streets away, but it wouldn't hurt to travel in style.'

Ada nodded. To arrive on foot would simply give the other guests more ammunition for gossip, and that was something she could well do without.

'There you are, miss,' said Milly, 'what do you think?'

Ada turned to face the mirror. Clad in a fashionable dress of silver-grey taffeta and with her hair artfully piled and pinned atop her head, she was pleasantly surprised by what she saw. Tall for a woman, and with the finely-honed features of her mother, Ada knew she looked striking, although she would hesitate to call herself pretty. Ashamed though she was to admit it, even with the suffocating help of a corset she still had little bust. It was not something she pondered on to any degree, but tonight there would be those who would make much of their womanhood, as if the amount of bosom on show was somehow linked to their worthiness as a person. She frowned and Milly gave her a gentle nudge in the ribs.

'Now, now, miss. Don't spoil it. You look most elegant.'

'That may be so, but I'd much rather be going to the music hall with Rory.'

'I'm sure we all would, miss.'

Ada grinned. 'Anyone would think you were sweet on Sergeant Canavan, Milly.'

The maid blushed scarlet. 'I'm sure I don't know what you mean,' she said, fiddling with the folds of her skirt.

'He *is* a handsome man, and I'm sure he would be pleased to know that you find him so. Now, if you would kindly help me button my boots, you may watch me walk to my doom.'

The Hunter residence was a grand townhouse in the most fashionable part of Shoreditch. Alighting from the carriage with the coachman's assistance, Ada took a deep breath before proceeding up the wide flight of steps. A be-wigged valet was in attendance, nodding deferentially and opening the door for her. Inside, all was light, music and the muffled giggling of young women.

'Ada, there you are.' She turned to see Dora Hunter gliding gracefully toward her across the lobby. Clad in a confection of burgundy silk and with her blonde chignon covered by a net of pearls, she looked magnificent.

'Hello, Dora,' she said, kissing her on both cheeks.

'I'm so glad you could come. I haven't seen you in so long.'

'I take it I don't have to explain why?'

'Indeed you do not,' said Dora, taking Ada's arm and leading her into the nearby salon. 'I cannot imagine how upsetting things have been for you, and I quite understand your need for solitude. And then your lovely father has to deal with this *ghastly* business in Limehouse. My father has been complaining it's affecting the efficiency of the docks. He can't get his ships unloaded fast enough.'

'I imagine that must be irritating for him,' said Ada. She loved her friend, but like most women of her class, Dora viewed what happened outside her immediate social confines as something distant, almost foreign.

'It's lovely to see you out of black. I imagine you'll be able to put on the most splendid dress once the formal period of mourning has passed.'

Ada wondered whether her friend was being deliberately offensive or simply dim. Knowing her as she did, Ada decided upon the latter. 'Mrs Crane chose this dress for me. Father will decide when I can finally lift my veil for good.'

'And on that day we shall celebrate your freedom from sartorial imprisonment,' said Dora.

'Let's get you some punch. Don't tell anyone, but I had a significant amount of rum put in it. I'm so decadent.' She chuckled at her own daring. Taking the proffered glass, Ada refrained from simply swallowing it in one go. She knew she could probably drink all the ladies present under the table, but tonight was hardly the time to prove it. Sipping as daintily as she could, she smiled and nodded as Dora steered her through the twenty or so women that filled the room. There were polite nods, curious looks and some small talk, but it was not as awful as Ada had expected it to be. In truth, part of her was actually enjoying it. For just one evening, the reality of mourning was distant enough to allow her to relax. Much to Ada's annoyance, her newfound equilibrium ended abruptly upon meeting Dora's newest acquaintance.

'Please let me introduce Josephine Schlecter. Her father is the German ambassador.'

Josephine held out a gloved hand. Ada shook it politely. 'How do you do, Miss Schlecter,' she said, putting on her best smile.

'I am content, for the moment.'

Ada disliked her instantly. Slim, with thin lips and heavy-lidded eyes, she carried herself with an arrogance born of self-indulgent privilege. There was an uncomfortably long pause as the two women studied each other, the deadlock finally broken by the sounding of the dinner gong.

'Let us proceed to the dining room,' said Dora, aware of the iciness that had suddenly crept into the air. More than happy to oblige Ada took a seat at the huge table. Dora was at her side – for which she was inordinately grateful – but her heart sank as she saw Miss Schlecter sit opposite. Ada did her best to appear unconcerned but she knew what was coming, she could see it in Josephine's face. It was tolerable at first; a strained yet civil back and forth of innocuous pleasantries, but it wasn't until the fish course was over that the real sparring began.

'I gather you are something of a bluestocking, yes?' asked Josephine, her expression one of curiosity, her tone one of contempt. The surrounding table went quiet as everyone stared at the two women. They smelled blood in the water, and were curious as to who would be the predator, and who the prey.

'That depends on how one defines the term,' said Ada. 'I'm highly educated if that's what you mean?'

'I too am educated,' said Josephine, 'but not so much that it prevents one from being a lady.'

Taking a sip of white wine, Ada ignored the jibe. 'I don't view the two concepts as mutually exclusive,' she replied, eyeing her opponent over the top of her glass. 'How can we earn the right to vote if we take comfort in the familiarity of ignorance? *Scientia potentia est*, Miss Schlecter. Knowledge is power, is it not?'

Josephine snorted. 'Ah, yes, I see the influence of your Mrs Pankhurst. In Germany we are content to leave such matters in the hands of those better suited to politics.'

'I take it you refer to men?'

'Yes, of course men. A lady has far more important things to do than wave placards and make a nuisance of herself.'

Such as dying post childbirth from puerperal fever, thought Ada.

'Still,' Josephine continued, 'one should not belittle a modicum of learning. I am proud to be able to speak two languages in addition to my native tongue. It means I can converse with people of quality wherever I am in Europe. French and English are so useful.'

'I quite agree. I also find that Spanish and Russian have their merits, in addition to Hindi and a smattering of Mandarin.' Ada was only lying about the Mandarin, but this shrew wouldn't know that.

All eyes turned to Josephine, wondering how she would counter such a salvo. Her mouth drew itself into a cold and empty smile, and Ada steeled herself for whatever veiled insult came next. She needn't have worried, there was nothing veiled about it.

'I gather you are currently in mourning,

hence your somewhat drab appearance. My condolences on your mother's passing, I'm sure you miss her despite the manner of her death. I gather she went mad, attacked her maid with a razor then slit her own wrists; such a tragedy. How is the maid by the way? It's so charitable of you to keep her in your employ, despite her disfigurement. Were she part of *my* household, we would have to let her go. Nobody wishes to see such ugliness over breakfast.'

There was an audible gasp from those present. Such a blatant breach of etiquette was beyond the pale for polite company. Ada physically shook with rage. She wanted to knock Miss Schlecter off her chair, demand the satisfaction of public contrition, but all she could do was stare at her plate and try to conceal how deeply wounded she felt.

'Ada?' said Dora.

'What?'

'Are you all right?'

Ada shook her head. 'I... I should go,' she said, getting to her feet. Her chest felt tight, the corset barely giving her room to breathe. She left the room with as much decorum as she could muster, willing away the tears that threatened to run down her cheeks. Dora caught up with her by the front door.

'Please, Ada, don't go. That was unforgivable of Miss Schlecter. She will never be invited to this house again!'

'How did she know so much about my mother?' asked Ada, knowing the answer. 'I assume the circumstances of her death have provided hours of entertainment; gossip for those who have nothing better to do than wallow in the misfortune of others. Your Miss Schlecter is *schadenfreude* personified, Dora. I need to go home, I'm tired.'

'Let me call you a carriage at least. You can't walk home alone, it's not safe.'

'I have walked in far more dangerous places than Shoreditch. Besides, I need some air. The atmosphere in here is... suffocating.' Leaving a shocked Dora in her wake, Ada strode off into the night, the heels of her boots drumming on the pavement. Josephine's outrageous comments rang in her ears. Belittling her mother's suffering was bad enough, but to direct her vitriol toward Milly, an innocent who could not fight back, was cruel in the extreme. She imagined her grandfather's response had someone dared to say such a thing to him. There would have been blood, followed by a swift and grovelling apology. She wished such an option were open to her, but striking another woman, even after such extraordinary provocation, would only bring more shame to her family.

With every step Ada took the anger began to fade, replaced by a sense of hopelessness that left her drained and weeping. Upon reaching the end of her street she came to a stop, leaning against some railings for support. 'Damn you all,' she said, reaching into her purse for a handkerchief with which to dry her eyes. The last thing she wanted to do was enter the house with smudged cheeks. Mrs Crane would demand to know what had happened, and Ada did not wish to revisit such an awful experience so soon.

Taking a deep breath, she composed herself and walked on. As she did so, she heard another set of footsteps; they were behind and to her right – likely on the opposite side of the road – matching her stride beat for beat. Ada increased her pace, and a moment later so did her pursuer. Her skin prickled. In her desire to flee Miss Schlecter she had forgotten the clear and present danger of a madman on the loose. The safety of home was so close, and breaking into a run Ada covered the last few yards in a state of barely suppressed terror, almost crying with relief when she reached the threshold. With shaking hands, she opened the front door and swiftly locked it behind her, berating herself for such carelessness. She would not make the same mistake again, whatever the circumstances.

Quietly making her way upstairs she bumped into Milly. Duster in hand, the maid was cleaning the gas sconces along the landing. Upon seeing Ada, her beautiful, scarred face broke into a welcoming smile.

'You're back early, miss. Did you have a good evening?'

'Not really, Milly. I wasn't feeling well so I came home. Would you please help me undress?'

'Of course, miss.'

Once she was alone and in bed, Ada tried to still her racing mind. She was sure that someone had been following her, and if she had been attacked there would have been little she could have done. Such vulnerability was unacceptable, but there was a solution. Ada closed her eyes, seeking comfort in darkness. 'Whoever you are, you will not find me easy prey,' she whispered. 'I have learned from the best, and your garrotte is no match for a bullet.' Wishing nothing more than to put the evening behind her, she waited for sleep to take it all away.

CHAPTER 7

Beloved

C lad only in a nightdress Ada stood in her mother's old room. It was bare of furniture, the walls decorated with the soot-stained halos of where paintings used to hang. The shutters were open and bright moonlight crept in, creating a stark silhouette for the man standing at the window, his back to Ada as he looked out over a sleeping London.

'You must think me harsh,' he said.

Ada took an involuntary step backward. That voice was unmistakable; it was him, the man in the mask who had made her watch as he killed her father. She shivered, the floorboards cold against her bare feet. The man turned and walked over to her. Removing his cloak, he gently draped it about Ada's shoulders. It weighed nothing yet warmth enveloped her, as if she were wrapped in firelight.

'I do not wish to see you suffer,' he said, 'but I had to know.'

'Know what?' asked Ada, hands held tight to her chest.

'What lies beneath,' he replied, his breath

warm and sweet against her neck. 'It is only when faced with fear itself that a person's true nature is revealed. Suffice it to say, you demonstrated significant promise. In the face of tragedy you refused to yield, and when pitted against an implacable foe you denied him his prize. Such passion is both rare and impressive.'

'I'm so glad I could live up to your expectations,' said Ada, unable to keep a caustic edge from her voice. 'What is it you want from me? Why do you keep haunting my dreams?'

The man cupped her chin with his gloved hand, peering at her from behind his mask. 'I am not haunting you,' he said. 'I am doing that which must be done. I am only here tonight because in your sadness you called out to me.'

'I did no such thing.'

'Not consciously perhaps, but you did so all the same.'

'And why would I do that?'

'You already know the answer,' said the man. 'Perhaps it would be more pertinent to ask yourself why we are standing *here*, rather than at your mother's graveside?'

Ada was about to protest that it was irrelevant where they were but stopped herself. He was right, these four walls held more meaning for her than she cared to admit; it was in this very room that the last vestiges of childhood had been stripped away. She sighed heavily. 'What happened that night broke my heart.'

'I know,' said the man, 'but the human heart is quite extraordinary. It is stronger than anyone would believe. It can even keep on beating for a time when cut from the body. Feel the strength in *yours*, Ada; let slip the memories that keep you mired in the past. It was not your fault, believe me.'

'Perhaps,' she said, turning to look at where her mother's bed had been, 'but it is no easy thing to forget.' Ada could almost see Clara's emaciated form writhing on the sheets, clawed hands tearing at her scalp as piece by wretched piece her sanity slipped away. Ten long years of watching her mother fall into the abyss. Her ravings had always been consistent, an imaginary assailant, a man of shadows, a slow yet inevitable erosion of reality: infernal variations on a familiar theme.

"I can feel them pecking at me, a murder of crows tearing at my soul," Clara had said. "They're carrying it away and giving it to him. He's always there, my demon, my *ravener*. He won't let me go. Make him stop, please."

Ada had cradled her mother as she wailed and cursed, cried and pleaded, stroking her hair and speaking in hushed and comforting tones. None of it had made the slightest difference. And then, on that fateful evening, Clara stole a straight razor from her husband's dresser. Milly came into the bedroom with a glass of water and a bottle of laudanum as she always did, only to have her devotion rewarded by lifelong disfigurement as Clara carved her madness into the maid's face.

'There was so much blood that it soaked through the carpet,' said Ada, unable to avoid looking at the dark stain on the floorboards. 'Mother was taken to Grandfather's sanatorium the following day. I never saw her alive again. When this room was cleared, I left the house. I couldn't bear the finality of seeing workmen carry her furniture downstairs to their cart.'

'An understandable reaction, given the circumstances,' said the man.

'It was pathetic. I sat in the British Museum and stared at the Rosetta stone for hours. I'm sure Father thought I was grieving, but in truth I was relieved. The nightmare was over and we could begin anew, or so I thought.'

'Forging a new path is never easy, but it is simple. All that is required is the courage to see where it leads, to spit in the eye of your fears.'

Ada turned to the man and gave him a sad smile. 'That sounds like something Grandfather would say.'

'Yes, it does rather, doesn't it?'

She reached up and gently touched the man's mask, running her fingertips down the cheek and across the lips, following the path his knife had taken across her own face. 'If I lift this, I think I know what I would see,' she said.

'And what might that be?'

'Myself. I have read Doctor Freud's treatise on dreams, and as terrifying as you first appeared I know what you are.'

'Do you indeed? Enlighten me, please.'

'You are not real. You are fragments, a phantom; pieces of guilt and memory given form. You are the part of my mind that wants me to survive, and in order to do that I *must* be stronger than my mother was.'

'So you believe you are talking to yourself?'

'In a way, yes.'

'And what if I were to say that you are mistaken, that I am something else entirely?'

'It would only be my own doubts made manifest. I am under no illusion as to the difficulty of what lies before me, but I will prove myself a match for any male doctor, regardless of how many others may wish to see me fail.'

'It is hard to argue with such logic,' said the man. 'You require evidence to refute your beliefs, and I have the means to open your eyes to what real and what is not.' He stepped in close, enfolding Ada in his arms. Behind his mask she saw the glittering of stars in the void. They filled her vision; she wanted to fall among them, a never-ending descent without care or suffering, wrapped in the comfort and safety of darkness.

'Know that I love you,' the man whispered. 'I have loved you since the day you were born. I have walked beside you all of your life, you just didn't notice me, until now. We have much to do, you and I. The scales need to be balanced. Twenty were taken and twenty will pay for that crime. Gather your strength, beloved, for you will need it.'

CHAPTER 8

Old Soldier

A da woke to the smell of freshly brewed coffee. Sunlight filled the room and she heard the sound of a match being struck. Lifting her head, she saw Milly kneeling by the fireplace.

'Good morning,' she said, rubbing the sleep from her eyes.

'Morning, miss. I thought I'd light a fire, it's quite chill outside. I was going to wake you but you looked so peaceful. There's a tray on your bedside table.'

Ada sat up and poured herself a coffee, pondering on her dream. There was sadness and regret but something had shifted inside her, something subtle yet fundamental. It felt as though a weight had been lifted, and as yet she wasn't entirely sure what to make of it. As for the man in the mask, her *phantom*, it made sense that he was simply a devil's advocate of own her own creation, a mental construct to help navigate events that would test even the strongest of personalities. His parting words were a puzzle, however. Still uncommonly sharp in her mind, they had the ring of both a promise and a threat, but try as she might she could not divine their meaning.

'Is there anything else you need, miss?'

Ada looked up to see Milly standing at the foot of the bed. 'No, thank you. That will be all for now.'

'Then I'll be about my duties.'

Ada nodded, and after finishing her coffee, ventured downstairs in search of breakfast. She found Mrs Crane sitting at the parlour table, poring over the domestic accounts ledger.

'Ah, there you are, miss. I hope you slept well? Your father sends his apologies. He had an early start and didn't want to disturb you.'

'That was kind of him, I did need the rest.'

'And how was Miss Hunter's party?'

Ada paused before replying; the housekeeper's tone indicated she was likely aware things had not gone smoothly. 'It was tolerable, apart from one particularly unpleasant guest. I must admit I came home early, I wasn't in the mood for rudeness.'

Mrs Crane nodded sagely. 'A note was delivered earlier by one of the Hunter's footmen. It's on the dresser, along with a telegram from your grandfather.'

Ada read the note. 'It's from Dora. She is profuse in her apologies for the actions of one Josephine Schlecter, and hopes that I will not be so offended as to decline further invitations to dine with her. I'll respond of course, it wasn't her fault that Miss Schlecter was such a vicious little trollop.'

'I am aware of Miss Schlecter,' said Mrs Crane. 'She is rapidly developing a reputation in London for being... uncouth, shall we say. Had I known she was attending Miss Hunter's *soirée*, I would have suggested you find an excuse not to go.'

Appreciative of the support Ada grinned at the housekeeper; it was reassuring to know they were both of a like mind when it came to such matters. Putting Dora's note to one side she opened the telegram.

"*ARRIVING MIDDAY STOP YOUR ATTENDANCE AT AFTERNOON LECTURE REQUIRED STOP MUCH TO DISCUSS STOP HAPPY BIRTHDAY. EH.*"

Ada glanced at the clock. 'Grandfather will be here shortly. Typical, he disappears to France for almost three weeks and the minute he's back, it's fix bayonets and advance at the double.'

'Some things never change,' said Mrs Crane.

Ada nodded. 'Indeed. I have missed him regardless, and we *do* have much to discuss.'

At the stroke of noon, the doorbell rang. Taking a last glance in her bedroom mirror to ensure she was presentable, Ada made her way downstairs, Milly following close behind. Rounding the final corner, she saw her grandfather standing in the hall next to Mrs Crane. He gazed up at her with undisguised affection and pride.

'Well now,' said Sir Edmund, handing his top hat to the housekeeper. 'Come here and let me look at you.' Doing her best to appear dignified, Ada walked slowly toward him, the hem of her dress brushing softly on each riser as she descended. 'Now that is a sight for an old soldier's eyes,' he said, taking her hands in his. 'You are exquisite, my granddaughter, even in black.'

Ada curtseyed and smiled at the tall man, pleased to see such happiness on his face. 'Thank you, Grandfather.'

'I'm sure you'll ruffle some popinjay's feathers at the lecture today,' he said, his silver-grey, mutton chop whiskers bristling with mischief.

'You'd love that, wouldn't you?'

'Me? Enjoy deflating the self-important bubbles that my young charges have encased themselves in? Whoever heard of such a thing? Just wait until you get the vote. There'll be apoplexy at my club on that day, I can tell you.'

Half-hidden behind Ada, Milly giggled.

'Why, Miss Fletcher, just the person I wanted to see. Step into the light so I can have a look at you.'

The maid did as requested, and with gentle, practised hands, Sir Edmund probed the skin on her face. 'Thanks to some fine stitching on my part you appear to be healing nicely. There'll be some tightness when you smile but don't let that stop you; smiling is good for the soul. Keep your face out of the sun for now and use that cream I gave you, it'll soften the scars and soon you'll barely notice them. By next spring you'll be stepping out with some fine young gentleman in Hyde Park.'

Milly blushed scarlet. 'Thank you, sir,' she whispered.

'Thank *you*, dear girl. Thank you for your service, bravery and discretion. It is much appreciated. Your mother sends her regards, by the way; her superlative cooking is what keeps my household going. Right, Granddaughter,' he said, turning to Ada, 'we need to be off. Time, tide and surgery wait for no man.'

'Enjoy your day, miss,' said Milly.

Collecting her hat and veil from Mrs Crane, Ada and her grandfather climbed into the smart carriage waiting by the kerb. 'The London Hospital please, Baynes,' said Sir Edmund.

'Righto, sir,' replied the coachman, and with a flick of the reins urged the horses into a brisk trot.

Sitting opposite her grandfather, Ada studied him as he stared out of the window, his brow furrowed in regal concentration. He'd left the army long before Ada was born, but even after all these years, his bearing was military to a degree that was unmistakeable to any who crossed his path. 'Thank you for being so kind to Milly,' she said.

Sir Edmund nodded. 'It's only fitting. Clara cut open that poor girl's face when all she was trying to do was help. I thank God the damage to her facial nerves was limited. She could have lost the use of her jaw.'

'I know,' said Ada. 'In some respects she was lucky, but I don't want anyone seeing her as damaged, ugly even.'

'I understand, and I will do my best to protect her. There is nothing like tragedy to remind one of what is important in this life.' He sighed and looked at Ada. 'You're all I have left now, dear one. With my wife and daughter gone, it falls to you to make this world a better place; hence my insistence on giving you the best education money can buy.'

'I'm grateful, Grandfather, really I am, but I need to talk to you about Papa. We spoke yesterday about him stepping down as coroner as soon as possible. He needs to rest, and he can't do that while he's wading through blood with Halloran nipping at his heels.'

'I'm aware of the situation,' said Sir Edmund.

Ada raised her eyebrows.

'I saw Henry this morning, before coming to see you. I had my concerns when I left for Paris, but with this… Strangler,' his mouth pursed in disgust, 'continuing his murderous rampage, I can appreciate the pressure your father is under. I know when a man is on the brink, Ada; I saw it many times while serving in India, and something does need to be done. However, for Henry to relinquish his role, especially when he is so badly needed, may not reflect well upon him. It shows professional weakness.'

'That's so unfair. Why should Father have to keep on suffering, simply for the sake of appearances?'

Sir Edmund raised a placatory hand. 'Hear me out, please. I am simply stating a fact. I am not blind to what he has gone through; don't forget that I lost my daughter too. My son-in-law is made of different clay from you and me. He does not have the ability to be ruthless when required, to be truly dispassionate when faced with impossible choices; it is simply not in his nature.'

'It makes him a good and loving father.'

'It does, and it made him the perfect husband for my beloved Clara. It's why I approved their match in the first place. I would not have seen my daughter married to someone who could not perceive her frailty.'

'Oh, I see,' said Ada, understanding that Sir Edmund was not belittling her father.

'You have faced similar challenges, Granddaughter, yet despite your grief you have risen above it, forged onward. You are a match for any man and superior to many, remember that.'

Ada smiled at him. Praise from her grandfather was rare; it meant a great deal to her.

'And as for Henry, please put your mind at rest. He needs to be far away from the rigours of Whitehall, and I can help with that. I have written to Thomas Bond in A division, asking if he would kindly act as interim coroner. There will be other strings to pull, but given time the matter should be settled with no loss of face. If, God forbid, there is another murder before Doctor Bond takes office, I shall be on hand to assist.'

'Thank you, Grandfather,' said Ada, genuinely grateful. 'My apologies for doubting you.'

'Think nothing of it. Family is everything.'

'I hesitate to ask more of you, but there is one other matter I wished to discuss.'

'And what might that be?'

'Please don't think me histrionic, but since attending the scene of Elizabeth Fellowes' murder, I have felt that someone is watching me. Last night I believe that I was followed home; I did not see them but I heard their footsteps. We do not know who the Strangler is; he could be anyone, and that puts him in a position of power. I may not be a newlywed bride, but taking my life would demonstrate just how impotent the authorities are to stop him. My point,

Grandfather, is that I'm afraid, and I do not like it.'

Sir Edmund nodded thoughtfully. 'I've learned many things over the years, and first among them is that it is perilous to ignore one's instincts. You have never been prone to flights of fancy, Ada, and I will not tolerate a threat to your person by anyone. What would you have me do? Ask, and it is yours.'

'I was wondering if I may avail myself of the armoury at Rookwood? I'm sure I can find something suitable yet discreet.'

Sir Edmund grinned. 'I was about to suggest the very same thing; an unorthodox solution, yet undeniably effective. You're an excellent shot and it's a simple matter to obtain a licence for you. I will have one signed in a couple of days, three at most.'

'Having the means to defend myself will be reassuring, although I shall need to practice. It's been some time since I held a firearm.'

'That's easily remedied. Fix a playing card to the old elm tree and take aim from the terrace, just like we used to.'

Ada nodded. 'Thank you for indulging me. I may be worrying about nothing but it never hurts to be prepared, at least until this killer is caught.'

'I quite agree. As for now, let us move from matters martial to academic. I had no doubt that Doctor Garrett-Anderson would accept you into her school, but that is no reason to rest on your laurels. Merely succeeding is not enough, I expect you to be an example and to lead. To that end,' he said, taking out his fob watch, 'you have two minutes to tell me everything you know about amputation.'

CHAPTER 9

Anatomy

'I trust you are all paying attention, gentlemen?' Sir Edmund surveyed the auditorium with eyes like a hawk. Tiered ranks of student doctors stared back at him, some arrogant, some pale and nervous, but all in awe of the man who would ultimately decide their futures.

Watching her grandfather hold court, Ada hid a smile behind her veil. The only woman in a sea of starch, she stood confident and aloof despite the glances that flicked her way. The resentment from the men that surrounded her was palpable, but she ignored it, safe in the knowledge that a single dishonourable word would likely end a career. In Sir Edmund's presence she was for all intents and purposes, untouchable.

'Today we are dealing with amputation,' he bellowed, 'specifically that of the leg below the knee. Thanks to advances in anaesthesia, we no longer have to trade speed for finesse. Mr Hampton, since your gaze appears to be fixed on my granddaughter as opposed to my good self,

74

would you be so kind as to enlighten us as to the procedure for rendering a patient insensible to pain?'

Ada looked at the man standing to her left. He positively radiated embarrassment, a pink glow spreading up his neck and across his cheeks as all eyes fell upon him. 'I... uh,' he stammered.

'In your own time,' said Sir Edmund, drumming his fingers on the tray of surgical instruments by the operating table.

'Chloroform,' he finally managed to say, his voice a strangled croak.

'Correct. We could also use ether, but chloroform is the more potent of the two, and is therefore the anaesthetic of choice for today's operation. And how do we apply said chemical? Do we pour it down the patient's throat with the aid of a funnel, perchance? Or maybe we dance in a circle, flicking the miraculous liquid from our fingertips and begging the gods of surgery to do our bidding?'

Ada felt a degree of sympathy for Mr Hampton as he struggled to recall the answer. Compared to the majority of those present, he at least had made the effort to be polite to her, even if it was mainly self-serving. The seconds ticked by and Sir Edmund rolled his eyes, heaving a dramatic sigh at the apparent idiocy of her neighbour. Ada shook her head; her grandfather was in a puckish mood today, his trip to the

Sorbonne had patently been good for him.

'Since your senses appear to have deserted you,' said Sir Edmund, 'I shall have to ask someone else. Miss Phillips, perhaps you would care to furnish me with the information I require?'

Ada gave a start. It was rare for her grandfather to address her directly, and to pit her against a colleague was unheard of. The auditorium fell deathly silent as every man present fixed their attention upon her. She knew they wanted her to stumble, to demonstrate her unsuitability for their chosen profession; it was an attitude she was more than happy to throw back in their faces.

'We would use a Snow Inhaler, sir,' she replied, her voice clipped, precise and unemotional.

There was a pause as he considered her response. 'Thank you, Miss Phillips, you are correct. Gentlemen, gentlemen, you have been bested by a mere woman of twenty-one years. What am I to do with you?'

Nervous laughter rippled its way round the auditorium, those present unsure whether Sir Edmund was teasing or berating them. Inwardly Ada bristled with indignation. She had offered the correct answer, and yet she was still referred to as a *mere* woman. She knew her grandfather was simply trying to encourage the other students to work harder, but she would still have words with him later.

'So,' said Sir Edmund, 'now we have established the means by which one is spared the agonies of surgery without anaesthesia, we can begin the operation.' With a sweep of his arm he gestured to the man on the operating table, his body covered from the neck down with a white sheet. 'The patient is Mr Albert Short, a thirty-six year old male sewer-worker. He suffered a crushing injury to the lower leg, resulting in extensive tissue trauma and severe damage to both tibia and fibula. Infection has set it and threatens to become gangrenous. Amputation is the only option if we are to save this good man's life. Mr Short, are you ready for me to begin?'

The patient nodded. 'Yes, sir. This won't hurt, will it?' His eyes were wide, his fear obvious.

'You won't feel a thing,' said Sir Edmund reassuringly. 'Believe me, you're in the best of hands. When the mask is put over your face, I want you to breathe slowly and deeply. Before long you'll be asleep, and when you wake up you'll be as right as rain.'

Ada watched in fascination as the chloroform did its work. She'd witnessed this procedure many times, but it never seemed other than miraculous; in less than twenty seconds Mr Short was completely unconscious. She couldn't imagine what it must have been like for a patient before the discovery of anaesthetics. To have a limb cut off without any pain relief – beyond a bottle of whiskey and a strip of leather to bite on – would have been appalling.

An orderly removed Sir Edmund's frock coat, before rolling up his sleeves and slipping a white apron over his head. More theatrics, thought Ada, a demonstration of the power her grandfather wielded. He was perfectly capable of dressing himself for surgery, but it was more effective to have someone else do it for him. It left no question as to *who* was in charge.

Sir Edmund pulled back the sheet, revealing the injury to the patient's left leg. The wound was large and festering, the surrounding flesh rapidly becoming necrotic. The splintered ends of the tibia and fibula were clearly visible, and no amount of carbolic spray was going to halt the infection. Ada agreed wholeheartedly with her grandfather's diagnosis; amputation was indeed the only option. Sir Edmund tapped the shin just below the knee. 'I will make the initial incision here. Speed of the operation is still a factor; blood vessels such as the popliteal and posterior tibial arteries will need to be clamped and sutured in order to minimize blood loss. Please be aware that sufficient skin and calf muscle need to be retained in order to close the wound properly. Once that is done we get to the easy bit, sawing through the leg bones; simple carpentry really.

Any questions?'

A hand went up at the back. 'What size scalpel would we use, sir?'

'Good question. Given the volume of tissue one is cutting through, I prefer a larger knife for an even incision. Today I'm using a catling; it's robust, and the double-edged blade is helpful in lifting the periosteum away from the bone. So, let us get to it.'

Ada leaned forward, carefully noting every detail of her grandfather's technique. The knife a blur in his hands, there was no hesitation as he drew it round the circumference of the limb. Flesh parted, and the major arteries and veins were tied off in turn. The sheets beneath the patient's leg turned crimson, and Sir Edmund's forearms were soon covered in blood. Ada was surprised to find herself recoiling at the sight. She was not squeamish in the slightest, but since attending the Limehouse killings, the stark image of blood-spattered linen had a more visceral context for her. No longer just a by-product of lifesaving treatment, it could also be the result of savage butchery. Given the manner in which the Strangler had murdered his victims, his arms too would have been red to the elbows, soaked in arterial spray as his garrotte did its awful work. Ada closed her eyes for a moment, forcing herself to breathe slowly, to focus on the here and now. For once she was actually grateful for her veil; it hid her discomfiture from the men around her.

'With the soft tissue dealt with,' said Sir Edmund, wiping his hands on a clean cloth, 'we proceed to the amputation proper.' Reaching for the bone saw, he gripped the knee tightly and with rhythmic strokes was through the lower-leg in seconds. Returning the instrument to the tray, he held up the severed, dripping limb for all to see. 'And that, gentlemen, is how quickly you should be able to...' There was a thump from the stalls as one of the students fainted, crumpling to the floor in a well-attired heap. Rather than being concerned for his welfare, Ada was simply glad that it hadn't been her. Showing such weakness in front of these men would do serious harm to what standing she had earned so far.

'Leave him be,' Sir Edmund barked as two men made to raise their fellow to his feet. 'If you don't have the fortitude for this kind of thing, better we find out now.' He handed the leg to an orderly before picking up a needle and reel of suture thread. 'That was the easy part,' he said, 'closing the wound requires significant care. If it isn't done properly, then the patient has little chance of being able to use a prosthetic. Watch closely.'

Ada's admiration for her grandfather's skill grew each time she watched him work. Over dinner she had heard many grisly tales of his exploits as an army surgeon. It was clear to her that he'd cared deeply about the men in his charge, and had tried his best to make the loss of a limb as bearable as possible under the circumstances.

'And so we are done,' said Sir Edmund, standing back to admire his handiwork. 'Comments?'

A handful of technical queries were answered with military efficiency, and with notes taken, the lecture was closed and attendees dismissed. Ada waited patiently while the men filed out, doing her best to ignore their backward glances.

'My apologies for any embarrassment caused, Miss Phillips,' said Mr Hampton as he shyly collected his papers. 'I find it refreshing to have a woman present. I wish we had more; it would render the environment far less like a gentleman's club.'

'Thank you, Mr Hampton. It may please you to know that I will be starting my degree with Doctor Garrett-Anderson in the spring.'

'Then I wish you the success you have so patently earned. Unlike some of my colleagues, I feel you are eminently suited to this profession. I cannot see *you* fainting at the sight of blood.' He caught Sir Edmund peering up at him. 'I had best take my leave. Good day to you, Miss Phillips.' The young doctor scurried off, clutching his notes to his chest and trying not to trip on the stairs.

'So,' said Sir Edmund as Ada joined him, 'what do you think of my efforts?'

'I think you're a frustrated actor, and that you enjoy teasing your students far too much.'

'Hah!' he said, patting the severed leg that lay on the table next to him. 'You see far too clearly for one so young, but then again I would expect nothing less from you.'

'Despite me being a *mere* woman?'

'You know I didn't mean it. I would never think of a woman as *mere.* Having you here helps keep the egos of my students in check. Some of them are simply too soft for this line of work; if they'd served the empire as I have then perhaps they would understand what it really means to make life and death decisions.'

'Are you referring to India?' asked Ada.

'Yes, very much so.'

She watched as a shadow fell across her grandfather's face, he suddenly looked very old and tired. Seeing Ada's scrutiny he collected himself.

'Still, let us not dwell on the past. Times may have changed, but it irritates me that the offspring of various moneyed families think their social standing entitles them to be surgeons.'

Ada was about to remind her grandfather that he too came from a wealthy and aristocratic family, when there was a sharp rap on the auditorium door.

'Come,' said Sir Edmund.

The orderly who'd assisted him earlier poked his head inside. 'Your carriage is waiting out front, sir,' he said.

'Thank you, Hobson, we'll be there shortly.' He turned to Ada. 'I won't be a moment; I just need to clean myself up.' He disappeared into a side room to scrub his hands, and reappeared looking every inch the Victorian patrician, his tall frame clad in a frock coat, and with a top hat and kid gloves tucked under his arm.

'Despite being used as a stick to beat your students with,' said Ada, 'I know you only have my best interests at heart.'

'I should hope so too,' he said, raising his eyebrows, 'your education is costing me a fortune. Some of the older members at my club have mutteringly referred to me as a *progressive*. It's quite too much for them. Perhaps I should go on one of Mrs Pankhurst's marches, just to see which of the old hounds keels over first.'

Ada laughed, and was about to take her grandfather's arm when a smartly-dressed man entered the auditorium.

'Edmund, I'm glad to have caught you. An urgent matter has arisen and your assistance is required.'

'And what could be so urgent as to interrupt a belated birthday supper with my granddaughter? Come to think of it, I don't believe you've been properly introduced to each other. Ada Phillips, this is Sir Frederick Treves, director of this august establishment.'

'An honour, Sir Frederick,' said Ada, shaking his hand. 'I read your treatise on the treatment of Joseph Merrick with great interest. I was saddened to hear of his passing in April.'

'Thank you, Miss Phillips. Joseph was indeed an extraordinary individual. It is rare to meet someone who demonstrates such grace despite their challenges. However, much as I would like to discuss the case history with you, the matter in hand requires immediate attention.'

'Of course. I shall leave you to talk with Grandfather.'

'Quite the contrary, Miss Phillips, your presence is most fortuitous; it saves me having to send for you. What I have to say concerns you both.'

'What is this about, Frederick?' asked Sir Edmund.

'I have just come from a meeting with Sir Kerr McDonnell. He asks that you return to your sanatorium at Rookwood immediately.'

'Sir Kerr is the private secretary to the Prime Minister,' said Ada.

'Indeed he is. I trust that indicates the need for complete discretion?'

Ada nodded.

'You have new patient, Edmund, and she

requires treatment away from public view. She is apparently suffering from acute psychological distress, and has harmed herself physically.'

'Very well,' he said, 'but what I don't understand is what this has to do with my granddaughter.'

'The young woman in question has asked to speak to Ada. In fact she has insisted that Ada is the *only* person she wishes to speak to.'

'Why would she want to speak me?' said Ada. 'Who is she?'

'She's the daughter of the German Ambassador,' said Sir Frederick. 'Miss Josephine Schlecter.'

CHAPTER 10

Schadenfreude

'Are you familiar with this woman?' Sir Edmund asked Ada.

'I met her for the first time last night, at Dora Hunter's party. She was the reason I left early.'

'I see. Well, under the circumstances it would be impolitic not to go and see her immediately.'

'I hoped you would say that,' said Sir Frederick. 'I see your carriage is already outside. Please do your best to reassure the ambassador, Edmund. This is a particularly sensitive matter. He is waiting for you at the sanatorium.'

'Then let us be on our way. I shall report back in due course.'

Sir Frederick nodded, and Ada and her grandfather hurried to their carriage.

'What exactly occurred at this party last night?' asked Sir Edmund once they were underway. 'I'm sure it has no bearing on the current situation, but I would rather be in possession of all the facts.'

'I was introduced to Miss Schlecter,' said Ada, 'and found her to be irksome. She is vain, arrogant, and when we sat down to dine she publicly insulted both me and our family. Rather than retaliate, I left with as much decorum as I could muster. It's why I ended up walking home alone. I was deeply upset.'

'It sounds as though you behaved impeccably. Had she the temerity to say such things to me, I doubt I would have shown such restraint.'

'The thought did cross my mind at the time,' said Ada, 'but she wanted me to react. I chose not to give her the satisfaction.'

'I am proud of you. Unlike Miss Schlecter, your conduct does you credit. You could be forgiven for taking some measure of satisfaction as to the predicament the girl currently finds herself in.'

'I have no love for Miss Schlecter,' said Ada, 'but neither would I wish someone harm on the basis of an insult. I must admit that I am curious as to what illness has suddenly befallen her; she appeared in rude health last night.'

'And now it falls to us to investigate the matter. Fate is a curious thing, is it not? Given that she wishes to speak to you, perhaps she wishes to offer an apology?'

'That is a possibility,' said Ada, 'but from what Sir Frederick said I think there is likely more to it. We shall find out when we examine her.'

'I shall be interested to hear your diagnosis,'

said Sir Edmund. 'Forgive me for asking this of you, but when we arrive, please don't speak to the ambassador unless he addresses you directly. He has a reputation for being fractious, and with relations with our Teutonic cousins being somewhat tense of late, I would rather this matter did not escalate.'

'I understand,' she said. 'It will give me a chance to talk to Josephine without interruption.'

Arriving at the sanatorium, Ada and Sir Edmund were greeted by an orderly and taken inside. Ada always found herself impressed by what her grandfather had created. A decade earlier he had repurposed a hunting lodge, adding new wings and installing the most modern of equipment. Catering exclusively to military personnel, the hospital treated those who had been grievously wounded in both body and mind. Here in the quiet woodland of the Rookwood estate, the damaged produce of the British Empire's relentless expansion could hopefully find some measure of peace. For all its merits, the building held challenging memories for Ada. Her mother had been brought here after her attack on Milly, and shortly afterwards had taken her own life, opening her wrists with a shard of ceramic from a broken teacup. It was a harsh truth that even the best of care was sometimes insufficient to prevent tragedy.

Sir Edmund came to a stop by the

administrator's office. 'Would you be so kind as to wait outside please, Ada?' he asked. 'Fitz will escort you to see Josephine.'

Ada nodded and her grandfather disappeared inside. She heard muffled voices, and moments later a tall, athletic man with thinning fair hair and wire-rimmed glasses came out to greet her. He wore a dark, three-piece suit, and eschewing the fashion for sideburns, he instead sported a neatly waxed moustache.

'Good afternoon, Fitz,' she said.

He smiled and took her hand in greeting. 'Ada, how lovely to see you. You are looking well.'

'Thank you. I should apologise for not coming to see you after the funeral, but…'

He held up a hand. 'There's no need to explain. I'm sure you would rather not be here under the circumstances.'

She nodded, grateful for the doctor's understanding. John 'Fitz' Fitzpatrick ran the establishment in partnership with her grandfather, and Ada held him in the greatest of esteem. Also an ex-military man, he attended to the day-to-day operation of the sanatorium with an uncommon blend of efficiency and empathy. Fitz was also the one to find her mother as she lay dying, and Ada knew that he still blamed himself.

'I gather we have a patient that is asking for me?' she said.

'Yes,' said Fitz. 'This is all rather unusual.

It's probably easier to show you.' He led her to the secure wing. Behind a barred gate, rooms had been built to house the most disturbed patients. Lined with quilted material, they were designed to prevent the occupants from harming themselves. Upon reaching the last door on the row Fitz lowered his gaze. 'I'm sorry, but it was the only one we had available. I have deliberately avoided using it until now.'

Ada sighed. This was where her mother had spent her last days. Just like her room at the house in Shoreditch, she had left the floor covered in blood. 'It's all right, Fitz,' she said, 'it's just a room, not a mausoleum.'

'I was concerned that this might be difficult for you, so I am relieved to hear you say that. However, I should caution you that Miss Schlecter was most disturbed upon her arrival. She had cut her forearm quite badly and was incoherent. She would not speak English and my German is rather poor, I'm ashamed to say, so I had difficulty understanding her. Her desire to speak to you was clear though. She has been restrained, so you are in no danger. Are you still willing to see her?'

Ada nodded, although given the choice she would rather be anywhere else. The fact that Josephine now occupied the same space as her late mother was an unsettling synchronicity. Fitz unlocked the door and ushered her inside. In the centre of the room was an iron-framed bed; Josephine lay upon it, eyes closed and her wrists secured with thick, leather straps. She was dressed in the same clothes she had worn to the party, and her left forearm was wrapped in a bandage. Next to the bed was a plain, wooden chair.

'If you would like to take a seat,' said Fitz, 'I'll be waiting just outside.'

'Thank you. I'm sure I'll be fine. I am curious as to what she has to say to me.'

Fitz smiled and withdrew, leaving her alone with her patient.

'Josephine. It's Ada Phillips. Can you hear me?' There was no response; the young woman appeared to be asleep, her breathing soft as her chest rose and fell in reassuring rhythm. Not wishing to alarm Josephine by rousing her abruptly, Ada decided to examine the injury she had inflicted upon herself. As gently as she could, she removed the bandage. Carved into the delicate skin on the inside of Josephine's forearm was a word, the capital letters neatly incised with a sharp blade of some kind. The cuts were deep enough for the edges of the skin to part, yet not so deep that they would cause profuse bleeding. The scarring would be significant. It read, "SCHADENFREUDE".

Ada frowned. She remembered using the same word to describe Josephine to Dora the previous evening. The literal translation was harm-joy, taking pleasure in the misfortune of others. 'What on earth possessed you to do such a thing?' said Ada, taking Josephine's hand in hers. She may have been offended by Miss Schlecter's comments, but it was clear the young woman was very disturbed, a condition that Ada would not wish upon anyone. She lifted her head and saw that Josephine was looking straight at her, a faint smile on her lips.

'I am sorry for what I said. I see now that I caused you pain.'

'I accept your apology, Miss Schlecter, but why did you do this to yourself?'

Josephine's smile widened to alarming proportions, her eyes rolling back in her head. She gripped Ada's hand tightly, as if seeking to anchor herself with physical contact. 'He said that my heart was not black enough to take, but that recompense was still required; a demonstration of contrition.'

'Who said such a thing to you?' asked Ada.

'He did not tell me his name, but he gave me a message. He wants you to know that you are stronger than your mother was.'

A knot formed in Ada's stomach, her skin prickling as the temperature in the room dropped suddenly. Josephine's breath steamed as it left her mouth. Pulling Ada in close, she whispered in her ear.

'*Sei gewiss, das ich dich liebe. Ich habe dich seit*

dem Tag deiner Geburt immer geliebt. Dein ganzes Leben lang bin ich an deiner Seite gewesen, du hast mich nur nicht bemerkt... bis jetzt!'

Ada tore her hand from Josephine's grasp.

The young woman laughed hysterically, tears running down her cheeks to soak the rough cotton of the pillow beneath her head.

'Witness my art,' she screamed out, fixing her gaze upon Ada, 'fear my wrath!' Her body convulsed, thrashing against her restraints as Ada jumped up and backed away, knocking over the chair with a clatter. Fitz burst in, and seeing Josephine's distress he rushed over to hold her down.

'Please wait outside, Ada. I need to sedate her.'

She nodded dumbly, turning away and almost running from the room. Alone in the corridor she leaned against the wall, her mind reeling. Josephine had spoken the exact same words as the masked man in her dream. "Know that I love you. I have loved you since the day you were born. I have walked beside you all of your life, you just didn't notice me, until now." How was that possible? It made absolutely no sense.

'Are you all right?' said Fitz, coming to stand next to her. 'You aren't hurt in any way?'

Ada shook her head, but for a moment she found herself unable to speak. The vehemence of Josephine's outburst had shaken her deeply.

'When you said she was disturbed, Fitz, I did not think it would be anything so extreme. It reminded me of what Mother was like in her last days.'

'I am so sorry. Perhaps it was a mistake to bring you here?'

'No, you did the right thing. A good doctor does not avoid a patient just because the circumstances are challenging. Please do not worry, I shall be fine once my heart stops racing.'

'Thank you for being so understanding,' said Fitz. 'I really had no idea she would react in such a fashion. When she was brought in she was upset, confused; there was no indication she might become violent. I fear she may have suffered a seizure. She should remain unconscious for some time, but I will sit with her for a while, make sure the sedative takes hold. Oh, and before I forget, an orderly brought me a message from Edmund. The ambassador wishes to speak to you.'

'I see,' said Ada, trying to ignore the sinking sensation in the pit of her stomach. Leaving Fitz to minister to his patient, she did her best to compose herself; her grandfather would be furious if she appeared anything less than professional. Taking a deep breath, she knocked on the office door and entered. Sir Edmund was standing next to a short, impeccably-dressed man with fair, thinning hair and a neatly trimmed beard. He looked at her with pale-blue eyes, his face lined with worry.

'Fräulein Phillips,' he said, bringing his heels smartly together and bowing from the waist.

Ada curtsied in response. 'Your Excellency.'

'Herr Schlecter is deeply concerned for the welfare of his daughter. It would be of great help if you could offer some words of comfort.'

Ada understood what her grandfather was asking of her. His tone indicated she should choose what she said next with the greatest of care.

'Josephine is resting at the moment. Her arm is a matter of concern, but the injuries are clean and will heal.'

'Why did she wish to see you?' he asked.

Ada paused; this was what he really wanted to know. How she answered him was of paramount importance. 'Josephine and I had a minor difference of opinion at a party last night; more a problem of translation than anything else. It troubled her that she may have inadvertently caused offence, and wished to apologise. There was no need to of course. I reassured her that I held no ill will, and wished her the most rapid of recoveries. Josephine is in safe hands, and if I may be of service in any way I am at your Excellency's disposal.'

Herr Schlecter nodded and gave Ada a warm smile. 'I gather you are training to be a doctor, yes?'

'That is correct. I have two exceptional mentors in both my father and grandfather.'

'That is a worthy aim, and thank you both for coming to my family's aid.'

'It is an honour to assist, Herr Schlecter,' said Sir Edmund. 'Both myself and Doctor Fitzpatrick will be in attendance upon your daughter. Rest assured she will receive the best, and the most discreet, of care.'

'Danke schön, Sir Edmund.'

'Ada, I will stay with Herr Schlecter until he is satisfied his daughter is comfortable. Please continue on to the main house and I will join you presently. Hargrave will attend to anything you may require. The fire in my study will be lit, so please feel free to ensconce yourself.'

Relieved to be politely dismissed, Ada curtsied to the ambassador and returned to the waiting carriage. It was only a short walk to Rookwood itself, but she didn't trust her legs to carry her. She was met at the main door by Hargrave, the senior butler. Elderly and courteous, he greeted her warmly and showed her into the study.

'May I bring you some refreshments, miss?' he asked.

'No thank you, Hargrave, I shall wait for Grandfather.'

'As you wish, miss. There is a bell-pull to the side of the mantelpiece if you require me.' With a brief nod he left.

Removing her veil, Ada poured herself a brandy and sank gratefully into an armchair by the hearth. What Josephine had said defied all logic; it was a riddle, and an unsettling one at that. And then there were her parting words, "Witness my art, fear my wrath." Ada didn't know if it was just the ravings of an unbalanced mind, or if there was more to it. To find out she would need to speak to Josephine again, but after being sedated she would not be lucid until morning at the earliest. With Fitz and her grandfather keeping a close eye on their patient, Ada knew she would have to tread carefully. Josephine's wellbeing was their primary concern, and they may be reticent to allow visitors for fear of another violent outburst. Ada decided to speak to Fitz when the opportunity arose; if Josephine's condition had improved, hopefully he would grant her access. Until then, her questions would remain unanswered.

Heaving a sigh of frustration, Ada took a sip of brandy and closed her eyes, letting the warmth of the fire seep into her bones. She was on her second glass when her grandfather strode in.

'Are you all right?' he asked, bending over to kiss the crown of her head.

'Yes,' she said, smiling at him.

'You handled that well. Fitz told me what happened. Your poker face is as good as mine.' He sat in the chair opposite, joining Ada in supping on a brandy. 'The ambassador has put his faith in us. There is a great deal at stake and we must do our utmost to help his daughter; should her health deteriorate while in our care, the consequences could be dire.'

'Is that likely?' asked Ada.

'I sincerely hope not, but loathe though I am to admit it, I have no idea what ails the girl. Did she say anything that may explain the cause of her distress?'

Ada knew she would have to lie; if she told her grandfather the truth, he would no doubt question both her fitness to practice as a doctor, and her sanity. For the time being obfuscation was the safest option. 'No, Grandfather. As I told the ambassador, she simply wished to apologise for her poor conduct last night. As to what led her to harm herself, I cannot speculate.'

'Perhaps she took some form of illicit substance?' he suggested. 'Opiates are rife among the gentry, especially laudanum, and in high enough doses can certainly affect one's state of mind. If that is the case, then there is no reason Josephine should not make a full recovery.'

'I hope you are right, Grandfather. It was unpleasant seeing her so distressed, and in that room too.'

Sir Edmund nodded. 'Yes, that cannot have been comfortable for you. It is testament to your character that you dealt with it so professionally. To that end, I have something which may lift your spirits after our unexpected diversion.' He got up and reached behind his desk. In his hands he held a large box of stiff, white card, tied with a blue ribbon.

'Is that for me?'

'Yes. While I was in Paris I went shopping, safe in the knowledge that you would be starting your degree. Happy belated birthday, darling Granddaughter, you make both me and the family proud.' He gave the box to Ada. Opening it, she found an exquisite dark-blue dress; it was simple, elegant, and made from the finest cotton and lace.

'These are fashionable with French female doctors at the moment,' said Sir Edmund. 'Apparently they are easy to clean, which will be a prerequisite for your attire, believe me. I have two more for you upstairs.'

'Thank you, Grandfather, it's beautiful.'

'Wearing black until you start your degree will be more than sufficient,' he said, 'then it shall be time for you to spread your wings.'

Ada leaned forward and kissed him on the cheek; it was a most thoughtful gift.

'I'm pleased you like it. Let us have something to eat, then I'll send for a carriage to take you home. I shall be busy this evening.'

'I understand,' said Ada.

After a light supper she was driven back to

Shoreditch. Milly and Mrs Crane made much of her new dress, but the one person that Ada really wanted to show it to was absent. 'Do you know when Father is coming home?' she asked.

'No miss,' said Mrs Crane, 'he didn't say.'

'I see. In that case I may as well retire; it's been a long day.'

'Of course, miss.'

Trudging wearily upstairs, Ada prayed that her father had the strength to keep going until Doctor Bond became coroner. All that was needed was a few more days without incident, without the spilling of blood. Perhaps then they could finally be a family again.

CHAPTER 11

For Whom the Bell Tolls

H is huge frame wreathed in bright sparks, the anvil rang as Thomas Quick forged a new horseshoe. Fingers stiff with age and injury gripped the hammer, each carefully placed stroke a single note in a glorious symphony of iron and sweat. His brow furrowed in concentration as he worked, singing the song his father had taught him.

'Tommy was a piper's son
And fell in love when he was young
But all the tunes that he could play
Were o'er the hills and far away.'

Once the glowing metal was shaped to his satisfaction, he punched holes for the nails and quenched it in a bucket of water. There was a sharp hiss, a cloud of steam, and his job was done.

'How are preparations, Thomas?' said a voice from behind him.

The blacksmith turned to greet his visitor. ''Ello, sir, I didn't hear you come in.'

'That's all right. I didn't wish to disturb your labours, and it's always a pleasure to hear you sing.'

Thomas smiled shyly. 'It helps me think, sir; stops the noise in my head.'

'I know,' said the man, gently touching the livid scar than ran across the side of Thomas' shaven scalp. 'I had hoped your suffering might lessen, but some wounds are more difficult to heal than others.'

'I think you're right, sir, but those pills you gave me make it better.'

'I am glad. I do not like to think of you suffering.'

'No need to worry about me, sir. I've just got some shoeing to do and then I'll be ready.'

'Wonderful, Thomas, you have been of great assistance. I always knew the horses would take to you.' He looked fondly at the two, midnight-black mares waiting patiently in their stalls. Nearby stood a finely-appointed Clarence carriage, its lacquer gleaming.

'They're good girls, sir. Mari and Uma may be old, but they still have some fire in them.'

'As do you, my friend. The army may have discarded you after years of service, but I shall give you purpose again.'

'They said I was going to die, sir. After coming back from Africa I almost wanted to, but here I am. I will do my duty.'

'I am pleased to hear it. Have you thought upon what we discussed, about what I shall ask of you? If you are to be part of my great work it must be of your own free will. Your soul is pure and I do not wish it darkened by doubt.'

'I understand what you want me to do, sir, and I will help in any way I can, for Martha, and my little Gracie.'

'Your wife and daughter would be proud of you, Thomas. They were cruelly taken and yet you were denied justice. They never caught the man who killed them, did they?'

'No, sir. It was just some thief, stealing what little we had. He didn't have to take them from me too.'

'He did not, and the choice to do so shows the wickedness that can hide within a human heart. Vengeance is a cold and shining thing, Thomas. It is both righteous and necessary. Come now, night has fallen and we must be about our business.' He handed the blacksmith a long, double edged knife. 'This is called a catling; I need it to be as sharp as a razor. Would you be able to help me?'

Thomas nodded. Seating himself at his bench, he unwrapped a bundle of oil-soaked muslin; inside was a whetstone of the finest quartz. With gentle strokes, he rasped the blade back and forth, honing the steel until it hummed beneath his fingers. Once finished, he cleaned it with a dry cloth and handed it back.

'Very good, very good indeed. This will do nicely. I shall wait while you finish your other tasks.'

'Of course, sir, I shan't be long.' Swiftly replacing Uma's shoe, Thomas harnessed the horses and opened the coach-house doors. 'Where are we bound, sir?' he asked.

The man smiled at him from the dark recesses of the carriage, white teeth bathed crimson in the dying glow of the forge.

'A photographer's studio in Limehouse; I have an appointment and I don't wish to be late. I am so very hungry, Thomas. One could even say I was... ravenous.'

'Ah, you're awake.'

Harold Price opened his eyes and tried to scream, but the rag stuffed into his mouth muffled the sounds of his distress.

'There is no point crying out,' said a voice from the darkness. 'There is nobody to hear you.'

Price flicked his gaze left and right, up and down. There was no mistaking his predicament. His naked body dangled in mid-air, bound wrists looped over a hook attached to a pulley high above. A stout wooden platform surrounded him on three sides, and beneath his feet gaped the maw of a vast ceramic crucible. Flickering orange light from oil lamps and banked fires gave his surroundings a hellish tint.

'Take out his gag and turn our guest to face me, Thomas.'

A gnarled hand reached out and swung Price

round. The rag was pulled roughly from his mouth and he coughed, trying to find some saliva to moisten his dry lips. In front of him stood a tall man, smartly dressed and with a white, velvet carnival mask covering his face.

'Who are you?' Price snarled. 'Why are you doing this? I'll have you arrested. I work with the police you know.'

'I'm well aware of what you *do*, Harold,' said the man. 'It's who you really *are* that interests me. I have something you may wish to see.'

'I'm not doing anything while you've got me tied up like this,' he hissed.

'I think you may change your mind. You have such an interesting hobby after all.'

'Are you an actor or something?' said Price. 'Is this supposed to be a joke? Some of the crew from Wilton's Theatre having a bit of after show fun?'

'All the world's a stage, as the Bard said. Are we not all actors? Do we not wear different faces, different masks, depending on who is watching? Where is your true face, Harold? I've wanted to look upon it for some time.'

'You're not making any sense,' said Price.

'Then maybe this will clarify matters,' said the man, turning up the wick on an oil lamp. Price blanched as he saw what was laid out before him.

'The Chapman field camera with tripod,' said the man, 'a fine choice for recording the scenes of crime. Light, portable, it provides excellent detail in a wide range of light, perfect for recording the results of suffering.'

'I'm a photographer,' said Price. 'It's what I do, take photographs.'

'Oh, you do yourself a disservice; capturing the likeness of a subject is the least of your achievements. Take the contents of your fine equipment bag for example.' The man gestured to a leather Gladstone sitting open next to the camera. 'What treasures I found therein. Spare silver-emulsion plates, a wide-angle lens, bottles of cleaning fluid, and… these.' The man held out his hands. Resting upon them were a portfolio of developed photographs, a piano-wire garrotte and a short, narrow-bladed knife.

'I ask you again, Mr Price. Take off your mask and show me your true face.'

The photographer hung his head, remaining silent for a moment before his chest began to heave. A slow, viscous chuckle crawled from his mouth as he raised his eyes. All trace of righteous indignation was gone, replaced by a thin-lipped sneer and the coldest of expressions.

'Ah, there you are,' said the man. 'Welcome home, Mr Price, or should I say, The Limehouse Strangler.'

'That was the papers. I didn't ask for some ridiculous title.'

'Ridiculous it may be, but it was rather apt

don't you think? You choked the life from four new brides then disfigured their bodies.'

'They got what they deserved,' Price spat.

The man sighed. 'Oh, Harold, I fear your self-importance has only fed your evil, along with the syphilis that is currently eating you away. Is that why you did what you did? Revenge for your condition? Could your fragile manhood not stand being jilted at the altar by the fiancé who infected you?'

Price's face contorted with rage. 'They're all the same. They lead you on, promise you the world then turn you into a laughing stock. They deserved every ounce of pain I could give them.'

The man opened the portfolio and carefully – almost reverently – turned the photographs inside. 'They're all here,' he said, 'Catherine Foster, Jane Hart, Susan Read and poor, young Elizabeth Fellowes. You took their wedding portraits, noted their addresses, and then took their lives in a manner designed to torture and humiliate them, even in death.'

'They were as ugly on the inside as they were on the outside.'

'I disagree, Harold. They were beautiful, and more importantly they were innocent. Four, simple, ordinary women, married to decent men who treated them with respect and love.'

'They… were…fucking… whores!' screamed Price.

'They were people,' said the man, 'and in murdering them you destroyed their families too. That kind of atrocity deserves a pithy response.' Reaching into the black-leather medical bag at his feet, he took out an ebony-handled amputation knife. Holding it up, he inspected the steel as it shone in the lamplight. 'My friend Thomas here has a skilled hand; I doubt I have seen a finer edge.'

Price heard a satisfied grunt from somewhere in the darkness behind him. 'Are you like me then?' he said, sweat beading on his forehead. 'Perhaps you're no stranger to killing.'

'I am certainly no stranger to killing,' said the man, 'of that you can be sure, but I am nothing like you. You are, at best, a diseased animal, revelling in the suffering of others and the violent taking of life. Your heart is black and filled with sin, and that, my dear Harold, means that you are *mine*.'

'What do you mean yours?' said Price. 'You're going to hand me over to the police, aren't you?'

'No, I am not handing you over to the police. They will simply arrest you; give you to the Courts for trial and your subsequent execution by hanging. That would be wholly insufficient for your crimes. I have work to do, you see; a great undertaking that requires much sacrifice. A wrong was done to me that can only be answered in blood. London may be an unwilling pupil, but there is a lesson that must be learned; you will make a fine start, and an even finer example.'

'You don't have to do this,' begged Price. 'I have money, you can have it all, just don't cut me.' His eyes darted wildly, desperate to find a means of escape.

The man leaned in close and inhaled. 'You stink of fear, Harold. It is quite exquisite.'

'Just let me go. I won't hurt anyone else, I promise.' Tears began running down Price's cheeks.

'I quite agree, Harold,' said the man. 'You will not hurt anyone else ever again, that I can promise you.'

Price thrashed in his bonds, screaming impotently for help. Trickles of blood ran down his forearms as the skin on his wrists tore, but his efforts achieved nothing. Eventually his struggles ceased. Hanging limp and exhausted, he stared at his captor with wide and terrified eyes.

'It is not my purpose to inflict suffering,' said the man. 'I have it in my gift to take all the pain away, but the dead cry out for vengeance and their agonies must be paid for. If you feel yourself aggrieved at your circumstances, Harold, remember what you did to Elizabeth Fellowes. You even kept her eyes as a souvenir. They're in a bottle at the bottom of your equipment bag.'

'Mercy, please,' Price sobbed.

The man in the mask shook his head. 'You

are deserving of many things, Harold, mercy is not among them. Just like the great bells that were forged in this very building, my message will ring out loud across the city of London. Only through example will my beloved Ada come to know the truth. Now, Mr Price,' he said, raising the catling, 'shall we begin?'

CHAPTER 12

The Foundry

'I didn't hear you come back last night,' said Ada, joining her father at the breakfast table.

'I was rather late. Halloran ordered a re-examination of Elizabeth Fellowes' body, not that it revealed anything pertinent.' The utter weariness in his voice was palpable; it made Ada want to seek the chief constable out, shake him, scream at him, force him to leave her father alone. The day he left Whitehall for good could not come soon enough.

'I gather you've spoken with Grandfather,' she said, stifling her anger.

He nodded. 'Edmund made a good case. You won't have to be concerned about my health for much longer. I was reticent to hand over the reins, but I think it is time to do so. He made that quite clear.'

Ada smiled at him. 'It's for the best, Papa.'

The doorbell rang, and Mrs Crane swept along the hall to answer it. There were muffled voices, and moments later the housekeeper entered the parlour. Ada's heart sank. Although she was doing her best to hide it, the expression of concern on Mrs Crane's face spoke volumes.

'It's a Constable Bennett, sir. He asks that you accompany him immediately. He has a carriage waiting. He would not say what the matter entailed but he appears agitated.'

Ada watched in despair as her father crumpled in upon himself. Grey and trembling, he offered the housekeeper a resigned nod. 'Please tell the constable that I will be five minutes. I need to collect my things first.' With visible effort he got up and turned to leave.

'I'm coming too, Papa,' said Ada. 'Whatever this is we'll deal with it together.'

'Thank you, darling,' said Henry, 'I'll meet you outside.'

Ada rushed upstairs, collected the journal she used for observations, and on the spur of the moment decided to take her new medical bag. If I'm going to be a doctor I'll damn well look like one she thought, making her way out to the carriage. Waiting next to it was the young constable she had met at Station Row; from his sickly pallor it was clear to Ada that something was very wrong indeed.

'Morning, Miss Phillips,' he said. 'Sorry to disturb you so early.'

'What's happened? Has he killed again?' The prospect of discovering another bride had been murdered filled her with dread.

'I'm not supposed to say, miss, but it's not a

young lady if that's what you're asking. Sergeant Canavan said to come and get Doctor Phillips immediately. He's also sent for your grandfather.'

'Where are we going?'

'The Whitechapel Bell Foundry. It's bad, miss, really bad.'

'I'm ready, constable,' said Henry, emerging from the house. Ada helped him into the carriage. His shoulders were hunched, his tired eyes held low; it was as if he carried the weight of the world on his shoulders.

'So, Bennett, what grim news do you have for us?' Henry asked as the carriage sped toward Whitechapel. 'Has the Strangler claimed another victim?'

'No, sir.'

'That is welcome news, but if it isn't that then why the urgency?'

'It's hard to explain, sir,' said Bennett. 'Dear Lord, I could do with a brandy right now.'

'Surely there must be something you can tell us?'

'It's the chief constable, sir. He's taken control of the scene. He gave orders that nobody was to talk about what we've found, and then be brought in Special Branch. Scary buggers they are, excuse my French miss, they've got the whole place locked up proper tight.'

Henry rubbed his hand over his face and sighed. 'That's all I need, Halloran throwing his weight around, and why would he bring in Special Branch? Aren't they supposed to be dealing with the Fenian threat?'

'I don't know anything about that, sir. I just do what I'm told.'

You're terrified, thought Ada, watching Bennett as he wiped sweat from his brow. What could possibly scare you so? Her mind raced as the rocking carriage thundered along Whitechapel Road. If it wasn't another murdered bride, then what could be so serious that Halloran would leave his office to attend in person? The carriage came to a sudden stop. 'We can't get any further, sir,' the driver called down. 'The street's jammed with people, all wanting a gawk no doubt.'

'Very well,' said Henry, 'we'll have to walk the rest of the way.'

Following her father and Bennett out of the carriage, Ada stepped into a cauldron of noise, stench, and simmering chaos.

'Henry, Ada, there you are. I was waiting for you.' She turned to see her grandfather striding toward them. 'Do either of you have any idea as to why we've been summoned?'

'No, said Henry, 'though I'm glad you're here, Edmund. Halloran is inside; apparently he has Special Branch with him.'

'Has he indeed? How curious. I don't wish to intrude on your purview, Henry, but would you like me to take the lead with this?'

Ada knew what her grandfather was doing. He could see that her father was at the point of collapse, and wished to offer assistance without injuring his son-in-law's pride.

'I… I should be able to carry out my duties,' said Henry, taking a deep breath and squaring his shoulders. 'I'm just tired, that's all.'

'Quite understandable,' said Sir Edmund. 'I am available to help in whatever fashion you require. First we have to actually get there. Would you allow me to forge a path for us?'

'I would be most grateful,' said Henry. Ada took his arm, as much to support her father as for her own protection. The anger and frustration of the mob that surrounded the foundry was obvious. If they decided to riot, anyone who looked to be in a position of authority would be a target.

'The entrance is that way, sir,' said Bennett, pointing over the heads of the crowd. Sir Edmund nodded and began to push his way through, Ada and her father close behind him.

'Ooh, you're a fine one,' screeched a woman as Ada brushed past, her gaudy yet ragged clothing marking her as a prostitute. 'Left your palace to come see 'ow the other 'alf die, eh?'

'No, it's not like that, I…'

The prostitute spat at her, leaving a gobbet of tobacco-laced phlegm running down her veil.

'Get out of it, you!' snarled Bennett, shoving

the woman aside. 'Are you all right, miss?' he asked.

'Yes,' said Ada, wiping her veil with her sleeve, 'she's just angry that's all, and with good reason.'

With a muttered apology for the familiarity, Bennett deftly steered Ada and her father back to the relative safety of Sir Edmund's wake. The old soldier was an imposing figure, and when the crowd saw him coming, they shuffled nervously out of his way. Ada had seen it before; her grandfather was a kind man, but there was something in his eyes that said he was no stranger to violence, and anyone that met his gaze knew it.

The police cordon opened to let them through, and Bennett showed Ada and her father to a side door guarded by two officers. 'It's through there,' he said.

'You lead the way with Henry,' said Sir Edmund, placing a reassuring hand on Ada's shoulder. 'I shall be right behind you.'

She nodded, and taking a firm grip on her father's arm, she stepped over the threshold and into a tiny corner of hell.

The cavernous interior of the Whitechapel Bell Foundry was gloomy and still, wan daylight struggling to pierce the soot-covered windows set high in the walls. Pigeons fluttered among the rafters, and the air was thick with the cloying smell of oil and ash. Up ahead, Rory stood waiting at the foot of a huge wooden scaffold. Ada walked over to greet him, feeling the unsteady weight of her father as he braced himself against her.

'Good morning, sergeant,' said Sir Edmund. 'Would you kindly explain to the coroner the reason for being summoned in such a peremptory manner?'

'Of course, sir. Good morning, Doctor Phillips, Ada. Look, the guvnor's in the manager's office over the other side of the casting hall, talking to the chief constable. I don't think Halloran wanted you here, but the inspector told me to send for you anyway. There's a body you need to see.'

Henry nodded, but the moment he let go of Ada's arm he stumbled and almost fell. Sir Edmund deftly steadied him without fuss. 'One needs to watch the floor in here,' he said, 'it's quite uneven. Sergeant Canavan, may I suggest I wait here with the coroner while you escort Ada to the scene. She will take notes on her father's behalf as part of her training, if that is amenable to you, Henry?'

'Of course, part of her training, yes.' His breath was quick and shallow, his voice barely more than a dry croak.

'You have everything you need, Ada?' asked Sir Edmund.

'Yes' she said, tightening her grip on her medical bag.

'Good. We shall await your observations.'

'Follow me, lass,' said Rory, 'we have to go to the top of the scaffold to see things clearly.' He mounted the stairs and Ada followed him, the wooden treads creaking softly underfoot. Oil lamps held the shadows at bay, and as she climbed ever higher, Ada could not help but wonder just what scene waited to greet her.

'We're here,' said Rory, and stepping aside gave Ada an unrestricted view of utter butchery. She had expected to find a body, but not something as appalling as this. 'Dear God,' she said. Taking a deep breath, she placed her bag on the floor and took out her casebook. She had never been so glad of her veil; yet, if she was to do her job, she had no option but to lift it.

'Are you all right?' asked Rory.

She nodded, and clearing her throat began to record the necessary details.

'The victim is male, likely aged between thirty and forty years. He is naked, and his wrists and ankles are tightly bound with leather straps. He hangs suspended by a rope and pulley, attached to the straps on his wrists with a metal hook. There is a neatly-cut hole in his chest some eight inches square, revealing his heart. Around his neck, embedded beneath the surface of the flesh, is a wire garrotte.'

Ada turned to look at Rory. He raised his eyebrows, but said nothing to interrupt her interpretation of the scene.

'On the floor to the right of the body, a collection of photographer's equipment has been neatly arranged. There is a tripod camera, a portfolio of developed photographs and an open Gladstone bag.'

Ada knelt and picked up the portfolio, carefully turning over the photographs: four weddings, four happy couples, four pictures of murdered brides. She held the most recent in her hands, a stark, monochrome image of Elizabeth Fellowes on her death bed, a crumpled, white sheet on the floor next to her. He didn't even bother to replace it, thought Ada. She turned her attention to the open bag, lifting out the contents and placing them to one side. Two items were of interest – a short knife with a narrow blade, and a small glass bottle containing a pair of human eyes, suspended in a clear liquid. The irises were blue, cornflower blue.

'Bastard,' she whispered, doing her best to quell the anger she felt growing in her chest. She stood to examine the face of the hanging corpse; with the mouth wide open in a silent rictus of agony she hadn't recognised him at first, but now she did. Her memory of the murder scene at 2 Station Row was crystal clear, as was the moment the police photographer was ushered inside after she and her father had finished their work. 'It's Price, isn't it? He was the Limehouse Strangler.'

Rory nodded. 'He was right under our noses all this time. The evidence is all here. He did other jobs as well as working for us, weddings mainly, that's likely how he chose his victims. He knew where they lived, and after picking a time when he knew each woman would be alone, he killed them. And then of course we ask him back to take pictures of his own damn handiwork. Jesus Christ, what kind of evil fecker do you have to be to want to do something like that?'

'That's why Halloran is here,' said Ada. 'He can't allow such a thing to be made public.'

'Can you imagine the outcry?' said Rory. 'We've been under enough pressure with trying to catch him. If the mob outside discovers the Limehouse Strangler was actually one of us, then we might as well set light to a barrel of gunpowder while sitting on it. There'll be fecking carnage.'

'That's as may be,' said Ada, 'but I have a job to do, for Papa.'

'Aye, you do. Can I help you with anything?'

'Would you kindly hold one of those oil lamps for me? I need to take a closer look at the wounds.' Rory did as asked, and leaning over the balustrade Ada peered at the body. 'The garrotte appears to be similar, if not the same, as that used on the four murdered women. As with them, it has partially severed the windpipe and the main vessels in the neck, but there is little evidence of blood loss. This would suggest the injury was incurred post mortem.'

'Why in name of Saint Patrick would anyone garrotte a corpse?' said Rory.

'Perhaps Price's killer wished to make a statement,' said Ada. 'Perhaps he is linked to the murdered brides in some way and is taking revenge? He clearly knew all about Price and what he was doing.'

'Wonderful,' said Rory. 'We've just exchanged one lunatic for another.'

'If this is the work of a lunatic, then he's a very organised one.' She studied the gaping hole in Price's chest. 'The ribs close to the sternum have been cut vertically. There are no striations to indicate that a saw was used; the edges of the bones are partially crushed, as if a sharp implement was pulled through them with great force. Lateral incisions were then made through the muscle tissue, and the ribs pulled open and back to reveal the heart. From the volume of blood present within the chest cavity, and the manner in which it has run down the body and thence to the ground, it would seem likely that Mr Price was alive during the procedure.'

'Holy Mary, mother of God,' said Rory, the lamp shaking slightly in his hand.

'There's something else,' said Ada. 'The

amount of congealed blood pooled around the lungs is substantial. The only explanation for that would be if...'

'What? What does it mean?'

'I think that whoever killed Mr Price left us a present. If I am right, he has skill, Rory, far greater skill than I originally thought.' Removing her glove, Ada carefully reached into the wound, gripping the exposed heart with her fingertips. A gentle tug was all it took, and the heart came neatly away to sit in the palm of her hand.

'Feck me,' said Rory.

'It's as I suspected. There's simply too much blood for the vessels to the heart not to have been severed,' said Ada, 'but the incisions are so fine, so neat, it was difficult to see them in this poor light.'

'Why would the killer cut out Price's heart and then put it back?'

'I don't know,' said Ada. 'Perhaps they wanted to make sure attention was drawn to it?' She turned the bloody organ in her hand, assessing its condition. 'Look, here on the dorsal side, there's a piece missing.'

'Perhaps he wasn't so good with his knife after all?' said Rory.

'I don't think that's the case,' said Ada, tasting bile in the back of her throat.

'How so?'

'The marks round the edge of the excised piece; they weren't made by a sharp implement.'

'Then what did make them?'

'Teeth, Rory, human teeth. Whoever killed Price took a bite from his heart.'

'I think I might actually puke.' The sergeant turned away, leaning against the balustrade and taking deep, slow breaths. 'Fecking hell, Ada, is there no end to this?'

'We can but hope, Rory,' she said, carefully replacing the heart in Price's chest. Cleaning her hand with alcohol from her medical bag, Ada took a step back, forcing herself to be as dispassionate and objective as she could.

'This scene is almost theatrical. Whoever did this was making a point, turning Price into some ghastly exhibit. The killing was methodical, not frenzied. It was carried out with great skill and significant knowledge of anatomy, added to which all the evidence of Price's guilt has been handed to you on a plate. You may have a vigilante on your hands.'

Rory groaned. 'Well, I suppose he's done us a favour, however gruesome. If he doesn't eat anyone else then I may buy him a drink, as opposed to hanging him.' He gave Ada a weak smile.

She nodded. 'I have all I need to write up my notes. We should return to Father. I want to get him away from this place and back home as soon as possible. I will not allow him to become involved in this. Grandfather will understand; I shall ask him to either take over himself or press for Doctor Bond's immediate appointment. I don't care how it appears.'

'I agree wholeheartedly,' said Rory. 'I will do whatever I can to help.'

'Thank you,' said Ada, lowering her veil. 'Let us be gone from here.' Taking a last look at the remains of the Limehouse Strangler, she made her way down the stairs. She had just reached the last flight when someone shouted at her.

'What the hell are you doing? Get away from there now!' A thin, sour-faced man stood waiting at the base of the scaffold, hands on his hips. It was Chief Constable Halloran, and it was clear to Ada that he was apoplectic with rage.

'Sir James, please moderate your tone when addressing my granddaughter,' said Sir Edmund.

'This has nothing to do with you,' snapped Halloran. 'I did *not* request your presence at this murder scene. The case has been handed over to Special Branch. Soames here will take control of it from now on.' He gestured to a man standing patiently to his right. Soames gave no indication that he had been referred to, he just stared straight ahead with cold, grey eyes. It struck Ada that this was a man who was capable of anything. He would follow any order, however morally questionable, and sit down to dinner with his family without breaking stride. He turned his head a fraction to study her, a jagged scar on his cheek clearly visible through his salt-and-pepper beard. He leaned in to Halloran and whispered something.

The chief constable stared wide-eyed at Ada. 'Explain what this *girl* has been doing here?' he barked at Henry.

'She... she has been assisting me with my work,' he replied.

'And you look as though you need it,' snarled Halloran. 'You can barely stand, man. Consider yourself relieved of your position through incapacity. Go back to Harley Street and leave the real work to men who can cope with it.'

'But I'm duty bound to file the coroner's report,' Henry gasped, his face ashen. 'I must, it's the law.'

'The law be damned,' said Halloran, jabbing a finger in Henry's chest. 'You will do exactly as you're told. Take yourself and your daughter away and *forget* that you were here. If you breathe a word of this to anyone, I will see you hanged.'

'But... but...' Clutching at his chest, Henry's legs gave way and he slumped to the ground.

'Papa!' said Ada. Running over she knelt by her father's side, putting an arm round his shoulders. He moaned softly, eyes squeezed shut as he grimaced in pain.

'Someone fetch a wagon and get him to Whitechapel police station,' said Halloran, more irritated than concerned.

'I think not,' said Sir Edmund. 'My son-in-law comes with *me*. I shall take him to my sanatorium where he can be cared for properly. As for what we have seen here, you may rest assured that it will not be spoken of in public. I trust you have no objection to us leaving immediately?'

'I... uh,' Sir James stammered.

'Then the matter is settled. I bid you good day.'

Ada could see that her grandfather's interjection had thrown Halloran off balance. He hadn't been expecting to come up against someone of at least equal authority.

'Let me help you, lass,' said Rory.

'Thank you,' she replied, and between them they raised Henry to his feet.

'I wouldn't trust a Mick with the coroner, sir,' Soames said to Halloran. 'You never know where their loyalties lie. They're all Fenians underneath.'

Rory turned, colour rising in his cheeks. 'What did you say, you miserable shite?'

'Ignore him,' said Ada, 'he's baiting you, that's all.'

'Insubordinate to the core,' sneered Soames. 'I'm surprised Sergeant Canavan is sober enough to understand that he's addressing a senior officer.'

'So I'm a drunkard as well am I? Perhaps I should teach you some fecking manners?'

Soames laughed. 'You wouldn't dare. Be off with you, playing nursemaid is all you're fit for.'

'Bastard,' said Rory, and before Ada could stop him he punched Soames full in the face. The Special Branch officer staggered back, blood gushing from his nose.

'Arrest that man,' ordered Halloran.

Struggling to hold her father upright, Ada watched helplessly as four uniformed officers pinned Rory to the floor. He met her eyes briefly, offering a mute apology for losing his temper. For a moment she was torn; leaving Rory in such dire straits was the last thing she wanted.

'I can't interfere with this,' Sir Edmund whispered in her ear. 'I'll do what I can later. We need to get out of here, now!'

'I know,' said Ada sadly, and with Constable Bennett clearing the way she and her grandfather half-carried the stricken coroner to the waiting carriage.

'I hope he recovers quickly, miss,' said Bennett, helping them inside.

'As do we all,' said Ada. 'Please keep an eye on Rory, let him know we'll be back as soon as we can. We will not abandon him.'

'I will, miss.'

The carriage set off, rocking on its suspension as Baynes drove as fast as he could toward Rookwood. Ada felt for her father's pulse; it was thready but it was there. That was something at least. 'I'm here, Papa,' she whispered, and behind her veil, tears ran down her face.

CHAPTER 13

Through a Glass Darkly

'**P**lease do not worry about Henry. Fitz will take good care of him,' said Sir Edmund, handing his hat and gloves to Hargrave.

'I know he will,' said Ada. 'It's not quite how I imagined it, but Father finally has the peace and quiet he needs.' Following her grandfather into the study she seated herself by the fire. He handed her a brandy and sat opposite, lighting a cigar. 'So,' he said, through curls of aromatic smoke, 'what are your observations on the discovery at the foundry? The officers at the scene were unwilling to go into detail, but I gather the victim was none other than the Limehouse Strangler himself.'

'Yes, of that I am in no doubt. The evidence of his guilt was laid out in the most... helpful manner. It transpires that our murderer was none other than Harold Price, the police photographer.'

'Ah,' said Sir Edmund. 'That would explain the chief constable's aggressive tone. He will no doubt wish to hide that particular fact from the public.'

'Rory was of a similar opinion,' said Ada.

'It was not a pleasant sight, Grandfather. Price's heart was cut out while he was still alive, and a bite taken from it.'

Sir Edmund sat bolt upright, eyes wide and coughing as he inadvertently inhaled cigar smoke. Ada made to get up but he raised a hand to forestall her.

'Are you all right, Grandfather? Shall I fetch you some water?' He shook his head, taking a mouthful of brandy to clear his throat.

'Apologies,' he said. 'You caught me unawares. All murders are grim, but I haven't heard of something like that before.'

'It was truly grotesque. While it is difficult to have any sympathy for a man such as Price, I cannot but wonder who did this to him, and their motivation for such an act.'

'Indeed. We find one killer, albeit indirectly, only for another to take his place; at least on this occasion the victim was no innocent. I take it you have detailed notes of the crime scene in your casebook?'

'Yes,' said Ada, 'although I don't know of what use they will be with Father removed from office.'

'Sad though I am to say it, they are of no use at all, in fact they may be a serious liability. Forgive me for asking this, but I would like you to tear out those pages and burn them.' He nodded toward the fireplace.

'But why?'

'It's for your protection. As far as Halloran is concerned, any leak of information regarding this killing is tantamount to treason. If your notes are destroyed, I can tell him that no evidence regarding Price's murder exists outside of the official investigation. You will therefore be above suspicion should anything go wrong. Do you understand?'

She nodded. 'I will do as you ask, Grandfather. I have no desire to aggravate the chief constable, especially with Rory's liberty at stake.'

'Precisely. This matter now rests with Special Branch, Ada, and they are not men to be trifled with. They are the ones the government use for tasks that stray into areas of dubious morality. The man that Rory struck, Frank Soames, has a chequered history. His methods of dealing with the Fenian uprisings in Ireland were viewed by Whitehall as somewhat extreme; hence he was recalled to the mainland.'

'He does seem a rather unpleasant character.'

'That would be an understatement. I know his type – a bully to the core. It was easy to deal with them in the army. I just made them dig latrines until they toed the line. Special Branch is a very different animal, Ada. Avoid them please, for me.'

'Of course, Grandfather, but given what you

say about Soames, will he hurt Rory?'

'Not openly, but striking him in front of Sir James – even though it was entirely warranted – was a stupid thing to do. Rory may hail from one of the more *interesting* areas of Dublin, but he needs to keep that temper of his in check.'

'That he does,' said Ada.

'And to that end I need to go and see Halloran as soon as possible. Not only do I have to negotiate with him as regards Rory's punishment, but perhaps I can smooth things over by nudging Doctor Bond into accepting the position of acting coroner for H division.'

'He would be a fine replacement for Father, given his experience with the Whitechapel murders,' said Ada. 'I've attended several of his lectures and he strikes me as an honourable man. He has always treated me with respect.'

'Hence he is my first choice,' said Sir Edmund. 'Hopefully Halloran will agree.' He finished his brandy and got up to leave. 'I will no doubt be gone for the rest of the afternoon, so please make yourself at home. Oh, and further to our conversation yesterday, if you still wish to avail yourself of the armoury, Hargrave has the keys. I find that shooting inanimate objects is just the tonic when one is irked in some way.'

'Thank you, Grandfather. I will see you at dinner.'

'Good. Don't forget to burn those notes, and

ask Mrs Fletcher to prepare some venison. It always puts me in a good mood. After seeing the chief constable, I fear I shall need it.'

Once her grandfather had left, Ada went to stand by the bay window behind his desk. Looking out over the vast deer park, stark in its winter glory, she tried to marshal her thoughts. The Limehouse Strangler was dead, and her father – though gravely ill – was far from Halloran's reach. Fitz had assured her there was every chance Henry would make a full recovery, which was heartening to hear, yet despite her relief Ada could not ignore the pervasive sense of unease that dogged her heels.

Her mind kept returning to Josephine. While her grandfather may ascribe the young woman's condition to the misuse of opiates, Ada was far from convinced. Her gut told her there was something else at play, something she had missed. It was Josephine's sudden descent into madness that troubled her most; it had manifested overnight, mere hours after her uncouth behaviour at dinner. She had carved a statement of redress into her arm with a knife; for a person to do such a thing required dire reason indeed. It was as if the devil himself had whispered in Josephine's ear, urged her to apologise in the most awful of ways. Punishment, Ada thought – that's what it looks like, for taking joy in my misfortune.

And then there was what Josephine had said during their meeting in the sanatorium. Try as she might, Ada could not think of how the young woman knew the contents of her dreams. One statement in particular kept coming back to haunt her: "He knows you are stronger than your mother." For Josephine to say such a thing, strapped to a bed in the very room where Clara had taken her own life, was both painful and deeply disturbing. Until her nightmares began, her mother had been the most gentle of women, kind, delicate, pure of heart, but Ada would never have described her as strong. Clara had always found the iniquities of the world difficult to face; she had hidden behind walls of privilege, tending to her orchids while refusing to acknowledge the suffering that lay outside her very door. What would happen to such a fragile mind, Ada wondered, if it was suddenly visited by a man in a mask, demanding that fears be faced, agonies endured? The more she considered the concept, the more she let herself remember, the sicker she felt. "He's always there, my demon, my *ravener*. He won't let me go. Make him stop, please."

The delicate sound of thunder filled Ada's head as a terrible diagnosis presented itself. What if she had been wrong all this time? What if her mother had been driven to insanity, wholly unable to accept the horrors shown to her? And now Josephine, plunged into madness and self-harm. Was the man she referred to the same as the one Ada saw in her dreams, the one that may have haunted her mother for so long too?

'Oh this is insane,' she said, rubbing a hand over her face. She couldn't believe she was considering such outlandish concepts. She approached life with logic, rationality, empiricism; she did not believe in a world separate from the one she occupied, a place of spirits and shadows. To seek answers in such fantasy was madness in its own right, and yet there were still things she could not explain. Price's death only added to the mystery; his was far from some run-of-the mill murder. It was a grotesque and deliberate act, carried out with the utmost precision by someone with the hands of a surgeon; a dark gift to the people of the East End. In that regard Josephine's words had proven strangely prophetic: "My heart was not black enough to take, but recompense was still required, a demonstration of contrition." Price's heart had been as black as they came; it had not only been taken, but devoured. His contrition had been absolute, and fatal, yet whoever killed him was flesh and blood. A phantom could not wield a knife.

'Witness my art, fear my wrath,' Ada muttered.

'I'm sorry, miss, what did you say?'

She spun round to see Hargrave standing behind her, a curious expression on his face.

'I was just wondering if you needed anything, miss,' he said. 'Some food perhaps, or shall I prepare a room for you to rest? I gather you have had a most challenging morning.'

'Thank you, Hargrave,' said Ada, hoping the old man did not think her unhinged for talking to herself. 'That is most thoughtful, but I must admit I have no appetite at the moment.'

'That is understandable under the circumstances, miss.'

'However,' she said, 'there *is* something you can help me with, and for that I need the keys to the armoury.'

Ada stood on the wide terrace to the rear of Rookwood. On a trestle table at her side sat an open wooden box, lined with red velvet. Nestled within were a Webley Mk 1 revolver and a box of .455 calibre ammunition. It had been a gift to her grandfather from a colleague at his club, and was the perfect distraction from questions to which Ada had no reasonable answer. Her grandfather had taught her to shoot, insisting that the concentration required to hit a distant target would be of benefit when she held a scalpel – and therefore a patient's life – in her hands.

Ada had come to enjoy the impromptu competitions Sir Edmund had organised.

Sometimes Fitz had joined in, but usually it was just the two of them, each with one of a matched-pair of Purdey duelling pistols. The target was always a single playing card, pinned to the trunk of a dead elm some twenty paces from the terrace. At first Ada had been unable to even hit the tree. The pistol – even with its small calibre – had been heavy, and with an unrifled barrel it was notoriously inaccurate, but she had persevered. She enjoyed the preparation as much as taking the shot; the careful insertion of wadding, gunpowder and lead ball was vital; performed incorrectly it could lead to a misfire, or in the worst case, an explosion.

'Think of it as readying yourself for an operation,' Sir Edmund had said. 'A failure to lay out the correct instruments may cost you dearly.'

Once the recoil and the explosion of smoke were no longer a surprise, Ada's aim gradually improved. The moment she hit the playing card for the first time was one of immense satisfaction, and her grandfather had gifted her the duelling pistols to mark his approval of her progress. Today she held an unfamiliar weapon; Price may be dead but his killer was still at large, and Ada had no intention of leaving herself vulnerable. If the Webley was to be of any use, practice was required.

Loading the revolver, she placed the foresight directly on the playing card, exhaled slowly and squeezed the trigger. There was a sharp crack and her hand jerked upward, the bullet tearing into the bare branches of the dead tree. The kick was far greater than she had expected. Placing her left hand over her right wrist, Ada took careful aim and once again squeezed the trigger. This time the shot slammed home just above the playing card. She nodded, instinctively knowing what was required to handle the weapon effectively. The next shot went low, but the fourth struck the playing card dead on. Smiling to herself, Ada emptied the final two chambers, hitting the card both times. Putting the revolver down, she recovered the remains of her target from the tree – an ace of hearts, shot to pieces from twenty paces.

Striding back to the terrace, she noticed movement behind one of the nearby windows. The sun was low, and reflections in the leaded-diamonds of old glass made it difficult to see. She walked closer, recognising the window as belonging to the India Room, the gallery where her grandfather kept all the trophies and treasures from his time in the army. Shielding her eyes, she stepped as close as she could. From inside the room, barely inches away, another face returned her stare. It wore a mask of white velvet, and the eyeholes glittered as if filled with stars.

CHAPTER 14

Haunted

Holding her breath, Ada returned the unreal gaze of her phantom tormentor. Slowly, the man raised a kid-gloved hand and placed it, fingers spread, on the inside of the glass. Unwilling to show fear by refusing the invitation, Ada copied the motion, placing her hand upon his. A sudden drowsiness took her, and for a moment the window between them slipped away. She could feel the gentle pressure of his fingers on her skin, the soft knap of his gloves. It was as if she were inside a painting, reaching out into a world more real than the one she inhabited. The man in the mask nodded to her, and in a swirl of black he was gone.

Tearing her hand from the glass, she ran along the terrace and through a side entrance next to the kitchens. Servants dived out of her way as she rushed past, the heels of her boots ringing on the flagstones. Reaching the India Room, she took a deep breath and swung the door wide. The space beyond was long and narrow, lined with display cases and filled with the spoils of a young man's life spent adventuring in the East. Jewelled daggers, tiger skins, intricately woven rugs – there was even a baby elephant on a wooden plinth, its tusks tipped with gold and a miniature howdah sitting proudly on its back. Everything was in its place, just as she remembered, but on a table at the far end of the room, close to where she had seen the man in the mask, sat an object that Ada did not recognise.

Stepping inside, she peered into every corner. There was no one to be seen, but dust motes swirled in the sunlight as if disturbed by the rapid passing of another. Casting wary glances to either side Ada walked toward the window, the watchful eyes of stuffed animals following her progress. She had disliked taxidermy as a child and her opinion had not changed. There was something unnatural about remodelling the dead; far better to remember something as it was, she thought, rather than give it the pale imitation of life. Suppressing a shudder, she reached the table under the window and stared at the object that rested atop it. It was a statuette of a naked woman riding on the back of a lion, carved from the purest white alabaster and inset with gemstones. She had four arms, and in her hands she held a sword, a cup, a trident and a severed head. Her face was both serene and incredibly beautiful.

'Kali,' said Ada, recognising the Hindu goddess. She reached out, gently running the tips of her fingers over the soft stone. A wave of sadness filled her; it was as if a child wept in the darkness, howling into a void with no prospect of comfort, joy or hope. Ada thought she understood the nature of grief, but the pain that lay within the statuette was of a magnitude she could barely comprehend. She pulled her fingers away, holding them to her chest. They were numb, cold, tingling with the echoes of loss.

'Exquisite, isn't she?' said a familiar voice from behind her.

Ada spun round, her heart pounding. There was nothing there, but the sensation of someone being present yet unseen was incredibly strong.

'You are not real,' she said, 'and I am not mad.' She did not know if the words were a statement of fact, or simply a means to reassure herself of what she hoped was true.

'You may have one or the other, not both,' said the man in the mask. His voice flowed from every nook and cranny of the room, from the mouths of the animals sitting frozen in their cages of glass. 'If you are truly mad then of course I am not real. I will simply be a boon companion as you lie alone in your cell, strapped to a bed like Josephine. But what if you are completely sane? If that is the case, use your skills to give me a diagnosis.'

Ada struggled to find some flaw in his logic, but try as she might there was only one conclusion to be drawn. 'If I am not mad then you must be real; but that is fantasy, you cannot be so.'

'Believe me, I am not some product of a fractured mind. As I said, I am someone to watch over you. Take Mr Price, for example.'

'What about him?'

'He was going to kill you. He followed you home from the party at the Hunter residence, and I in turn followed him. He heard my footsteps as you heard his. If he had believed himself alone, you would have felt the touch of his garrotte about your neck. Are you not grateful?'

'Price was butchered by a vigilante, not some apparition from my dreams.'

'Cannot the two things be one and the same? Price's death at my hands was inevitable, and his desire to take your life only added impetus to my actions. One might even say he made it personal. He was a cancer that needed removing, and there are more such operations ahead. You of all people should understand that metaphor; you yearn to be a surgeon, do you not?'

Ada covered her face with her hands; it felt as though her head was splitting in two. Is this how it starts, she thought. Do I stand on the brink of the abyss, trying not to throw myself in while secretly yearning to do so?

'And let us not forget Miss Schlecter,' the man continued. 'I found her hubris offensive. She insulted you in public. Did you not wish to see her suffer for that?'

'I would have wanted her to apologise, nothing more. I had no desire to see her so terrified that she maimed herself.'

'So you admit the possibility of my involvement then?'

'I admit nothing! Josephine took opiates, and in a fugue state cut herself out of guilt. There is nothing more to it.'

'You so want to believe that don't you,' said the man, 'yet it doesn't explain how she knew what we discussed the last time we met. Still, you need not worry about Miss Schlecter. She will recover, unharmed by her experience yet hopefully the wiser for it. It was simply a demonstration of what I can offer.'

'Stop it, please,' said Ada, backing away until she was pressed against the windowsill. 'If that is what you offer then I want nothing to do with it.'

'Your mother said something very similar.'

'How dare you insult her memory,' cried Ada. 'Can you not let her rest in peace?'

'Not until you accept what you already know in your heart. All you need do is say it aloud and I will leave you be.'

Ada swallowed hard. What she had dismissed as impossible now made the most awful sense. Even so, it took everything she had to force the words from her mouth. 'It's you, isn't it? This *Ravener* my mother spoke of. The one who plagued her dreams and drove her to suicide? You say you love me, but if you are responsible for destroying my family then know that I *hate* you.'

'Ravener,' said the man, 'such an interesting word. One who ravens or plunders, just like a bird of prey, yes? I rather like it.'

'You didn't answer me,' snapped Ada, rage blossoming in her chest.

He sighed. 'I offered Clara the same thing that I'm offering you. Sadly she was unable to accept it.'

Ada let his words wash over and through her; there was something hidden beneath the surface of his speech, something he did not wish her to know. It felt like regret.

'It is time for me to leave now, beloved; there are matters that require my attention. But fear not, proof of my existence will be with you soon enough.'

'Why are you haunting me?' Ada screamed. 'Tell me, damn you!' Her only reply was distant and fading laughter. No longer knowing what to believe or even trusting in her own sanity, she strode angrily from the room, slamming the door behind her.

Seated in a chair by the fire, Ada half-heartedly perused a medical textbook. She had hoped that by concentrating on the mundane she would feel less adrift, but time and again her thoughts turned toward fear of madness, of following her mother into oblivion. The possibility that she was hallucinating due to some abnormality of the brain was terrifying, but try as she might she could think of no other explanation for her experiences. To have her dreams crushed, her faculties stripped away until there was nothing left but an empty shell; the unfairness of such an outcome made her want to weep.

'That posturing little shit!'

Ada looked up as her grandfather stormed into the study. Pouring himself a large brandy, he sank heavily into the chair opposite.

'Things went well with Halloran I take it?' she said, grateful for the distraction.

'It depends what you mean by *well*. Being thankful for small mercies, I managed to persuade Doctor Bond to put himself forward as coroner for H division. Halloran accepted without hesitation of course, given Bond's experience with the Whitechapel murders.'

'Then why are you so angry?'

'I am angry because despite smoothing the way for your father's absence, Halloran knew he had me over a barrel as regards Sergeant Canavan, so I've had to buy him off.' He frowned, drumming his fingers on his knee in irritation.

'What did you have to do?'

'I had to sponsor his membership application to my club, the club – I might add –

that Fitz and your father also attend. Halloran's wanted to join the Carmichael for years but nobody likes him, odious little yes-man that he is. He said that he would *overlook* Sergeant Canavan's indiscretion if I put him forward, knowing full well that my word would be enough to guarantee acceptance. Now we'll have to listen to Halloran braying about himself while we're trying to relax over whiskey and cigars.'

'Oh,' said Ada.

'Oh, indeed. Still, it means that Rory's punishment is far less severe than it could have been. He's suspended for two weeks without pay, but his record remains untarnished. He needs to watch his back though; Soames is unlikely to be so forgiving, and may well decide to take revenge regardless of what Halloran says. Hammer the point home with Rory when we see him tomorrow, Ada. He'll likely pay more attention to what you say than I.'

'I'll do my best,' she said, 'the last thing I want is to see him hurt.'

'Good, in that case we should eat.' Sir Edmund rang the bell by the fire, and after a brief wait Hargrave appeared. 'Sir?'

'Please tell me Mrs Fletcher has prepared venison for dinner?'

Ada smiled at her grandfather's tone; it almost sounded as though he were pleading.

'Indeed she has, sir. Would you and Miss Ada

prefer to move to the dining room?'

'No, here would be fine, Hargrave, thank you.'

'As you wish, sir.'

Ada ate dinner in pleasant silence, surrounded by the soft sounds of the old house. The crackling of the fire, the ticking of the longcase clock, the distant murmuring of the servants – for a brief time she could almost pretend everything was normal.

'I sent a message to Mrs Crane,' said Sir Edmund. 'She knows you'll be staying here tonight.'

'Thank you. I wouldn't want her to worry. Where will I be sleeping?'

'You could have your mother's old room if you like? It's been kept aired and the bedclothes are clean.'

Until now Ada would have chosen one of the guest suites; they held no pain, no reasons to revisit the past. However, with her father so ill she found the idea of being close to her late mother oddly comforting. 'I would like that,' she said.

'Good, then that's settled.' Swirling the brandy in his glass, Sir Edmund pointed to the book Ada had been reading. 'And I see you found my copy of Gray's Anatomy.'

'Yes,' she said. 'I thought that studying might take my mind off things, but I admit it is hard to concentrate under the circumstances.'

'I quite understand, and it is to your credit that you made the attempt. I know I have been something of a martinet as regards your education, but I hope you understand why. It irks me that women are treated so poorly, especially when they have a mind as fine as yours. Your grandmother was very much of the same opinion. She would have adored you, you know.'

'You always speak of her so fondly,' said Ada, looking at the portrait of her grandparents that hung over the fireplace. They had just come back from India; Sir Edmund was in his captain's uniform, and sitting next to him his wife was resplendent in a crème taffeta dress.

'Charlotte has been gone a long time now,' he said. 'Bloody malaria, horrible disease. Another reason to study medicine. Maybe you'll discover a cure for it one day.'

'That would be a fine thing,' said Ada.

'You're the only family Henry and I have left; remember that if we seem a little over-protective at times.'

There was a distant jingling from the lobby as the doorbell rang, and Ada heard Hargrave's measured steps as he went to answer it. After a brief, muffled conversation, the butler entered the study with a visitor in tow.

'It's a Constable Bennett, sir. He says he has an urgent matter to discuss with you.'

'Thank you, Hargrave,' said Sir Edmund. 'Come in, Bennett, join us please.'

Dressed in a plain, tweed suit and with a brown derby hat clutched in his hands, the young constable did as asked, seating himself on a stool next to Ada. 'Thank you for seeing me, sir, miss,' he said, nodding to them both.

'So, to what do we owe this unexpected visit?' asked Sir Edmund.

'In all conscience I needed to speak to you, sir. I didn't have the chance at the foundry this morning, not with Soames and his men about. Is your father all right, miss?' he said, turning to Ada. 'Me and the lads wanted to ask as he's always treated us with respect.'

'He is resting peacefully, George,' she said. 'Thank you for your concern.'

'While it is heartening to know that Doctor Phillips is held in such high regard,' said Sir Edmund, 'I'm sure you didn't come here this evening just to ask after his health. What is it that you wish to speak to me about?'

Bennett fiddled with the brim of his hat, trying to stop his hands from shaking. 'I've seen some strange things in my short time on the force, sir, but this... well, it makes my skin crawl. I was on late duty last night; graveyard shift we call it. Dawn had broken and I was about to clock off when I heard some shouting from the bell foundry. It was the night watchman; he was staggering about in the street, clutching his head and moaning about 'orrors and suchlike. I ran over and tried to get some sense out of him, but he just sat down against the wall and started crying like a child.'

'That sounds like severe shock,' said Ada, looking at her grandfather. He nodded in agreement.

'Since I couldn't get anything out of the poor bloke, I left him where he was and went inside. There weren't many lights on but there were enough to see Price's body. I climbed up the scaffold and saw what the killer had left for us to find. Did you see it all?'

'Yes,' said Ada. 'It was unpleasant in the extreme.'

'But there's something you didn't see. There was a letter stuffed in Price's mouth. It was covered in blood and I didn't want it to get ruined, so I carefully pulled it out and read it. It was written really neat like, in black ink on thick paper. I made a note of what it said in my pocketbook. It's a good job I did, because when the chief constable arrived he took it off me and told me to forget I'd ever seen it.'

Ada shook her head, inwardly admonishing herself for not having checked Price's mouth. It was an elementary error that in other circumstances may have yielded useful evidence.

'I take it this letter was from Price's killer,'

said Sir Edmund. 'What did it say?'

'Give me a minute, sir; I've got my notes 'ere.' Bennett fished inside his jacket for his pocketbook, and as he did so Ada's skin began to prickle. She wanted to know what the message said, yet feared what it might reveal. Finding the right page, Bennett read out what he had jotted down.

"*Twenty were taken, twenty will pay. This creature is but the first of my gifts to you. The innocent should not be afraid of my hunger, however ravenous I appear. But for those who harbour evil in their hearts I have a message. Hear it, and hear it well, for my face will be the last thing you ever see. Witness my art, fear my wrath.*"

Ada felt as though she'd been punched in the stomach. The letter contained phrases spoken to her by both Josephine and the man in the mask. What he had said in the India Room was true after all; here was the proof he had promised, delivered right into her hands. She was not mad, and in defiance of all rational thought this vigilante, this *Ravener*, must therefore be real. If she was to believe everything he had said, then not only had he saved her life by butchering Price, but he had defended her honour by forcing Josephine to maim herself. And then there was Clara. By his own admission he had been the catalyst for her fall from grace, the shadow that had driven her to self-destruction. What kind of a monster would indulge in such brutality, yet still profess his love? Rory had been right, Ada thought, one lunatic had replaced another, and from the contents of his letter he was just getting started.

'Now that is a most unnerving missive,' said Sir Edmund. 'However, while this is of no doubt serious concern for the police, why risk your career bringing this information to me?'

Bennett wiped sweat from his forehead. 'It was the paper it was written on, sir. It was headed with the name and address of a London gentleman's club.'

'Which one?'

'The Carmichael, sir. Your club.'

Ada watched as her grandfather's face grew pale in the firelight.

'Doctor Phillips often spoke of the Carmichael, sir, and of how you were both members, so I thought you should know.'

Sir Edmund cleared his throat. 'You were right to bring this to my attention, Bennett. You have my sincere thanks. Rest assured I shall not mention your actions to anyone. That Price's killer used notepaper from my club is a matter of great concern to me. It's no wonder Halloran took the original letter from you; the last thing he'd want is a potential scandal at a club he wants to join. I will make some discreet enquiries, although I cannot imagine any member of the

Carmichael being capable of such an atrocity. Anyone could have taken that notepaper.'

'I'm glad I could help, sir.'

'I'll have Baynes drop you wherever you wish, it's the least I can do to reward you for your efforts.'

'That's very kind of you, sir, I'll wait out front.' With a polite nod Bennett got to his feet and left the room.

'Now what do you make of that?' asked Sir Edmund.

'I'm not sure,' said Ada, unwilling to discuss what was uppermost in her mind. 'If you will excuse me, Grandfather, I think I shall retire, I can barely keep my eyes open.'

'Of course, my dear. Sleep well.'

Eager to put the day behind her, Ada kissed her grandfather goodnight before making her way to her mother's old room. As she climbed into bed, she saw a framed photograph of a young Clara on the nightstand. She looked happy, and there was no hint in her expression of the agonies to come. 'I miss you,' Ada said as she turned down the light. Lying there in the darkness she waited for sleep to take her, but the more she thought about her mother's absence, the angrier she became. If this man of shadow, this *Ravener* that Clara had spoken of, was indeed the same phantom that now dogged Ada's footsteps, then there would be a reckoning. Nestled in her purse was a loaded, short-barrelled Webley revolver, and, if she deemed it necessary, she would not hesitate to squeeze the trigger.

CHAPTER 15

A Fresh Start

T he following morning Ada sought out her grandfather in the Rookwood orangery. Built some twenty years earlier, it was a semi-tropical paradise designed to mimic the hothouses that had become so popular at Kew Gardens. A myriad scents drifted lazily around her, dominated by the Lady of the Night orchids that her mother had loved and nurtured. Their sweet fragrance brought to mind childhood memories of standing on clay pots to help Clara plant seedlings: the feel of loam in her hands, the wonder of seeing the extraordinary plants grow.

'Ada, is that you?' said Sir Edmund from behind a huge fern.

'Yes, Grandfather,' she said, walking over to greet him. He was seated in a wicker chair, a copy of The Times open on his lap. He was still wearing the clothes of the previous day and looked shockingly tired.

'Please forgive my dishevelment but I fell asleep in my study. I didn't rest particularly well.' He looked up at Ada, dark rings prominent beneath his eyes. 'I hope you did though?' She nodded and he favoured her with the faintest of smiles. 'I was just reading this morning's paper. The front page is positively awash with speculation about the murder at the foundry, but few actual facts. It seems Halloran is making good on his promise to keep this contained.'

'Does he really have the power to suppress what happened?'

'Oh yes. It's not a murdered bride; it's simply another death in an area where life tends to be cheap. All the press knows is that a body was discovered. It wouldn't surprise me if Halloran leaks his own, carefully constructed version of events to the press in due course. Perhaps it may end up being a tragic *accident*?'

'So he would create a lie to protect himself?'

'It's in his interest to be economic with the truth. He knows the Limehouse Strangler is dead so he can rest easy on that account. There'll be no more young women butchered by his hand. The mob will continue baying for blood, but if there are no new bodies their anger will fade over time. From now on I think it likely Halloran will bend his efforts toward finding Price's killer.'

Ada nodded, although given what she knew, she had her doubts as to how successful Special Branch would be in that regard. 'So,' she said, 'when are we going to rescue Rory?'

'In a couple of hours. There are a few matters I need to attend to first, washing and changing being primary among them.'

Ada chuckled. 'Good, I want to see Papa before we go. Would it be all right if I took him some orchids?'

'Of course. Those ones your mother was so fond of always smell like oranges to me. I'm sure Henry would appreciate them, they'll help to brighten up his room. Take him the paper too; he needs to be aware of the requirement to be discreet. I know the prospect of having to remain silent will annoy him, but he is not naïve. This is a matter he will have to accept, regardless of any ethical qualms he may have.'

'I understand,' said Ada. 'I will talk to him about it.' Leaving her grandfather to his duties, she cut some flowers and made her way to the sanatorium. Heading for the staff wing where her father was quartered, she bumped into Fitz as he left his office.

'Good morning, Ada. I was just about to start my rounds. You've come to visit your father I assume?'

'Yes, how is he?' she asked.

'Much improved. He was asking after you.'

'May I see him?'

'Of course, I'll walk you over.'

'That would be most kind,' said Ada, 'and if it is not inconvenient, may I visit Miss Schlecter too? I was hoping to talk to her again.'

'I was just on my way to see her in fact. I

make no promises, but if I deem her condition to be stable then I have no objection. Come and find me once you're done.'

'I shall do so,' she said, 'and thank you.'

Arriving at the staff wing, Ada entered a bright, clean room with a view of the grounds. The morning sun streamed in through muslin curtains, and lying in a comfortable bed was her father, propped up with pillows and smiling at her.

'You have a visitor, Henry,' said Fitz. 'I'll get back to my patients,' he whispered in Ada's ear, 'leave you two alone for a bit.' He patted her arm affectionately and left, closing the door behind him.

'Hello, Papa,' said Ada, barely able to keep her voice from breaking.

'Hello, child,' he replied, opening his arms to her.

Ada placed the flowers and paper on the bed and sat next to him, gently laying her head on his chest so he couldn't see her cry.

'There, there,' said Henry. 'Fitz informs me that I'm going to be fine, so it must be true.' He stroked his daughter's hair and kissed her forehead. 'You were quite magnificent yesterday, I am so proud.'

'Thank you.' She sat up and wiped the tears from her face. Her father looked tired, but he had colour in his cheeks which was a great comfort.

'I've brought you some of mother's flowers.'

'Lady of the Night,' he said, inhaling their scent, and for a moment his eyes misted up too. 'Thank you, darling, they'll mask the smell of carbolic soap.'

'And I have this.' She handed him that day's Times. 'I thought it important that you see it.'

Laying the flowers to one side Henry took the paper. 'I thought this outcome likely,' he said, once he had finished reading. 'What does Edmund think?'

'He views it as inevitable, however ethically dubious it may be.'

'Given the number of people that know what happened, it will be difficult to stop someone from talking. Then again, Halloran has Soames and his men. They can be quite persuasive by all accounts.'

'So Grandfather says. He warned me to keep away from them.'

'He's right,' said Henry. 'I shall convalesce while you return to your studies. There is no need to involve ourselves in this any further. Still, I am glad that Price was stopped. I worked with him often; I cannot believe that I couldn't see him for what he was.'

Ada gave his hand a squeeze, glad that he was taking the news so well.

'How's Rory? I gather he got himself into some trouble.'

'Grandfather and I are off to collect him shortly. Halloran only agreed to release him if he was sponsored for membership of the Carmichael.'

'Dear God, is nothing sacred. I'm sure Edmund is livid.'

'That would be an understatement,' said Ada, 'but at least we get Rory back in one piece.'

'Let us be thankful for small mercies.'

'Indeed,' said Ada. She paused before speaking again. She had come to a decision on the way to the sanatorium, and wasn't sure how her father would react. 'There is something I would like to do and I wanted your blessing.'

'And what might that be?'

'I will of course continue to wear black, but I would rather not cover my face in public anymore. If you have no objection, I would like to cease that aspect of mourning.'

Henry nodded and smiled at her. 'Given what we have been through, I see no reason to refuse your request. I will not force you to do anything that makes you uncomfortable.'

'Thank you, Papa. I do not wish to appear disrespectful to Mother's memory, but I will not hide behind a mask.'

'I understand, and you have my blessing. Perhaps now we can all have a fresh start? Leave the past behind?'

'I think that would be lovely,' said Ada, but

at the back of her mind she doubted it would be so simple. One monster had been replaced by another, and that was the kind of fresh start they could all do without. Something unearthly was waiting in the shadows, offering love and death in equal measure, and as yet she had no idea what to do about it. Promising to return the following day, she kissed her father goodbye and left him to rest. She had almost reached the door to Fitz's office when he called out to her.

'Ada, I have some news you should hear.' He ran along the corridor, his face flushed.

'What is it?'

'It's regarding Miss Schlecter.'

'Please tell me her condition hasn't worsened.'

'Far from it. She has woken and is in full control of her faculties. She has no recollection of anything that happened after leaving the Hunter residence.'

'Nothing at all?'

'It appears not. I asked if she remembered speaking with you, but she denied such a thing ever took place. I do not feel that she is dissembling either. She presents some degree of confusion, but that is only to be expected. Whatever afflicted her has vanished like morning dew; it's highly unusual for such a thing to occur but not unheard of. However, it is the wounds on her arm that concern me.'

'In what way,' said Ada, a sudden chill running down her spine.

'They are healing at an inexplicable rate,' said Fitz. 'In all my years of practising medicine, I have never seen the like. By rights Miss Schlecter should suffer significant and permanent scarring, yet you can barely see the letters she carved into her skin. I admit that I am at a loss as to how to explain this, although I'm sure her father will not mind in the slightest. I have sent for him, and he will be here shortly to collect his daughter.'

Ada didn't know how to respond. While it was a relief to hear such news, it simply served to underline the Ravener's sincerity. He had not lied about Josephine's recovery, so why would he lie about anything else? Such knowledge did little to ease Ada's fears over what would come next. It was a burden she would have to bear alone; sharing such thoughts would lead to her being placed inside the very cell that Josephine was about to vacate. 'That is wonderful news,' she said, forcing a smile, 'even if it does border on the miraculous.'

'Miraculous indeed,' said Fitz. 'Perhaps your mother is watching over us and interceded with the Almighty on the poor girl's behalf? That would be very like Clara.'

Ada knew that Fitz was simply trying to be kind, but she did not wish to dwell on the concept of her mother's ghost. Wherever her soul was now, Ada hoped that Clara was at peace, far away from the malign entity that had wormed its way into their lives. 'Please give Miss Schlecter my regards,' she said, 'and let her know that when she feels herself to be fully recovered, she is welcome to call upon me if she so wishes.'

'I would be happy to,' said Fitz. 'Right, I shouldn't keep you any longer. Good luck with rescuing your friend.'

'Thank you,' said Ada, 'let us hope Rory is still in one piece, otherwise he may end up in the room next to Father.'

'Whitechapel police station please, Baynes,' said Sir Edmund, rapping on the roof with the head of his cane. The carriage set off down the drive, open parkland giving way to the streets of Blackheath as it made its way north.

'Will Halloran be there to gloat?' asked Ada.

'No, he has what he wants. He'll let us clear up the mess, as it were.' He paused a moment, staring out of the carriage window. 'Ada, I was thinking...'

'Yes?'

'How would you feel about having Rory as a houseguest until Henry recovers?'

Ada smiled. 'I was about to suggest a similar arrangement,' she said. 'The company would be most welcome with Father *in absentia*.'

'Good. I was hoping you would say that. I

have much to do over the coming days and won't be able to see you as often as I would like. I know you are perfectly capable of running the household by yourself, but I would prefer that your studies don't suffer unduly. I trust Rory to observe propriety and help out as required. As he is suspended without pay, I'm sure he will appreciate a modest stipend from me. Just as importantly, he will be less vulnerable in Shoreditch than if he stayed at his usual lodgings.'

'Do you really believe that Soames will seek further reprisal,' said Ada, 'given that Halloran has already rendered judgement?'

Sir Edmund sighed. 'Not only is the chief constable a weak man, but he has a tiger by the tail. As I said last night, if Soames is intent on revenge, then Halloran may not be able to dissuade him. If that be the case, then I have no option but to deal with the matter myself.'

Ada's eyes widened. 'You don't mean...'

'It is a question of honour, Granddaughter. I promised Rory's grandfather that I would keep the boy safe. One does not ignore the request of a dying man, especially when his life was given to save mine. Hopefully my concerns will prove groundless, but if my hand is forced then I will treat Soames as I would any rabid animal. I have the means to put him down swiftly and without mercy, and I will not hesitate to do so, regardless of the consequences.'

Ada nodded. What Sir Edmund said disturbed her, but she understood it all too well. If one could not reason with a foe, then a confrontation was all too inevitable. The weight of the purse in her lap was a salient reminder of her own fears, and as the carriage sped toward Whitechapel, she hoped that Rory would listen to what she had to say. If there was anyone who could help her make sense of the nightmare she found herself in, it was him.

CHAPTER 16

A Friend in Need

T he lobby of Whitechapel police station was utilitarian and dimly lit, sunlight struggling to pierce the high, smoke-stained windows. On the far side of the room, close to the staircase leading down to the cells, Ada was pleased to see the reassuring bulk of Duty Sergeant Osborne. Perched on a stool behind a raised desk, he was filling in the admittance register in a neat, delicate script that quite belied the size of his hands. She knew Osborne well. He was blunt, gruff, and could out-drink any man in the station, but he had never been anything less than courteous to her.

'Good afternoon, Walter,' she said, standing in front of his desk, 'we've come to collect Rory.'

He looked up, peering at her with bloodshot eyes. 'And about time too.' He waited a moment before allowing a crooked smile to peek through his impressive beard. 'It's good to see you, miss. Our mutual friend is waiting for you in his cell. Feels wrong him being there but it's his own fault, the pillock. Shouldn't mess with the higher-ups, however much they deserve a slapping.'

'I couldn't agree more. Still, we are here now so hopefully that will be an end to the matter.'

Osborne leaned over and lowered his voice. 'You ought to know that chap from Special Branch came in a few minutes ago. Said he wanted to have a chat with Rory. You may want to intervene sooner rather than later.'

Ada looked at her grandfather. 'We should get down there,' she said.

Sir Edmund nodded.

'The keys to the cells are on the wall next to the charge sheet,' said Osborne. 'You know the way.'

'That I do. Thank you, sergeant.'

At the bottom of the stairs was a green-tiled hallway, lit by gas lamps and lined on one side with vertical iron bars. Soames was standing in front of Rory's cell, arms folded across his chest. He glanced at Ada, his face wearing the same cold expression she had seen in the foundry.

'It appears you have friends in high places, Canavan. Rest assured that I will be watching you regardless.'

'Feck off,' grunted Rory. 'You're all bark and no bite.'

'Unfortunate choice of words,' said Soames, chuckling mirthlessly under his breath. 'Enjoy your freedom while you can.' He turned and walked toward Ada and her grandfather, offering them a curt nod as he strode past. For just a moment, the fingers of his gloved hand brushed against Ada's wrist. His touch filled her with revulsion, and it took all of her self-control not to pull away. The policeman had almost reached the exit when Sir Edmund turned and called after him.

'Mr Soames, in the interests of justice, know that I shall be watching you too.'

'As you wish, sir' he replied, but his tone was one of challenge, not acquiescence, and without a backward glance he strode off upstairs.

Fetching the key from its hook Ada opened the door to Rory's cell, noting the bruises on his face and the fear he was trying to hide.

'I'm sorry,' he said to her.

'It's all right, you're safe now. It's time to go home.'

'How's your da?'

'I saw him this morning. He looks well – far better than you in fact.'

'Ah, I've had worse. They weren't gentle getting me in here. I'll be fine in a few days.' He stood up, grunting in pain as he did so.

'You owe me a favour for getting you out of here, Sergeant Canavan,' said Sir Edmund, shaking Rory's hand, 'and I'm collecting it immediately.'

'Of course. Anything you want.'

'Good man. I'll let Ada explain on the way to Shoreditch. You won't be seeing your lodgings for a while, and given the demeanour of your previous visitor I hope you understand why.'

'He'll be staying in one of the servant's rooms I take it?' said Mrs Crane.

'Of course I will, ma'am,' said Rory, handing her a posy of flowers he'd chosen from the florist at the end of the street. 'These are for you, to make up for the inconvenience.'

'Well, I suppose it wouldn't be too untoward under the circumstances. You are a policeman after all, and with Master Henry away it would make sense to have a man in the house, for security's sake.'

'My thoughts exactly,' said Sir Edmund. He bent to kiss Ada's cheek. 'Sleep well tonight, dear one. We'll take good care of your father so please don't worry. He'll be back with you soon.'

Ada smiled at him and returned the kiss. 'Thank you,' she said.

'And you, sergeant; please assist Ada and Mrs Crane in any way you can.'

'I won't let you down, sir,' said Rory.

'Right, I must away. I'll send a telegram if I need to inform you of anything.' With a polite nod to Mrs Crane he left the house, leaving her to shut the door behind him.

Hamlet padded into the hall, snuffling gently at Rory's hand. 'Hello, boy,' he said, 'you going to join me in keeping an eye on things?' The dog gave a soft bark.

'Fine, that's settled then.'

'Go through to the parlour, Rory,' said Ada. 'I'll fetch you something for that bruising.'

He nodded, and on her return she found him sitting at the dining table. 'Hold this to your face,' she said, handing him a knotted teacloth filled with crushed ice. He did as asked, wincing as the cold leeched through his skin.

'Would you like me to take a look?' she asked, seating herself next to him. 'You may have a fractured cheekbone.'

'If you wouldn't mind.'

Ada raised her hands, but as she did so they began to shake uncontrollably.

'What's the matter, lass?' asked Rory.

Ada stared at her friend, unable to answer as the tears finally came. Putting the ice pack aside, Rory took her hands in his. She leaned forward and rested her head against his shoulder, silently sobbing as she let slip all the terror she had been holding inside. This is what love feels like, Ada thought, it is kind and selfless, it does not make grand declarations on one hand, while offering violence and death with the other.

'I… I am sorry,' she said, sitting up and hoping that Rory did not think her weak. She had never displayed such raw emotion in front of him before.

He smiled at her, gently drying her cheeks

with the edge of his thumb. 'In your own time, lass,' he said.

'Thank you.' She took a deep breath, trying to still her racing heart before speaking. 'Do you remember our conversation in the park the other day, when I said that I was scared?'

'Yes. You had good reason to be under the circumstances.'

'Well, much has happened since then. What I dread most of all is that you will not believe what I have to tell you, that you will think me some histrionic child.'

Rory chuckled. 'You know very well that I would never view you as such.'

Ada smiled in return. There was a subtle relief to be found in honesty, however difficult the subject. 'I need you to promise me something, Rory.'

'Aye, anything.'

'Please listen to what I say with an open mind. It will sound far-fetched in the extreme, but it is true nonetheless.'

'Of course. Tell me what it is that has you so upset.' The Irishman sat back in his chair, waiting for her to speak.

'The nightmare I had was just the beginning,' said Ada. Haltingly at first, then with increasing assurance, the words spilled from her lips: a torrent of impossible experiences, all seemingly tied to one man of shadow, one

Ravener. She finished, and with a dry mouth sat waiting for Rory's response.

There was a long pause in which he opened his mouth then closed it again, as if not knowing what to say. Eventually he met Ada's eyes. 'You haven't got anything to drink by any chance?' he asked.

Ada got up and poured them each a whiskey. 'Tell me that you don't think I'm mad,' she said, handing him a glass.

'You're not mad, lass, but feck me, I can see why you feel scared. I bloody would too.'

'Witness my art, fear my wrath,' said Ada. 'How could Josephine have known those words would be in the letter stuffed in Price's mouth?'

'I have no idea,' he said, 'perhaps she is involved with the killer in some way, and was putting on some elaborate act to toy with you?'

'You didn't see her, Rory. Even Fitz was rattled by her behaviour, and there's no aspect of mental ill-health that he hasn't witnessed first-hand. Something terrified her into cutting herself as an apology to me, yet as of this morning she is apparently sane and unharmed, her injury almost gone. I don't believe in ghosts but I feel haunted just the same. I'm not sure what is real anymore.'

'Given what you've just told me that's perfectly understandable, but playing devil's advocate, could it be that what you've experienced is simply a mixture of grief, exhaustion and strange coincidence?'

'I told myself the same thing at first, but with each new horror such a pedestrian explanation seems less and less likely.'

Rory nodded. 'It's clear that something strange is happening, you wouldn't be so unnerved if it wasn't, but the evidence that connects it to Price's death is still far from solid. All you have is what Josephine said during her mania, and the dreams in which this Ravener speaks to you, taunts you almost.'

'Taunting is exactly what he does, but don't forget the India Room. I was wide awake when he spoke to me then.'

'Could somebody have been hiding behind the panelling? Whispering to you from some secret passage or suchlike. It is an old house.'

'It's possible I suppose, but who would do such a bizarre thing?' Ada rubbed a hand across her face. 'God, I am so tired, but it's a weight off my mind to share this with you.'

'Think nothing of it, lass. You've been through enough and you don't have to shoulder this alone anymore. I'll be with you come what may. I am concerned about that letter, though. Whoever this vigilante is, Price may well be the first of many.'

'Twenty were taken and twenty will pay,' said Ada. 'It sounds like a declaration of war.'

'I agree, but much as though I would like

to pursue the case, it's Special Branch's problem now.'

Ada took a sip of whiskey and nodded. 'Working on the assumption that I am not insane, I cannot for the life of me fathom *why* this is happening, Rory. Why would the Ravener punish Josephine so harshly over a few poorly chosen words? Why would he butcher Price in such a brutal manner, if indeed he is the killer? He implied that he did it for my benefit, but how could anyone believe that such actions would result in my approval? And then there is what he said about Mother. Why would he drive her to madness and death yet profess to love me? All those years I spent resenting her, hating her at times; now it seems her illness may have been caused by the same creature that seeks to test me. I didn't know it was possible to feel such guilt.'

'But if your theory is correct, then how could you possibly have known, lass?'

'That is true, Rory, but it doesn't take the pain away.'

'No, it's cold comfort at best. As for Clara, if she *was* visited in her dreams by this man, perhaps he didn't drive her mad intentionally? I knew your mother well, Ada. She was a lovely woman, full of grace, but she didn't have your strength, or your character.'

'That had occurred to me. If Mother was living in constant fear, what damage would that have done to her mind?'

'It would likely destroy it,' said Rory. 'I know what it's like to be afraid, truly afraid, and it can eat you away until there's nothing left. Perhaps Clara was overwhelmed by what the Ravener was saying to her as she slept. Perhaps she became so afraid of him that it drove her insane?'

'But why would he have been speaking to Mother all those years? What did he want from her? What does he now want from me?'

'With Clara in her grave it's not as if we can just ask her,' said Rory. 'Then again...'

'What?'

'Ah, it's just *my* mother speaking now, superstitious old bat. She was always one to believe in spirits and the world beyond this veil of ours. I used to laugh at her as a child, but there were times when she saw things before they happened, knew things that I couldn't explain.'

'And how is that supposed to help me?'

'Just hear me out, lass. She was no medium, my mother, but I know of someone who is. It's only a suggestion, but why don't you book a private appointment with Madame Blavatsky? Apparently she has quite the reputation.'

'The Russian psychic? I've never given that kind of thing any credence, however lauded certain individuals might be.'

'It may be clutching at straws, but what have you got to lose? At least we get out of the house for a bit. She has a spiritualist lodge over in Holland Park, so it's not far to go.'

Ada sighed. Faced with such a curious and frightening set of circumstances, the thought of asking her late mother for help was a seductive one, however nonsensical it sounded. 'Very well, despite my reservations we shall do as you suggest. However, if I think that she is exploiting my grief for financial gain, I will not hesitate to tell her so.'

'Fair enough,' said Rory, 'I'll go and see her tomorrow. I'm sure your story will pique her interest.'

'I doubt she will have heard anything so outlandish, but if there is a chance she can help then I am willing to suspend my disbelief for an hour or two.'

'That's the spirit.'

Ada couldn't help but smile at him. She was fully prepared for Madame Blavatsky to be a charlatan, but deep down she hoped that was not the case. To be able to speak to her mother again, to have the opportunity to say sorry for not believing her, would do much to ease the ache of loss that lay wrapped round her heart.

CHAPTER 17

The Corsairs

'**C**ome with me, Ada, there is something you need to see.'

She tried to ignore the summons, but like a stern parent with a recalcitrant child, it refused to be denied. Taking her by the hand, it led her from the deepest slumber to somewhere she did not recognise. The darkness fell away, leaving her standing on planks that were sodden with seawater and despair. It was the hold of a ship, the air thick with the smell of spices and lamp oil, timbers creaking as the vessel rolled slowly with the swell.

'Can you not leave me be?' she asked. 'I am tired of being your plaything. Why do you torture me so?'

'This is not torture, beloved,' said the Ravener, 'it is an awakening.' He sat on a crate of China tea, head cocked to one side as if wondering why Ada was so reticent to hear what he had to say.

'After what you did to Josephine, to my mother, you still expect me to listen to your monstrous prattling?'

The Ravener sighed. 'You have come to a conclusion without all the evidence. You sound like some tuppence-ha'penny defence lawyer, arguing a case that you know deep down to be false.'

'And you are the prosecution, I take it?'

'Oh Ada, I was not always thus, but the actions of others have left me little choice. My hand has been forced and it is high time you understood the true nature of evil. It began with Mr Price and it continues here. Welcome to the Pegasus, and all who sail in her.'

Somewhere deep in the ship's gloomy hold a woman cried out, pleading in a language Ada couldn't understand. It sounded like Mandarin but she couldn't be sure. 'What is this?' she demanded.

'It is a study in suffering, proof that I am no phantom.'

The woman began to scream then; whether in pain or desperation, Ada could not tell. 'Who is that? We need to help her.'

'Of course,' said the Ravener. 'You must always follow your heart.'

Ada turned and ran toward the bow of the ship, the wooden planks rough against her bare feet. With cargo stacked on all sides there was no easy way through, but she refused to be thwarted. Clambering over a pile of hessian sacks she saw a pool of light ahead, but before she could reach it the sounds of distress suddenly ceased. Silence filled the hold, and Ada knew in her bones that she was too late. Stepping out from behind some crates, she saw the body of young Chinese woman – barely more than a girl – lying on the deck. Her plain, cotton shift had been torn open, exposing her breasts, livid finger marks encircling her neck testament to the manner of her death. Her eyes remained open and accusing, begging for retribution. Standing at her side, staring at the body, were three sailors.

'You shouldn't 'ave been so rough with 'er, Bill,' said one. 'That's coming out of your share of the profits.'

'Like 'ell,' said another. 'We always 'ave a bit of fun with the cargo, you know that. This 'un just put up more of a fight.'

'That don't matter,' said the third. 'The whorehouse don't mind 'em being roughed up a little, but we don't get paid for bringin' 'em a corpse.'

'Dear God,' said Ada, 'what have you done?'

The men didn't seem to hear her. One of them picked up the body, slung it over his shoulder and walked away, while the others filled their pipes and sat down for a smoke. Ada made to fling herself at them, to vent the rage she felt at such a callous murder, but her feet remained rooted to the deck.

'There is nothing you can do,' said the

Ravener. 'What you see here is but a shadow, a memory of what was. That poor girl lies at the bottom of the ocean, as do many others. Would you have it continue so?'

'No,' said Ada. 'I would have the authorities made aware of such atrocity, have these animals arrested.'

'Their activities are well known. Bribes are offered and accepted, eyes turned away, and so the helpless remain hopeless. If this is to be stopped, more... radical measures are required. Come seek me on the morrow, Ada, and witness the truth. Midday at Tower Bridge, don't be late.'

Ada turned to remonstrate, but there was nothing in sight but the crammed and stinking ship's hold. The scene dissolved as sleep wrapped its arms round her, pulling her away. Her last thought was of the young woman, sinking through fathoms of dark water, arms reaching out for help that never came.

The Ravener waited on the Wapping dock, ignored by the drunken stevedores that lurched past to spend their pay in taverns and opium dens. The schooner Pegasus, docked and half-unladen, sat huddled against the wooden pilings. She reeked of shame, the despairing cries of her unwilling cargo clinging to her hull like barnacles. It was time to put the ship out of her misery.

'Thomas?'

'Yes, sir?'

'Please keep watch and ensure I am not disturbed.'

'Of course, sir.'

'I realise that dealing with Harold Price was not the most pleasant of experiences, but an example had to be made. London must know my name, and for that it needs to be shaken awake with a rough hand. Do you understand Thomas? Are you still content to assist me in this work?'

'Yes, sir. Price was an evil man, he needed to be stopped. No more of them poor ladies will die now.'

'That is true, dear Thomas. I only ask because it is vital that your help is freely given, not forced from you under duress. It is a matter of pride and necessity that this be so. If you wish to stop then all you have to do is say so, and I will let you go in peace. You have nothing to fear from me.'

Thomas nodded, his eyes meeting those of his master. 'I will do my duty, sir,' he said. 'I will help you.'

'You were a fine soldier, Thomas, and now you are an even finer man. This path may be dark, but it leads to somewhere brighter than you could possibly imagine. I thank you for your efforts. Now, it is time for me to be about my duty. Wait here, I will call for you when I need your assistance. My instruments please.'

Thomas handed over the black leather bag, its contents a means to an end: justice and death. The Ravener took it, striding out of the fog and up the gangplank. He paused to inhale the scent of the Thames, the relentless tide of effluent that flowed out to sea, cleansing the metropolis of its filth. Smiling beneath his mask, he headed toward the main companionway. The ship was quiet. Most of the sailors were ashore, enjoying the many delights and vices that Wapping had to offer. The Ravener had been patient, waiting for the right moment. The three he sought were still below decks, congratulating themselves on yet another profitable voyage, another journey enriched by the suffering of the innocent. His shoes made barely a sound as he trod the boards, descending into the bowels of the ship like a wraith.

Muffled voices came from the far end of the hold. The Ravener paced slowly toward them, the edges of his cloak caressing the bolts of silk that lay stacked on narrow benches to either side. His quarry was close now. They had no idea what lay ahead and the thought was intoxicating. Reaching his destination, he looked at the cage that had been built into the space under the fo'c'sle. Inside it, five young Chinese women huddled together in abject misery. The clothes they wore were stained and ragged, the stench from the bucket in the corner of their prison speaking volumes as to how they were regarded by their captors.

Three sailors stood near them, deep in conversation. 'Now you listen to me,' said one. 'If I want to take…' He stopped mid-sentence as he noticed a black leather bag sitting atop a nearby crate. Next to it were a top hat, and a neatly folded cloak.

'Whose are those?' he asked his compatriots. They all turned, watching in astonishment as the Ravener stepped out of the shadows. 'Gentlemen, gentlemen, what have you done?' he asked.

'We ain't done nothing,' said one.

'The question was rhetorical,' replied the Ravener. 'You are stained with death. All of you. How many innocents have you tortured and killed in your relentless pursuit of pleasure and coin?'

The sailors looked at each other, curiosity turning to low cunning in the blink of an eye.

'You shouldn't have come down here,' said one. 'We can't have you interferin'.'

'I am not here to interfere, gentlemen,' said the Ravener, 'I'm here to kill you. I have no particular preference as to the order of your deaths, but you, William Trench,' he pointed to one sailor, 'will be the last.'

The men looked at each other and laughed.

'Do you 'ear that, Billy? He's gonna save you for afters.'

'Shut it, Silas,' said Trench. 'Just deal with this ponce, will ya?'

The sailor nodded, taking a lock-knife from his pocket and making great show of opening the blade. 'I'm going to cut that mask off your face,' he said, smiling to reveal a mouth full of discoloured teeth.

'You are welcome to try,' said the Ravener, standing perfectly still as Silas advanced upon him in a half-crouch, knife at the ready. The moment he was two paces away he lunged, stabbing at the Ravener's chest. His arm was caught mid-thrust, stopped with such force that his elbow dislocated. With a sweeping, almost dismissive motion, the Ravener delivered an open-handed blow to Silas' face, shattering his jaw. The sailor slumped to the deck, writhing on the filthy planks as he moaned in agony.

'What about you, Mr Quinn?' said the Ravener to the man at Trench's side. 'You believe yourself skilled in the art of violence, do you not? Perhaps if you try really hard you will fare better than your ill-fated shipmate.'

'Fucker!' howled Quinn. Grabbing a bale-hook he ran forward, swinging it in a wide arc in an attempt to disembowel the Ravener. His clumsy attack cleaved nothing but air as his target sidestepped with unearthly grace. Thrown off balance, Quinn crashed against the bars of the cage.

'Not as impressive as I would have hoped, lacklustre even. Is that all you have to show me?'

With a bellow of rage Quinn threw himself at the Ravener, the bale-hook a blur as he tried to gut the man who taunted him. Again and again he swung, but his efforts were futile; it was as if he fought a plume of smoke.

'Enough,' said the Ravener, driving a gloved fist into Quinn's midriff. Unable to draw breath he doubled over, only to have a hand grip him by the throat and lift him clean off his feet. Slamming him against a post, the Ravener tore the bale hook from Quinn's grasp and drove it through the sailor's shoulder, pinning him to the wood. Quinn screamed, blood staining his shirt as he writhed, the hook gouging deeper into his flesh with every movement he made.

'It's quite apt, don't you think?' the Ravener said to Trench as he cowered against the hull. 'The young woman you raped and suffocated, you called her your little butterfly until she fought back. Mr Quinn makes a rather good exhibit, doesn't he? An insect pinned to a display board. Hardly a butterfly though, more a cockroach.'

Trench could only stare in horror at the consummate ease with which his colleagues had been incapacitated.

'Give me the key,' said the Ravener.

Trench nodded dumbly, rummaging in his jacket with a shaking hand before tossing it over. Unlocking the cage, the Ravener knelt and held out a hand to those huddled within. 'Go to the main deck and leave the ship by the gangplank,' he said in perfect Mandarin. 'There is a man waiting who will take you to a place of safety. You need not fear.'

On weak, shaking legs, the young women got slowly to their feet, eyes wide in both astonishment and gratitude. Offering a bow to their rescuer, they fled the place of their imprisonment. The last one to leave paused, turning to look at the Ravener. There were tears on her cheeks. 'The girl he killed, she was my sister.'

The Ravener nodded his understanding. 'Judgement is come,' he said, opening his hand to show her the perfectly-honed catling. The young woman reached out, gently pressing her fingers to the lips of his mask. Giving him a sad smile, she ran after her fellow captives. When the sound of her footsteps had faded, the Ravener turned to Trench. 'Any last requests?' he asked.

'Please,' he begged, 'we can make a deal, I 'ave money.'

'I have no need of more money,' said the Ravener, taking slow and measured steps toward the terrified sailor. He tilted the blade of the knife, catching the lamplight and flicking it into

Trench's eyes. 'I still need payment though, my pound of flesh, as it were.'

'Just tell me what it is you want, I'll give it to you.'

The Ravener chuckled, running the tip of the catling over the skin of Trench's cheek. 'Ah, little butterfly, I simply wish to eat your sins.' With his free hand, the Ravener took off his mask.

'Oh, Jesus Christ!' Trench screamed.

Up on the dock, Thomas helped the frightened girls into the waiting carriage. He could hear the muffled sounds of his master at work and nodded in approval. Their calling, their sacred duty, had finally begun in earnest.

CHAPTER 18

A City of Blood

'It was *real*,' said Ada, facing Rory across the breakfast table. 'It wasn't some disjointed nightmare. Whatever he's done, it has already happened; he wants me to come to Tower Bridge at midday.' She watched as her friend frowned and scratched his head. He had listened while she described her encounter with the Ravener, but still seemed reticent to believe her.

'Are you sure this wasn't just a dream about our chat last night?' he asked.

Ada shook her head. 'No. He has killed again, I know it. He wants me to witness his work, to prove he isn't some ghost.'

'I see,' said Rory, although he sounded far from convinced.

'I need you to trust me. I'm not making this up and I am most certainly not delusional. I have to go to the bridge and see for myself.'

Rory glanced at the clock on the mantelpiece. 'Very well. We have a couple of hours before we need to leave so how about I make some enquiries? What did you say the name of that ship was again?'

'The Pegasus.'

'It sounds familiar but I can't remember the details. I think the boys over Wapping way investigated it last year – something about an alleged slavery ring. Nothing was ever proved from what I recall.'

'So it does exist,' said Ada.

'Possibly, but for all we know it could be halfway to China. Why don't I send a telegram to the station, ask Osborne if he can get a runner to check what ships are currently moored up?'

'That would be helpful. Maybe then you'll stop looking at me as though I'm completely unhinged.'

An hour later the doorbell rang. Rory answered it and came back to the parlour carrying a note. 'You were right,' he said. 'The Pegasus is moored up in east Wapping, one of the smaller docks. No doubt it's trying to avoid attention if it's carrying contraband. My apologies for doubting you.'

'I would be sceptical too were our roles reversed,' said Ada. 'We should be off, there's not much time left.'

Hailing a cab, Ada and Rory made their way to the vast construction site of Tower Bridge. A large crowd had gathered on the abutment overlooking the river and Ada felt her pulse quicken. The proof she sought was within her grasp, she could feel it, but the manner in which it might be delivered still filled her with dread.

'Just here all right?' asked the cab driver.

'Yes, thank you,' said Ada. With Rory at her back, she pushed her way through the mass of people until she found a space by the parapet. In front of her, three policemen in a rowing boat fought against the current, aiming for base of the nearest tower.

'What's happening?' she asked a young, smartly dressed man standing next to her, a notebook and pencil in his hands.

'Workers found something; scared the wits out of them apparently. Rumour has it we have a new killer in town.'

'What makes you think that?'

'It appears someone offed a photographer in the Whitechapel Bell Foundry the other night – quite messily by all accounts. Nobody wants to talk about it which means there's a story to be had. I'm hoping today might provide some fresh leads. Still, where are my manners? Joseph Hazell, correspondent for The Evening Standard at your service, miss.'

'Oh, you're a journalist.'

'You make that sound like a crime,' he said, chuckling to himself. 'People love a good murder, it sells papers. If I can connect whatever's going on today with the death at the foundry, I'll get a pay rise.'

'Looks like they're about there,' said Rory,

pointing at the boat.

Ada watched as the policemen moored up to one of the great wooden pilings mid-stream. Climbing a ladder lashed to the side, they reached the top of the pier and stood looking at a pile of discarded clothing. Gulls perched on the surrounding scaffold, watching the policemen in turn. They can smell death, thought Ada; they're hungry and there are bones to pick clean.

The crowd went silent as a constable lifted a rumpled seaman's jacket from the top of the pile. He drew back, a hand over his mouth as he saw what lay beneath. As one the assembled throng let out a cry – of excitement or disgust, Ada couldn't tell. There, neatly arranged on a bloodstained white shirt, were three human hearts.

'Oh, this is just marvellous,' said Hazell. 'I'll lay odds that each of those hearts has a bite missing. My editor is going to be ecstatic.'

Ada's head swam. Only the gentle pressure of Rory's hand at the small of her back kept her from falling. Shielding her eyes from the sun, she watched with growing horror as inch by inch the outgoing tide revealed the bodies of three men, bound to the pilings with rope. Their grey-skinned faces wore expressions of agony, filthy water pouring gargoyle-like from their gaping mouths.

'What the feck is this?' said Rory, holding

Ada tight against him.

The crowd let out a roar as they realised where the hearts had come from. The men were stripped to the waist, and in each of their chests was a gaping hole, crawling with shore crabs. With raucous delight the birds descended, tearing at the sodden flesh, hungry, vicious, relentless. The policemen stood aghast, unsure of what to do.

Ada stared at the corpses, rotting evidence that her nightmares were real. Her mother, Josephine, Price, it was all connected to this man in the mask. What he wanted from her she did not know, but she was not going to give it to him without a fight.

'Ravener,' she spat, the word leaving a foul taste in her mouth.

'Now that's a name I can work with,' said Hazell, tucking his notebook into his jacket.

Ada had forgotten he was there. She felt nothing but revulsion as she looked at him, gloating at these fresh deaths, eager to create a new myth.

'Good day to you, miss.' He touched the brim of his hat and scurried away.

'Come, Ada,' said Rory softly. 'We've seen enough.'

She nodded, allowing him to guide her away from the mob and into a waiting cab.

'Jesus, you were right all along,' he said, his

face pale.

'I take no joy in it. All I have is evidence that someone, or *something*, is trying to manipulate me. I don't think the Ravener means me harm, quite the opposite in fact, but there are questions I need answered, especially as regards what happened to Mother.'

'I know, lass. Tell you what, I need to go back to my lodgings, pick up my things, but once I've done that I'll go and see Madame Blavatsky, ask if she would kindly grant us an audience.'

'That would be wonderful,' said Ada. 'Thank you.'

'It's the least I can do. I should have trusted your instincts in the first place. I'm supposed to be your friend.'

'You are my friend,' she said, taking his hand. 'And promise me you'll be careful. If Grandfather is concerned about Soames, you should be too.'

'Ah, I'll be fine. He has the Ravener to deal with now; I doubt he'll give me a second thought.'

'Let us hope that's the case,' she replied.

Ada sat in the parlour and tried not to fret. Rory had been gone for almost four hours. Even allowing for a trip to Holland Park, he should have been back some time ago. She jumped as the front door opened and moments later Rory strode in. 'Oh thank God!' she said, placing a hand on her chest. 'I was about to send a telegram to

Grandfather.'

Rory took a seat next to her and smiled apologetically. 'Sorry for taking so long, but things didn't go entirely to plan.'

Ada raised her eyebrows. 'Dare I ask?'

'I got to the end of my street and saw someone watching the front of my house. Lawson I think his name is, Soames' second in command. Vicious little shit by all accounts.'

'Please tell me you didn't confront him?'

Rory shook his head. 'I'm not daft, lass. I went round the back and used the kitchen door instead. When I got in I found my landlady, Alice, sitting by the fire and weeping. It seems that Lawson barged in and threatened her earlier today, demanding to know where I was. When she said she didn't know the fecker blacked her eye.'

'That poor woman. Is there anything we can do to help her?'

'It's already taken care of. I gave her enough money to go and stay with her sister in Clerkenwell for a while. Her neighbours will keep an eye on the house, and if Lawson comes calling again I told Alice to mention that I was skipping town, all the way back to Dublin in fact. With any luck that'll keep them off my back for a while.'

Ada sighed. 'I knew Soames wasn't going to just give up.'

'Well, there's not much I can do about it

except keep my head down and pray. Oh, and that journalist we met at Tower Bridge has been busy. I bought a copy of the Evening Standard on the way back. Have a look at the front page.'

Ada took the paper, rolling her eyes at the sensational headline and the article beneath.

A City of Blood

According to confidential sources, the body found recently in the Whitechapel Bell Foundry may well be that of the notorious Limehouse Strangler. The corpse was apparently mutilated, with the heart cut out and partially eaten; a violent, perhaps fitting end for the murderer of four, innocent young women. Speculation as to the Strangler's identity is rife, but no statement has been released to the public as yet. It may be that the unexplained disappearance of local photographer, Harold Price, is connected to the case. He had close links with the police, but the authorities have refused to comment.

In a disturbing development, the bodies of three sailors were found tied to the pilings of Tower Bridge this morning, their injuries almost identical to that of the foundry victim. Enquiries point to the sailors being part of a slavery ring, procuring young women from the Orient for use in prostitution. Once again the police have refused to comment, but indications are that London may have acquired a vigilante, dispensing his own brand of justice in a manner both brutal and uncompromising. The local populace has even given him the name 'Ravener', an apt title for one who is apparently preying on those who would seek to harm others.

'It reads like a penny dreadful,' said Ada, pursing her lips in distaste, 'but Mr Hazell got the story he wanted. I even gave him the killer's name. Halloran will be furious when he finds out someone has talked.'

'It'll certainly keep him occupied,' said Rory. 'With any luck he'll forget about me completely.'

'A grim silver lining, but welcome nonetheless. However, while I dislike such lurid prose I think Mr Hazell may be on to something. The Ravener appears to be choosing his victims with care, only taking the lives of those who are themselves murderers.'

'He's no ordinary vigilante, that's for sure. I've dealt with a few in my time and they didn't eat people's hearts. That smacks of someone trying to make a fecking point, but exactly *what* point is beyond me.'

'I agree,' said Ada, 'but there is something that I don't understand. The Ravener was speaking to Mother in her dreams for years. If he was killing during that time, then why haven't other victims been found? It's not as if he's trying to hide his activities.'

'He certainly has a flair for the dramatic. It's

almost as if he's taunting the authorities, like the Ripper did back in the day.'

'Except the Ravener isn't targeting innocent women. He's methodical, he plans; he's not some run-of-the-mill butcher. There must be a reason for what's happening. I just don't know what it is yet.'

'I may have some good news on that front,' said Rory. 'After dodging Lawson, I took a cab to Holland Park and made an appointment with Madame Blavatsky for eight o'clock this evening. Once I explained what had happened, she was quite eager to meet you, she's even sending her carriage to collect us. I'm sure it makes a change from people asking her to contact their dearly departed, to find out where they buried the family silver.'

Ada nodded. 'Well, charlatan or not, we shall see tonight, won't we?'

Through several hands of whist and then supper, Ada watched the clock as it ground slowly onward. It felt good to be doing something proactive, however strange. She hoped this Russian psychic was indeed genuine, that she could shed some light on what this creature of shadow wanted with her, and on what he had done to cause Clara's suicide.

At half past seven the carriage arrived. Fetching her coat, Ada bade goodbye to Mrs Crane, saying that she and Rory were going to the theatre.

'Are you ready for this?' he asked, as a dark and misty London sped by.

'Yes,' she said. She needed answers, and at this moment she could think of nowhere else to turn.

CHAPTER 19

Waking the Dead

'Well, this is the place,' said Rory.

Ada stared at the imposing townhouse. At the top of a short flight of steps sat a huge oak door, framed by flaming sconces. The flickering light illuminated an intricate design carved into the wood. Two interlocking triangles, similar to a Star of David, were encircled by a serpent swallowing its own tail. In the centre was an Egyptian Ankh, and above were written the words: "There is no Religion higher than Truth." The building radiated a primal air, and Ada wondered if this was just for show. She was sure that visitors would no doubt feel they were entering somewhere bohemian and mysterious, but she was no simpering debutante to be impressed by parlour tricks.

Climbing the steps she gave the bell-pull a gentle tug. Footsteps sounded from within, and moments later the door was opened by a tall, smartly-dressed man. He smiled at Ada and extended a hand. 'Welcome to my home, Miss Phillips,' he said warmly. 'I am Bertram Keightley. Please, come in, both of you.'

'Thank you,' she replied. Taking Rory's arm, Ada stepped into an entrance hall almost as grand as that at Rookwood. The floor was polished marble, tapestries hung from the walls, and candlelight filled the room with a soft, golden glow.

'Madame is waiting for you in the library,' said Mr Keightley. 'I must admit that it is unusual for her to grant such an audience. Her health has been poor of late and she rarely sees anyone.'

'Then I am most grateful for her time.'

Mr Keightley nodded, apparently satisfied with her response. Ada sensed no malice in him, only concern for a friend; it was something she understood all too well. 'Have you known Madame Blavatsky long?' she asked.

'Since I was boy. My grandfather was a student of her teachings, so he built this house to provide her with sanctuary when she visited London. Every stone was laid according to the tenets of sacred geometry. It is a place of stillness, of power, and I am honoured that she has chosen to stay here while she convalesces.'

The sincerity of his words was clear to Ada, but she was not willing to simply accept them at face value. Having loyal followers was no guarantee of veracity. However, despite her scepticism, Ada resolved to hear the medium out. If there was even the slimmest chance that she could speak to her mother, beg her forgiveness, then the journey would not have been wasted.

'Keep an open mind and all shall be well,' said Mr Keightley, seeming to read her thoughts. 'I shall not be in attendance for the ceremony, but I will be available if needed. Now, if you would kindly follow me.' Leading his guests to a door at the rear of the hall, he opened it and ushered them inside.

Ada found herself in a large, dimly-lit room, ringed with a balcony. Oak bookcases lined the walls, and close by the fireplace a diminutive figure sat hunched in a wheelchair, hands resting in her lap. Behind her stood a tall woman in a fashionable dress, her face impassive, her bearing regal.

'Welcome, Miss Phillips,' said the woman in the wheelchair. 'I am Helena Blavatsky. I have been looking forward to meeting you.'

'Thank you, Madame,' said Ada.

'And this is my companion and secretary, Countess Constance Wachtmeister. She will assist me this evening.'

'Lady Wachtmeister,' said Ada, inclining her head.

The Countess returned Ada's nod but remained silent.

'And it is good to see you again, sergeant,' said Madame Blavatsky, 'your tale has me very intrigued.'

'It's not my story, but Miss Ada's, Madame.

I hope you'll be able to help her unravel such a disturbing mystery.'

'I shall try. Please, come and sit by me, both of you.'

Once she and Rory were seated on chairs that had been set out for them, Ada took a moment to study the famed medium. She appeared both frail and vulnerable, her legs hidden beneath a blanket and her head draped with a rustic shawl. Age lined a face that had seen much, and large, strikingly-blue eyes regarded Ada in turn.

'Tell me everything,' she said. 'Leave nothing out, however trivial. Sergeant Canavan has told me some of what you have experienced, but I need to hear it from your lips. It is the only way to divine the truth.'

The trace of a Russian accent was evident in the medium's voice, and Ada found it unexpectedly soothing. Taking a deep breath, she began to speak of her mother. She half-expected Madame Blavatsky to recoil in horror as she described the contents of her dreams, the scenes of carnage she had witnessed, but the medium simply nodded, her brow furrowed in concentration.

'I no longer have any doubt that this Ravener is real,' said Ada. 'Somehow he is both flesh and phantom, an impossibility yet the facts speak otherwise. I need to understand why he drove my mother to madness and death, and what he now wants from me? Why is he haunting my family?'

'Those are the questions to which we shall seek answers,' said Madame Blavatsky. 'I must admit that in all my travels I have never encountered anything so ruthless or manipulative. Entities that can speak to us in dreams or affect the physical world rarely show such intelligence. They tend to be beings of instinct, remnants of memory that cannot let go of this realm. This Ravener of yours appears rather unique in his abilities.'

'Then what am I supposed to do?' said Ada, feeling utterly drained now she had told her story. What Madame Blavatsky was saying went against everything she knew, a world of science and rational thought colliding with the supernatural. A week ago Ada would have dismissed such assertions out of hand, but evidence was evidence, and the consequent diagnosis was something unearthly indeed. Torn between two utterly different points of view, all she could do was wait and see what transpired. It was an uncomfortable place in which to find herself.

'We need to speak to Clara,' said Madame Blavatsky, 'and in order to do that we will hold a séance. There are times when only the dead hold the key, and this, is one of them.'

'Is such a thing really possible? Please say

that you are not using my grief against me. I could not bear it.'

'Oh, my child, I would never hurt you so. I am no toe-cracking fraud, pretending to have spirits rapping on my table. If you truly wish it I will try to summon Clara, but I must caution you that the process is not without peril, for either of us. There is a reason the living and the dead inhabit separate worlds; bringing the two together can have dire consequences.'

'What could happen if something goes wrong?'

'If the ritual is not conducted properly there is always loss of some kind,' said Madame Blavatsky, smoothing the blanket over her withered legs. 'I know this to be true. In July of 1871, I was travelling from Greece to Egypt on the SS Eumonia, following in the steps of an ascended master. One of our party sought to contact this master's spirit, ask him for guidance, but he was careless in his summoning and terrible destruction was the result. An angry and malicious entity reached through the veil, and in doing so it destroyed the ship. Out of 200 passengers only 16 survived, myself among them. I have not been able to walk unaided since. Now do you understand what you ask?'

'I believe so,' said Ada, taking the medium's hands in hers. 'If you are willing to aid me, then I will do whatever you ask.'

Madame Blavatsky gave her a sad smile. 'I do not say these things to frighten you, my child, but sometimes it is healthy to be frightened; it can keep you alive. I won't be taking your money either, my good sergeant,' she said, turning to Rory. 'I am a seeker after knowledge, not a carnival sideshow.' She pointed to an envelope that sat on the mantelpiece. 'You may take it when we are done. As for you, Miss Phillips, I have only one request. Whatever happens during the séance you must not interfere, however much you may wish to do so. Listen to the countess' instructions as if they were my own and obey them without fail.'

Ada nodded.

'Good,' said Madame Blavatsky, 'then we shall begin. First, I need a drop of your blood.'

'My blood? Why?'

'Do not be alarmed, this is not vile Satanism, it is sympathetic magic. Your mother carried you in her womb; you are of the same flesh and like always calls to like. Clara will sense that connection. It will help guide her back to us, to you.'

'Very well,' she said, holding out her hand.

Pulling a pin from her hair, the medium pricked the tip of Ada's index finger; a drop of blood welled up. 'Draw a circle upon my forehead with it.'

Ada did as asked. She felt a strange, tingling

sensation, as if static electricity coursed through the old woman. Madame Blavatsky closed her eyes, her breathing slow and deep.

'Constance, assist me please.'

Apprehensive yet utterly enthralled, Ada watched as the countess pushed the wheelchair across the library floor. She hadn't noticed it when she came in, but a ring of unfamiliar script – some twenty feet across – had been set into the boards by an expert in parquetry. The detail was exquisite, and inside it was a compass created with the same consummate skill. Leaving Madame Blavatsky in the centre of the circle, the countess fetched four large candlesticks from the corner of the room. Placing one at each of the cardinal compass points, she lit them before coming to stand at Ada's side.

'The writing is Enochian,' said the medium, her voice sounding distant and strangely hollow. 'Do you know what that is?'

'It's the language of the angels,' said Rory. 'My mother spoke of it.'

'We will need their protection. This circle is not for my benefit, it is for yours. It does not prevent the dead from challenging me; it stops them from leaving and attacking you.'

Despite the warmth emanating from the fire, Ada shivered. The air in the room felt oppressive, thick and heavy as if waiting for a storm to break. Reaching out she clasped Rory's hand, reassured to find that it was as clammy as hers.

'Michael to my South,' said Madame Blavatsky, 'give me your courage.' The laughter of children echoed round the room, joyous and innocent.

'Uriel to my North, give me your wisdom.' A gentle breeze filled the library; it held the scent of spring, of apple blossom.

'Gabriel to my West, give me your mercy.' From somewhere high above, a single white feather drifted down in lazy spirals, coming to rest in the medium's hands.

'Raphael to my East, give me your strength.' The candles flared impossibly bright, a shining bulwark against the darkness. Madame Blavatsky bowed her head, face hidden by the folds of her shawl.

The countess placed a comforting hand on Ada's shoulder. 'Be brave,' she said.

'I will try,' she replied, wondering if the countess spoke not only to her, but also to the medium who sought to pierce the veil of death on her behalf. For long minutes nothing happened and Ada had to remind herself to breathe, her hand gripping Rory's so tightly that her knuckles showed white.

'Clara. Clara Phillips. I am here with your daughter. I beseech thee, hear my plea. Follow the light of my candles, the path of your blood, speak to us of what ailed you and share your pain.'

Madame Blavatsky's words hung in the air, repeating themselves in a manner at odds with physics. Ada closed her eyes, sending her own thoughts to her mother, begging her to share what she knew. All the sadness, confusion and loss that surrounded Clara's illness and death came flooding back, and Ada let the tears run freely down her face.

The old house shifted on its foundations, groaning as if placed under some unimaginable weight. Books tumbled from their shelves, and sprites danced in the fireplace as dislodged soot rained down. The temperature in the library plummeted, and with a soft, crackling sound, hoar frost rippled its way across the walls and floor. Ada's breath steamed as she exhaled, her skin prickling with cold.

'Help me,' said an achingly familiar voice, 'I cannot see.'

Clapping a hand to her mouth, Ada stifled the cry that threatened to burst from her lips. Inside the circle, the wavering image of Clara Phillips coalesced in front of Madame Blavatsky. Born of smoke and candlelight, the funeral-garbed shade clawed at her scalp, her face agonised, her eye sockets empty.

'He won't let me go,' she wailed. 'He won't let me go!'

The room shook with the force of her

distress. Ada made to stand but the countess stopped her. 'Do *not* interfere,' she hissed. 'There is more than one soul at stake.'

Ada nodded, but the urge to go to her mother was overwhelming. 'Dear God, Rory, it's her.'

The sergeant crossed himself. 'Hail Mary, full of grace, the Lord is with thee,' he whispered, over and over again.

'Be at peace, Clara,' said Madame Blavatsky. 'Your daughter has asked for my help. She is assailed by the same entity that binds you.'

'Ada? She is here?'

'Yes. She is safe for now, but seeks understanding of what she faces, of what you still face; the nature of the beast that holds you in thrall.'

'I cannot pass on,' cried Clara. 'I would not accept his gift and now he punishes me.'

'What did he promise you?'

'He offered me vengeance. I was to be his instrument, both sword and scales, to wreak havoc on those who hurt him. Who would want such a terrible thing?'

'And you refused?'

'Yes. I fought with every ounce of strength that I had, but it was not enough. I have failed you, my daughter.' Lifting her head, Clara gave a howl of such anguish that the enochian script flared white, struggling to contain the forces unleashed within it.

On seeing how much her mother suffered, even in death, Ada's grief shifted upon its axis. Tears became calm, calm became anger, anger became cold resolve. The Ravener had torn her family apart, and for that there would be a reckoning.

'Who is he?' asked Madame Blavatsky. 'Where can he be found?'

'He is…' Before Clara could answer, a sword blade as pale and insubstantial as her ghostly form punched its way out from the centre of her chest. Her body went rigid, blood pouring from her mouth and wrists. Shockingly stark in the candlelight, it flowed down her dress and across the floor, covering the wood inside the circle completely. Madame Blavatsky sat motionless in her wheelchair, seeming to float on a pool of crimson.

'No!' Ada cried. 'Stop torturing her, you bastard.' Unable to just sit and watch such atrocity, she leapt up and ran toward her mother.

'For God's sake, stop her,' said the countess.

Bolting from his chair Rory sprinted across the room. 'Jesus Christ, lass,' he said, grabbing her round the waist, 'don't do it.'

'Let me go,' she screamed. 'I have to save her. I have to.'

Hanging limp and bloody in the air, Clara turned to face her daughter. 'I will always love you,' she whispered, holding out a beseeching hand. Ignoring the warnings she had been given Ada reached out to take it, her fingertips crossing the ring of enochian script. A wave of blue flame engulfed her, and with a sound like cannon fire the protective enchantment surrounding Madame Blavatsky exploded outward. Flung violently away, Ada tumbled across the floor like a rag doll. Gasping for breath and with her ears ringing, she struggled to rise as the countess dashed to her side.

'Do you know what you have done?' she said, her face aghast. 'You have let it out!'

'I didn't mean any harm, I just wanted to...' the words stuck fast in Ada's throat as beneath her the floorboards began to flex and splinter. The house groaned again, more loudly this time, as if trying to stop itself from being rent asunder. Suddenly, from out of the darkness, came a deafening bellow of rage. Ada covered her ears; she had never heard anything like it, the vehemence, the power, it was terrifying. It reverberated back and forth until every of pane of glass in the library shattered. Dragging himself to her side, Rory put his arm round Ada's shoulders, shielding her as glistening shards rained down. Burying her face in his chest, she prayed that her reckless actions had not doomed them all.

As quickly as it had arrived the awful sound faded away, leaving behind it the silence of the grave.

They were no longer alone, Ada could feel it. Somewhere, hiding just out of sight, was a man in a mask.

'I know you are here, Ravener,' said Madame Blavatsky, lifting the shawl from her head. 'Cease your torment of this poor woman.'

The voice from Ada's dreams spilled from the shadows. It plucked at her nerves, ran clawed fingers down her spine.

'I will not. How dare you interfere with my reckoning?'

'I interfere because it is right to do so. My body may be failing but my mind is not. Your anger blinds you to that which is right and just.'

'Do not speak to me of what is right and just. Clara's soul is mine. She is repaying another's debt and it *will* be met in full, of that you can be sure. This is my first and only warning, Ada. Do not try and summon your mother again. If you do, the consequences will be dire indeed. I bid you farewell... for now.'

Clara turned to look at her daughter. Her ghostly face bereft, she mouthed a silent 'help me' before slowly fading away. Heaving a weary sigh, Madame Blavatsky nodded to the countess; shoes crunching on broken glass, she carefully pushed the medium's wheelchair to where Ada and Rory sat huddled on the floor.

'I am so sorry, Madame,' said Ada, wiping tears from her eyes, 'I could not help myself. To see Mother like that was... heart-breaking.'

'I know, my child, but all is not as it appears. What you saw was only a half-truth. This Ravener of yours is hiding something, and that grotesque display was an effort to dissuade you from finding out what it is. Behind his threats I sense desperation; he needs you, and therein lies his weakness.'

'But what does he need me for?'

'Only you can answer that, and to do so will require great courage on your part. I have never encountered such a creature. Both spirit and flesh, he carries within him such implacable will, such hatred. It makes him a formidable adversary, but he is not invulnerable.'

'I am not afraid of him,' said Ada, trying to sound braver than she felt.

'You should be. He wasn't lying when he said there would be consequences if you tried to stop him. His perverse affection may prevent him from harming you directly, but those who are close to you have no such protection.'

'Then what am I to do? How do I save Mother?'

'You must tread carefully,' said Madame Blavatsky. 'Clara is trapped in a room without doors or windows. She batters herself against the walls, helpless and alone until her jailer chooses to set her soul free. It is an insult to the natural order of things and cannot be allowed to continue. If you are to wrest her from the Ravener's clutches, you will have to do something extraordinary, something that he will not expect.'

'And what is that?'

'Love him.'

Ada gasped. 'After all the damage he has caused, the blood he has spilled, how could I possibly do such a thing?'

'This is a game; a deadly one, yes, but a game nonetheless. It requires both wits and determination, qualities you have in abundance. The Ravener craves your attention, your approval, so why not give it to him? Let him believe you are his, gain his confidence, and when the opportunity presents itself destroy him utterly. Only then will Clara finally find peace.'

Ada nodded. She felt sick and light-headed, but clarity of purpose helped steady her nerves. 'Thank you,' she said, taking the old woman's hand and kissing the back of it. 'The reality of what I face is not easy to stomach, but I will try my best to follow your advice.'

Madame Blavatsky smiled. 'You shall not flinch…'

'In the face of horror,' said Ada. 'How did you know what I was thinking?'

'I hear echoes of your grandfather. His bond with you is unusually strong. It is as if he stands by your side, a soldier at the ready, and that is no bad thing.'

'He is a force to be reckoned with, but he would understand none of this.'

'Few have the capacity to open their eyes to a world beyond the mundane, however brave they may be. For your sake as well as theirs, I suggest you tell no one of what you have experienced here. This is for you and you alone to confront, with the support of Sergeant Canavan of course.'

'I will help in any way I can,' said Rory, getting to his feet, 'though God knows what use I will be.'

'A steadfast heart is often enough when a loved one needs you. Remember that.'

'I shall, Madame.'

'I am pleased to hear it. Now, the hour grows late and I must rest. Plan your next steps carefully, there is much at stake. My door is always open should you need me.'

'Thank you, Madame. That is good to know.' Bidding goodnight to the medium and Countess Wachtmeister, Ada took Rory's arm and returned to the waiting carriage. Her head was awhirl with everything she had seen and heard, but as she journeyed home her resolve began to fade. Knowing that she must confront the Ravener to save her mother was one thing. Finding the strength to do it was another matter entirely.

'Feck me, I need this,' said Rory, downing a glass of whiskey before pouring himself another.

'Bring me one too, please,' said Ada, from her chair by the parlour fire.

He handed her a tumbler and sat opposite, staring into the dying flames. Curled up in his bed by the dresser, Hamlet whined softly. Ada held out her hand but the dog stayed put, his dark eyes twinkling in the firelight. 'He knows something has happened,' she said.

'They do say that animals are able to sense things we humans can't.'

She nodded, turning the glass in her hands, watching the rich liquid as it clung to the sides. 'I am afraid of the Ravener, Rory,' she said, 'but not for myself. Madame is right. If I move against him, he could well do something to hurt you, Father, anyone that I hold dear.'

'Possibly, but in doing so he would drive you further away from him. From what Madame said, that is the last thing he wants.'

'Perhaps, but it is a risk nonetheless.'

'Aye, it is, but it is one worth taking I think.'

'Do you really mean that?'

Rory smiled at her. 'If my mother was in his grasp then I would move heaven and earth to free her. After what you saw tonight, can you honestly say that you are willing to do anything less?'

'No,' said Ada. 'Death is supposed to be a release. The thought of allowing such cruelty to continue while I sit on my hands is unbearable.'

'Then you have your answer.'

'I know, but a doctor is supposed to do no harm. I will do what I must to save Mother, Rory, but the thought of taking a life when my own is not threatened does not sit well with me, even if it is for the most noble of reasons.'

'That's as it should be, lass. I'm sure your grandfather would say the same thing.'

'Yes, I think he would. However, I very much doubt he would approve of me carrying this.' She reached into her purse and drew out the Webley.

Rory raised his eyebrows. 'And where did you get that?'

'I borrowed it from the armoury at Rookwood, after the Ravener spoke to me in the India Room. Grandfather gave me permission to arm myself while Price was still at large, but as far as he is aware I didn't take up his offer.'

'And you can hardly tell him why you need it now.'

'Precisely. If I'm to face the Ravener I cannot do so empty handed. Appealing to his better nature is unlikely to carry as much weight as him staring down the barrel of a gun.'

'And how do you propose to track him down? Will you follow Madame's advice?'

'I find the concept of returning this creature's *love* repulsive, Rory, yet I see no other way to get close to him. The killings will continue, of that I have no doubt, but the more I learn, the greater the chance of finding out who and where he is. Perhaps then I have a chance of stopping him.'

There was a soft snuffling at her knee. Looking down she saw Hamlet, sitting on his haunches and peering up at her.

'Shall we go hunting, boy?'

Placing his chin upon Ada's thigh, Hamlet growled his assent.

CHAPTER 20

Dire Mother, Dire Father

T hat night, when she felt the Ravener reach out to her, Ada offered no resistance. Wrapped in the dread warmth of his presence, she followed him to a narrow, dimly-lit corridor where rats skittered across the floorboards. The musty smell of damp filled the air, and from somewhere nearby came the mournful sobbing of a child.

'What you did was foolish,' he said. 'More than that, it was unnecessary.'

'Would you have done any different were our roles reversed?' Ada replied. 'All I wanted was to see my mother's face, hear her voice. Is it so wrong to miss the woman you took from me?'

The Ravener sighed. 'Perhaps I spoke in haste. You have every reason to hate me yet I ask for your patience. There is much you do not comprehend. The truth, were I to reveal it to you now, would break your heart.'

Ada didn't know what to say. By rights she should tear the mask from his face, claw out his eyes in payment for all he had done, but something quelled the turmoil inside her. A doctor's compassion, she thought, or is it something else? Perhaps tonight would be different; perhaps it would show another side to this man of shadow, offer some clue as to what he wanted with her? 'Where have you brought me?' she asked. 'What is it you want me to see?'

'You stand in a foster home for orphans,' said the Ravener, 'run by a Mrs Margaret Foyle and supported financially by the parish, a *haven* for the young and unwanted.'

Ada could almost taste the venom dripping from his words.

'You were lucky, beloved. Born into wealth and comfort, you have never known want such as the inhabitants of this drear house. Many young dreams have been crushed here, snuffed out like the candles in Christ Church across the way.'

So we are in Spitalfields, thought Ada. The Ravener was either being bold or careless. 'At least these poor children have somewhere to live, however rudimentary it may be,' she said. 'Better that than freezing to death on some street corner.'

'Better? Oh, Ada, it is time for you to open your eyes, to understand the trials of those less fortunate than yourself.'

'But I do understand. It's why I have studied so hard, so I may help alleviate the suffering of others.'

'An honourable and worthy aim, but it will do nothing to stop the evil that hides in plain sight, wearing a smiling mask all of its own. The sailors that I dealt with are a perfect example. You may find my methods abhorrent, but you cannot deny they are most effective. Some infections need to be cut out.'

'Witness my art, fear my wrath?'

'Oh yes. The people of London will come to understand my work, and when they do they will lay flowers in the streets.'

'A royal progress for a killer,' said Ada. 'Does that not strike you as perverse?'

'I agree that taking life makes one a killer,' said the Ravener, 'but it does not necessarily make one a murderer. This is war, Ada. The *reason* for the taking of life is paramount, as you will come to realise.'

'I doubt that very much,' she replied.

'You may surprise yourself. Look now, the dire mother approaches.'

Ada turned to see a tall, thin woman advancing toward her along the corridor. Clad in a worn, black dress, her face was pinched and humourless, deep-set eyes only adding to her cadaverous appearance. A ring of keys jangled softly at her belt, and tucked under her arm was a stained pillow.

'Observe how death masquerades as love,' said the Ravener.

The woman stopped outside a door next to Ada, opening it to reveal a mean, little room, lit by the stub of a candle. On a narrow cot a young boy lay sleeping, his clothing old and patched, but cleaner than that of the urchins who ran wild in the East End streets. The boy's breathing was slow and shallow, his face pale, and half-clutched in his hand was a battered, pewter mug, its contents spilling onto the straw-filled mattress.

'Bathtub gin laced with laudanum,' said the Ravener, 'an effective, albeit indelicate anaesthetic.'

With growing unease, Ada watched as the woman walked over to the boy, poking him in the ribs with a bony finger. He moaned in his sleep but did not wake. Nodding to herself, the woman took the pillow from under her arm and placed it over the boy's face.

'Stop her!' Ada cried.

'I cannot change the past,' said the Ravener, sorrowfully. 'Like so many before him, he is already lost to us.'

With a scream of anger Ada fought to move, to rip the pillow from the woman's hands and save the child, but her body betrayed her. She was on the other side of the mirror, hammering ineffectually at the glass, unable to do anything but act as horrified witness. Weeping hot tears, she sank to her knees as Mrs Foyle pushed down with all her strength, suffocating the boy. Legs thrashed, hands clawed weakly at the pillow, but held in thrall by alcohol and narcotics his little limbs had no strength. Moment by awful moment the child's struggles lessened, until at last he lay still.

Ada bowed her head in despair, fists clenched and fingernails drawing blood from her palms.

'Do you not desire retribution for such an act?' asked the Ravener. 'Does your heart not cry out for vengeance on his behalf?'

'Yes, but not in the way that you would have it. You are as much a monster as she.'

'I would beg to differ,' said the Ravener. 'We are not finished yet.'

'Job done?' asked a deep, rasping voice.

'Aye,' said Mrs Foyle. 'It's your turn to off the next one.'

A burly man stepped into the light; he wore the smart uniform of a parish beadle. 'It'll be my pleasure,' he said. 'I'll have a replacement here in a couple of days, meantime I'll dump him in the sewer out back as usual. All the other's asleep?'

Mrs Foyle nodded. 'They like their gin, think it's a treat, keeps the little beggars quiet.'

'Good,' said the man. 'Nobody wants a fuss, it's bad for business.' Unrolling a hemp sack, he entered the room and shut the door behind him. Getting to her feet, Ada shook with impotent rage.

'The boy's name was Charles,' said the Ravener. 'He was ten years old. He had a withered arm, so he couldn't work as hard as the others when he was sent to the workhouse to pick oakum. He had become a liability.'

'But why would they do such a thing?' asked Ada, filled with grief for the child she had just seen murdered.

'Being upstanding members of the community, they get paid by the parish for all the orphans they take in. They also get a share of the income from the work the children do. If one of them becomes ill or infirm...'

'They kill them,' whispered Ada.

'And so the wheel grinds on. Think on that when your maid brings you your morning tea. Come with me, there is something else you need to see.' He held out a kid-gloved hand and Ada hesitantly took it. The gloves were soft and warm to the touch, and with gentle pressure he led her down the corridor and into the kitchen.

A large, oak table sat in the centre of the room, scarred and stained with years of use. On it lay Mrs Foyle and her male associate, bound and gagged with strips of linen. They struggled to free themselves, but their efforts were sluggish, uncoordinated.

'And so we come to the subject of vengeance,' said the Ravener. 'Forgive my presumption, but I thought it best to deal with the mundane matter of incapacitation before your arrival.'

'What have you done to them?' she asked.

'I gave them something to drink – a high dose of laudanum mixed with gin. I thought it apt under the circumstances. They are aware, yet helpless, just as the children were when they were smothered.'

'And do you intend to kill them in turn, rather than sending them to the hangman?'

'Of course. How else could I eat their sins?'

Ada shuddered. It took little imagination to know what he was referring to.

Letting slip her hand, the Ravener walked to the head of the table. 'Here we have Albert Ford, parish beadle these fifteen years: mason, civic dignitary, upstanding member of the community, procurer of child labour for profit and murderer. I see you, Mr Ford,' he said, running his index finger over the man's sweat-beaded forehead. 'And you, Margaret Foyle – you act the role of caring foster mother so well. Fêted for your good works, your tireless efforts on your charges' behalf, your... sacrifices. Do you not understand that taking the life of a child is an insult to creation itself?'

The two captives moaned, eyes bulging as they heard the Ravener's words. They were terrified, yet Ada found it hard to summon any pity. The sounds made by the dying boy still rang in her ears, and the knowledge that he was but one in a long line of victims was almost too much to bear.

Fetching a wooden chest from a cupboard beneath the sink, the Ravener lifted the lid to show Ada what lay within: a small fortune in gold, silver and copper coins. He scooped up a handful, letting them trickle through his fingers. 'How many?' he asked. 'How many children do you think they killed in order to amass this nest egg? How did they justify such actions to themselves?'

Ada could only shake her head in disbelief.

'I shall leave the ferryman his payment once I am done, but now it is time for me to balance the scales.'

'I do not want to see this,' she said.

'Yet you will, you must. You cannot flinch in the face of horror, after all.' There was a note of amusement in his voice.

'Damn you,' said Ada, unable to avert her gaze.

'My damnation is not in your gift, but your education is in mine. Shall we begin?' A black medical bag sat on the worktop. Opening it, he took out a long-bladed amputation knife. 'I'm sure you recognise this?'

Ada nodded. She knew all too well what such an instrument could do to the human body.

Tearing open Mr Ford's shirt the Ravener plunged the knife into his chest, severing the ribs with a swift, downward motion. Ada heard a muffled scream as blood poured from the wound, coating the Ravener's gloves and spilling onto the table. A knife should not be able to cut through bone like that, she thought, clinging to scientific observation for the sake of her sanity.

With deep, lateral incisions, the Ravener cut away the pectoral tissue, allowing the ribcage to spring open like some ghastly jack-in-the-box. Reaching into the chest cavity, he swiftly removed Mr Ford's still-beating heart, holding it up for Ada to see. Black and diseased, it dripped smoking malice to the floor.

'Dear God,' she whispered, 'what is that… thing?'

'It is evil made manifest. This is what happens when a soul rots.'

The stench made Ada retch. Raising a hand to her mouth she took deep, slow breaths, trying her best not to vomit.

'You have seen enough for one night, I think,' said the Ravener. 'There will be other opportunities for you to see how strong you really are. Goodnight, beloved, sweet dreams.'

Ada could not bring herself to answer him. She did not know which was worse – cold-blooded murder, or the vile fruit that was born from it. The bonds that held her slipped away, and with a profound sigh of relief she fell headlong into blessed darkness.

'Be gentle with them, Thomas, they have endured

much.'

'Of course, sir,' he replied. One by one, he carried the sleeping children from their humble beds to the waiting carriage. Once all were comfortably stowed, the Ravener handed him a wooden chest.

'Take the little ones to the address I gave you, along with this coin. No questions will be asked, do you understand?'

'Yes, sir. I'll take good care of them.'

'Good man. I shall meet you as arranged on the stroke of three. Be on your way now.'

Climbing into the driver's seat Thomas clucked at the horses. Without fuss, Mari and Uma walked slowly on, as if they too wanted to ensure the safety of their precious cargo. Once the carriage was lost to view, the Ravener returned to the foster home kitchen. 'Now then, Mrs Foyle,' he said, picking up the bloodied catling, 'where were we?'

CHAPTER 21

Further Education

'That poor boy, smothered by hands that should have been caring for him.'

'Christ almighty, lass,' said Rory. 'All murder is sin, but there's a special place in hell for those who kill children.'

The hansom cab clattered along half-empty streets, an early-morning mist – backlit by the rising sun – lending the city an ethereal air.

'It confirms what we thought about the Ravener,' she said. 'He is only killing those who take the lives of others. Were it not for the fact that he drove Mother to suicide, I could almost see a perverse righteousness to his actions.'

'Nobody has the right to be judge, jury and executioner. It's why we have Courts and hangmen; it's why we have policemen like me.'

'And for that I am grateful, yet these atrocities still continue, tacitly accepted because it is expedient to do so. What if the Ravener is right? Is terrorising those who would commit such heinous acts the only way to stop them?'

Ada could see the way Rory looked at her. He was worried, but not for her safety. 'I need to see the bodies,' she said, changing tack. 'These killings have a degree of ritual about them. If I can understand why he is mutilating his victims, I'll be a step closer to finding him.'

'It's as good a place to start as any,' said Rory, 'but Special Branch will likely be at the scene. They have a mass murderer on their hands. Halloran will do all he can to limit the damage, especially after that article in the Evening Standard. They're not going let you anywhere near the evidence and I'm still on Soames' blacklist.'

'It is a risk, I know,' said Ada, 'but if luck is on our side we may find help from an unexpected quarter.'

The cab turned into Brushfield Street. As it drew closer to the great church at the centre of Spitalfields, Ada saw people whispering to each other on the pavement. 'Let's get out here,' she said, 'lose ourselves in the crowd. If Soames' men are about they'll have a harder time spotting us.'

'Agreed,' said Rory.

Warily making their way forward, it didn't take long to reach the towering edifice of Christ Church. The main door was framed by four, huge columns, and tied to the innermost were two bodies, one male, one female. A white sheet was spread on the steps between them. At its centre sat two, glistening human hearts. Painted in blood on the sheet were the words: "*The Wages of*

Sin".

'He's not one for subtlety, is he?' said Rory.

'I think that's the point. He needs people to know what he is doing. It's as much a message as it is murder.' Ada looked more closely. The two victims were certainly Mr Ford and Mrs Foyle, but their eyes were missing. She wondered if birds had taken them, but the bodies could not have been here that long. The Ravener must have done it, but why?

She turned her attention to the two hearts. In the cold light of morning they bore no resemblance to the revolting object she had seen in the foster home. Ada thought back to what the Ravener had said to her during his nocturnal visits, the way he viewed the world, the corruption he said that he found there. Perhaps it is a matter of perception, she wondered. If he believes himself surrounded by evil, then it would go some way to explaining his desire to kill. What would I do in his place? Does he see clearly when the rest of us do not?

'Look who's here,' said Rory, pointing to Ada's left.

It was the journalist she had met at Tower Bridge. He was drinking in every horrific detail, scribbling frantically in his notebook with eyes alight at what a good story this would make.

He glanced up from his work, meeting Ada's gaze. 'Ah, hello,' he said, walking over. 'We appear to be making a habit of meeting at scenes of tragedy.'

'*Do* you think it's a tragedy, Mr Hazell?' she asked.

'Well, it's certainly newsworthy. These ne'er-do-wells were scamming the parish, bumping off the orphans in a local foster home for profit. The remaining children were delivered to a convent early this morning, along with money for their care and a letter detailing what they had suffered. Perhaps our vigilante has an altruistic bent? I should thank you for coming up with the name 'Ravener' by the way; it's quite appropriate given his dietary inclinations. What made you think of it?'

Ada wished she hadn't said anything at the bridge, but there was no taking it back, and the last thing she needed was anyone poking their nose into her affairs. 'As you say, Mr Hazell, the killer has very specific appetites. Seeing those gulls descend on the sailor's corpses brought the word to mind.'

He nodded. 'I must admit I'm having mixed thoughts about him; I don't know whether he's a maniac or a saint.'

Maniac or saint, Ada thought, now there was a choice.

'Curiously enough the public seem to be warming to him. After being terrified by Saucy Jack and then the Limehouse Strangler, they're actually cheering this one on. It's like he's some angel of vengeance, come to cut out the evil in London's heart, no pun intended.'

Ada winced, the journalist's glee was nauseating but she couldn't fault his logic. She looked at the crowd around her; there was horror, curiosity and confusion, but the one thing that was absent was fear. They did not *fear* the Ravener, or rather, only those who had reason to were looking over their shoulders, wondering if they would be next.

'I'd best be off,' said Hazell, disappearing into the crowd, 'there's much to do if I'm to meet my deadline. Make sure you buy a copy of this evening's paper. I'm going to create a new legend for London!'

'I'm sure that's exactly what he wants,' Ada muttered.

'You mentioned something about unexpected help,' said Rory.

'I did indeed. I'm hoping that... ah, there he is.' She nodded toward an ambulance parked by the church railings. An immaculately-dressed man carrying a medical bag was standing next to it, watching intently as a group of uniformed officers began the gruesome work of cutting down the bodies. 'Isn't that Doctor Bond, one of your father's colleagues?'

'Yes. Now he has taken over as coroner for H division, he may, God willing, be able to provide the assistance I need.'

Rory glanced casually about him. 'I can't see any of Soames' men. Why don't we go and speak to him while he's alone?'

'My thoughts exactly. Follow me.' Keeping a close eye on the crowd, she walked over to the ambulance. 'Doctor Bond. My apologies for the intrusion but may we speak with you?'

'Miss Phillips, Sergeant Canavan, what on earth brings you here?'

'We happened to be passing, and were curious as to the reason for such a commotion.'

'I trust your curiosity has been thoroughly assuaged,' he said, pointing at the bodies as they were lifted onto canvas stretchers.

'Are these more victims of this Ravener, as the papers are calling him?' asked Ada.

'Highly likely. I'm taking them to the mortuary, but in the morning they'll be handed over to Special Branch. The chief constable has been most insistent that all evidence in this case be stored at Scotland Yard. Irritating, but at my age one does not wish to rock the boat.' He gave Rory a knowing glance.

'I know it's somewhat irregular,' said Ada, lowering her voice, 'but would it be possible to view these two bodies before you release them?'

'Why would you want to look at the remains of these two unfortunates?'

Ada paused, hoping that her reasoning was

sound. 'I start my degree in the spring, and I'm sure Father would want me to get as much experience as possible, as part of my training you understand.'

'Well, since you assisted Henry with that godawful mess at the foundry, I suppose it wouldn't be *too* untoward, although I think it best that Halloran didn't know of your visit. He is being unusually proprietorial about this case.'

'I think that a degree of discretion as regards the chief constable would be advisable,' said Ada.

Doctor Bond nodded. 'I concur wholeheartedly. May I suggest you visit the Golden Lane Mortuary at, say, one o'clock? The coast should be clear by then, as it were. I don't wish my examination room turned into a pugilist's den.'

'Oh, so you heard then?' said Rory.

'Yes, sergeant, you've become quite the topic of discussion. Mr Soames is nursing a bruised jaw, and, infinitely worse, a bruised ego. Be careful.'

'We will, Doctor, and thank you,' said Ada, inclining her head. 'A short visit this afternoon would be quite acceptable.'

'I will see you then,' he replied. 'Now, if you would excuse me, I have the dead to deal with.'

Ada looked at the approaching stretchers, their covering sheets already stained black with congealed blood. 'We'll leave you to your duties, Doctor,' she said. With a polite nod he strode off, barking orders at the approaching policemen.

'Are you sure this is a good idea?' said Rory.

'Yes. I need to know the facts, not just what the Ravener wishes me to see, and the only way to do that, Sergeant Canavan, is to get my hands dirty.'

'Impressive, isn't it?' said Doctor Bond, ushering Ada and Rory into his inner sanctum, clusters of gas lamps bathing the mortuary in a bright, warm light.

'It beats the cellars under Scotland Yard,' said Rory.

'Absolutely, everything we need under one roof thanks to the Corporation of London. Then again, we did have to wait until we were knee-deep in decomposing corpses before they would part with a penny. Now I can actually see what I'm doing, and I don't have to tie a carbolic-soaked rag over my nose and mouth to mask the smell.'

'Yes,' said Ada, 'I remember it well.' She had visited the police mortuary under Scotland Yard with her father, and it was medieval in comparison. In front of her were eight tables, topped with polished granite. Six were empty, but the two nearest cradled the sheet –draped forms of the Christ Church victims.

'I've already examined them both,' said the doctor. 'They were almost certainly killed by the same man responsible for the foundry and Tower

Bridge murders. See if you can tell me why. Miss Phillips, meet Mrs Margaret Foyle.' He pulled back the sheet on the nearest slab, uncovering the woman beneath to her waist.

Ada stared at the ravaged corpse. 'The facial mutilation is new,' she said. 'Did he cut out her eyes?'

'Nothing so delicate – he used penny coins to crush them instead. They were so deeply jammed against the back of the sockets I didn't see them at first; had to fish them out with a pair of forceps.'

'Were they crushed post mortem?' she asked.

'I believe so. The cause of death was exsanguination following excision of the heart, so there was little haemorrhaging from the orbital cavities.'

Ada nodded. She could sense the Ravener's presence. It permeated the body, dripped menace from every pore. Blinding the corpse with money gained from the murder of children was both ghastly yet fitting. The Ravener had done similar things to both Price and the sailors, garrotting the first and drowning the latter, the punishment matching the crime.

'It appears that our killer wanted to ensure his victims had the ferryman's fee,' said the doctor. 'Tuppence each, quite a modest fare really. What else do you see?'

Ada focused her attention on the gaping hole in Mrs Foyle's torso. The damage was identical to that she had seen inflicted upon Mr Ford. 'It is customary to use a bone saw or cutters to gain access to the chest cavity,' she said, 'but there are no serrations on the rib ends that I can see. The bones are crushed as much as cut, just as they were with Price.'

'I agree. It's most unusual. I've never seen anything quite like it. I would suggest the killer used a sharp and sturdy blade to sever the ribs, although the physical strength required to do so would be quite extraordinary.'

Ada couldn't help but replay Ford's murder in her mind and the way the Ravener had cut into his body with no apparent effort. 'Do the wounds on the Tower Bridge victims follow the same pattern?' she asked.

Doctor Bond nodded. 'Whoever is doing this is very skilled. None of the hearts were damaged prior to their excision, showing that our killer has an excellent grasp of anatomy.'

'And do all the hearts display signs of cannibalism?'

'Yes. I'll take some plaster impressions to confirm my findings in due course, but on preliminary examination I think the same person did the biting. The teeth marks match in every case.'

Ada nodded. 'I think I've seen enough. I do have one request though.'

'And what might that be?'

'May I take one of the coins you found in Mrs Foyle's skull?'

Doctor Bond raised his eyebrows. 'I didn't expect you to be a collector of morbid keepsakes, Miss Phillips.'

'Far from it,' said Ada, 'I have a theory I wish to put to the test.'

'Very well, although I don't know what you hope to glean from it. There are no obvious markings beyond normal wear and tear, and it's already been cleaned in alcohol.' He fished a coin from a glass beaker, wiping it with a cloth before handing it to her.

'Thank you,' she said. 'Oh, take this.' She fished in her purse for a similar penny. 'Under the circumstances, Halloran won't know the difference.'

Doctor Bond smiled and shook his head. 'No, I don't suppose he will.' He glanced at the clock on the wall. 'I don't wish to appear rude, but I do need to finish my work before Soames arrives. I doubt you wish to be here when he does.'

'Indeed not,' said Ada.

'While I hope this exercise has been instructive, I would ask you to be discreet. I'm doing this as favour to your father. Please send him my regards and wish him a speedy recovery.'

'I will,' said Ada, 'and thank you for your time, it is much appreciated.'

Bidding him good afternoon, Ada and Rory

left the mortuary and walked slowly along Golden Lane.

'Did you discover anything of interest?' Rory asked.

'Possibly. Something the Ravener said to me feels pertinent.'

'And what might that be?'

'I've been asking myself why he takes a single bite from the hearts of those he kills. Last night, when I spoke to him, he mentioned something about eating sin. Perhaps it provides him with some form of absolution for his actions, or, since we are considering more esoteric avenues, what if he is literally taking their sins into himself.'

'It's an interesting hypothesis,' said Rory, 'although how you prove it is beyond me. And what about that coin you asked for? Doctor Bond gave you a very odd look.'

'I wasn't lying,' said Ada. 'I do have a theory, but I need to think about it for a while.'

Rory nodded. 'Fair enough. Given that we left home in such a hurry, may I buy you a late lunch? There's a Lyons' Tea House at the end of the road.'

'That would be most welcome,' said Ada, 'I am rather hungry.' The prospect of tea and cake was a pleasant one, but at the back of her mind the image of teeth biting into a human heart lingered on, and for a moment, if only from a purely scientific point of view, she wondered what it would feel like.

'This has to be stopped!' shouted Halloran, throwing the report across his desk.

'I quite agree, sir,' said Soames, his face impassive as the chief constable worked himself into a fury.

'The last thing we need is another fucking madman on a killing spree. I'm not giving anyone another excuse to mock the police, that's *why* I ordered Price's identity obscured.'

'This one is different though, sir,' said Soames. 'He's targeting murderers; that's obvious enough.'

'I don't care who he's targeting,' said Halloran. 'I just need you to stop him. The mob is turning him into a folk hero. We go from them being terrified and threatening to riot, to laughing at us because we have some vigilante gutting people. We're becoming a joke. That bloody journalist from the Evening Standard isn't helping matters. He's even given this new one a name. What did that graffiti in Limehouse say again?'

'Long live the Ravener, sir,' replied Soames.

Halloran pounded his fist on the desk, the veins in his forehead throbbing. 'They're cheering him on. We try to keep order and they're actually cheering him on. Ungrateful bastards. Nobody saw anything I suppose?'

'No one has come forward, sir.'

'How did he manage to dispose of Price, those sailors and now these two from Spitalfields without anyone seeing anything? It's ludicrous. Somebody *must* have seen something. I don't care who you have to lean on, what methods you choose to employ, just find me a lead so we can stop this lunatic!'

'I'll do my best, sir.'

'See that you do.'

'One more thing,' said Soames as he turned to leave.

'What?'

'The Irishman. Lawson said he was leaving the country, but I can't see him running away like that, he's far too proud. He's bound to be lurking about somewhere, and with your permission I'd like to deal with him. He made me look a fool and that simply won't do.'

'If you insist,' said Halloran. 'Find me the identity of this Ravener and you can indulge your need for petty revenge as much as you like. Don't waste manpower though; the current investigation is far too important. And if you do happen to find Canavan during the course of your enquiries, then for God's sake be discreet.'

'Absolutely, sir,' said Soames, allowing himself a crooked smile. 'I shall be the soul of discretion.'

CHAPTER 22

Josephine

On returning to Shoreditch, Ada found a telegram and letter waiting for her in the parlour. The telegram was a brief missive from Sir Edmund. He said that her father's health was improving and invited both her and Rory to dinner in two days' time. Ada smiled. Good news had been in short supply of late and it was most welcome. Putting the telegram aside she picked up the letter; the envelope was of the finest quality, heavy and textured. It must have been delivered in person as there was no stamp, and the only writing on the front was her name, penned in elegant copperplate. She turned it over, eyes widening as she saw the wax seal, embossed with the imperial eagle or *reichsadler* of the German empire.

'Milly?' she called.

'Yes, miss,' said the maid, appearing in the doorway.

'This letter – who delivered it?'

'It was all very unusual, miss. It came about ten. A footman handed it to me. There was a smart carriage waiting for him, but I didn't see who was inside.'

'How curious. That will be all, Milly, thank you.'

Carefully prying open the envelope, Ada withdrew a single sheet of cream paper.

Dear Miss Phillips,

Please forgive my writing to you, but there is a matter of great importance that we need to discuss. As you are no doubt aware I was released from the sanatorium, and although my injuries have healed and my mind is clear, remnants of my experience still remain. They are fading, and I do not want to forget before I can share them with you. My father has ordered that I return to Germany tomorrow, to recuperate at our jadgschloss, so I must meet with you tonight.

I do not understand what I see, but in my heart I believe it imperative that you have this information. I do not think he would want you to know it, and that is precisely why I must tell you. I think you know to whom I refer. Soon I will be across the sea and in the mountains, yet even then I do not know if I will be beyond his reach.

It is too complicated to set down in words, but face to face I can at least try to explain the rage and horror that still lingers inside my head. If you have experienced anything similar, then you have my deepest sympathy. Nobody should have to bear this.

I ask that you meet me outside the park gates

on Pitfield Street at eight o'clock tonight. My carriage
will take me there, but I cannot stay long as my
father is ever watchful. I pray that you will come.

> *Your obedient servant,*
> *Josephine Eleonore Schlecter*

Utterly astonished, Ada re-read the letter to
ensure she had fully grasped its importance.

'What's wrong?' asked Rory.

'Nothing's wrong. Here, see for yourself.'

'You're going, I assume?' he said, once he'd
finished reading.

'I have to, I owe it to her. That poor girl went
through hell on my account; the least I can do is
listen to what she has to say. It may be that she
can tell me nothing more than I already know, but
what if she has information that could be of use? I
would be a fool not to find out.'

'I agree,' said Rory, 'but I'm coming with you.'

'I don't think you should. She sounds scared
and she doesn't know you. I have one chance to
talk to her before she leaves and I don't want to
jeopardise that. Please understand.'

'But I promised your grandfather I would
keep you safe.'

'I know, but I'm not going far. Pitfield Street
is what, ten minutes away at most?'

Rory nodded, but he looked far from happy.

'Don't worry so, I shall be fine. Price is dead,
remember?'

'I know, but the Ravener isn't.'

'He doesn't want to hurt me,' said Ada. 'I think you're being overly cautious.'

'Perhaps, but it's something to consider. And what if Josephine is still unwell? What if she's trying to lure you out so she can attack you, take some revenge for what the Ravener put her through?'

'Now you're being ridiculous,' said Ada. 'You read the letter. Those are not the words of a madwoman, they are a cry for help and I will not brush them aside. I appreciate your concern, Rory, but my decision is final. I am going to meet Josephine alone and that is the end of the matter!'

The hours ticked by in awkward silence. Once the clock on the mantelpiece showed quarter to eight, Ada got slowly to her feet. 'Wish me luck,' she said, trying to lighten the mood.

'Just be careful, lass,' said Rory, slumped disconsolately in his chair. 'I can't explain it but something doesn't feel right. If anything happens to you, Sir Edmund will have my guts for garters. Do you have the revolver?'

'It's in my purse, but I have no intention of shooting the daughter of the German ambassador; I have enough on my plate as it is.'

'All right then, but if you're not back in an hour I'm coming to find you.'

Ada smiled at him. 'Very well, but I doubt I

shall be that long. I'll see you soon.' Kissing him on the cheek, she left the house and made for Pitfield Street. The night air was chill, a thin fog muffling the noise of the city. Street lamps had halos, and the smoke from coal fires made the air taste of ash. Ada didn't have far to go, for which she was grateful. Even with Price dead, she still felt vulnerable walking alone; not that she would admit as much to Rory.

Reaching the park gates she found them closed and locked, the attendant having retired for the evening. Josephine had not yet arrived, so Ada stood beneath a lamppost and waited. Shivering with cold, several minutes passed before she heard footsteps tapping their way toward her. She heaved a sigh of relief as Josephine Schlecter stepped into the light. Wrapped in a thick coat and with her hands covered by a fur muff, the young woman looked tired and afraid.

'Miss Phillips, thank God you are here. I did not know if you would wish to see me after everything that happened.'

'Given the contents of your letter I could hardly do otherwise, Miss Schlecter. It gladdens me to see you recovered, it was an awful thing to witness your distress in the sanatorium.'

'I thank you, even though I do not think I deserve it.'

'Miss Schlecter... Josephine, your actions did

not warrant such awful treatment. A simple apology was all I required, not for you to be brutalised by this creature that haunts my family. It is I that should ask your forgiveness.'

Josephine smiled, a measure of tension leaving her face. 'I have seen the newspapers,' she said. 'This Ravener, as they call him, is a monster whose touch is like a knife in one's mind. It is he that I wish to speak to you about. I cannot stay long; my carriage waits at the end of the street, and my father will doubtless be wondering where I am. I did not inform him as to where I was going or why.'

'Then please, Josephine, tell me what you know. It does not matter how strange you think it, for I have experienced much of late that makes no rational sense.'

Josephine nodded. 'It is difficult to know where to start. All I have are images, feelings, all filled with such terrible anger. There is a sense of him knowing you, of familiarity, as if he has been close to you for a long time. He views himself as family.'

Ada frowned. The Ravener had spoken to her of many things, but one phrase in particular sprang to mind. *"I have walked beside you all of your life, you just didn't notice me, until now."* 'He has alluded to such,' she said, 'although I still don't understand how that can be.'

Josephine lifted her hands to Ada's face,

cupping her cheeks in a gesture of tenderness. 'There is more at stake than you realise. He covets you, loves you in his own, twisted way. He wishes for you to believe in what he does, to become like him.'

'But why?'

'I do not know but he is desperate. He will stop at nothing to cleave you to him.'

'He tried to do the same thing with my mother,' said Ada. 'It is what drove her to take her own life.'

'That is something I understand all too well.' She paused, lowering her eyes.

'What is wrong, what are you not telling me?'

'It is madness of the most awful kind. I do not think you will believe me if say it.'

'After all I have seen this last week I am prepared to believe anything if it brings me peace,' said Ada. 'Tell me, Josephine, please.'

The young woman took a deep breath. 'This Ravener, he is not a...'

There was a sudden cry from the far end of the street, closely followed by panicked whinnying and the harsh clatter of wheels on cobblestones.

'What is that?' asked Josephine, clutching at Ada's arm.

The awful sound grew rapidly in volume, and with terrifying speed a carriage erupted from the fog. The horses were screaming, their hooves slipping on the wet road as they thundered onward. Fighting to regain control the coachman heaved desperately on the reins, but his efforts availed him nothing. Ada could only watch in horror as the nearest horse lost its footing and plunged downward, snapping its neck. Behind it the carriage heeled over, swinging wide before striking a lamppost. Wood split, glass shattered, and thrown violently from his seat, the coachman's flailing body stuck the cobbles with a sickening crunch. He moaned and tried to rise but his legs lay at impossible angles, bone protruding from a tear in his breeches.

'Johann!' cried Josephine. She made to run forward but Ada stopped her.

'Wait,' she said, 'it's too dangerous.'

With eyes wild and flecks of bloody foam covering its nostrils, the remaining horse bucked and reared in its harness. Tearing itself free, its iron-shod hooves struck the fallen coachman as it galloped into the fog.

'Stay here,' said Ada, taking Josephine's shoulders. 'I will help him.'

She nodded and Ada ran into the road, kneeling beside the injured man; his chest had been crushed and his mouth was filled with blood. She felt for his pulse but there was nothing, he had gone. Running feet sounded to her left as Rory tore out of the fog.

'Jesus!' he said. 'Are you all right?'

'I'm fine, Rory, unlike this poor soul. What are you doing here?'

'I'm not good with following orders, as you well know. I was keeping an eye on things from down the street. What the hell happened here anyway?'

'I don't know. This is Miss Schlecter's carriage. Something must have frightened the horses and the driver lost control.' She stood up, turning to Josephine where she waited by the park gate. 'I'm so sorry. Your driver is dead, I...'

The young woman stared at her, hands pressed to her neck. From between her fingers a torrent of blood poured forth, soaking the fur of her coat.

'No!' screamed Ada. Dashing over, she caught Josephine as she sank to her knees. Her throat had been cut clean across, severing both windpipe and arteries.

'I'm here,' said Ada, cradling her, knowing there was nothing she could do to stop the inevitable.

'Don't...let...him...in,' said Josephine, and with a soft groan she breathed her last. Holding the young woman's limp body in her arms, Ada sobbed as blood pooled on the pavement beneath her.

'I warned you,' said the Ravener.

Ada looked up. There, hanging in the

darkness behind the bars of the park gate, a white velvet mask stared down at her, its expression more disapproving than ever.

'Jesus, Mary and Joseph,' gasped Rory, eyes flicking between the corpse in Ada's arms and the apparition that loomed before him.

'It is good that you have faith, Sergeant Canavan,' said the Ravener. 'You will find it most useful in the days ahead. I bid you farewell.' Turning away, he disappeared into the night.

'We need to go, Ada,' said Rory. 'We need to go now!'

Lights began to bloom in the windows of nearby houses, and the shrill piping of a police whistle echoed down the street.

'I can't just leave her.'

'You have to, lass. You can't be found holding the murdered daughter of the German ambassador.'

Ada knew Rory was right, the scandal would be appalling. There would be uncomfortable questions, unwanted attention for her family, even Special Branch might become involved. She would never be able to pursue the Ravener under such scrutiny. As she wiped the tears from her eyes, she gently lowered Josephine's body to the ground. Kissing her on the forehead, she took Rory's hand and ran with him into the fog.

CHAPTER 23

Sympathy for the Devil

Milly screamed as Rory half-carried Ada into the kitchen.

'It's all right, it's not her blood,' he said.

'But, miss, you're soaked in it.'

'Please don't fuss, Milly, I'm fine.'

'What on earth has happened?' said Mrs Crane, rushing in.

'We were out walking and there was an accident,' said Rory, thinking on his feet. 'A carriage overturned and both the driver and passenger were killed. Ada tried to save them, but there was nothing she could do.'

'Good gracious, miss. You are not hurt I take it?'

'No, Mrs Crane, but I need to get out of this dress.'

'Of course. Milly will assist you.'

Ada nodded, mouthing a silent 'thank you' to Rory as the maid led her upstairs. After handing Milly her soiled clothes, she cleaned herself up, put on a dressing gown and went in search of her friend. She found him sitting by the fire in the parlour, face pale, hands wrapped tight round a whiskey glass.

He looked up as she entered. 'How are you feeling?' he said.

She sank wearily into the chair opposite. 'Numb. I just washed that poor girl's blood off my hands, but it is not truly gone is it? I am stained by her death. Were it not for me she would still be alive.'

'You can't think that way, lass,' said Rory. 'It was the Ravener that chose to kill her. All she did was try to help.'

Ada sighed. 'I should have listened to you. Had I not responded to her letter then she would have left the country and been safe from his wrath. I have no words to describe how much I hate him at this moment. For all his vaunted declarations of love, his sanctimonious prattling about vengeance, he is nothing more than a butcher after all. Josephine knew something about him, something important, so he murdered her before she could tell me.' Swallowing hard Ada blinked back tears. 'We left her there, Rory. We left her alone to be found like that by strangers. What does that make us?'

'I don't like it either, but we had no choice. Her death will have serious repercussions.'

'I know, but it doesn't make me feel any less of a coward. All I can do to honour her sacrifice is keep going forward, try and find a way to stop this nightmare.'

'Did Josephine say anything that might help?'

'Yes, she did. My approval is not the only thing the Ravener seeks. It appears that he also wishes me to join him in his crusade, to mould me in his image.'

'Christ, how could he possibly believe you would do such a thing?'

'Had he shown *you* the brutal murder of a child, you might be less certain of your convictions. The desire for vengeance is seductive, especially when faced with such terrible evil. I saw the way you looked at me this morning when I said I could almost see righteousness in the Ravener's actions.'

Rory hung his head. 'I'd be lying if I said that I wasn't worried about the effect he's having on you.'

'And for that I am glad,' said Ada. 'You are a constant in my life, and I would be lost if you were not here to steady me.'

'I'm glad I can help, lass.'

'And I don't want you to worry; I have no intention of becoming what he wants me to be. If we ignore all conscience and morality, then his argument has weight. Fear is a powerful tool in stopping injustice, but the cost is too high. In killing Josephine he has shown his true colours. There is nothing noble in his actions, whatever he may say.'

'I couldn't agree more, but how do we stop him? He's a damn shadow.'

'As to that I have an idea.' Reaching into the pocket of her dressing gown, she brought out a penny coin. 'Remember this?'

'Is that the one Doctor Bond gave you?'

'Yes. When we saw Madame Blavatsky, she talked about the concept of sympathetic magic, how my blood would call to my mother's, bring her to me. I've been wondering if I could do the same thing with the Ravener, if only I had something connected to him, something he had touched. He pushed this coin into Mrs Foyle's skull with his thumbs, Rory. It was part of her punishment and I can feel his anger in it.'

'Feck me, lass, you don't want to bring him to you, he warned you to never try something like that again. He doesn't take kindly to being thwarted, look what happened tonight.'

'I'm not going to bring him to me, Rory, I'm going to go to *him*. With Madame Blavatsky's help I want to see if I can reach out, touch his mind without alerting him. If I know where he is going to strike next then I can be there, lying in wait. He may not wish to harm me but I have no such constraints. If he refuses to release his hold upon my mother, then I have no avenue left but to kill him. One way or another, Rory, I will free her soul from this monster.'

The following morning Ada made her way to Holland Park, hoping that Madame Blavatsky would consent to see her. Greeted by Mr Keightley, she was shown into the conservatory at the rear of the house where the medium was resting.

'It is a bold and clever move,' said Madame Blavatsky, once Ada had explained her plan. Leaning back in her wheelchair, she held the coin between thumb and forefinger, concentrating on it intently. 'His touch is faint, but it is there. If I may be honest, I am relieved that it is not more strongly connected to him. I do not know if I could face him again so soon.'

'I don't want to put you at risk,' said Ada, 'but with your guidance I may be able to find him, glimpse but a fraction of what poor Josephine had to endure.'

'I was shocked to hear what happened to her, and I will keep that information in confidence, but it only serves to confirm my opinion that this Ravener must be stopped.'

'And if I do kill him, will I be damning my mother's soul to some other purgatory?'

'It is only his implacable will that holds her captive. Whatever he is – and I admit that I am not sure of his true nature – if you destroy his body then he will no longer have the strength to restrain her. A soul *must* pass on, it is a universal law.'

'Thank you,' said Ada, deeply relieved to hear such reassurance. 'It has been weighing on my mind since I conceived this course of action.'

'Then be at peace with your decision. The fact that you are here speaks volumes as to your strength of character. I have met many people in my travels, but you, my child, shine very brightly indeed. I believe that may be the very thing that pulls him to you, and, God willing, it will be his downfall.'

'I can but hope,' said Ada. 'So, Madame, what must I do?'

'It is quite simple. Close your eyes and take my hand. Let go of the day, listen to my voice and my voice only as we walk strange paths. Be mindful, however, if you pry too deeply he will sense you, and this endeavour will have been for nothing. You have one chance, so use it well. Shall we begin?'

'Yes,' said Ada, breathing deep and settling into her chair.

'You are standing at the top of a flight of stairs,' said Madame Blavatsky, her words soft and calm. 'They lead to a place between worlds but there is nothing to fear. Walk slowly downward as I count to ten. When you reach the bottom be still and wait. He will reveal himself if you are patient.'

The medium began her count, and with each step Ada felt her body become lighter, buoyant even, as if her spirit wished to shed the flesh that housed it.

'Ten,' said Madame Blavatsky. 'Now, be one with your senses, embrace whatever comes to you.'

Ada found herself standing in a vast and lonely void. Glittering shards hung all around her, jagged fragments of thought and memory, windows into the Ravener's mind. With only her need for answers as a guide, she hesitantly reached out to touch one. It was cold and razor sharp beneath her fingers, as if she ran them across a tray of scalpels. 'He's afraid,' she said. 'I don't know what of, but that is the source of his rage. Time is against him. I see sand pouring through an hourglass, it has almost run out. Whatever he is doing, he has to finish before it is too late.'

'Keep going,' said Madame Blavatsky. 'Let him reveal what lies behind the mask.'

Ada tried again. There was pain this time, a slow, piercing ache that set her nerves aflame. 'I hear screaming, many people all at once. There is crimson on steel. Bodies lie all about me, and at my feet there is a young woman, an awful wound in her chest. Twenty were taken, twenty will pay; in his grief this is what he swears.'

Filled with the most terrible despair, Ada felt tears rolling down her face.

'Do not cling to it,' said Madame Blavatsky,

'seek his vengeance instead. Let it show you what his gaze is fixed upon.'

Ada nodded, letting herself dwell on all the deaths she had witnessed, the hunger that lay behind them. Without conscious choice, her hand closed upon another shard. It writhed in her grip, gouging its way into her palm.

'There are bells,' Ada groaned, 'and a choir singing. Beneath their feet lies horror, hidden under stone and begging for release.' Her body shook as the Ravener's anger rose up like a wave. Relentless and without pity, it threatened to smother her in suffering.

'I will eat your sins you hypocrite. I will show them exactly what you look like, on the inside.'

'No!' she screamed, tearing herself free. Gasping for breath she stared wide-eyed at Madame Blavatsky, heart hammering wildly inside her chest.

'It's all right,' said the medium, gently stroking her hand, 'you are safe now. He does not know that you were with him.'

'Dear God, I thought I was drowning.'

'That is understandable. This Ravener feels emotion in the most powerful way. You barely touched the surface of him, yet even that was almost too much.'

'It is no wonder Josephine lost her mind,' said Ada. 'To have his wrath directed toward you with intention would be unbearable.'

'Did you find what you were looking for?'

'Yes, right at the end, a single image that I recognised. I know where he will be tonight, Madame. When he arrives, I shall be waiting for him. Only then shall we find out whose will is the stronger.'

'You just missed Sir Edmund,' said Rory, looking up from his paper. 'He's not in the best of moods. He asked if you knew anything about Josephine's death.'

'And what did you tell him?' said Ada.

'We told him nothing,' said Mrs Crane, placing a tray of tea on the table. 'It would serve no purpose to do so. This family has been through enough. As far as Milly and I are concerned you had an early night.'

'Thank you,' said Ada.

'There's no need to thank me, miss. You were asleep, after all.' Giving Ada a knowing look over the top of her spectacles, the housekeeper left the room.

'Was he angry?' Ada asked, taking a seat next to Rory.

'No, just concerned. The incident has caused uproar with the authorities. There seems to be some confusion over the manner of Josephine's death. The police are taking the line that an attempted robbery caused the driver to lose control of the horses, and that both he and

Josephine died in the crash.'

'How do they explain a slashed throat?'

'Glass from the carriage window as she was flung from the wreck.'

Ada shook her head. 'Lies upon lies. It all has to stop.'

'Did your visit to Madame Blavatsky bear fruit?'

Ada paused. She had thought long and hard on her journey home about what she would say to him, and Rory wasn't going to like it. 'He is going to kill again tonight, and I know where.'

'That's great news. Finally we steal a march on him. When do we leave?'

'*We* don't,' said Ada, unable to meet his eyes. 'The Ravener is driven by something that I do not understand, but it is all-consuming. If anyone gets in his way he will not hesitate to kill them. Look what he did to Josephine.'

'But...'

'No, Rory. I am not pushing you aside, I am trying to save your life. Losing you would break my heart and I will not risk that. The Ravener says that he loves me, but I cannot guarantee that such love will keep me safe. If I present him with a fait accompli he may decide to kill me regardless. Mother is dead because she would not accept him, and I could well suffer the same fate. As you so succinctly put it, he will not tolerate being thwarted. If he stays his hand long enough I have a chance to stop him, but he would sweep you aside without a second thought. You know that, don't you?'

Rory gave her a reluctant nod. 'Losing you would break my heart too, you know.'

Ada smiled and took his hand. 'Yes, I know, but this is my fight, and if I lose I will need you to explain everything to Grandfather.'

'If that happens I'll be swiftly joining you in the afterlife,' said Rory, swallowing his pride.

'Then let us work on the assumption that I can end this tonight,' she said. 'The Ravener will pay for what he has done, and if that payment has to be made in blood, then so be it.'

CHAPTER 24

Unintended Consequences

A t six o'clock Ada left, telling Mrs Crane that she was visiting Dora Hunter. The fact that Rory was not accompanying her only added veracity to the deception. Hailing a cab, she cast a backward glance at the house. Rory stood in the doorway, arms folded across his chest and a pensive expression his face. She nodded to him, silently willing her friend to believe in her.

Once underway, Ada reached into her purse for her veil. It rested upon the revolver, and for a moment she considered the strange combination they made; one, a symbol of mourning, the other, an instrument for bringing such a condition about. Believing it sensible to keep her identity obscured, she affixed the veil and tried to relax. The thought of what she was about do was terrifying, but to finally be pre-emptive, to not feel subject to the perverse whims of another, gave her courage.

It did not take long to reach her destination – a mere twenty minutes if that – but as she stood alone on the pavement home seemed very far away indeed. Tiny flakes of snow drifted through the air, melting as they struck her veil. He would be coming soon, and she had to be ready when he did.

Saint Mark's Church, Islington, was a solid, Norman building, sitting in extensive grounds and with a vicarage to one side. Warm candlelight illuminated the stained glass windows, and from within Ada heard the delicate sounds of a choir. Thomas Tallis, she thought, mournful and exquisite. By the lych gate was an elegantly-painted sign, listing the times of service and the names of those who would officiate. This was what she had seen in her vision, this had been her guide.

Making her way to the main door, she carefully lifted the heavy, iron latch and slipped inside. In an alcove across the nave a confessional booth sat empty; with the congregation intent on their prayers, Ada managed to reach it unseen. Drawing the curtain behind her she sat back, listening as the choir sang *spem in alium*. Their voices rose and fell in beautiful counterpoint, and Ada could not help but let her mind dwell on Christmases past, of midnight mass and a time when her family was whole and together. Another life in another time, she thought. Taking the revolver from her purse, she laid it in her lap and waited for the devil to show his face.

The minutes turned to hours, and cradled by warmth and the sounds of worship, Ada struggled to stay awake. She had barely slept the previous night and her body was weary to the point of exhaustion.

'*For the wrath of God is revealed from heaven against all ungodliness and unrighteousness of men, who by their unrighteousness suppress the truth.* Was that not in your sermon this past Sunday, Father?'

Ada came to with a start. She had been drifting in the grey space between wakefulness and dreams, and the voice that roused her was one she knew all too well. *He* was here, and already about his business. Inwardly berating herself for making such a fundamental error, Ada opened the confessional curtain and peered out. The congregation and choir had gone, but in the space beneath the tower the parish priest stood on a chair, hands bound behind his back and a gag in his mouth. Round his neck was one of the bell ropes, tied in a hangman's knot.

'Come now, Father, surely Romans 1:18 strikes you as fitting? In your unrighteousness you have certainly suppressed the truth.'

The Ravener was standing not ten paces away, a monster made flesh at last. In his gloved hand he held a catling; the priest had only moments to live, of that Ada was sure. Heart in her mouth, she took soft, slow steps to the centre of the aisle, aiming the revolver at the back of the Ravener's head. With blood pounding in her ears she thumbed back the hammer, the metallic click ringing loud in the silent church.

'Oh you clever girl,' he said, turning slowly to face her. Beneath the top hat, glittering eyes peered at her from behind his mask. 'I see you are wearing your veil. Are you attending a funeral?'

'Possibly. Please do not move or I will shoot you where you stand.'

'Of that I have no doubt,' said the Ravener, 'but I would rather you didn't. You would regret it most profoundly.'

'Release my mother,' said Ada. 'I do not wish to kill, but I shall if I must. If your death means her soul goes free, then so be it.'

'My death *would* free her,' said the Ravener, 'but I am not ready. I have work to do as you can see.' He gestured to the priest standing shaking on the chair, eyes wide and pleading for mercy.

'And what he has done that requires your obscene attentions?' asked Ada.

'He takes in fallen women under the guise of Christian charity, has them perform domestic tasks in his vicarage. His parishioners hold him in high esteem for his work with such unfortunates. However, despite his vow of celibacy he finds himself tempted all too often, not even mortification of his own body is enough to quell such desire. He drugs the women, rapes them, and, desperate to hide the evidence of his crimes, he poisons them with arsenic. The old crypts beneath your feet are full of their rotting corpses, hidden inside old sarcophagi and doused with quicklime. Do you still wish me to stay my hand?'

'He is helpless and cannot avoid justice,' said Ada. 'Leave him for the police.'

'No,' said the Ravener, 'I shall not. He must pay for what he has done.'

'Like Josephine? You preach about the wages of sin and yet you killed her because she wanted to help me. She saw something in you, a secret that you wish to keep hidden.'

The Ravener sighed. 'She was no murderer. There was no sin in her heart beyond hubris but she left me no choice. All she had to do was remain silent, slowly forget what she thought she knew, but her actions decided her fate.'

'How dare you accuse her of hubris when *you* are the one who took an innocent life.'

'As I said, I had no choice. You are not yet ready, Ada. You will have all the knowledge you crave, but you must be prepared.'

'I am not your damn puppet!' she shouted.

'We are all puppets, Ada, in our own way.'

'What is that supposed to mean?'

'It means that we have roles that need to be played out, whether we like it or not. Very soon you will have a choice to make. You will need my help. The decision whether to ask for it or not rests solely with you, as do the consequences.'

'I am sick of your riddles,' said Ada.

'Then learn to unravel them. All you have to do is let me in when the time comes.'

Josephine's dying words rang inside Ada's head. 'I will never let you in. Now, free my mother, you bastard. I shall not ask again.'

'You make me very proud,' he said, opening his arms wide as he walked toward her.

'I do not care,' said Ada, tears spilling from her eyes as she squeezed the trigger. With a sharp, reverberating crack the revolver bucked in her hand, but she was ready for it. Her aim was perfect, her resolve to finish him, absolute.

With extraordinary speed the Ravener stepped aside, so fast that Ada's eyes could barely register the movement. It was as if he flowed through the air, effortless, graceful, lethal. Directly behind him the bullet struck the helpless priest full in chest, passing through his body to bury itself in the ancient stone of the tower. He jerked backward, falling from the chair. Hanging by his neck he began a slow descent, legs crumpling beneath him as he reached the floor. From high up in the tower, a deep, sonorous tolling began.

Ada could only stare in horror, smoke curling from the revolver as the bell rope lifted the priest's limp body upward once more.

'You should run,' said the Ravener.

She remained rooted to the spot, unable to

comprehend what she had just done.

'I said run, girl!' he bellowed.

Ada recoiled as if slapped. Grabbing her purse from the confessional, she stumbled to the door and into the graveyard. The frozen, snow-covered gravel crunched beneath her boots as she ran beneath the lych gate and into the empty street, desperate to get away from the church. Behind her, the bell rang out across Islington, summoning the faithful to witness the most awful of revelations.

CHAPTER 25

Taken

A da did not reach home until the early hours. Numb in both body and spirit she quietly let herself in, not wishing to wake anyone. Hoping there may still be warmth in the grate, she made her way to the parlour. Hamlet lay curled up in his basket and Rory was fast asleep in an armchair, an empty glass on the table at his elbow. She sat opposite, studying her friend's face in the glow from the dying fire. I pray your dreams are more pleasant than mine, she thought.

The circulation was just returning to her hands when Rory woke. 'Feck me, thank God you're back,' he said softly. 'Are you all right, lass?'

She shook her head, chest heaving as she began to sob. Rory got up and came over. Taking her in his arms, he waited patiently as her sorrow ran its course.

'What happened?' he asked as Ada dried her eyes.

For a moment she could not speak, the enormity of what she had done, albeit inadvertently, was only now hitting home.

'I killed someone tonight, Rory,' she said,

mouth dry and the words sticking in her throat. 'Once again there is blood on my hands.'

'The Ravener?'

'No,' she said, and taking a deep breath she told him what had transpired in the church.

'Oh, lass, I'm so sorry. It is no small thing to take a life, I know, but it was an accident. You were not aiming at the priest.'

'And yet he is still dead. It is a stain on my conscience that I cannot erase. Even if what the Ravener said about the man was true, it was not my place to be his executioner.'

'But you went there to kill the Ravener,' said Rory.

'That is different and you know it. He has made this personal, and under the circumstances I have more than enough reason to end his life. All he had to do was set my mother free and I would not have pulled the trigger. No one needed to die.'

'I understand. You have every right to be angry.'

'That's what bothers me. I was angry and he knew it, yet he showed no malice toward me in return. He did not expect to see me, yet he was actually proud I had tracked him down. If he had not shouted at me to run, I may have still been standing there in shock when the police arrived. He did not want me to be caught. Try as I might, I cannot fathom what lies behind that mask.'

Rory leaned forward and took her hands.

'You did a brave thing going to face him like that. It was hard to just let you do it but you were right, I would not have been any help.'

'You are more help than you realise,' she said. 'I don't need a white knight, I need a friend, and you fulfil that role most admirably.'

He reddened about the cheeks. 'Ah, feck it, now look what you've done.'

Ada gave him a sad smile.

'So what happens next?' Rory asked.

'I am unsure. He will be on his guard now, so I doubt I'll be able to find him again. All I can do is wait until he makes his true intentions known, and hope that when the time comes I am strong enough to resist him.'

'This choice he said you will have to make?'

She nodded. 'The circumstances would have to be dire indeed for me to ask for his help – let us hope that such a thing does not come to pass. If it does, then my mother's soul will not be the only one held in thrall.'

Ada had just finished her breakfast when Milly entered the parlour, telegram in hand. It was from Sir Edmund, confirming dinner for eight o'clock that evening.

She sighed. 'I had forgotten he invited us. I must admit that I do not feel like attending, but we really should go. I would like to see Father, and he may even be well enough to join us.'

273

'Perhaps it may serve to distract you, if only for a brief time,' said Rory, 'and I would like to see Henry too.'

'Very well, I shall put on a brave face and pretend that I am not beset by chaos. Do you have anything suitable to wear? Grandfather is a stickler for formality.' She had meant it lightly, but saw that Rory paled at the thought of attending dinner without decent apparel. 'Father has some suits here you could borrow?' she suggested. 'You're of similar build, and there's a tailor a couple of streets over if we need alterations made.'

'That's a fine idea,' he said, visibly relieved. 'No time like the present. Show me where they are and I'll try them on.'

She led Rory to her father's room and presented him with a wardrobe full of formalwear.

'What do you think?' he asked, once properly attired.

'It's not bad, not bad at all. It needs a nip and tuck here and there, but overall you are quite presentable.'

'I look like a penguin,' said Rory.

'Well, you make a very dashing penguin,' said Ada, 'and it won't take long to make it fit perfectly.'

The tailor's shop was in a secluded courtyard, set

back from the street with a wide, bay window full of mannequins. A bell rang softly as Ada opened the door. Seated at a worktable, a young man with a *yarmulke* on his head was chalking some material prior to cutting. He looked up, and upon seeing Ada, smiled broadly.

'Miss Phillips, good morning,' he said.

'Good morning, Jacob. I hope you don't mind but I have a favour to ask. Sergeant Canavan here needs a suit altered for this evening. Would you be so kind as to attend to it as a matter of urgency?'

Jacob nodded. 'Of course. Oh, and may I ask how your father is? It was sad news to hear that he had been taken ill.'

'He's recovering well, thank you.'

'Please pass my good wishes to him,' said Jacob. 'Now then, sergeant, let's see what we can do for you. Please follow me to the fitting room.'

Rory looked at Ada. 'Off you go then,' she said. She found it strange that Rory was so worldly in many ways, and yet in others he was almost childlike; it was quite endearing. Seating herself near the window she peered between the mannequins, watching the inhabitants of London as they passed by. She envied their normality, their humdrum ordinary lives – it was so far removed from where she was now. Death surrounded her, yet she remained relatively unscathed. How long that state of affairs could last was matter of debate.

Shifting her gaze, she caught the eye of a man leaning against the street-side of the courtyard. He looked away just a shade too quickly, trying to appear nonchalant as he picked at his nails. A cold certainty settled into the pit of Ada's stomach. Despite Rory's misdirection, it appeared that Soames had extended his search to Shoreditch after all.

There was a cry of pain from the rear of the shop, closely followed by a muffled crash. 'Oh, God, no,' said Ada. Dashing into the fitting room, she found Jacob lying motionless on the floor, a nasty gash on his forehead bleeding profusely. The door to the back alley was open, and beyond it she heard the sound of something heavy being dragged. Without hesitation she ran outside, only to be met with a slap across the face that drove her to her knees. Through watering eyes she could see Rory's unconscious form being bundled into a carriage by two men. Above her towered Soames, the look on his face one of utter contempt.

'Well, well,' he said. 'I wondered where the mick had got to. Seems he was playing doctors and nurses at your house all along. I hope you don't mind if we take him for a ride? The sergeant and I need to have a little chat about his conduct while on duty. I doubt you'll be seeing him again.'

Ada wanted nothing more than to strike

him, but she knew such action would be futile. She was no match for him physically, and he would have no qualms about leaving her battered and bleeding on the cobblestones. Hoping that someone might come to her aid she opened her mouth to scream, but before she could do so Soames grasped her round the throat with a black-gloved hand. There was a soft click, and the blade of a lock-knife appeared against her cheek, the point so close to her eye that she couldn't focus on it.

'Listen to me you stuck-up little whore. If you so much as whimper, I'll cut that nose right off your pretty face. I don't care who your grandfather is. There's only so much he can do and I've gone up against greater than him. So, ask yourself if you want to play nicely. Do you understand?'

Ada nodded. While she was only too aware of what the Ravener was capable of, she no longer feared him. She feared Soames however, very much.

'Good,' he said, releasing the hold on her throat. 'Now, if you try to interfere in any way, I'll have some fun with that virginal little quim of yours before I open you up like a kipper. I trust I make myself perfectly clear?'

'Yes,' said Ada, her voice barely more than a whisper.

'Then I shall bid you a good day, Miss

Phillips.' Putting the knife in his pocket, he strode off and climbed inside the carriage. Within seconds it was gone, leaving Ada kneeling on the ground and shaking with rage. A single thought remained uppermost in her mind – if she didn't do something, and quickly, Rory was going to die.

Getting to her feet, Ada took a deep breath to steady her nerves; panic would be of no help. Re-entering the shop she found Jacob leaning against a table, head in his hands.

'Are you all right?' she asked.

'I think I'll live. I'm Jewish – it's not the first time I've been assaulted. Who were those men? Why did they take your friend?'

'It's best you don't know. I didn't think they'd be so brazen as to take Rory in broad daylight.'

'They certainly don't lack chutzpah.'

'I'm so sorry, Jacob.'

'Ach,' he said, waving off the apology. 'It's not your fault.'

'I would stich you up myself but I have to go.'

'Don't worry about me – I have people I can call on. You go and find your friend, but for God's sake be careful.'

'I shall,' said Ada, 'and thank you.' Leaving the tailor to tend to his injuries, she made her way out to the street. The first thing she needed to do was find out where Soames had taken Rory. Her thinking still addled from the slap she'd received, it took precious minutes to decide on a course of action. Raising a hand she hailed a hansom cab.

'Where to, miss?' asked the driver.

'Whitechapel police station as fast as you can, please,' she said, trying to formulate a plan as the cab wove smartly through traffic. She would need her grandfather's help but that would take time, time that Rory may not have. Soames must know that taking him would bring down Sir Edmund's wrath, which meant that he didn't care. The only reason for that would be if he had tacit permission from Halloran, no doubt wanting to prove to Sir Edmund that he wouldn't be bullied now he was also a member of the same club.

'Damn the arrogance of little men,' she said.

Every second the cab took to get to Whitechapel was agony. Ada hoped that Soames would want to spend as much time as he could taunting Rory before getting down to the business of killing him. It actually gave her a chance of getting there before the fateful moment.

On arriving at the station house, she asked the driver to wait while she ran inside. Hugely relieved to see Sergeant Osborne's huge frame perched behind his desk, she walked over and leaned in so only he could hear.

'I need help, Walter, and I need it to be discreet.'

Osborne didn't blink; he simply nodded as

if the request was the most natural thing in the world.

'Special Branch has Rory. They took him away in a carriage and I don't know where they've gone. Soames said that he was going to kill him, and me too if I interfered.'

The sergeant's pen briefly faltered in its way across the duty ledger, a smudge of ink marring the otherwise perfect script. 'Well, that sounds untoward,' he muttered, flicking his eyes left and right to ensure that nobody was eavesdropping.

'Where would Soames take him?' asked Ada. 'Nothing gets past you. There must be some gossip about Special Branch, they're the police version of a fireside ghost story.'

'And if I was to say that I did know something, and I'm not admitting it, mind you, hypothetically speaking, what would a young lady like yourself do with such knowledge?'

'Knowing that she couldn't involve the police, she would send a telegram to her grandfather. She would ask him to meet her at a certain location, and bring with him a group of staff from his house, all armed to the teeth of course.'

'That would be a sensible approach under the circumstances,' said Osborne, blotting the ink from his ledger. 'And of course, a lady would never divulge how she came to know the location of a Special Branch safe house.'

'A lady would never do such a thing,' said Ada. 'It would be unconscionably rude.'

'That's what I thought. So if I was to mention that a sewage pumping station –specifically the one in East Limehouse – had a large cellar with thick walls, would that be of use?'

'It would indeed.'

'Then please give my regards to your father,' said Osborne loudly, ensuring that those nearby would hear him.

'Thank you, sergeant, I will.' It took great effort not to run out of the station, but now Ada knew where Soames was, her path became clear. Climbing back into the cab, she asked the driver to take her to the post office at the end of her street.

'Can I help you, miss?' said the clerk as Ada walked in. He sat behind a small window, the wall behind him lined with pneumatic tubes.

'I'd like to send a telegram, please.'

He handed her a slip of paper, and Ada jotted down the message she had already composed. It was short, but her grandfather would know how important it was. Hopefully he wouldn't take too long to respond.

"RORY TAKEN BY SB STOP MEET EAST LIMEHOUSE PUMPING STATION SOONEST STOP BRING MEN SUITABLE ATTIRE. ADA."

After paying the clerk she walked briskly home. Milly was about her duties and Mrs Crane was out, which suited her perfectly. Unlocking the bureau in her room, Ada reached for the revolver that lay within. She paused a moment, her hand resting on the cold steel. The last time she held it she had killed someone, but without it she would be at Soames' mercy, as would Rory. With a heavy sigh she slipped it into her coat pocket, the Ravener's words in the foster home coming back to haunt her. "This is war, Ada. The *reason* for the taking of life is paramount, as you will come to realise." She had denied him then, sure in the strength of her morality, yet now, faced with the prospect of her friend's imminent demise, she had to admit that she may have been wrong.

Making her way downstairs, she roused Hamlet from his basket. Having the old dog by her side would be a comfort while she waited for her grandfather.

'You off out again, miss?' asked Milly, appearing from the kitchen with an armful of linen.

'Yes,' said Ada, putting on an amiable face, 'just taking Hamlet for a walk. It's a nice day so we may be some time.'

'Is Sergeant Canavan not going with you?'

'He's… busy at the moment, Milly.'

'Righto, miss. I'll see you later.' Ada felt a pang of unease at lying but there was no point doing otherwise. Putting a lead on Hamlet she left the house, hoping that when she returned

Rory would be with her.

'East Limehouse pumping station, please,' she said, hailing a cab.

'Oh, want to 'ave a gander at one of Mr Bazelgette's wonders, eh?' said the driver. 'He's done miracles that chap. I remember the Great Stink of 1858. I was just a kid, and we would throw stones at the turds floating by. Gawd, the Thames was nothing but a great big sewer then.'

The driver continued to reminisce as Ada only half-listened to him. He was right though – the Thames had been nothing more than a cesspit, a breeding ground for cholera, typhoid and dysentery. Over thirty thousand people had died from such diseases before the city commissioned Joseph Bazalgette to build the new sewerage system. All it took was for the government to have been inconvenienced by being forced to abandon the Houses of Parliament due to the stench from the river. The injustice of it all simply fuelled Ada's anger. The pumping stations had breathed new life into London, and now she was going to one in order to save her friend. She wondered what Mr Bazalgette would think if he knew what purpose Special Branch were putting it to.

'Hold on, Rory,' she said, the revolver lying heavy against her thigh. 'I'm coming.'

CHAPTER 26

Industrial Revolutions

H idden in the shadows of a nearby alley, Ada made careful study of the Limehouse pumping station. A temple to Victorian ingenuity it sat behind a high wall, its cream-coloured brick in stark contrast to its dour neighbours. Despite housing two, massive beam engines, the building seemed unusually quiet and still. The gates were open, and during the last hour she had seen nobody enter or leave.

'Where are you, Grandfather?' she whispered, trying to quell the growing sickness in her stomach. Soames would expect her to raise the alarm, despite his threats, but then again he couldn't know that she would discover his location. She hoped that Osborne's information was correct, and that Soames – safe in his arrogance – wouldn't hurry to fulfil his promise to kill her friend.

As the minutes ticked by and Sir Edmund failed to arrive, Ada's fear grew. If anything happened to Rory due to inaction on her part she would never forgive herself. Eventually she could bear it no longer; she would have to go in alone, whatever the risk. Praying that she wasn't making a terrible mistake, she took a firm grip on Hamlet's lead and made her way to the station entrance. With every step she half-expected Soames' men to see her and come running, but mercifully her luck held, and on reaching the door she opened it just wide enough to slip quietly inside.

The cavernous pumping hall was empty save for a lone man in overalls, working on one of the beam engines. At his back, a spiral staircase led down to what Ada assumed was the cellar, but getting to it unnoticed would be a problem. The man didn't look like he was part of Special Branch, but Ada made no assumptions. As far as she was concerned, anyone in this building apart from her and Rory was a potential enemy. In front of her, a decorative iron lattice – beautifully painted in rcd and gold – formed a ring round the centre of the hall. Using it for cover, Ada crept slowly toward the stairs.

'Right then you stubborn bastard,' said the man, 'let's see what you've got for me.'

Ada froze behind a pillar, watching him from the corner of her eye. Wiping his hands with an oily rag, he opened a valve and stood back. A cloud of steam billowed round his legs, and with a deep, grinding sound the huge engine came to life. The spoked flywheel – a good fourteen feet across – began to rotate, slowly at first but with increasing speed. Startled from its hiding place by the sudden noise, a sewer rat scurried across the floor close to Hamlet. The dog lunged toward it and barked, almost pulling Ada off her feet.

'Who's there?' said the man, turning round to peer at the lattice. 'This is private property, show yourself.'

Ada's heart sank. For a moment she considered running, but if Soames realised his safe house had been discovered, he would not hesitate to execute Rory. If she was to save him, her only option was to behave like her grandfather, face the enemy head on and damn the consequences. 'I'm so sorry,' she said, striding confidently into the open, 'I was just passing and thought I would come in to have a look. I love steam engines and I've never seen one of these working before. My apologies if I behaved inappropriately.'

The man frowned. 'It's somewhat irregular, miss. We're not open to the public except on special viewing days. These machines are dangerous – they'll take your arm off if you're not careful.'

'I'm sure they could,' said Ada, taking firm hold of the revolver in her pocket.

'Well, no harm done. I'm Harris by the way.'

'Pleased to meet you, Mr Harris, I'm Ada Phillips.'

'Are you here on your own?'

'Just me and my faithful hound,' she said. 'I have no wish to interrupt your work if you're busy.'

'That's all right, miss, I've just finished as you can see.'

'And what is it you were doing?'

Harris gestured toward the beam engine. 'This monster is the Prince William. He's been a temperamental beast since he was first installed twenty years ago, and most of my time is spent trying to keep the damn thing running. The station's in mothballs for the moment, problems with the foundations or something. They have me in to keep things ticking over while they sort it out.'

'How fascinating,' said Ada.

'I'd be happy to stay and talk, miss, but I do have other matters to attend to. If you don't mind, I'll show you out.'

'Of course, Mr Harris, I don't wish to keep you. There's just one more thing I need to ask.'

'And what would that be, miss?'

In one swift, fluid movement, Ada drew the revolver and pressed it to Harris' forehead. 'Soames brought a man here earlier. Where is he? He's a good friend of mine and I am keen to ensure his safety.'

'I don't know what you mean, miss,' he stammered.

'I think you do,' she said. 'I know damn

well this is a Special Branch safe house. You're not stupid – you know exactly what I'm talking about.' Ada forced Harris backward, pressing him against the guard rail surrounding the beam engine. Scant inches behind him, the flywheel cut the air like a knife. 'As you say, these machines are dangerous.'

Sweat beaded on Harris' forehead. 'I will give you to the count of three,' said Ada, hoping that her bluff was convincing. She had no wish to hurt the man but there was no time for subtlety.

'One.'

'He'll kill me if I say anything.'

'And I will kill you if you don't. Two.'

'All right, all right. Soames brought some chap in an hour or so back. They took him downstairs. I'm not one of them; I just get paid to look the other way.'

Ada felt a surge of relief. Osborne had been right. A muffled shout came from the stairwell and for one brief moment she turned her head. Seeing his chance, Harris swept her arm aside and lunged forward. 'Bitch,' he spat, punching her hard in the stomach. Gasping for breath Ada sank to her knees, crying out as the revolver was wrenched from her hand.

'Whoever you are, I doubt Soames wants you here. If I deal with you myself, I may even get a bonus.'

'Please,' said Ada, 'don't do it.'

'It's nothing personal, love, but you're in the wrong place at the wrong time.' Aiming at her heart, his finger tightened on the trigger. With a growl Hamlet leapt at him, jaws closing round Harris' wrist with a sickening crunch.

'Christ!' he shrieked, 'Get this thing off me.'

Ada struggled to her feet, knowing that any element of surprise was long gone. To have come so close only to be stymied by this underling, this bootlick, was unacceptable.

'He wants to kill you,' the Ravener whispered in her ear, his voice soft and sibilant as a cobra. 'Let us show him the error of his ways.' Ada felt him reach inside her, his chill touch laden with the unfettered desire for vengeance. She fought him with everything she had but his will was all consuming, all powerful. Hatred ran in her veins, burning with such intensity that all rational thought fled before it. Empathy and compassion were stripped away until nothing of the Ada she knew remained. In its place, something terrible was born.

'Leave him, Hamlet!' she shouted. Releasing his grip, the dog trotted obediently to her side. Harris clutched at his wounded arm, moaning in agony. 'You're not getting out of here alive,' he snarled.

'I beg to differ,' she replied. Striding forward, Ada grabbed his overalls and shoved him hard against the beam engine's guard rail, lifting him clean off his feet. The revolver clattered to the floor as he flailed wildly, trying to stop himself from falling.

'What...what...no, stop, please!'

The look of terror on his face pleased Ada greatly. 'You were wrong,' she said, teeth bared in a manic smile, 'this is very personal indeed, *love*.' Letting go of Harris she stepped away, watching expectantly as he toppled backward. One of his hands caught against the flywheel, and with shocking speed he was dragged into the machine, a merciless, spinning guillotine that cut him to pieces. Blood and viscera flew in all directions, spattering Ada as she stood – arms wide – basking in such a magnificent death.

'Do you see how easy it is when you desire it? How effective such measures are against those who would stand in your way?' With a sigh the Ravener withdrew his presence from Ada's mind. The awful rage left with him, leaving her numb and shaking. Gore trickled down her face; she could taste it on her lips, smell it on her hair. 'Dear God,' she said, staring open-mouthed at the shredded remains of what used to be a man. There was no comfort in knowing that the Ravener had been controlling her actions, only shame that she had not been strong enough to resist him. I have taken two lives in as many days, she thought, I am truly damned.

A shot rang out, and Hamlet gave a pained

yelp as a bullet tore into his abdomen. Back legs buckling beneath him, he slumped to the floor panting violently.

'No!' screamed Ada. She turned to find Soames standing behind her, a revolver of his own pointed at her head.

'My, my,' he said, 'aren't you full of surprises? Look at the mess you've made. If it wasn't so inconvenient I'd actually be impressed. How did you find me?'

'I'm telling you nothing.'

'That's only to be expected I suppose. You'll sing a different tune soon enough. Now, place your hands behind you if you please.'

Knowing that Soames would have no qualms about shooting her on the spot, Ada did as she was told. The beam engine was still running, Harris' remains adorning it like ghastly festival decorations. She swallowed hard as bile rose in her throat. 'Did he have a family?'

'Not that I know of. Why, is your conscience pricking you?'

Ada didn't reply. There were no words to explain how wretched she felt.

'It's of no consequence,' said Soames, seemingly unaffected by the carnage that surrounded him. 'He was just some corporation employee we had nicely in our pocket. However, thanks to your interference we'll need to find a new safe house. Luckily I have somewhere in mind. Sergeant Canavan is waiting for you in the cellar, so if you'd kindly lead the way we can bring all this unpleasantness to an end.' He gestured toward the spiral staircase.

Casting a last, sad glance at Hamlet's prone body, Ada trudged downward on leaden feet. She was under no illusions as to what would happen next. Unless her grandfather arrived soon, both she and Rory were going to die. Soames pushed her into a dimly lit room, the walls lined with oak benches and tools of all kinds. In the centre of the floor a man sat tied to a chair, his face bloody and head bowed.

'Oh, Rory,' she gasped.

At the sound of her voice he lifted his head and groaned. 'Ah, Ada you mad fecker. Why on earth did you come after me?'

Soames gave a disparaging laugh. 'She came because she's so infatuated with a poteen-soaked mick that she signs her own death warrant. I warned her what would happen if she tried to intervene. Miss Phillips, you told your grandfather where you were going I assume?'

Ada glowered at him.

'I'll take that as a yes. No doubt Sir Edmund will soon be here, his beard bristling with righteous anger. That would be awkward. So, Miss Phillips, Sergeant Canavan, the only question is, what shall I do with you before he arrives?'

'Not much further,' said Fitz, trying his best to sound reassuring.

Sir Edmund glared at him, every inch of his face etched with fury. 'Baynes! Can't you go any faster?' he bellowed. Cracking his whip, the coachman urged the horses on, the carriage thundering through the East End with reckless abandon. 'If I hadn't been in the middle of an operation we'd have arrived an hour ago.' Sir Edmund pounded his fist against the seat in frustration.

'Your staff knows very well not to disturb you during a procedure, and they would never read the contents of a telegram,' said Fitz. 'What's done is done. Let's just focus on the rescue shall we?'

'Very well. Jessop, are you and your colleagues prepared?'

'Yes, sir,' said one of the four sanatorium orderlies that shared the carriage. 'Guns and knives, as you requested.'

'Good. You all served her majesty in India, so you know what I expect of you. My granddaughter and Sergeant Canavan are in the gravest jeopardy. They are to be protected at all costs.' The men nodded their understanding.

'Do you think Ada will be waiting for us?' asked Fitz.

'After so much time has passed I think it

unlikely. She will behave exactly as I would under the circumstances; go on ahead and learn what she can about the enemy. Damn her.'

'You can hardly criticise the girl for behaving like a soldier.'

'No, I cannot, but she is the very heart of me. If she is hurt or... worse, then you know what I will do.'

'Yes,' said Fitz, 'and I will be at your side, old friend.'

'Pumping station ahead, sir,' Baynes called down.

'Pull up outside, there's no need to conceal our presence. If they are watching, let's put the fear of God into them.'

Baynes reined-in the horses and the carriage doors banged open. Sir Edmund and Fitz went first, revolvers in their hands. The men fell into line behind them, ready to fight as soon as the order was given.

'What was that?' said Sir Edmund. 'I heard something.' He stopped, checking the grounds either side of the gravel path. A soft whining came from behind a large shrub. 'Watch the windows, Fitz.'

The doctor signalled the men to take up position beside him, and with one eye on the pumping station Sir Edmund walked over and bent down, pulling back the undergrowth. He groaned when he saw what had made the noise.

Hamlet lay on his side in a pool of blood, an awful wound in his stomach. The Great Dane's eyes were clouded, his tongue lolling from the side of his mouth, coating itself with dirt and grass.

'There, there, old boy,' he said, patting the dog's head. Hamlet whined and tried to lick the proffered hand, but he had no strength left. The dog's chest heaved once, and then he was still.

'What is it, Edmund?'

'It's Ada's dog. Some bastard shot him.'

'There's a trail of blood, sir,' said Jessop, 'looks like it goes to the main door.'

'It's likely he was hurt inside and dragged himself out here to die,' said Fitz.

'He wouldn't leave Ada unless he had no choice,' said Sir Edmund. 'Follow me and be at the ready.' He entered the pumping hall; the building was eerily quiet and there was no one to be seen. 'Jesus Christ!' he said, all colour draining from his face as he looked at one of the beam engines. The great machine was covered in blood, tatters of flesh and bone hanging from the flywheel. 'For the love of God, tell me that's not her.'

'Jessop, watch my back,' said Fitz. 'The rest of you, fan out and quarter the hall. If anyone offers resistance, shoot them.' Without question the men did as ordered, swift, silent and efficient. Swallowing hard, Fitz walked over to the beam engine. In the shallow maintenance pit beneath it, the remains of a body lay half-submerged in oily water. Despite his revulsion at such a sight, he could only heave a sigh of relief. The victim was clearly male and clad in overalls.

'It's not Ada,' he said. 'It's likely a waterworks employee, poor beggar.'

Sir Edmund wiped a hand across his face. 'Thank you,' he said.

Moments later Jessop returned. 'All clear, sir. No sign of anyone.'

'They must be downstairs,' said Fitz, pointing to a staircase sunk into the floor.

'Then let us introduce ourselves,' said Sir Edmund, treading softly on the iron steps as he descended. 'There,' he whispered, pointing to a set of partial, bloody footprints. They led to a closed door in the side wall. With their weapons drawn the men lined up, three to either side. With a nod from Sir Edmund, Fitz turned the handle and pushed, swinging the door wide. The room beyond was as silent as the pumping hall. In the centre of the floor lay an overturned chair, a length of rope at its feet and drops of blood spattering the concrete.

'They were here, I know it,' said Sir Edmund, an uncharacteristic tone of despair in his voice.

'There's a hatchway to the sewers over here, sir,' said Jessop, 'more blood on the floor too.'

'Open it.'

The reek of raw sewage billowed into the room. 'I can't see any further tracks, sir, the water's washed everything away. They could have gone anywhere.'

'Damn it!' Sir Edmund turned to Fitz. 'Soames must have known I'd come. That knowledge may stay his hand awhile but he's not going to stop. There's no point trying to find them in there – we could spend weeks searching and never catch up.'

'What are you going to do?'

'The only thing I can. Take this matter up with a higher authority.'

Chief Constable Halloran sat hunched over his desk, scrutinising case papers in the hunt for the Ravener. The door to his office swung open and footsteps approached across the wooden floor.

'I said I wasn't to be disturbed, Davies,' he mumbled, not bothering to look up. A leather-gloved hand gripped the back of his head and slammed it onto the blotter.

'You snivelling little wretch!' hissed Sir Edmund. 'Do you know what you've done? You've let your hound off the leash and now he's gone rogue. He has Sergeant Canavan *and* my granddaughter. Don't try to deny it or by God I'll cut out your eyes.'

Halloran blinked, the tip of a shining, steel blade hovering perilously close to his face. 'I told Soames he could deal discreetly with Canavan,' he whimpered. 'I don't know anything about your granddaughter.'

'She saw Rory being taken and went after him. The pumping station in Limehouse, I'm sure you know the one?'

'Yes,' he said.

'It's a damn bloodbath in there. Some engineer is in pieces after being fed through a beam engine. I assume that will be explained away as an *accident*. Soames took Rory and Ada into the sewers before I arrived. Where have they gone, Halloran?'

'I don't know. The pumping station is the only Special Branch safe house I'm aware of. I leave local arrangements to Soames.'

'Then this is what you are going to do,' said Sir Edmund, leaning over so his mouth was next to Halloran's ear. 'You are going to use every resource at your disposal to get hold of Soames. I don't care how, but rein him in. If Ada and Rory are returned to me unharmed, I'm prepared to forget this matter ever happened. Do you understand?'

Unable to nod, Halloran grunted his assent.

'However,' said Sir Edmund, his voice calm, cold and measured. 'If anything happens to either of them, I will find you, take you, and dissect you on my operating table without anaesthetic. You will feel everything, and I will keep you alive long enough for you to witness your own dismemberment. I have seen and done things that would make you vomit, Chief Constable. Pray do not test me on this.'

Releasing Halloran he raised himself to his full height, towering over the craven policeman. 'You have until midnight,' he said. 'I will be at the Phillips' house in Shoreditch. If Ada and Rory are not returned to me safe and sound by then, I will destroy you, Halloran, of that you can be sure.'

With a snort of contempt Sir Edmund strode from the room, slamming the door behind him. Hunched in his chair, a shaking Halloran reached for a pen and began to write. He knew exactly what would happen if he failed to stop Soames. Swallowing his pride, he racked his brain for a way in which to bring his hound to heel.

CHAPTER 27

The Patriot

A ngry, scared, and so very tired, Ada sat handcuffed to a chair, head lolling on her chest. She had been dragged through sewer tunnels for what seemed like hours, effluent up to her knees. It caked the skirt of her dress and the stench was appalling. In front of her sat Rory, trussed with rope and barely conscious after the beating he'd received. Through a haze of pain she could dimly hear Soames and his men talking; she had no doubts about her fate, she had seen too much and was now a liability. This dank room, deep beneath the streets of London, would likely be the site of her execution.

'I'm so sorry, Father,' she mumbled, 'this will break your heart.'

'Be silent!' barked Soames, dealing her a vicious slap across the face that split her lip. She barely had the strength to moan. Her limbs felt numb and the blessed release of oblivion called. She ached to give in to it, but was afraid that if she closed her eyes she would never open them again. A pair of kid-gloved hands rested themselves gently on her shoulders, the leather soft and warm against her skin.

'Have you come to gloat?' she asked.

'No, beloved, I am here to offer my services. I told you a choice would be coming and here it is.'

'We will soon be dead, Rory and I. Soames is going to rape me then shoot us both. Our bodies will float into the Thames on a tide of filth, food for crabs and gulls.'

'That would be a sorry end indeed,' said the Ravener, 'but it does not have to be so. All you have to do is let me in willingly, and I will grind your enemies beneath my feet.'

'Why would I do that? You are nothing but chaos, destroying my family piece by piece, taking the life of anyone that dares to cross your path. I will be glad to be rid of you.'

'You know that you would likely have died back there in the pumping hall, had I not intervened.'

'You invaded my mind, forced me to do your bidding.'

'Are you sure? Perhaps I simply called to that which lies within you, clamouring to be set free.'

'I would not have killed Harris had you given me the choice. All you had to do was knock him unconscious, shoot him in the leg if you thought it necessary. Pushing him into that machine was nothing more than deliberate butchery.'

'He threatened you, and that is something I will not tolerate. Can you truthfully say you felt no satisfaction when you took his life? Was it not glorious to be strong enough to make a difference, to be able to fight back?'

Ada wanted to say that he was wrong, that such feelings were anathema to her, but she could not. She hated herself for it but the Ravener was right; for one brief second she had stared into the abyss, and had embraced it. Are we really just animals beneath the skin, she thought, willing to rend and tear at a whim, blind to the suffering it may cause?

'Your confusion is only to be expected,' said the Ravener. 'As yet you are not in possession of all the facts. If you give me the opportunity I will explain everything, but that requires time, a commodity that you do not have. In Soames you face a man whose heart brims with violence and lust. He is, by far, the most evil soul I have encountered in this stinking city. Every murder he commits – and there have been so very many – is done in the name of queen and country, or so he tells himself. The truth is far more pedestrian.'

'And yet you would let him kill me?'

The Ravener paused, weighing his words with extraordinary care. 'The decision is yours to make. If you refuse my offer you condemn us both. Believe me, I have as much to lose as you.'

'I cannot bear it,' said Ada. The Ravener tightened his grip on her shoulders, holding her steady, helping her balance on the razor's edge between this world and the next.

'You are so strong, beloved. Will you take my hand and live, or will you let this man triumph? What a waste that would be.'

'Why do I have to ask? What difference does that make? You could just help me anyway, as you did with Harris.'

'That was but a taste of what I can offer. There are rules, child. If I am to open myself to you completely, share everything that I am, then I need your consent. I cannot force my gifts upon you, I will not. You are my salvation, and such a precious thing can only be given freely.'

'Soames killed my dog,' said Ada, weeping silently in the darkness.

'Yes, he did. Will you let Hamlet's death be in vain? Choose, beloved, we do not have long.'

Bereft of will, all Ada had left was anger. It burned blue inside her, stark illumination for all the injustice she had witnessed. Innocent women were strangled and mutilated, others treated as slaves, mere chattels to be used and abused. Children were smothered for coin, and good people like her father and Rory sacrificed their health and even their lives in an effort to make the city a better place for all. The images spun and wheeled behind her eyes, a kaleidoscope of bitterness. She would tolerate this no more.

'Help me,' she whispered.

'Thank you,' said the Ravener. There was

no triumph in his words, only the deepest of gratitude, but Ada knew she had made an unearthly bargain nonetheless. At some time, and in some way, that debt would have to be repaid. She gasped as freezing water drenched her body, snatching her from the limbo in which she drifted.

'Wake up,' said Soames.

Ada peered at him through ropes of sodden hair. 'Take my advice and run. You'll regret it if you don't.'

Soames turned to the two men standing a few paces behind him. 'Shall we run, gents? Shall we beg for mercy?' The suggestion was met with derisive laughter. 'No, Miss Phillips, that is not Special Branch's way. It is you who will be on your knees, praying for deliverance, praying for a swift end to your suffering.'

'I very much doubt that.'

'Defiant to the last, eh? Well, night has fallen and it's time for all good children to be in bed. My family is waiting for me. Supper will be on the table and a glass of port sitting next to it. I'm eager to be done with you both. This is nothing personal you understand, it's simply business.' Opening his lock-knife he began to cut away the bodice of Ada's dress. Lace by lace, thread by thread, the blade carved its way upward, baring her flesh to his leering gaze.

'You have earned what comes next,' hissed

Ada, unable to hide her disgust as Soames ran his fingers over the swell of her breasts.

'As have you,' he grunted, reaching for his belt.

On the far side of the room, Ada glimpsed a flash of steel in the darkness. A strangled gurgling began, only to be cut short by a sickening, wet crunch.

'What the hell was that?' said Soames.

Thrown into the wan pool of light in which she sat, Ada watched as a severed head rolled to a stop at her feet. The cut across the neck was clean and precise – no ragged edges, no splintered bone, a masterpiece of battlefield surgery.

'I told you to run,' she said, 'but it's too late now. Hell is empty and all the devils are here.'

'Lawson? Christ!' Soames dropped the knife and drew his revolver. 'Who have you got helping you, bitch? Is it your fucking grandfather?'

Ada favoured him with a grim smile 'Why spoil the surprise?'

'Ramsay, where are you? Talk to me.'

A muffled cry was the only response. Moments later Ramsay staggered out of the gloom, face deathly pale and hands pressed to a wide gash in his belly. Slumping to the floor, oily ropes of greyish bowel spilled from between his fingers, a ghastly lesson in anatomy.

'And then there was one,' said Ada, drinking in the look of shock on Soames' face.

'Who are you?' he cried out, blind panic evident in his voice. 'You don't scare me.'

Liar, thought Ada.

'But I should scare you,' said a voice at Soames' back.

The policeman swung round, firing blindly. The bullet did nothing but gouge a hole in the rotten brickwork of the far wall.

'You will need to do much better than that,' said the Ravener.

'It's you, isn't it? Our new killer – a replacement for Price and his garrotte.'

'Hardly a replacement, think of it more as… evolution.'

'You don't know who you're dealing with,' said Soames, his breathing shallow and rapid.

'I think I do. I know all your dirty little secrets. Quite the patriot, aren't you?'

'I do what needs to be done, for her majesty, for stability of the empire.'

'Ah, just following orders; the traditional defence of the weak-minded, the gutless and the black of heart.'

'I believe in doing my duty.'

'A zealot then, filled with all the fire and brimstone of righteous cause. What a pathetic excuse for murder.'

'I'm no murderer.'

'Oh yes you are. You were about to add these two young people to your tally, were you not? Your justifications are meaningless, a vain attempt to explain your penchant for death. Do you remember Fenton Street? That night in Dublin?'

'How do you know about that? You've been through Special Branch files, haven't you? That's a hanging offence.'

'Do I seem bothered by the concept?'

Through simmering hysteria, Ada watched as Soames tried to track the Ravener's voice. Try as he might he couldn't locate it. The words flowed from every shadow, oozed from the very stone under her feet. The single, dim gas lamp did little more than illuminate the centre of the room; all else was filled with midnight, pregnant with menace.

'I asked if you remembered Fenton Street?' said the Ravener.

'Of course I do.'

'You committed an atrocity that night.'

'I took out a cell of Fenian bastards.'

'You did. In addition, you also killed twelve families living in the tenement rooms above the men you were hunting. Sixty three innocents all told, twenty of them children. You knew they were there, sleeping peacefully, yet you still set fire to the ground floor with incendiary explosives.'

'It was war,' growled Soames.

'It was murder,' said the Ravener. 'Do you

know what it is like to be burned alive? The most fortunate suffocated before the flames reached them, but the others had to watch their loved ones as the flesh melted from their bones, even as they themselves were consumed. Only one person survived that inferno; a young girl, thrown from the top floor by her mother in the hope that she might live. Despite a broken back she did. Even after all these years she still has nightmares about falling. You cowered in a doorway and watched as they died, your need for revenge blotting out their cries for help.'

'Revenge? It was a sanctioned operation.'

'That may be the case, but the men you targeted were those that set the Clerkenwell Prison bomb in 1867. Correct me if I am wrong, but didn't the explosion kill your little brother and give you that scar on your face?'

'Nobody knew that, not even Halloran. How could you?'

'I told you,' said the Ravener. 'I know everything.'

'I've had enough of your shit. Come out, you coward. Fight me like a man, I dare you.'

'Now why would I do something like that?'

'Because she dies if you don't.' Soames turned to Ada, placing the barrel of his revolver against her forehead. The cold metal dug painfully into her skin, but she smiled at him nonetheless.

'How does it feel to be afraid?' she said.

'I'm not afraid.'

'The sweat running down your face indicates otherwise.' She could see his fingers twitch, tighten on the trigger.

'Show yourself,' Soames demanded.

'Very well, if you insist.'

The Ravener stepped into the light at Ada's side, the darkness peeling away from him like wisps of smoke. He seemed taller than she remembered, thinner too, like some unholy, well-dressed scarecrow.

'So this is what has London in uproar,' said Soames, 'a gentleman in a mask. Did you get lost on your way home from the theatre? Let's see your face, shall we?'

'No,' the Ravener replied.

'I'll kill her if you don't do as I say.'

'I disagree. Miss Phillips is precious to me. She has a destiny, and I will not suffer interference from one such as you.'

'Have it your way,' said Soames, pulling the trigger.

It happened so quickly that Ada didn't have time to blink. Just as he had in the church, the Ravener flowed through the air, a blur in the lamplight. His hand closed round the revolver, the hammer clicking softly against leather of his glove. Soames froze, mouth agape as the man in the mask towered over him.

'How did you…' the policeman gave a choked gasp as the catling entered his back. Ada heard the grating of bone as Soames's spine was severed just above the pelvis. Legs crumpling beneath him, he fell to the floor, moaning piteously.

'You watched that little girl lying on the cobbles, unable to move and crying for her mother. This is what it felt like.' Taking the revolver from Soames' hand, the Ravener threw it across the room.

'They will hunt you down for this, you bastard. You can't just kill someone like me.'

'Oh, but I can. You and your compatriots are part of my design, mere steps along the path to resurrection. Be silent. I will deal with you shortly.' The Ravener turned to Ada, kneeling before her and gently cupping her chin. 'You are safe now, as is the good sergeant.'

'What have I done?' she asked him.

'The inevitable, beloved. Rest now; we will see each other again very soon.'

As he stood up, the Ravener's cloak brushed against Ada's face, a silk-lined promise of a horror yet to come. Knowing she could finally let slip the reins of consciousness, she fell headlong into exhausted sleep. Somewhere in the distance a man was screaming in agony, but Ada paid it no heed. She and Rory were alive, and at that moment it was all that mattered.

CHAPTER 28

Hung Parliament

C lawing her way through layers of suffocating fog, Ada slowly surfaced to a new day. Opening her eyes she saw the comforting confines of her bedroom, rather than the foetid cellar in which she and Rory had been held prisoner. She had no memory of being found or returning to Shoreditch, but there was only one person who could have engineered her rescue. She had no idea how the Ravener had done it, but hopefully it hadn't involved revealing his existence to her grandfather.

Swinging her legs out of bed, Ada shuffled to the bathroom and gingerly washed her face. Her stomach ached terribly, and on lifting her night dress, she saw a livid bruise across her abdomen, a parting gift from Harris. She tried not to think of his gruesome end. He hadn't deserved it, regardless of the Ravener's justification for taking control of her faculties. In retrospect, it was as much a violation of her person as that threatened by Soames. She wondered what had happened to the policeman, but given the Ravener's penchant for public display, she doubted it would be anything less than brutal.

Muffled voices came from downstairs, Sir Edmund's loudest among them. Ada knew there would be questions, and pulling on her dressing gown, she steeled herself to lie. In the parlour she found Mrs Crane, Doctor Fitzpatrick and her grandfather standing in conversation, empty teacups on the table between them.

'Darling!' said Sir Edmund, seeing her in the doorway. He rushed over and enfolded her in a gentle bear hug. 'Say nothing,' he whispered as he kissed her cheek.

Ada returned the hug, smiling at Fitz and Mrs Crane. 'Where's Rory?' she asked.

'He's in his room, sleeping. He's in a poor way and Fitz has been attending to him.'

'That would be a significant understatement,' said Fitz. 'Had Sergeant Canavan received further injury, it is likely he would have died. He has a fractured skull, four broken ribs, a re-broken nose and multiple contusions. In addition I am concerned that he may have internal injuries, but as yet it is too early to tell. It's been a long time since I saw anyone receive such a vicious beating.'

'Is his life in danger?' asked Ada.

'I hesitate to answer that,' said Fitz, 'but I believe he will live as long as complications do not arise. The injury to his head is the most serious matter. Try not to worry though; he is young and as tough as they come. If anyone can put himself back together, it's Rory.'

'Thank you,' said Ada, offering up a silent prayer for her friend's recovery. She turned to her grandfather. 'How did we get here? I can't remember anything.'

'I shall explain on the way to Rookwood. Your father has been asking for you. Fitz has kindly offered to remain here to keep an eye on Rory, aided by the invaluable Mrs Crane of course.'

'I will offer any assistance I can, sir,' said the housekeeper.

'Thank you, everyone,' said Ada. Returning to her room she found Milly waiting for her, a fresh dress laid out on the bed.

'Sir Edmund asked me not to bother you, miss,' said the maid, wringing her hands, 'but are you feeling all right? When he brought you both in late last night, Mrs Crane almost had an attack of the vapours. I washed you as best I could and put you to bed. I had to throw your dress away, it was beyond saving.'

So it was Grandfather who brought us home, thought Ada. How much does he know? What did he see in that cellar? 'Thank you for your kindness, Milly,' she said, 'I'm just tired. It's Sergeant Canavan who needs our attention now.'

'You're not wrong there, miss. Was it those Special Branch types he got on the wrong side of?'

'It's best not to speculate, Milly. It's over now.

I'm leaving for Rookwood shortly to see Father, so while I'm away please help Mrs Crane look after Rory. It would mean a lot to me.'

'Of course, miss.'

Once dressed Ada looked at herself in the mirror. She would have to invent some accident to explain the split lip to her father, but apart from the dark rings under her eyes and the bruising to her cheek she looked reasonably presentable. Leaving Rory in Fitz's capable hands, she climbed into her grandfather's carriage and waited for him to speak.

'What *do* you remember?' he asked, as Baynes clucked on the horses.

Ada took a deep breath and recounted the events of the day before, starting with Rory's abduction. 'I waited for you as long as I could,' she said, 'but when you didn't arrive I had to go in. Please don't be angry with me.'

'I'm not angry with you, darling, just very relieved. Fitz upbraided me yesterday for expecting you to do anything else. You are what I have pushed you to be, and I cannot criticise you for that.'

Ada nodded. 'What about Hamlet? He was shot by Soames.'

'Sadly he succumbed to his wounds. I found his body outside the pumping station. We brought him home with us, brave old soldier that he was. I buried him in your back garden. I hope that was the right thing to do?'

'Thank you, Grandfather,' she said, wiping a tear from the corner of her eye. 'He *was* a brave old soldier, he saved my life.' There was a moment's silence before Ada asked the question that was uppermost in her mind. 'How did you find us?'

Sir Edmund scowled. 'When we left Limehouse I went to see Halloran. I threatened to gut him if he didn't return you safe and sound by midnight, then I went back to Shoreditch and waited. Just before midnight a note from Halloran arrived, giving me the address of a slum dwelling on the edge of Whitechapel. He reassured me that you were relatively unharmed.'

'I'm glad he decided to help you find us, Grandfather,' she said, 'especially given how badly Rory was hurt.'

'Indeed, the threat of extreme violence can work very well if applied with conviction. So, what do you recall about your time in the cellar?'

Ada groaned inwardly. This was what her grandfather really wanted to know. Luckily she had given some thought as to how to respond. 'I remember very little. Soames hit me so hard that I lost consciousness. The next thing I knew I woke up at home.'

'Then we must thank God for small mercies,' said Sir Edmund, seemingly satisfied with her answer. 'When Fitz and I arrived we found you and Rory lying on blankets, battered and bruised but alive. There was a great deal of blood about but no bodies. Someone left us a present though – Soames' bowler hat was sitting upside-down in the middle of the floor. Inside it were a set of male genitalia.'

Ada winced at the thought. 'How do you know it was Soames' hat?'

'His name was embroidered on the headband. As to whether the... contents of the hat were his I cannot comment.'

Ada said nothing, but she knew it was Soames who had suffered the emasculation; he had been about to rape her after all, and the Ravener would hardly let such a thing go unpunished.

'Are you sure there's nothing else?' asked Sir Edmund. 'No clue as to what befell Soames and his men?'

Ada shook her head. 'No, Grandfather, I'm sorry.'

He smiled at her. 'There is no need to apologise. You have been through a terrible ordeal. All that matters is that you and Rory are home, and I don't have to make good on my threat to disembowel Halloran. Perhaps he decided to deal with the matter of Soames *in-house* to avoid any embarrassment.'

'That is possible,' said Ada, knowing it couldn't be farther from the truth.

'And before I forget, I recovered my Webley

from the pumping station.' He dug into his coat pocket and handed the revolver to her. 'I'm somewhat disappointed that you took it without permission. You don't have a license yet, and with Price dead there's no reason for you to carry a firearm. However, if you return it to the armoury then I'm prepared to overlook your lapse in judgement.'

'Thank you, Grandfather,' said Ada, slipping the Webley into her purse. While relieved that he hadn't pressed her as to why she took it in the first place, she had no intention of returning it just yet. This battle of wills with the Ravener was far from over, and while the revolver might be of limited use against such a creature, it was better than nothing.

'Oh, and one more thing,' said Sir Edmund. 'In his note Halloran asked me to meet him on Westminster Bridge at two o'clock. He said he had something of interest to show me. A curious request, don't you think?'

'Very curious,' said Ada, her tender stomach tying itself in knots beneath her corset.

'We're stopping there on the way to Rookwood. It won't add anything to our journey so I hope you don't mind indulging me? It seems a small price to pay to have you back.'

Arriving at Westminster, Baynes brought the carriage to halt and climbed down to open the door. The bridge was busy so Ada and her grandfather waited for Halloran by the parapet. The tide was out, and the mud banks at the river's edge gave off an unpleasant reek. Sir Edmund took out his fob watch and flipped it open. 'I hope he isn't wasting our time,' he said, 'it's almost two.'

'Ah, there you are.'

Ada turned and saw Halloran, hovering somewhat cautiously out of arm's reach of her grandfather.

'Good afternoon, Chief Constable,' said Sir Edmund. 'I received your note. Though it pains me to do so, I must thank you for resolving our little problem.'

Halloran looked confused. 'I am most relieved to see Miss Phillips at your side,' he said, nodding politely to Ada, 'but I didn't send you a note. I haven't been able to locate Soames. My men scoured the city last night, I can assure you, but he seems to have disappeared. I came here because you sent *me* a note, saying that Ada and Rory were safe, and that you wished to ensure there was no further animosity between us.'

Sir Edmund frowned. 'I sent no note.'

'Then I don't understand,' stammered Halloran. 'Who invited us here?'

Inside parliament's clock tower, the great bell began ringing the Westminster Quarters. Ada wondered just what demonstration of his *art* the Ravener had planned for them. Whatever it was, it would not be pleasant. With Josephine dead, Rory incapacitated and her grandfather still unaware of the truth, she had never felt so alone.

As the chimes began for two o'clock, pedestrians stopped to check their watches. The bell struck once, twice, and to the consternation of all kept striking all the way to twelve. The bridge came to a standstill as everyone looked up. Big Ben never struck wrong, it was a matter of national pride.

'What on earth is that?' said a well-dressed man to Ada's right. Her heart sank. So this was the reason for the notes: the Ravener wanted a very public message to be sent, one that struck at the very heart of the establishment. Trussed securely with rope, three bodies dangled from the hour hand of the clock. One hung by his feet, his head missing. The other two were suspended by the neck, and even at this distance Ada could see the dark hole in the centre of each man's chest, let alone their other, equally horrific injuries. Once again the Ravener's perverse sense of humour tailored the punishment to fit the crime. Just following orders, she thought, the defence of the mindless, the gutless, and the black of heart.

'Dear God,' said Halloran, sweat beading on his brow, 'are those my men?' Without a word of farewell, he ran toward Westminster as the crowd began to murmur and shout. Ada knew what was going through their minds. They would be speculating as to whom these men were, and why the Ravener had chosen them to be his next victims.

'It was him,' said Sir Edmund, his gaze fixed upon the bodies, 'the Ravener. He rescued you, sent those letters and then did this.' He pointed at the blood-soaked evidence adorning the clock tower. 'There's no other explanation.'

'I think you may be right,' she said, trying to sound as horrified as her grandfather.

He turned to Ada, searching her face for any sign of obfuscation. 'Are you sure you remember nothing?'

She shook her head, hating herself for having to withhold the truth from a man she loved so much.

'I am sorry,' said Sir Edmund, heaving a sigh. 'This has all come as rather a shock. Witness my art, fear my wrath – there is something quite dreadful about it. Seeking vengeance is a terrible thing, even if it is justified. I've seen men consumed by it, eaten alive until there was nothing left. If you ever meet anyone like that, promise me you'll run the other way and never look back.'

Ada wasn't prepared for this sudden change in her grandfather's demeanour; it was unsettling in the extreme.

'Promise me,' he said again, taking her hand

and gripping it tightly.

With a sad smile she leaned forward and kissed him on the cheek. 'I promise,' she lied.

CHAPTER 29

The Point of No Return

The journey to Rookwood was a silent one. Ada watched her grandfather as he stared out of the carriage window, seemingly lost in thought. The revelation that the Ravener had been the one to save her would no doubt be playing on his mind, but there was nothing she could say to allay his fears. If she told him what had been happening, not only would he not believe her, but he may well assume that she was following her mother into madness and death. Ada knew how much he doted upon her, and strong as he was, the prospect of losing yet another loved one could very well break him. This is my burden, she thought, and I will bear it alone for as long as I can.

The carriage came to a stop outside the sanatorium. 'I'll meet you at the house later,' said Ada. Sir Edmund nodded absently, his face pale and drawn.

'Are you sure you're all right, Grandfather?'

'Yes. I'm just tired, that's all. It's been quite some time since I slept. A brandy and a nap is what I need. Go and see Henry, he's missed you.'

It felt like a polite dismissal but Ada did not object. There would be time for talking later. Climbing out of the carriage, she made her way to her father's room. He was sleeping peacefully, a copy of that day's Times lying open on the bed. She sat at his side, heartened to see that his pallor was much improved.

'Hello, Papa,' she said softly.

Henry Phillips opened his eyes, smiling as he saw his daughter. 'Hello, darling,' he said, 'I was just dreaming about you.'

'Something nice I hope.'

'You were little, and you were bringing your mother some flowers we'd bought from the market. It might have been a memory but I'm too drowsy to tell.' He frowned as he noticed the cut on her lip. 'What happened to your face?'

'Oh, it's nothing, I managed to trip over my skirts and catch it on the side of the dresser; entirely my fault for not paying attention to where I was going. Anyway, how are you feeling?'

'Much better, thank you. Fitz is pleased with my progress. He says I should be able to come home in a week or so if I continue to improve.'

'That's wonderful,' said Ada. 'The house will be ready and waiting for you.'

'I've been keeping abreast of the news too. This Ravener business is gathering a worrying degree of momentum. The papers are all but singing his praises. I can't say I agree with them;

he's a vigilante after all. I wonder how the chief constable is coping with it?'

'That's Halloran's problem, Papa, not yours.'

'I know,' he said, 'but old habits die hard. Still, I will have my practice to attend to soon enough.'

'Indeed you shall.'

'And don't forget that you need to prepare for the start of your degree. It will come round sooner than you think.'

She nodded. He was right, but with everything that had happened she had barely given it a second thought.

'And how is Hamlet? I must admit that I'm looking forward to taking him for a walk.'

Ada's heart sank. 'I'm sorry, Papa, but he passed away yesterday.'

'What?'

'It was all very sudden. It seems that old age finally caught up with him.'

'Oh, that is a blow. I'll miss the old fellow. He didn't suffer I hope?'

'No,' she said, silently screaming inside. 'He just died in his sleep. We buried him in the back garden. I hope that was the right thing to do?'

'Of course, he was family.'

Ada smiled at him. 'I thought you would approve. Oh, and speaking of family, I'm going to visit Mother's grave tomorrow. It would be good for me I think. Perhaps I should bring her some fresh flowers, just like in your dream.'

'That's a lovely idea,' he said, his eyelids drooping.

'Rest now, Papa. I will see you soon.'

Giving her hand a squeeze, Henry settled back into his pillows. By the time she reached the door he was fast asleep.

It was growing dark when Ada left the sanatorium. A chill wind had risen, stripping the leaves from the trees and sending them tumbling across the parkland. Hurrying up the drive she found Hargrave waiting for her in the lobby.

'Good evening, miss,' he said. 'May I take your coat?'

'Thank you. How is Grandfather?'

'He is working, miss. He said he had important papers to review for tomorrow, and asked that he not be disturbed. If he requires anything he will summon me.'

'I see,' said Ada. 'In that case, may I take supper in the library?'

'Of course. I'll bring it through to you at seven. Would you like a pot of coffee in the meantime?'

'That would be splendid.'

As Hargrave went about his duties, Ada stared at the firmly-shut door to her grandfather's study. His reaction at the bridge worried her. He had sounded desperate, scared even, and that was something she had never witnessed before. She considered ignoring his orders, bursting in and asking him outright what was on his mind, but ultimately decided against it. She knew him too well – granddaughter or not, such behaviour on her part would elicit nothing but the most curt of responses.

With a heavy sigh she entered the library. Seating herself on the chaise longue by the fire, she peered into the flames as they danced in the grate. Her body ached, a salient reminder that the previous night she had faced death at Soames' hands. The Ravener's intervention may have saved both her and Rory, but she dreaded what he would demand in recompense. "He wants you to become like him." That's what Josephine had said. It was clear that was what the Ravener was trying to do. By repeatedly showing her the evil that lay beneath the surface of everyday life, he no doubt hoped that she would come to see things as he did. She shook her head. One could not be judge, jury and executioner, whatever the provocation.

'Your coffee, miss,' said Hargrave, appearing at her side with a tray. Ada thanked him, and after pouring her a cup he left as quietly as he had arrived. Craving distraction from her troubles, Ada cast her eyes over the books left piled on the nearby coffee table. There were the expected medical and scientific journals, but hidden among them she found a recently published, leather-bound volume by the philosopher, Friedrich Nietzsche. Picking it up, she ran her fingers over the gilt-embossed title, *Jenseits von Gut und Böse*: Beyond Good and Evil. As she flicked through it, the pages fell open at a chapter bookmarked with a slip of paper. The text was in German but she could translate it well enough. *"He who fights with monsters might take care lest he thereby become a monster. And when you gaze long into an abyss, the abyss also gazes into you."*

A chill ran down her spine as she recalled her encounter with Harris. The Ravener had shown her what could happen when vengeance was allowed free rein. Untempered by mercy it was nothing more than callous self-indulgence, a means to an end that gnawed at the very fabric of society's rules. We all have the capacity for violence, she thought, but most of us choose not to act upon it, to turn our back on the abyss' dread gaze. Curious as to why her grandfather had marked that specific page, Ada resolved to speak to him about it. If there was something playing on his mind, perhaps the book had some bearing on what it might be?

Feeling her eyes begin to close, Ada set the book aside and lay back on the chaise longue. Her battered body demanded sleep and there was no reason to deny it. Piece by ragged piece the day fell away, and warmed by the fire she drifted slowly into darkness.

'Ada. You need to come with me now,' said a familiar voice.

'Please let me be,' she begged, 'I am so tired.'

'Alas I cannot, there is something I wish you to see.'

Unable to resist his compulsion, Ada got to her feet. She was still in the library, but the French doors leading to the front of the house were open. A gentle breeze rippled the silk curtains; beyond them stood the Ravener, hand extended in invitation.

'Where are we going?' she asked wearily.

'To your final test, beloved. If you succeed then my work will be almost complete.'

'And if I fail?'

'Then I will fade into memory, and the weight of regret will lie heavy on your shoulders.'

A carriage was waiting some distance down the drive. Gravel crunched softly underfoot as Ada walked toward it, the night air stroking the folds of her dress. She knew she was dreaming but it all felt so real. The door to the carriage stood open, and after helping her inside the Ravener sat opposite. He felt more present this time, less ethereal, as if her choice to let him in allowed him to be fully inside her head.

'Do you approve of what I did with Soames and his men?' he asked.

'I am grateful that you saved our lives,' said

Ada, 'but I do not understand your need to defile the bodies of your victims. You eat their hearts.'

'That is not true,' said the Ravener. 'I take but a single bite. That is all I require to restore myself to what I was.'

'But *why* do you eat from their hearts?' said Ada. 'It is loathsome.'

'It is necessary,' said the Ravener, his voice even and patient. 'The sin they contain is powerful. By consuming it I make it mine.'

'And why do you need such power?'

'I cannot fulfil my purpose without it. I am still but a shadow, and the souls of the faithful cry out for vengeance. I am simply righting an old wrong, Ada.'

'And what kind of wrong could justify the suffering you have caused my family?'

The Ravener sighed. 'Know that I had no choice. When one is faced with oblivion, any avenue of escape is better than the alternative.'

'Tell that to my mother. I saw the agony she endures at your hand, yet you still insist that you love me, that you have walked beside me all of my life. How can you expect me to have any sympathy?'

The Ravener shook his head. 'You saw what I wanted you to see. Clara does not suffer in the way Madame would have you believe. From the beginning I have been so very hard on you, but every trial you faced was necessary. Your will, your strength of character, your desire to make a difference – you have proved yourself time and again. Once my work is complete you shall be my last chance at redemption.'

'I will not become you. You are nothing more than a demon in fine clothing.'

'You wish to be a doctor, do you not? How can you make a diagnosis without all the facts? As I told you in the foster home, when you finally know the truth it will indeed break your heart.'

Ada didn't reply. It was difficult to fault his logic and his sincerity was clear.

'I make you a vow,' said the Ravener. 'Tomorrow night I will stand before you and explain everything. If you truly desire to end my life, I shall let you. One way or another, Clara will be free.'

'After everything you have done, you would just let her go?' asked Ada, incredulous.

'Yes, but before that happens we have an appointment to keep at The Marylebone Cholera Hospital. Our quarry is a nurse called Anna Hyde. On the surface she is a veritable Florence Nightingale, dutiful, self-effacing, tending to the most acute cases when other staff dare not enter the room.'

'And what has she done that warrants death at your hand?'

'She is deliberately infecting people with the disease.'

'That cannot be,' said Ada, 'it makes no sense.'

'Evil rarely does. She mops the brows of her patients as they die in agony, savouring every moment.'

Ada felt nothing but revulsion; such actions went against everything she believed in, everything her grandfather had taught her. 'But she's a nurse, why would she do something so appalling?'

'There is a hunger inside her that cannot be sated. She craves the attention of the afflicted, their worship even. When the cholera outbreaks stopped due to the efforts of Mr Bazalgette, she watched as her unwilling congregation grew ever smaller. The solution to this dilemma was quite simple. She took samples from those still in her care, from their blood, their urine, their excrement, and used it to contaminate a public drinking fountain. The effects were short lived, but it was long enough for eight people to be stricken with the disease. Miss Hyde was overjoyed. She had new patients to tend to, new sickness to wallow in.'

'Dear God,' said Ada.

'When she realised that nobody knew what she had done, she decided to do it again, and again, all over London. Rich or poor, old or young, she did not discriminate. Over the last decade she has killed ninety four people, and permanently sickened many more.'

'She must be mad!'

'Quite the opposite,' said the Ravener. 'I would not harm someone who has no volition over their actions. Miss Hyde is completely sane, but she *chooses* to do harm when others would find it abhorrent.'

'And you intend to stop her, I take it?'

'Would you prefer that I left her alone? She would never be tried for her crimes, there is no evidence. In the eyes of the public she is a heroine of sorts. If I do nothing she will continue to kill. She may get careless and be caught one day, who knows, but are you willing to let more innocents die to soothe your conscience? What if the next fountain to receive her blessing is on your street? What if Milly takes a sip as she returns from shopping? Will you stand at her graveside and weep tears of hapless regret?'

Ada bowed her head, horrified at the concept. She wished that Hargrave would wake her up, save her from such terrible realities, but that would only delay the inevitable. Her mother's soul was at stake; all she could do was face whatever test was coming. She remained silent for the rest of the journey, ignoring the Ravener as he watched her from behind his mask.

'We are here,' he said, as the carriage came to a stop outside the hospital.

'Are you not concerned that someone will

notice you?' she asked him, 'you are hardly inconspicuous.'

'I find that people ignore things they don't wish to see,' he replied. 'Stay close, Miss Hyde's personal fiefdom is not far.' Ada followed the Ravener inside. Despite them passing close to the main desk, the night porter sitting behind it didn't so much as look up. The quarantine ward was easy to find. The astringent tang of disinfectant could not disguise the stench of human waste that filled the corridor.

'A piteous sight is it not?' said the Ravener.

Ada saw a long, high-ceilinged room, ten beds to each wall. Five were occupied, and in the nearest lay an elderly man, a nurse sitting by his side. 'Is that her?' she asked.

'Yes. That poor man will die soon, along with the others. When they are gone you know what she will do. She could not stop herself, even if she wanted to.'

Ada walked over to Miss Hyde, looking for some outward sign of the evil that lay within her. There was nothing. She was just an ordinary woman, holding a damp cloth to the forehead of a dying man. 'How do you know that she is guilty?' she asked. 'How can you be so sure that she is a murderer?'

The Ravener chuckled. 'You will find out soon enough.'

The nurse looked up, meeting Ada's gaze.

'Who are you?' she said. 'You're not supposed to be in here. Leave at once or I shall call an orderly.'

'You… can see me?'

'Of course I can see you. Are you suffering from some disorder of the mind?'

Ada's head swam, a combination of the cloying miasma in the ward and utter confusion. If the nurse could see her, there was only one conclusion to be drawn; she had made an assumption, and she was very, very wrong. Swallowing hard, she turned to the Ravener. 'I'm really here, with you, aren't I?'

He nodded. 'Your physical presence is required on this occasion.'

'Who are you talking to?' said Miss Hyde. 'You are clearly disturbed. I shall fetch someone to deal with you.' She made to leave but the Ravener swept forward, his cloak billowing round him like a death shroud. Placing his hand upon the nurse's forehead, she fell unconscious into his arms. Picking her up as if she weighed nothing, he carefully laid her limp body on an empty bed.

'What did you just do?' asked Ada, still shocked by the realisation that she was not dreaming.

'I have given Miss Hyde something I withheld from the other murderers. It is in my gift to ensure that even the worst of them does not endure the same pain as their victims. My purpose is to remove their sin from this world, not to create more suffering. In my anger, my desire for vengeance, I felt justified in giving those that came before some measure of hell, but there is no need for it now. I have hope, and that is enough.'

The Ravener reached into his medical bag and drew out the catling. Bile rose in Ada's throat. 'I will not kill for you,' she said, utterly resolute.

'I would not expect you to do such a thing.'

'Then why go to the trouble of bringing me here?'

'It is a matter of perspective. I wish you to see the world as it is, not as you believe it to be.' He sliced open the nurse's uniform, baring her chest. 'You do not have to watch, but you may not run, even if every fibre of your being screams out to do so. I need you here.'

Ada heard his words as if through fog, muffled and soft. The tone was not that of an order, more of a plea. 'I cannot stop you, but please make it quick,' she said, averting her eyes.

'I always do.'

Ada could not shut out the sounds of Anna Hyde's death, but the Ravener was true to his word. It was over almost as soon as it had begun.

'This is why I require your presence,' he said, standing before her. 'Look at me – I have a gift for you.' In his cupped hands he held the nurse's heart; a pulsating lump of rotting flesh, it stank of wickedness. 'It is time for you to taste the nature of evil.'

Ada took a step back, repulsed by the thought of taking a bite from such a disgusting object.

'You misunderstand,' said the Ravener, seeming to read her mind. 'To consume it would drive you insane, drown you in hate. Merely touch it to your lips. Only then will you comprehend the nature of what I face.'

'I cannot,' said Ada. 'It is too much.'

'Please, take this final step. It will be the last thing I ever ask of you. Do this and I will set Clara free, I swear it.'

'How can I believe you?' said Ada, her mouth dry and tasting of ash.

'I have never lied to you, beloved,' said the Ravener, 'not once.'

'You will keep your word? Release my mother from her prison?'

'On my oath, yes.'

'Then I do this for her, you monster,' she said.

'I know,' he replied.

The urge to pull away was overwhelming, but Ada fought it with every ounce of strength she possessed. Bowing her head, she brushed her lips against the awful, dripping thing in the Ravener's hands. The nurse's sins poured into her, a wave of twisted emotion and thought, thunderous in their power. Shaking uncontrollably, tears ran down her face as she bore witness to every unholy act Anna Hyde had perpetrated. There was no empathy, no love, no consideration for the suffering of others, only the hideous desire to continue her work. Ada felt the death of all the nurse's victims, shared their fear, saw the grief of their families. If she had been able to scream, the whole of London would have heard her. Sinking to her knees, she wrapped her arms around herself and sobbed.

'This is what a true monster looks like,' said the Ravener, placing a gentle hand on her shoulder. 'This is what I seek to stop.'

'How do you bear it?' said Ada.

'It is my duty, but with such terrible knowledge comes a gift. Close your eyes, be still. Reach out and tell me what you see.'

Her mind still brimming with horrid imagery, Ada tried her best to do as he asked. At first she saw nothing, but as her breathing slowed and equilibrium returned, the strangest of sensations filled her. She could feel the pulse of the sleeping city, a vast, slow heartbeat. People walking the nearby streets had auras, flickers of colour that wreathed them like Saint Elmo's fire. Some were so bright, it was almost blinding. She wanted to hold them close, bask in the inherent glory of their souls, but scattered among them like cancerous cells were those whose auras were a putrid green or oily black. Ada recoiled, instinctively knowing such individuals had committed acts of atrocity.

'Murderers all,' said the Ravener. 'Can you not feel the surgeon in you reaching for the knife?'

'I… I do not know,' said Ada, unable to think clearly.

'Food for thought, perhaps? You are indeed a brave soldier, beloved, and have more than earned the answers you seek. There is one last thing I need to do, but once I am finished I shall stand before you and await your judgement. My life, Ada Phillips, will be in your hands.'

CHAPTER 30

Hard Rain

A da woke with a start. She lay on the chaise longue in the library, her neck stiff and a lingering bitterness on her lips. At her side, a plate of stale sandwiches sat on the coffee table, no doubt left there by Hargrave. The fire was out, the air was chill, and beyond the French doors dark clouds covered the sky. On the mantelpiece, the carriage clock showed it was gone midday. Wondering why no one had woken her, Ada got to her feet and entered the lobby. Apart from the soft sighing of wind in the eaves, the great house was utterly silent.

The door to her grandfather's study stood open so Ada walked over, hoping that he was ready to talk. To her dismay he wasn't there, but sanatorium files that he had been working on sat open on his desk, alongside a tumbler of brandy and a half-smoked cigar. 'Grandfather?' she called out. 'Anyone?' There was no response, and with a growing sense of unease she ventured downstairs to the kitchen. The range was still warm, but Hargrave and Mrs Fletcher were nowhere to be seen. The adjacent servants' quarters were also deserted, the chattering of chambermaids and the sounds of domestic activity conspicuous by their absence. 'What on earth is going on?' Ada muttered. 'Where is everyone?'

For one horrible moment she wondered if the Ravener was responsible, but just as quickly dismissed the idea. There was no evil within these walls, no reason to harm anyone. He wanted her understanding, her love, and striking at those she had known all her life would destroy any hint of sympathy she had. There must be a logical explanation for this, she thought, I just don't know what it is yet.

Berating herself for assuming the worst, Ada fetched her coat from the cloakroom. Some fresh air would do much to clear her head, and she had promised her father she would visit Clara's grave today. After that she would head to the sanatorium and seek out her grandfather. Not only did she wish to know where the staff had gone, but there was still the matter of what he had said at Westminster Bridge. The more she thought about it, the more Ada was convinced that he was keeping something from her. They had always shared everything, and for him to withdraw like this upset her greatly.

Making her way to the orangery, Ada cut a spray of orchids before leaving via the garden door. She had meant to do this for months, but had always found an excuse not to. Now things were different, her world had changed forever, and it was time to make amends. Walking past flowerbeds covered in winter straw, she pondered on her experience at the hospital. For one brief moment she had viewed the world through the Ravener's eyes, experienced a heightened level of perception she didn't think possible. He can actually see evil, she thought, and it drives him to kill, but why was it so important that he share that knowledge? She shook her head. If he had sought to sway her to his cause, he had failed. Knowing that someone was evil to their core did not give him the right to butcher them.

And then there were the Ravener's parting words. He had said that he had one last thing to do, and Ada dreaded what it might me. Time and again he had spoken of his need to balance the scales: that twenty were taken and twenty would pay. He had claimed eight hearts that Ada knew of, and if she was right he needed twelve more. Something truly monstrous was going to occur, and if the Ravener was to make good on his promise to reveal all this very night, it would happen soon.

Putting such grim thoughts aside, Ada followed the gravel path to her mother's grave. Just as it had in her dreams, it lay in the shadow of an ancient oak, enclosed by a wrought iron fence. The words carved into the headstone were supposed to bring comfort, yet they rang hollow for Ada, even more so now she knew the truth.

"*Clara Phillips. Wife and Mother. May She Rest in Peace at Last. Free from Suffering.*"

'But you're not free, are you?' she said, kneeling to place the flowers she carried. 'I spent so long hating you for your madness, for what you did to our family, to Milly, now I know better. I see clearly, Mother, and understand what tormented you. It will end soon, I promise. Then you can truly rest. I swear it.'

A peal of thunder sounded overhead as spots of rain began to drum on Ada's coat. She looked up at the sky; black clouds, backlit by flashes of lightning threatened a winter storm. It suited her mood perfectly. Touching her fingers to her lips she pressed them to the headstone. 'Pray for me, Mother,' she said, 'as I pray for you.'

A muffled whinny reached her ears. Turning her head, she saw a man riding a horse at speed toward the northern boundary of the park. At this distance it was difficult to make out who it was, but she recognised the black gelding. Eighteen hands high and with white fetlocks, it could only be Shiva, her grandfather's mount. Jumping to her feet Ada ran toward the stable yard. She would not tolerate being kept at arm's length any longer. If Sir Edmund would not come to her, she would damn well go to him. In one of the stalls Ada found her own mare, Chandi. Tacking her up as quickly as she could, she mounted side-saddle and kicked the horse into a gallop, heading for where she last saw Shiva. Thunder sounded again – closer this time – and the rain began in earnest, hammering down in vast, rippling sheets.

'Grandfather!' Ada shouted, but the rising wind snatched her words away. Half-blinded by the downpour she could see nothing but empty parkland, dotted with copses of trees. Soaked to the skin and with fingers growing numb on the reins, Ada pressed on. Long, uncomfortable minutes passed, and by the time she reached the edge of the estate she was shivering with cold. Desperate to get out of the rain, she followed the boundary fence in the hope of finding some shelter. She hadn't gone far when a glimmer of light caught her eye. Riding toward it as fast as she dared, a small, thatched cottage emerged from the gloom. Hitched to a post in the lee of the gable wall, was Shiva.

Furious at having to go to such lengths simply to have a conversation, Ada dismounted and burst in, not bothering to knock. She found herself in a sparsely furnished kitchen, an oil lamp burning brightly on the table. 'Grandfather, are you here?' There was no reply, but on the far side of the room a door stood slightly ajar. From behind it, Ada could hear the sound of a man weeping. It was soft at first, but as she listened the cries grew louder and more ragged, as if dignified mourning had turned to unbearable grief; pure despair given voice, a recognition that all hope, all love, had been torn away and ground to dust.

'Grandfather?' she said again, scarcely able to believe that he was capable of such raw emotion. The awful keening abruptly ceased as if a switch had been thrown. In its place, an ominous silence settled upon the cottage. Dry mouthed and shaking, Ada walked slowly over and pushed the door wide. Lit by a flickering candle, the room beyond was devoid of life, but resting on the coverlet of a narrow bed was an open, black-leather medical bag. At its side, lips pursed in the most extreme of disapproval, lay a horribly familiar velvet mask.

Ada froze, all thoughts of being warm and dry completely forgotten. Of all the things she had expected to find, this was not one of them. Forcing her reluctant feet onward she hesitantly approached the bed. Inside the bag, a finely-honed catling lay on a wad of folded muslin. Grasping the ebony handle, Ada carefully lifted the knife up into the light, turning it over in her hand. Made by Gardner of Edinburgh, it was the same model as that used by her father, and grandfather. I have one too, she thought, it sits in my room at home, waiting for me.

Returning the catling, she reached down and picked up the Ravener's mask. The velvet was soft to the touch, the design stern, yet beautiful. 'Why do you wear this?' she said, placing it over her face. 'What are you hiding?' A mirror hung on the wall, and turning toward it she stared at her reflection. Were it not for the hair draped in lank ropes about her shoulders, she would not have recognised herself.

A clap of thunder shook the cottage. Chandi gave a frightened whinny and Ada cursed herself for not taking the time to hitch her properly. Throwing the mask on the bed she dashed outside, taking firm hold of the horse's bridle while trying to calm her. 'There, there, it's all right,' she said, looking over her shoulder to check on Shiva. Her heart sank when she saw that he was gone. 'Damn it!' she shouted.

A flash arced across the sky, and for one brief second the landscape was rendered bright as day. Atop a rise some hundred yards distant, Ada saw a black-clad figure sitting astride Shiva. She couldn't make out their face through the downpour, and as darkness fell once again they turned and rode away. Vaulting into the saddle Ada set off in pursuit, trying to quell the panic that grew inside her. She didn't know if she chased the Ravener or her grandfather, and the fact that they might be one and the same was almost too much to bear. The Ravener's words came back to haunt her then, a mocking reminder that there was still so much she did not know. "The truth, were I to reveal it to you now, would break your heart."

Fighting back tears, Ada galloped headlong through the park. Deer scattered, copses of trees blurred past and all around her the storm vented its fury. With every roll of thunder Chandi grew more and more skittish, hooves slipping on the wet grass. The rain turned to hail, forcing Ada to shield her eyes as she searched desperately for Shiva. There was no sign of him, and howling in frustration she urged her horse onward.

Without warning, a jagged bolt of lightning struck the branches of a nearby oak. The huge tree was rent asunder with an ear-splitting crack, sparks and splinters of wood flying in all directions. Already unsettled by the storm, Chandi dipped her head and bolted. Dropping the now useless the reins, Ada dug white-knuckled hands into the horse's mane, sat tight in the saddle and prayed. The world around her shrank to a grey, frozen nightmare, hail raising welts on her skin as the panicked horse tore across sodden pasture.

After what felt like an eternity Chandi's pace began to slow, but suddenly, from out of the murk, a high wooden fence rose up to block her path. For one horrifying moment Ada thought the horse might attempt to jump it, but at the last second Chandi shied violently to one side, losing her footing on the icy ground and crashing to her knees. Ada flew from the saddle and landed hard, striking her head and driving the wind from her lungs. With a groan she rolled onto her back, limbs numb and the world spinning crazily around her. From far away she heard a deep voice ask if she was all right. She tried to answer but could not; her mind and body had slipped quietly away from each other. I was so close, she thought, so very close, then everything faded to black.

'They hurt you so badly,' said Ada, stroking the bruises on Rory's face.

'They did,' he said, giving her a sad smile. 'I miss you.'

Ada nodded, trying not to cry. 'I miss you too. I'm frightened. It all ends tonight and I do not know what the outcome will be. I wish you were by my side.' The air around Rory shimmered, an aura with all the colours of the rainbow. There was not a trace of corruption in it.

'I'll be at your side for as long as you want me, lass,' he said, taking her hand in his, squeezing it gently, 'but I doubt your grandfather would approve.'

'His approval is neither here nor there,' said Ada. 'I fear he has done something terrible, something I do not understand.'

'Sir Edmund does nothing without reason. Ask him if you are worried.'

'I have been trying, but he flees from me.'

'He cares for you deeply. He's watched over you since you were born.'

'So has the Ravener, Rory.'

'Do you truly believe they could be one and the same?'

'I no longer know what to think. I wait for the Ravener to tell me the truth, to reveal what lies hidden beneath the skin of my life.'

'I know a great truth,' said Rory.

'You love me, don't you?'

'Since the day we met, but I fear I may never open my eyes again. My head aches so badly and all is fever. Can we not simply leave, put this nightmare behind us? Is there not somewhere you would rather be?'

'I cannot run from this, Rory, but there is a place I would take you, if only to breathe a different air.'

'You sound like you're going away.'

'I may not have a choice,' said Ada.

'There is always a choice.'

'How I wish that were so.'

'Am I dreaming you or are you dreaming me?' he asked.

'Perhaps we dream each other,' she replied, kissing him softly on the forehead.

'Miss Ada? Can you 'ear me?'

Her eyes snapped open. Wrapped in a rough woollen blanket, she lay on a soft bed of sweet-smelling straw. Warmth washed over her, and at her side knelt a huge man, his craggy face full of concern. She tried to move but pain lanced through her skull.

'Easy, miss, you took a nasty blow falling off yer horse. Here, let me.' Putting an arm round her shoulders, the man helped her sit up. 'Take a sip of water,' he said, holding out a battered tin mug.

'Thank you,' she croaked, gratefully easing the dryness in her throat. 'Where am I?'

'You're in my forge, miss.'

'Oh, I see. My apologies but I don't think we've met. I don't know your name.'

The man smiled shyly. 'No, miss, we've never met. I'm Sir Edmund's blacksmith and farrier. My name is Thomas, Thomas Quick.'

CHAPTER 31

The Last Supper

'It's a pleasure to meet you, Mr Quick.' said Ada, 'How did you find me?'

'I heard your horse, miss, she cried out when she fell. Lucky for you it was just outside.'

'Where is Chandi? Is she all right?'

'She'll be lame for a few days but she didn't break her legs, which is a mercy.'

'Thank God,' said Ada, drawing the blanket tighter around her. As she did so, she realised her coat and dress were absent. All she had on were her corset and underclothes.

Thomas reddened about the face. 'I do beg your pardon, miss, but I had to remove your things. They were soaked through and you were freezing, it was the only way to make sure you didn't get ill. I've watched men die of the cold after they got wet, and I didn't want that happening to you.'

'That's quite all right, Mr Quick,' said Ada. She could see her coat and dress laid out by the glowing forge, steam rising in slowly-curling spirals. 'I take no offence, and thank you for your kindness, you may have saved my life. I was out riding and got caught in the storm.'

'Sir Edmund would be furious if I let anything happen to you, miss. I owe him a great deal and this is the least I could do.'

Ada nodded, but at the mention of her grandfather's name all the confusion and doubt came flooding back. She didn't want to believe that he could be the Ravener, but there was no way for her to discount the possibility. He had walked beside her all of her life. Had she really been so blind that she hadn't been able to see for him for what he actually was? Could he have made some infernal bargain of his own, played Faust to another's Mephistopheles in order to gain the preternatural skills the Ravener had demonstrated?

'Have you seen Grandfather today, Mr Quick?' she asked. 'I thought I saw him riding Shiva in the park, so I took Chandi out to join him. That's when I got caught in the storm.'

The blacksmith shook his head. 'No, miss. Not today. I've been busy making new horseshoes.'

'Ah, well, never mind. I'm sure I shall speak to him later.' The thought filled her with dread. There was a conversation to be had and the outcome could be devastating. 'So you work for Grandfather?' she asked, unable to stop herself shivering.

'Yes, miss. For three years now. Here, I'll

fetch you something to warm you up.' Taking a saucepan from the edge of the forge, he filled the tin mug with dark liquid. 'Beef tea,' he said, 'a soldier's remedy I swear by.'

She smiled and sipped on it gratefully. 'Were you a soldier then?'

He nodded. 'I was in Africa. A sergeant. I've always had a way with horses, so they put me in charge of looking after them. They're cleverer than most people think. They know who to trust, and they would always come to me when they were hurt.'

Ada watched him as he spoke. To her surprise, she saw a pale-white aura playing about his body. It was a tabula rasa of sorts, as if he were waiting for someone to write the story of his life upon it. There was no malice in him, only a yearning to be of use, to do his duty. Ada wondered how long this *gift* she had acquired would last. Was it permanent, or would it fade unless she drank the sins of another murderer?

'Are you all right, miss?'

'My apologies, Mr Quick,' said Ada, realising that she had been staring at him. 'I'm still rather dizzy. Tell me, how did you end up as Grandfather's blacksmith?'

'I got injured, miss,' he replied, pointing to a livid scar on the side of his head.

'That must have been an awful wound.'

'It was. I got hit with an assegai spear at

Rorke's drift. It cut into my brain.'

'Dear God, you were lucky to survive that battle.'

'Yes, miss. Surgeon-Major Reynolds thought I was likely to die, but somehow I didn't. They discharged me, shipped me 'ome, and when I got back to London I learned that my wife and daughter were dead. Some thief had robbed our cottage and killed them. I was a cripple, all alone and with nothing to live for, but then Sir Edmund found out what had happened. He brought me to the sanatorium, and once I was well again he gave me a job, let me live here with the horses. It made me very happy.'

'I'm sorry to hear of your misfortune, Mr Quick,' said Ada. 'You are a brave man, and I'm glad you have found somewhere to call home. It's so strange that we've never met.'

'I just keep to myself, miss. I don't really like company. I have the only friends I need right here, I'll show you.' Lighting an oil lantern, Thomas walked to the opposite side of the forge. Next to him, two midnight-black mares stood quietly in their stalls, chewing on bags of hay. 'This is Mari and Uma,' he said. 'They used to be Sir Edmund's carriage horses.'

'I wondered what had happened to them,' said Ada. 'I thought they'd been put out to pasture?'

'No, miss, Sir Edmund gave them to me to

look after, along with that.' He pointed to the silhouette of a finely appointed Clarence carriage. 'It needed repairs so I took the time to fix it, made new leaf-springs and rebuilt the axles. Good as new it is.'

Ada's skin prickled. The Ravener had a carriage take me to Marylebone, she thought. He would have needed a coachman too. Then again, London was full of both, and Thomas radiated such simple purity that it was difficult to see him as an accessory to murder.

'You are a marvel, Mr Quick,' said Ada, trying not to lose herself in wild supposition. 'I'm sure Grandfather appreciates your talents.'

Thomas nodded. 'We all need a purpose, miss. Without that what are we?'

'I quite agree. May I ask what time it is?'

'It's almost six, miss. You were dead to world for several hours. I was about to send to the sanatorium for help.'

'You have done me a great service,' said Ada, 'but I must get back to Rookwood. There are important matters I have to attend to and they can't wait.'

'I understand, miss, I have things to do myself. The storm's blown over so I'll walk with you. Chandi shouldn't be ridden for a few days.'

'Thank you. That would be most helpful.' Thomas turned aside while Ada dressed, and once she was ready, he took Chandi's reins and led them through the park. As she trudged across the wet grass, Ada steeled herself for what was to come. One way or another this nightmare would end tonight, and she couldn't decide whether the concept filled her with relief or utter terror. On reaching the entrance to the stable yard, Thomas took his leave. 'I'd better be getting back miss.'

'I cannot thank you enough for your help, Mr Quick,' said Ada. 'I hope we shall meet again very soon.'

'I'm sure we will, miss.' Nodding politely, he turned away and strode off into the night.

Returning Chandi to her stall, Ada noticed that Shiva was back in his usual place, coat shining and mane brushed. Had she not seen him earlier, she would not have known he had left the stables at all. Tired, sore, and filled with a growing sense of apprehension, she walked slowly across the yard and entered the great house. It was as silent as when she had left, the atmosphere still and oppressive as if the very stone was holding its breath.

Ada climbed the back stairs to her mother's old room, removed her filthy clothes and ran herself a bath. Once clean and with her hair pinned up, she unwrapped one of the dresses Sir Edmund had brought from Paris. Slipping it on she looked at herself in the mirror; it was both beautiful and practical in its simplicity, a uniform for a doctor and armour against the ills of the world. Barely a week had passed since her birthday, yet it felt like a lifetime. Taking the deepest of breaths she made her way to the lobby, hoping against hope that her fears were groundless. The lamps in her grandfather's study had been lit, and, summoning all her courage, Ada walked in. He was sitting behind his desk, his back to her as he stared out of the window.

'Good evening,' she said, more abruptly than she would have wished. He turned round, looking at her with hollow eyes.

'Ah, there you are. I was wondering where you'd got to.' His voice was soft, his tone one of distraction.

Ada wanted nothing more than to go to him, to hold the man she respected and loved, but she remained steadfast in her need for answers. 'Where are the staff, Grandfather? Why is the house empty?'

He paused, as if unsure of how to answer such a simple question. 'I sent them away for the day. They have all worked so hard.'

'That seems an odd thing to do.'

'It is my house and I shall run it as I see fit!' he barked.

Ada took a step back. He had never spoken to her so brusquely. 'Very well,' she said. 'As you say, Rookwood is indeed your domain. I fell asleep in the library last night, and when I woke there was no one to be found. I was concerned, that's all.'

'Forgive me,' said Sir Edmund, rubbing a hand over his face, 'I am very tired. I have been at the sanatorium all day, attending to a desperately ill patient. It has left me quite out of sorts.'

'I see,' said Ada, but she couldn't help but notice that he kept avoiding her gaze. He was hiding something, she was sure of it now. Just as she had with Thomas, Ada caught a glimpse of the aura that swirled around her grandfather. A sickly chartreuse, it did not speak to her of evil, but of an awful mix of guilt and fear.

'Mrs Fletcher left us some dinner in the pantry,' he said, 'I shall go and fetch it. You must be hungry.' Getting up from his chair he brushed past her, almost furtive in his manner as he scurried off below stairs.

Feeling sick to her stomach Ada took a seat by the unlit fire, mortally afraid of her grandfather's reaction when she told him of her discovery. He returned a short time later, a tray of cold cuts, bread and condiments in his hands. Placing it on the table between them he sat opposite, struggling to appear jovial.

'I thought we'd have a picnic of sorts before you return home,' he said. 'I'm sorry it's not up to our usual standard.'

'I thought I'd stay here tonight,' said Ada, refusing to be so easily dismissed, 'keep you company and see Father in the morning.'

'Oh, there's no need for you to amuse me,'

he said. 'I have a lot of work to do and I'll be glad of the peace and quiet. Fitz has a carriage at the sanatorium, I'm sure he won't mind you borrowing it for an hour.'

Ada hated herself for what she was about to do, but her grandfather left her no choice. She would have to challenge him, even if it meant becoming the target of his wrath. 'I took Chandi for a ride today,' she said. 'We were caught in the storm, and I took refuge in one of the estate cottages.'

'I hope the tenant didn't mind?'

'No, the cottage was empty. I did see something strange, however.'

Sir Edmund blinked rapidly. 'And what might that have been?'

'I saw someone riding Shiva. I assumed it was you.'

'As I already told you, I was at the damn sanatorium, and nobody but me touches that horse!'

'How curious,' said Ada, fighting to maintain her composure. 'I tried to catch up with this mystery rider, but the storm frightened Chandi and she bolted. I was thrown off and knocked unconscious.'

'Dear God, are you hurt?'

'I've suffered worse. Luckily a good Samaritan found me – Thomas Quick, your blacksmith.' To Ada's dismay Sir Edmund flinched as if struck.

'Thomas, yes, he's a good man, a very good man, knows the meaning of duty.' He nodded as the words tumbled from his mouth, as if to reassure himself that what he was saying was true.

'I'm not leaving until you tell me what is wrong,' said Ada, leaning forward. 'It has been a long time since I was a child, Grandfather, and I will not be treated as one. You haven't been yourself since we saw the bodies on Westminster Bridge yesterday. You have experienced far worse in your life – why would such a thing scare an old soldier like you?'

'It did not scare me.'

'Yes, it did!' Ada shouted. 'You reek of fear and I can smell it. I found a bag of surgical instruments and a carnival mask when I took shelter in that cottage. Were they yours? What have you done, Grandfather?' She found herself taken aback by the vehemence of her words; for one moment she had sounded just like the Ravener.

Sir Edmund finally looked at her, his eyes brimming with unshed tears. Ada reached out, taking the old man's hands in hers; preparing herself for what he might admit to.

'You mean everything to me,' he said, his voice barely more than a whisper. 'You are too young to have regrets, but I have so many that I cannot bear the weight of them.' He stared at the portrait above the fireplace. 'We were so happy, your grandmother and I. How swiftly the past comes back to haunt us.'

'What is wrong, tell me?' It was all Ada could do not to scream at him.

'I have done terrible things, my darling. If you turned your face from me, I think I may die. So much blood is on my hands, and yet…'

In the empty, quiet house, the sudden jangling of the doorbell made Ada jump. 'I should get that,' said Sir Edmund, and before Ada could object he strode from the study, leaving her slumped disconsolately in her chair. It seemed that her worst fears were indeed justified, and it was all she could do not to weep.

Muffled voices came from the lobby and moments later her grandfather returned. He came to stand by her side, a telegram in his hand.

'No doubt it's something at the hospital that requires my attention,' he said wearily, 'there's a carriage waiting for me outside.' He opened the telegram and read the contents.

Ada watched in horror as her grandfather's face lost every trace of colour. It wasn't just pale, it was ashen. Tears ran down his face and his mouth hung open, his expression one of utter despair. 'What is it?' she asked.

'I… I have to go. I'm sorry.' Crushing the telegram in his fist, he dropped it to the floor.

'Let me come with you.'

'No!' he shouted. 'You must stay here. Wait for me to come back.'

'But...' Ada's protestations fell on deaf ears as Sir Edmund stormed from the house, pausing only to grab his coat.

For a moment Ada was too stunned to move, but then the frustration at being denied answers became too much. 'Damn you, no, I will not wait,' she said, striking the arm of her chair. Picking up the crumpled telegram, she read the words that had so upset her grandfather.

"*YOU ARE CORDIALLY INVITED TO JOIN THE SURVIVING MEMBERS OF YOUR OLD UNIT FOR DINNER AT THE CARMICHAEL STOP IT WILL BE SO LOVELY TO SEE YOU ALL AGAIN STOP I GATHER THE FOOD THERE IS QUITE EXQUISITE.*"

Ada swallowed hard. The phrasing of those words, the menace that lay within them – it was the Ravener, and he had summoned her grandfather to his London club. To know that Sir Edmund was not the masked vigilante filled her with the most profound relief, but his reaction to the telegram was chilling. Coupled with his recent behaviour and her discovery in the cottage, she could think of only one possible explanation. Her grandfather was no stranger to the man in the mask; he may even know their identity, and he was terrified.

Ada shook with rage at such a betrayal.

Despite all his reassurances, all his twisted declarations of love, the Ravener had been toying with her all along. The scene was set for his grand finale, a grim harvest with which to sate his hunger. Not in her worst nightmares did Ada suspect that Sir Edmund might form part of such a lethal tally. In answering the ominous summons he could well be rushing to his death, and that was something she would never allow. 'Hurt my grandfather,' she hissed, 'and I will send you straight to hell, you manipulative, lying bastard!'

CHAPTER 32

Best Served Cold

A da ran to the sanatorium, praying that Fitz was still on duty. With every step she felt her grandfather draw closer to the Ravener's knife; if she was too late to save him she would never forgive herself. The Webley was still in her purse, and Ada thanked God she had decided to keep it. Whatever awaited her at the club, she would be ready.

Fitz looked up in surprise as Ada burst into his office. 'Good evening,' he said. 'You seem out of sorts, is something the matter?'

'Yes, I need your help. Grandfather is in danger.'

He raised his eyebrows. 'Danger? How so?'

'I think the Ravener is going to kill him.'

'What?'

'I'll explain on the way. Please, you have to trust me. We need to get to the Carmichael, now!'

'Of course,' said Fitz, grabbing his hat and coat. Setting a brisk pace, he led her to the stable yard where a carriage sat waiting.

'I wasn't expecting you this early, sir,' said the coachman, hurriedly stubbing out a cigarette.

'Apologies for the lack of notice, Hobson, but I have need of your services. The Carmichael on St James' Square, please, quick as you can.'

'Righto, sir.'

With a crack of the whip the carriage took off, rattling down the drive at speed. 'Now then,' said Fitz, settling into the seat opposite Ada, 'perhaps you would care to explain what's going on? Why do you think that maniac from the papers is going to harm Edmund?'

Ada hesitated before answering. 'It's a long story,' she said, 'but Grandfather has not been himself of late. He's been avoiding me since yesterday, and when I finally met him for dinner a telegram arrived. He became very upset and rushed off, ordering me to stay at Rookwood.'

'What did the telegram say?'

'It was an invitation to meet some army colleagues at the Carmichael. I'm positive it was sent by the Ravener.'

Fitz peered at her from beneath the brim of his top hat. 'Forgive my bluntness, but how could you possibly know such a thing?'

Ada sighed. 'I wish I knew where to begin. Please believe me when I say there is good reason to suspect the Ravener's involvement.'

'Very well. I cannot pretend this revelation does not come as something of a shock, but I shall do what I can to help. I have known you a long time and you would not be concerned without reason. Besides, Edmund is my friend. I will not stand idly by if his life is threatened.'

'Thank you, your assistance means a great deal to me.'

He gave her a reassuring smile. 'Let us hope that circumstances are not as dire as you think.'

'Hope,' said Ada, 'a commodity that has been in short supply of late.'

Swiftly leaving Blackheath behind, the carriage soon reached Westminster Bridge. Ada couldn't help but glance at the clock tower. The bodies of Soames and his men had long since been removed, but their deaths had marked a turning point, setting in motion a train of events she didn't understand. Only her grandfather had the answers, but if the Ravener took him from her the truth would die too, leaving her twice as bereft.

'Not long now,' said Fitz.

Ada nodded, watching the dark city as it flashed past outside the window. Every passing moment was agony but the horses had been pushed to their limits. All she could do was pray that she got there in time. Thundering along Pall Mall, the carriage swung violently into St James' Square and came to sudden stop, rocking on its suspension.

'We're there, sir,' said Hobson, climbing down and helping Ada to the pavement.

The Carmichael Club occupied a grand Georgian townhouse, overlooking formal gardens, and standing to attention at the entrance was a smartly-attired steward in scarlet livery.

'Has Sir Edmund Hearst arrived yet?' asked Fitz, 'I'm escorting his granddaughter to meet with him.'

'He came in about ten minutes ago, sir. He's in the dining room on the top floor.'

'Thank you, my good man.'

Taking Ada's arm, Fitz led her inside. 'Up there,' he said, nodding toward an ornately-carved staircase. Mouth dry at the thought of what she might find, Ada tried to remain calm as she made her way upward. It was all she could do not to break into a run, but the last thing she needed was the unwanted attention of club members. On reaching the final landing she saw a large door, panelled in red leather. To one side, a sign on a brass stand read '*Private Function*'.

'This must be it,' she said, taking the revolver from her purse.

'You came prepared, I see.'

'Grandfather would expect nothing less. You'd better stay behind me. If the Ravener is here I don't know how he'll react.' Taking a deep breath, she turned the handle and walked in.

'Jesus Christ,' gasped Fitz, 'what hell is this?'

'One that has become all too familiar,' whispered Ada, appalled at the wanton carnage spread before her. Candles flickered, cutlery shone and splashes of crimson covered everything. Eight men in dress uniform lay slumped in oak chairs at the end of a long dining table, their faces serene and gaping holes in their chests. In front of them, on a silver platter, was a glistening pyramid of human hearts. A motionless Sir Edmund sat with them, head bowed and mouth hanging open.

'Grandfather?' said Ada.

Slowly, as if waking from a dream, he turned to look at her, tears running down his cheeks and into his beard. Rushing over she threw her arms round him. 'Oh thank God, I thought I'd lost you.'

Sir Edmund didn't respond to Ada's embrace, he just stared in disbelief at the ghastly meal set out before him. 'They're all dead now. I'm the only one left.'

'Are you hurt, old boy?' said Fitz, coming to stand by his side.

'No,' he moaned. 'Seeing this slaughter is injury enough. I led them to this terrible end – he was never going to forgive us.' Rocking back and forth in his chair, he closed his eyes and sobbed.

'I recognise some of these men,' said Fitz. 'From what I recall they were under Edmund's command in India, when he was stationed in the Punjab up by the Tibetan border.'

Ada sighed. 'They were his comrades, his brothers in arms. I was wrong when I thought the Ravener intended to kill him. What he really wanted to do was make him suffer. It's why the telegram upset him so much, he knew what he was going to find.'

'But why? What possible reason could there be for such savagery?'

'Only Grandfather can tell us that.'

'That may be so,' said Fitz, 'but now is not the time. I've never seen him so distressed. You need to get him out of here and back to Rookwood immediately; we can't have him found like this.'

'I agree, but how do we leave without being seen?'

'There are service stairs over there,' he said, pointing to a door in the far wall. 'They'll take you to the alley at the rear of the club – hopefully you won't meet any staff on the way down. I'll send Hobson round to fetch you before notifying the board. Better I do it in person, as opposed to having them walk in and discover this slaughterhouse for themselves.'

'Thank you, Fitz. Are you sure you'll be all right?'

'Don't worry about me. The last thing the club wants is a scandal. They'll do everything they can to keep this matter private; the Prime Minister is a member after all. I'll meet you back at the house once I've finished here.' Taking a moment to compose himself he left the room, quietly closing the door behind him.

'Grandfather,' said Ada, helping the old man

to his feet, 'it's time to go home now.' He nodded dumbly, clutching at her arm as if he were a child. Carefully guiding him down the stairs, she breathed a sigh of relief when she saw Hobson waiting for her. The carriage was soon on its way to Blackheath, and Ada held her grandfather's hand as he huddled in the corner by the window, drained of all vitality and numb to the world. If the Ravener's intention had been to break him, she thought, he may well have succeeded.

Arriving at Rookwood, Ada led Sir Edmund up the steps to the main entrance. 'Wait for me in your study,' she said, kissing his cheek, 'I'll be with you shortly.' He shuffled inside like some wary visitor, overawed by a grandeur he had no experience of.

'Thank you for helping us, Hobson,' said Ada. 'Please return to Fitz as quickly as you can. Things may get difficult for him at the club.'

'He seemed somewhat alarmed, miss.'

'The Ravener has struck again,' she told him, seeing no point in dissembling. 'When the good doctor is able to get away, would you bring him here? Sir Edmund needs him.'

'Of course, miss.'

Giving him a tired smile, Ada turned and entered the house. The moment she stepped over the threshold she froze. Stark against the polished tiles, a set of bloody footprints led straight to the study. A chill ran down her spine. Her grandfather could not have made these marks; she had seen no blood on his shoes. Someone had reached Rookwood before her, and she harboured no illusions as to who that person might be. Taking the revolver from her purse, she followed the grisly trail across the lobby.

Sir Edmund sat behind his desk, head in his hands, a towering figure reduced to a shrunken, brittle shell. Ada glanced to either side. The fire was lit, the curtains drawn, but of the Ravener there was no sign. Hating to see her grandfather in such awful pain, she walked over and placed a comforting hand on his shoulder.

'I'm so sorry it has come to this,' he said. 'I tried everything to stop it, everything, but my sins were too great.'

'What do you mean?' she asked. 'Please help me understand.'

There was a soft click as the study door swung shut. Ada spun round, and before her stood a tall, slim, blood-soaked figure, dressed for the opera and wearing a white, velvet mask. Raising the revolver, she aimed it at the Ravener's chest.

'And here we are at last,' he said. 'Revenge is indeed a dish best served cold. I place my life in your hands, Ada, just as I promised. Ask of me what you will, there must be something you wish to know?'

Ada nodded. There was only one question in

her mind, but she was too afraid to voice it.

'Be brave,' he said, 'say the words. You have more than earned the right.'

'Who are you?' she whispered.

The Ravener chuckled softly. 'Do you remember what I said to you at the hospital? That people tend ignore things they don't wish to see?'

'Yes,' said Ada, heart hammering in her chest.

'You are no exception to that rule, beloved.' Taking hold of the mask, he slowly uncovered his face.

All strength fled Ada's body. She sank to the floor in a rustle of silk, the revolver spilling from her hand. The impossibility of what she saw tore at her soul, pushed her to the very brink of madness and forced from her lungs a cry of anguish that echoed through the house.

'Hello, Ada,' said the Ravener.

'Hello, Mother,' said Ada.

CHAPTER 33

Guilty as Sin

Ada stared at the figure before her, barely able to believe the evidence of her own eyes. Clara Phillips was dead, yet here she stood, a ghost made flesh. 'Is… is it really you?' she stammered, struggling to comprehend how such a thing could be.

'Yes, beloved, it is.' Reaching down, the Ravener gently helped Ada to her feet. 'This is no illusion, however difficult that may be to accept.'

With a trembling hand, Ada ran her fingertips across the soft skin of her mother's cheek. She knew this face as intimately as her own reflection, but the voice that spilled from its lips was not Clara's. It had not sung to her as a child, nor reassured her when she was afraid; it was male, and belonged solely to the phantom that haunted her. 'How can you be in her body?' she asked. 'What have you done to my mother?'

'I shall explain all,' said the Ravener, 'but we must go back to the beginning. There is a tale to be told, a sin to be atoned for. Perhaps your grandfather would care to enlighten you?'

Ada turned to Sir Edmund. His eyes burned

with rage, his lips pressed into a thin, bloodless line. 'You took them!' he hissed. 'That wasn't part of our agreement.'

'I don't remember specifying *which* lives I was going to take. Are you so naïve to think I would simply forgive and forget? Their hearts were in part-payment for the twenty lives *you* took from me.'

'What does he mean, Grandfather?' asked Ada, sick to her stomach at the confirmation that he was acquainted with the Ravener.

Sir Edmund stood, bracing himself against the edge of his desk. Pouring a large brandy he tossed it back. 'That... thing is not your mother. You cannot believe a word it says.'

'I have never lied to Ada,' said the Ravener, 'unlike you. I wish her to know what kind of man her grandfather really is, perhaps then she can decide which of us is the real monster? Answer her question. Retrace your steps all the way to India.'

Sir Edmund looked at Ada, his face full of regret. 'If I could change what I did, I would.'

'Just tell me what happened,' she said, clinging to the Ravener as the room spun round her.

'It was all so long ago. My regiment was stationed in the Punjab, near the border with Tibet. It was a wild place, untouched by the outside world. I wanted to make my mark and it was the perfect place to do it.'

'As a lackey of the East India Company,' said the Ravener. 'They were no more than pirates, their currency one of oppression, robbery, murder and rape.'

'Is that true?' asked Ada.

Sir Edmund nodded. 'Things are different now, but back then the British Army was paid by the East India Company to keep order. We were given commissions, and told to do our duty for the sake of the Empire. Rumours of strange deaths caught the attention of our commander, so my men and I were sent to investigate. We headed north, and after many days of riding found a secluded valley in the Himalayan foothills. At its centre was a temple, surrounded by a large, well-kept village. The people were happy and healthy, the fields were full of crops and everything appeared peaceful.'

'Until you came,' said the Ravener.

'Yes, until we came. A crowd was gathered round the temple, so we dismounted and pushed our way in. A group of men and women in saffron robes were standing next to a stone dais, an elderly man lying upon it, eyes closed and a look of contentment on his face. His chest had been cut open, and at his side a beautiful young woman was eating his heart. She looked at me as I walked over, her lips all bloody and smiling, and before I knew what I was doing, I ran her through with my cavalry sabre. She screamed once then fell to the floor, twitching in agony as she died.'

Ada thought back to Madame Blavatsky's séance, the spectral image of her mother crying out in pain as a sword ripped through her chest. Not only had the Ravener been demonstrating his power, he had been sharing a memory.

'And then the killing began in earnest,' said Sir Edmund. 'I gave no order to shoot, but my men took it upon themselves to follow my example. They opened fire on the temple occupants, all nineteen of them. They offered no resistance; they just stood where they were and one by one they were cut down. It was over almost as soon as it began. When the smoke cleared we saw the riches that lined the walls – gold and silver, precious gems, it was like Christmas day for the men. They ransacked the place, taking what they could and scattering the rest. I was no different. I had promised my father I would make my fortune in India, and I meant to live up to that boast. Filling my saddlebags with wealth, I went back for the one thing that sealed all our fates. At the rear of the temple, sitting on an altar, was a statuette of the Hindu goddess Kali. Wrapping it carefully in silk I carried it away with me, and as we left I ordered that unholy place burned to the ground.'

'Unholy?' said the Ravener. 'Who are you to decide what is holy or not? My temple had stood for millennia. You left it a charred ruin, filled with the bodies of those you had slaughtered.'

'I know that now,' said Sir Edmund, his head bowed. 'I have no excuse for what I did. Years passed, and after leaving the army I returned to my medical career. I wanted to display the statuette with the rest of my trophies, but there was something about it I found increasingly unsettling. In the end I couldn't bear to look at it. It was evidence of my crime so I locked it away.'

'Evidence indeed,' said the Ravener, 'which is why I fetched it from its hiding place. I wished your granddaughter to see it.'

'The India Room,' said Ada. 'That day I was shooting on the terrace. You left the statuette for me to find, but why?'

The Ravener smiled. 'Because I knew this moment would come, and I wanted to show you proof of your grandfather's sin.'

'I should have dashed the damn thing to the floor, shattered it into a thousand pieces,' said Sir Edmund.

'If you had then you would have destroyed me too,' said the Ravener, 'but your greed was too strong, thus you became the agent of your own undoing. You see, Ada, that statuette was my sanctuary. Only as the years rolled by did it become my prison.'

'I don't understand,' she said. 'How could it be your prison? What *are* you?'

He paused, weighing his response. 'I am a scion of Kali, her child if you will; a being of spirit, not flesh.'

Ada stared at him open-mouthed. 'You are the child of... a goddess?'

'Yes, is that so difficult to believe? There was a time when the world was young and filled with wonders; gods walked the earth and miracles were commonplace. My mother was the most fearsome of warriors, divine protector and scourge of evil. She birthed me to help fulfil her design, vengeance upon those whose hearts were filled with darkness. In consuming their sins I gained the power to keep my people safe from harm. Every life I took was a hymn of praise to Kali, sanctified with the blood.'

'And if I say that I believe your story,' said Ada, trying to make sense of what she was being told, 'how is it that you are wearing my mother's face? How do you account for the suffering you have caused my family?'

The Ravener sighed. 'It all began the moment your grandfather murdered my host, my beloved. Her name was Yauvani, and her purity was unmatched even by those who had come before. I was created to work in harmony with a shining human soul; always female, years of preparation and training were required. Only those who were strong enough to control my essential nature were considered. Once bound with me my host would not age, and for twenty years we would punish those who sought to do harm. At the end of her period of service my beloved would return to her family, knowing she had been part of something great and terrible. A new host would then be chosen, and for generations the cycle remained unbroken, until your grandfather severed it with a length of cold steel.'

Sir Edmund stood by his desk, body held rigid, face impassive. He was suddenly a stranger to Ada. In hearing what he had done, she wondered if she truly knew him at all.

'I still feel Yauvani's pain,' said the Ravener. 'As she died I was torn from her body, and for the first time in my existence I was alone. Both lost and afraid I fled to my mother's arms, my spirit sinking into her statuette. Helpless as a new-born child, I waited for the time when I could visit my wrath upon those who destroyed my home. Twenty were taken, and twenty would pay.'

'You were always there, lurking, I could feel it,' spat Sir Edmund. 'But you didn't come for me, did you? No, you sought out someone who couldn't fight back. Clara was born here at Rookwood, and on her twenty first birthday the nightmares began.'

'Why did you do such a thing?' asked Ada. 'My mother was innocent.'

'On my oath I did not wish Clara to suffer,'

said the Ravener, 'but I was dying, my spirit fading slowly away. To be one with another was all I knew, and she was a young woman of the right age. I reached out to her as she slept, seeking to make her my host, but despite her pure heart she was wholly unprepared for my intrusion. It terrified her. Piece by piece her sanity fell away, but once I had bonded with her there was no way back.'

'You tore her mind apart,' Ada cried. 'She hurt people, she hurt herself!'

'Yes,' said the Ravener, 'but there was no alternative. I was consumed by the need for revenge, and Clara was the perfect instrument with which to punish your grandfather. For so many years I tried to claim her as mine, but I was too weak to bend her to my will. Finally she could stand it no more, and overwhelmed by fear she tried to take her own life in the sanatorium. Expecting oblivion her soul fled, locking itself away in some deep, quiet place I could not reach.'

'So Madame Blavatsky was right,' said Ada.

'In a way. Clara *is* trapped, she just isn't dead. I kept her heart beating until her wounds could be bound, and at that moment I revealed myself to your grandfather. I gave him a choice. If he helped me, then I would restore his daughter to him, whole in both body and mind.'

'And if he refused?'

'Then I threatened to let Clara die, even

though it meant my own undoing. I did not have the strength to return to the statuette or seek another host; if her body failed, I would cease to exist.'

'What kind of choice is that?' shouted Ada. 'You may as well have held a knife to his throat!'

'Perhaps,' said the Ravener, 'but I was desperate, and if I was to survive I needed the sustenance that only sin could provide. You had to believe that Clara was dead for a time, only then would I be free to go about my business, to once again become my mother's son.'

Ada shook her head in disbelief. 'I'm so sorry, Grandfather. Had I been in your position, I would likely have done the same thing.'

'I hated deceiving you,' said Sir Edmund, his eyes downcast, 'but he insisted that I do so. I would have agreed to anything if it meant I could hold my child in my arms again.'

'And I will keep my word,' said the Ravener. 'Everything I have done, every life I have taken, was to ensure we three arrived at this moment. My work is almost complete, the scales *almost* balanced.'

'Almost balanced?' said Ada, bile rising in her throat.

'Come now, have you not been keeping count?'

Her mind raced, adding up the deaths she had borne witness to. 'You killed Price, the three sailors, the two who ran the orphanage, the priest, Soames and his men, the nurse and now the eight soldiers. That's nineteen hearts. You still need one more.'

'I do indeed,' said the Ravener, glancing at Sir Edmund.

'No!' said Ada. 'Grandfather may have done a terrible thing, but I won't let you take him from me.'

'That was never my intention; watching him suffer has been payment enough. In his arrogance it never occurred to him that I would take an interest in his granddaughter. When he saw my display on Westminster Bridge he realised that I was the one who had saved you from Soames, and that scared him, didn't it, Edmund?'

'You damn well know it did.'

The Ravener grinned. 'I must admit that I felt a degree of shameful joy in watching you squirm, so I decided to twist the knife just that little bit further by going riding with Ada. I wanted her to find my mask and bag, knowing that she would confront you after making such a shocking discovery. It made for a pleasing aperitif to the main meal at the Carmichael.'

'You engineered that chase across the park just so you could torment Grandfather?' said Ada, astonished at such callousness.

'Yes. I may not wish him dead, but I still require my pound of flesh, as it were. I am sorry that you fell from your horse; it was a miscalculation on my part, but I knew that you would be safe in Thomas' hands. I asked him to care for you and bring you home.'

'Thomas was working *with* you?'

'I have many gifts but I am not invulnerable. Thomas' assistance in regaining my strength was most useful. He understands the nature of loss, and would not have others feel the pain that he has endured. He is a far more willing soldier than your grandfather, but to give him his due, Edmund has done everything I asked of him. Desperation and fear are a wonderful source of motivation. He stole a cadaver from the hospital for Clara's fictitious funeral, hid my existence from Doctor Fitzpatrick and gave me the cottage to live in. He even sent the staff away so we could have this meeting in private. Nevertheless, I could not help but bait him when the chance arose, such as leaving that note on Carmichael Club paper at the foundry. I thought it was a nice touch, as well as a pithy reminder that he danced to my tune.'

'You are indeed most adept at manipulation,' said Ada, caustically, 'but if Grandfather is to be spared your depredations, then who have you chosen to be your last victim? Which murderer awaits the touch of your knife?'

The Ravener looked deep into her eyes. 'Your mother has suffered enough and it weighs heavily upon me. Her soul is locked in a prison of its own making. Without its guidance, its love, I am nothing more than hunger incarnate. Clara was right to call me a ravener. While I reside within this empty shell I am truly a monster. Here in this vile city I am surrounded by so much evil that I cannot stop myself from killing, even though I wish it otherwise. It is *your* heart I wish to take, Ada Phillips, but not to devour. I have walked beside you all of your life and you have qualities that are rare, even among women. It is why I have always had priestesses. Women understand pain in a way that a man never could, it makes them strong. I have tested you again and again and you have shown such promise. You are Yauvani's equal, and we could accomplish so much together.'

'You want *me* to…' Ada couldn't finish. What he was asking for felt monstrous, yet seeing her mother's face, knowing that Clara could come back to her family, was not something she could simply dismiss.

'This is not what we agreed,' cried Sir Edmund, clawing at his desk with white-knuckled fingers.

The Ravener fixed him with a look of contempt. 'And where did you think I was going to go? I can only release Clara if I bond with another, and I knew it had to be Ada the moment she was born. We all have to make sacrifices.'

Sir Edmund stared at him in horror. 'How

dare you speak to me of sacrifice?' Pulling open a drawer, he grabbed the revolver that lay within and aimed it at the Ravener. 'You can't have her, I forbid it!'

'Grandfather,' said Ada, slowly reaching out a placating hand. 'You'll never hit him, and you've seen what happens to those who get in his way.'

'That was true until now, beloved,' said the Ravener, smiling as he spread his arms wide, 'but as I promised, tonight is a time for judgement. I shall not move if he wishes to shoot. Clara's life rests in your hands alone.'

Ice filled Ada's veins. The thought of losing her mother for a second time, and in such an awful way, was too much to bear. 'Please, Grandfather,' she begged. 'Don't kill her, don't take her from me.'

'It is too late,' he whispered, 'it was always too late.' Wild-eyed and with spittle running from the corner of his mouth, Ada could only watch helplessly as the Ravener's taunting finally pushed Sir Edmund into the abyss. The stoic, rational doctor that she knew was gone, in his place, a crushed and hollow man consumed by guilt. 'God forgive me,' he said, and with a howl of anguish he squeezed the trigger.

CHAPTER 34

Inferno

'**N**o!' shouted Ada. Throwing herself at her grandfather, she struck his arm just as the revolver fired. The bullet missed the Ravener's head by inches, shattering a lit gas lamp on the wall. Flammable vapour poured from ruptured pipe, exploding as it touched the hot metal of the ruined sconce. A sheet of flame rippled outward, igniting the panelling, the drapes and everything else it touched. In seconds, the study was ablaze.

'Damn you,' said Sir Edmund, shoving Ada aside. She tripped and fell backward, crashing heavily to the floor. 'It lies, girl, don't you see? It was never going to give my Clara back. It will leave her a mindless husk if you agree to its demands. I would lose you both.'

With a mocking laugh, the Ravener threw the door wide and strode from the burning room. 'Time to choose, beloved,' he called out.

'I killed you once,' bellowed Sir Edmund, 'I can do it again.'

'You are welcome to try. I'll be waiting.'

'Grandfather, please,' said Ada, clutching at the hem of his coat. Ignoring her entreaty, he tore himself free and rushed off in pursuit of his nemesis. Retrieving her fallen revolver, Ada climbed to her feet and followed him into the lobby. Billowing smoke filled the room, stinging her eyes as she searched for Sir Edmund. A shot rang out, closely followed by the sound of breaking glass. A gust of cold night air rushed in, feeding the flames, and with a mighty roar the fire spread up the walls and across the ceiling. The orangery, thought Ada, and fighting for breath she ran to the rear of the house, raising an arm to protect herself as lumps of burning plaster fell all around her.

The door to the garden hung open, its window panes shattered; at its foot, a carpet of glittering shards lay strewn across the tiled floor. From outside Ada could hear her grandfather as he raged and cursed in the Ravener's wake, blind to anything but his misguided desire for vengeance. She knew where she had to go to. There was only one place the Ravener would make his final stand, a grim yet fitting locale for the fate of Clara Phillips to be decided. 'Please, God,' she said, sprinting along the moonlit path, 'don't let me be too late.'

On reaching the secluded clearing that held her mother's grave, Ada saw the Ravener standing defiant beneath the old oak, his white-gloved hand resting on the headstone. In front of him, no more than ten paces away, a panting Sir Edmund took careful aim.

'I have you now,' he said, his voice filled with manic triumph.

'Wait!' Ada called out, 'you don't know what you're doing.'

He shook his head. 'Are you so blind, Granddaughter? You would let this nightmare continue when all I seek is to end it? Clara is already gone; there is nothing left but this creature that wears her face.'

With slow, deliberate steps, Ada placed herself between the Ravener and Sir Edmund. 'Stand down, Grandfather,' she said, raising her revolver.

'He won't listen,' said the Ravener. 'Even now, with his temple in flames, he still cannot bring himself to pay his debt.'

'There is no debt,' snarled Sir Edmund. 'You have taken everything from me.'

'I beg to differ, I am letting you live.'

'Grandfather, I'm warning you,' said Ada.

He looked at her, eyes filled with misery. 'You would shoot me?' he said in disbelief. 'After everything I've done for you, you would side with this… abomination?'

'I'm not thinking about myself,' she said, tears running down her cheeks. 'I'm thinking about Papa and you, how much joy you would feel at having Mother returned to us.'

'Joy? There is no joy, only revenge. I love you,

Ada, do not do this.'

'I love you too, just as I love my parents. If there is even the slightest chance that I can save Mother, then it is a sacrifice I have to make.'

'I was right to choose you,' said the Ravener. 'You are magnificent.'

'She is not yours to take,' screamed Sir Edmund. 'Die, monster!'

There was a sharp crack, the smell of burnt gunpowder, and the old soldier fell heavily to the ground. Hand pressed to the hole in his shoulder, he moaned as blood trickled through his fingers.

'He left me no choice,' said Ada, weeping.

'I know, beloved,' the Ravener replied, 'and to my eternal regret neither have I. I hope you can forgive me, in time.'

'Forgiveness has to be earned. You have done a terrible thing to my family, but I understand your reasons. All that remains is to decide what happens now.'

'You know what you must do if you want your mother returned to you. For my part, I simply wish an end to my loneliness.'

'Are you sure that is enough for you, or will your thirst for death remain undimmed?'

'In all truth I cannot say, beloved. Only time will tell.'

Ada nodded. 'You insist that you have never lied to me, yet I cannot bring myself to fully trust you. Know this, if you ever try to control me I shall fight you every step of the way. If for one moment I feel that I am losing that battle, I shall not hesitate to end my own life, and in doing so take you with me from this world.'

'I would expect nothing less.'

Ada drew a deep, shuddering breath. 'Then I accept your terms. Promise me this will not hurt.'

The Ravener reached out, gently enfolding her in his arms. 'Cross my heart,' he said.

The dripping bullet fell with a dull chink into a kidney dish. Nodding in satisfaction, Ada neatly closed the wound in her grandfather's shoulder with suture thread.

'Will he be all right, miss?' asked Thomas.

'Yes. He will sleep for a while until the chloroform wears off. There was no damage to the bone, so a sling will suffice until the tissue heals. Thank you for your help in bringing him here; you said we would meet again soon, though I didn't expect it to be under such unusual circumstances.'

'I always do my duty, miss. I shall be here as long as you need me.'

The door banged open and Fitz strode in, his face pale, his brow furrowed. 'What the hell is going on? I got back from the Carmichael to find Rookwood on fire, and then one of the orderlies tells me Edmund was shot. How is he?'

'He is resting, Fitz. I dealt with his injury.'

Wiping her bloodied hands on a cloth, she got up and walked over to him. 'What is happening up at the house?'

'The men have the fire under control; they're using the sanatorium tender to pump water from the fountain. The east wing is a ruin but the majority of the building can likely be saved.'

'I'm glad. I would have hated to see it burn to the ground.'

'That's all well and good, but who shot Edmund?'

'I did.'

Fitz's mouth dropped open. 'Why?'

'You need to come with me,' she said, taking his arm. Leading him to the adjacent room, she pointed to a woman lying asleep on the bed, her long, dark hair spilling across the pillow. 'That is why.'

Fitz staggered, and would have fallen if Ada had not been there to steady him. 'How is this possible?' he gasped, 'I don't understand.'

'There are more things in heaven and earth, Doctor Fitzpatrick. You have been a good friend to my grandfather, better than he deserved I think.'

'What do you mean?'

Helping him to a chair, Ada sat on the edge of the bed, taking her mother's hand in hers. 'I know it has been a long day, but do you have the time to hear a story?'

Fitz nodded, unable to tear his gaze from the

sleeping Clara.

Ada smiled at him and began. 'Once upon a time, a young man went to India…'

CHAPTER 35

Bittersweet

*I*t's time to wake up now, Rory. Come back to us.'
The voice reached out to him, a lifeline to cling to, a reason to drag himself from the grey purgatory in which he languished. His head ached, but the fever that had wracked his body was gone. Slowly opening his eyes, he saw a blurry figure sitting next to his bed.

'Ada, is that you?'

'No, Rory.'

The room came slowly into focus. At his side was someone he had never thought to see again: piercing blue eyes, delicate features, and long, raven hair tied back with a ribbon. Dressed in a gown of lavender silk, she was just as elegant as he remembered. 'I'm fecking dead, aren't I?'

Clara shook her head. 'You came very close. Fitz says you developed meningitis after Soames fractured your skull.'

'Jesus, so that makes two of us who have somehow cheated the grim reaper. Forgive me, Clara, but given the luck of the Irish I can understand why I'm still breathing; you were six feet under. Coming back from that is quite an achievement.'

She sighed heavily. 'My death was a lie, one of many in fact. Much has happened while you lay ill, and there are things you need to know.' The sun had set by the time Clara finished her tale. Lighting the gas lamps, she waited for Rory to respond.

'That sounds like Ada,' he said, wiping tears from his eyes, 'stubborn, yet just as magnificent as you describe.'

'My daughter is indeed both of those things. She saved my life, and my love for her knows no bounds. She has gone away for a time. I do not know where, but I trust her need to be alone. She will reach out to us when she is ready; she cares for you deeply, and would not have you concerned for her wellbeing.'

Rory nodded. 'There was a time when I thought that *I'd* be the one protecting *her*, foolish man that I am.'

'It is hardly foolish to love someone and want to keep them from harm.'

He reddened about the cheeks. 'I'm glad you think so. I'm just a boy from Dublin after all.'

'You do yourself a disservice, Rory – there are qualities in a person that matter far more than rank.'

'Thank you, Clara. It really is wonderful to see you alive and well. After all that you went through, I had almost forgotten what you were like before…' he trailed off, unsure of his words.

'You need not worry about upsetting me; I remember everything that happened. It is as if I sat alone in a theatre, watching events unfold upon the stage. There is no longer any madness, nor fear, my daughter saw to that. I am the same woman that I always was, and yet in some ways I am not, it is difficult to explain.'

'My mother would call it a miracle. I can't imagine how Henry feels to have you back.'

Clara smiled, lighting the room as brightly as any lamp. 'Ada and I broke the news to him carefully, but once the shock had passed he held me tight and wept. Now he refuses to let me out of his sight, lovely man that he is. He's in the parlour now, reading the paper.'

'He's home? How long have I been ill?'

'About three weeks. It's Christmas Eve.'

'Jesus, no wonder I feel so bloody weak.'

'You did almost die, Rory, but Ada would not let you slip from this life. She has gifts, and it will take time for her to learn how best to apply them.'

'I'm sure it will,' he said. 'And what about Sir Edmund? Is he recovered from his injury?'

'Yes, but he has not spoken since that night. Fitz is caring for him, and reassures me that there is nothing physically wrong. I believe my father is simply ashamed of what he did, and is afraid that he has lost his family. I shall visit him soon, help him to understand that he is forgiven. Time heals all wounds, even his.'

'That would be a fine thing, from the sounds of it he's suffered enough. I'll come with you. I owe him a great deal.'

'I'm sure he'd be happy to see you, although I must admit that I am somewhat apprehensive about leaving the house. My sudden resurrection is likely to cause something of a stir among friends and acquaintances.'

'I imagine that's going to be a tricky thing to explain,' said Rory.

Clara smiled. 'To a degree, but the social circles that Henry and I move in have their own set of unspoken rules. Madness especially is something to be feared; it taints reputation and brings scandal. Pretending that someone has died – as opposed to being locked up for the rest of their lives   would be considered a mercy by some. My reappearance after being *cured* of my mania will no doubt raise a few eyebrows, but eventually the fuss will blow over, never to be spoken of again in polite company. This is England, and if there is one thing English families are good at, it is pretending that something did not happen. Mrs Crane and Milly know everything of course, and will guard the reputation of this household as they always have.'

Rory shook his head. 'I don't think I'll ever understand this country.'

'These are the masks we wear, my good

sergeant.'

'Masks,' said Rory, unable to suppress a shudder. 'I only saw it once, but the one you wore, I mean, that the Ravener wore, scared me rigid.'

'It was nothing more than velvet and glue,' said Clara, 'one of a pair I bought in Venice when Henry and I were courting: one smiling, one frowning. I thought we could wear them to a masquerade ball, but never got the chance. It was not the mask you were scared of, but what lay beneath.'

'What happened to it?'

'I burned it. I may be at peace with what happened to me, but I did not wish to keep something that has seen so much death. It is time to move on, Rory, and leave the past behind. Speaking of which, there is someone who is very eager to see you. I'll be back with some dinner later.' Kissing him lightly on the forehead she left, leaving the door open behind her. Rory heard muffled voices, and moments later Milly walked in. Her head was bowed, and in her hands she carried a small parcel, wrapped in brown paper and tied with string.

'Ah, Miss Fletcher, you're a sight for sore eyes and no mistake.'

'Hello, Rory,' she said, seating herself next to him, 'Miss Ada asked me to give you this when you woke up. Merry Christmas.'

'Thank you very much.' He carefully

unwrapped the parcel; inside was a book, *A Study in Scarlet* by Arthur Conan Doyle.

'It's about a detective,' said Milly, 'she thought it would keep you company while you got better.'

Rory ran his fingers over the binding. He could think of only one thing more precious than the book, and that was for Ada herself to be there to read it to him. 'It's perfect.'

Milly raised her head and beamed, and as she did so Rory saw what she had been hiding. 'Dear God, lass!' With a shaking hand he reached out and gently touched her cheek; the awful scars that had ruined her face were all but gone.

'Miss Ada gave me a Christmas present too.'

Rory lay back on his pillows, utterly astonished.

'Do you think she'll be all right, wherever she is?' Milly asked.

'I hope so, I don't like the thought of her being out there alone.'

'I don't think she *can* be truly alone anymore,' said Milly, 'not while she carries such a dread spirit inside her.'

'That may be so, but she has us. Let us hope that will be enough to keep her from falling.'

'Yes,' said Milly, 'let us hope.'

Sitting in bittersweet silence, they watched as snow fell softly outside the window, draping a pristine blanket across the grimy roofs of London.

EPILOGUE

Venice

16 January 1891

F ireworks bloomed into life above the Piazza San Marco, filling the night sky with light and thunder.

'What do you think?' said Ada.

'I've never seen anything like it,' replied Rory, 'it's quite beautiful.'

'I hoped I would get the chance to bring you here. Mother always talked about it so passionately, especially given the carnival is in full swing.'

The bells in the Campanile tolled midnight and all around them people cheered; dressed in festival costume and wearing the most outlandish of masks, they flirted and danced without a care in the world.

'There's something I've been meaning to ask you,' said Rory, taking Ada's arm and walking with her beneath the colonnade.

'And what would that be?'

'I don't remember much from when I was ill, but I have a clear memory of us speaking to each other in a dream. Did that actually happen or was it just some fevered imagining?'

'It was real, Rory. I had fallen from my horse and for a while I was unconscious. I think I reached out to you in the same way the Ravener would reach out to me.'

'Do you recall what I said?'

Ada rested her head on his shoulder. 'I do indeed.'

'I just wanted you to know that despite all that has happened, I would say exactly the same thing to you now.'

'I am glad to hear that. When I wrote to you, I was unsure of whether you would come to Venice.'

'Did you really expect me to abandon the woman I love?'

'No, but I could not assume your feelings would stay the same. I have no regrets about what I had to do; the right thing is often the most difficult, and I knew there would be a price to pay. I could spend the next twenty years fighting this battle by myself, but I would rather I had you at my side.'

'Then that is where I shall stay. Not only did you save my life but you healed Milly. Just think of the good you can do. In time you could be a doctor like no other.'

'Much is possible,' said Ada, 'but you know that one day I will have to take a life, it is inevitable. I can feel the Ravener wrapped round my heart; he sleeps now, content that he no longer faces oblivion, but when he wakes...'

'Whatever happens we will face it together. You are not alone, Ada Phillips.'

'And for that I am grateful beyond measure, Rory.'

He turned and smiled at her. 'Good, then may I suggest we forget about the future for a while and simply enjoy this night.'

'I would like that very much.'

Finding an empty table at a nearby café, Rory and Ada took a seat. An aproned waiter appeared at their side, notepad in hand.

'Signore, Signorina?'

'What would you like?' Rory asked.

'Surprise me.'

He ordered a bottle of Chianti and a plate of *Baccala Mantecato* for them to share. 'I hope the Signorina approves of my choice?'

'I'm sure it will be lovely,' said Ada, letting her gaze drift across the piazza. On the far side, leaning against one of the many columns, a gaudily-dressed man watched the crowd. The evil that flowed from him was palpable. Surrounded by a sea of joy and innocence, his soul was a shrivelled, noisome thing that reeked of darkness.

A loud cheer went up as the orchestra outside the Doge's Palace began playing a Strauss waltz. 'Shall we dance, good sir?' said Ada, taking

Rory's hand.

'Why not, this is a carnival after all.'

'Cover your face first.'

'When in Venice,' he said, donning a simple, black domino. Ada reached into her purse for something more elaborate; a finely-sculpted mask of white velvet, the lips drawn up into a playful smile. Together, they joined the swirl of dancers that filled the square. Over Rory's shoulder, Ada caught glimpses of the man with the black heart, and deep within her an age-old hunger began to stir.

'You're light on your feet, lass,' said Rory, his arm tight round Ada's waist as they stepped and spun, losing themselves amidst the festivities.

'You're no slouch either, Mr Canavan.'

'A couple of these waltzes and we'll have earned our dinner.'

'I shall no doubt be ravenous,' said Ada, eyes glittering behind her mask, 'but I can wait.'

AFTERWORD

Thank you to Rhiannon Lawson and Sarah Steele for taking the time to read early drafts, and for their support and constructive criticism. Thanks also to Jo Hall for carrying out such a thorough copy edit, and for schooling me in the appropriate use of subordinate clauses. Special mention should also be given to Rebecca for her help with the English to German translation throughout. Finally, my sincere gratitude to author and editor, Eve Seymour, at Jericho Writers. Her guidance was invaluable, and gave me the confidence to really bring the story to life.

Ravenous is a radical departure from the style and age-group of books I had written previously, and treading such unfamiliar territory was quite daunting at first. In choosing Victorian London for a location, and having a young woman as a protagonist, I set myself quite a challenge. I hope that I have done the story justice, especially as regards Ada. I wasn't sure what to make of her at first, only that I wanted her to be brave, clever and prepared to make a difference in a society dominated by men. By the end of the novel I felt that we knew each other well, and I was glad that she accepted the Ravener's offer, however hard that must have been for her.

Significant research was required in order to portray Victorian London as accurately as possible. For example, I had to rewrite the scene where the sailors are found tied to Tower Bridge. Originally they were discovered dangling from the towers, but then I discovered that the bridge wasn't finished until several years later in 1894, so into the river the corsairs went. Mourning the death of a family member by wearing black was also a common formality in Victorian society, especially as one rose in social class.

While it was fascinating to unearth the more unpleasant aspects of Victorian London, it did remind me how bad life there could be, especially if you had the misfortune to be poor. Until Joseph Bazalgette rebuilt the sewer system, cholera was rife, and claimed the lives of tens of thousands of people before it was eventually eradicated. There were no recorded cases of cholera in London after the late 1860's, so the character of Anna Hyde and her desire to create further outbreaks is entirely fictional.

Real names and places have been used where possible, such as the inclusion of Doctor Thomas Bond, a surgeon for the Metropolitan Police's 'A' Division. He was heavily involved with the Jack the Ripper case, and is considered to be an early example of a criminal profiler. Madame Helena

Blavatsky was also a historical figure, and did indeed have a temple of sorts in Holland Park, at the house owned by Bertram Keightley.

I really wanted Ada to be following in the footsteps of her father and grandfather, and I was therefore heartened to discover that Elizabeth Garrett Anderson (1836-1917) was the first woman to qualify as a doctor in England. She obtained her medical degree in Paris, but at the time was still refused entry to the British Medical Register. In 1872 she set up The New Hospital for Women in London (later called the London School of Medicine for Women). Due to her campaigning, an act of parliament was passed in 1876 that allowed women to enter the medical profession in England for the first time. It was only natural that Ada would study for a medical degree under Doctor Anderson's tutelage, if she wished to be a surgeon.

Special Branch does have a dark past when it comes to doing clandestine work for the government of the day. Created in 1883 and originally titled Special Irish Branch, its purpose was to combat the activities of the Irish Republican Brotherhood. In giving the character of Soames a basis for his obsessive and violent character, I linked him to the actual bombing at Clerkenwell Prison in December 1867. This act caused a public backlash in Britain, and was a setback to the cause of Irish independence.

Soames' subsequent revenge with an arson attack is fictional.

The deities of the Hindu pantheon are complex, beautiful and sometimes terrifying. Kali is portrayed in her earliest references as a destroyer of evil, and is often considered the kindest and most loving of all the Hindu goddesses. She is regarded by devotees as the mother of the universe, and because of her fearsome appearance is also seen as a great protector. I did not want to use Kali directly in the narrative, but instead invented a scion or child for her, a being whose purpose was to exact vengeance in her name against those who were truly evil at heart. This being, this demi-god, has no name, but takes a liking to the title Ravener given to him by both Clara and Ada. The Ravener and Ada have a long way to travel together, and London has not seen the last of them.

H. N. Pashley
Norwich
April 2022.

ABOUT THE AUTHOR

H N Pashley lives in Norwich, and when not typing furiously can often be found risking life and limb doing partner acrobatics. He also has an irrational dislike of brioche. Ravenous is his first book for adults.

He is also the author of a middle-grade trilogy: Gabriel's Clock, Sammael's Wings and Michael's Spear, under his full name of Hilton Pashley.

Work on 'Nemesis', the second book in The Ravener trilogy, is currently underway, and will take the reader to some very dark places indeed. If you would like to be kept informed of progress and be eligible for bonus content, then please sign up to my book club at www.hnpashley.com

Printed in Great Britain
by Amazon